GUARDIAN

THE GUARDIAN TRILOGY BOOK ONE

SARA MACK

Nicole –
until the
end of
forever

Guardian (Book 1 in The Guardian Trilogy)

ISBN: 9781724187512

Cover art and editing by Red Ribbon Editing Services

Created with Vellum

Dedicated to
Koz, Aubs, Bree, and Abbie Gale
Thank you for living in my fictional world

PROLOGUE

I sit and stare. My gaze is concentrated on a plant, an orchid. One single, curved stem holds six fuchsia flowers, each with a white center. The plant is beautiful. I allow a small part of my mind to wonder who might have sent it, while the rest of my consciousness blocks the reason why.

Faces blur in and out of my vision, and I hear muffled voices. They remind me of the old *Peanuts* cartoons that come on around the holidays, where the adult voices sound garbled. I know the blurry, muffle-voiced people mean well; they remind me of the "Great Pumpkin" episode in which all Charlie Brown gets trick-or-treating is rocks. Rocks. My chest feels full of them. It's hard to breathe.

My grandma takes a seat next to me. I can tell it's her because she takes my hand in hers and her skin feels like sandpaper. Grandma Ethel's skin has always felt this way. I can sense her getting settled in her chair when something hits my foot. Instinctively, I reach down to pick up the purse she has dropped. My concentration on the plant is broken, and I remember why I am here.

A scream rips through my throat.

CHAPTER 1

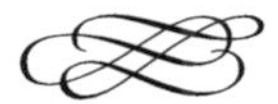

I lift my face toward the sun, its bright light illuminating the darkness behind my eyelids. I have escaped my house and walked to a nearby park with the excuse of needing to get out and enjoy the warmth while it lasts. Michigan weather is never predictable, so this excuse is accepted. My hope is the sun will burn me and redden my skin to replace the sorrow in my heart with physical pain. A pain that can be relieved and cured. Something I know has an end, something I can see healing.

"There you are."

Squinting, I see the outline of a person walking toward me. As it gets closer, my eyes focus on my best friend, Shel.

"Your mom told me I'd find you here." She produces two bottles of water and offers me one. "Thirsty?"

I shake my head.

She sits down next to me and opens her bottle. "It's warm for this time of year."

We sit in silence for countless minutes, staring at the park. A family of three plays in the sand by the water, taking advantage of the spontaneous warm weather. A few people hang out on a shaded picnic table; a jogger runs along the sidewalk. I play with the grass underneath my fingers as Shel follows my lead and watches what is going on around us. I've known Shel forever, since elementary school, and even she can't bring up what's happened. I suppose for fear of my reaction. But that's okay. I'd rather sit here in silence indefinitely than discuss it.

"So," she pushes her sunglasses up into her hair. "When are you going back to school?"

"I'm not," I turn to look at her. "I'll be finishing from home."

Her brown eyes widen. "Oh. Online?"

I nod. "You heading back this weekend?"

"Saturday."

"I'm sorry I haven't been much company."

"No worries," she says and lounges back on her elbows. "I'll be coming home for the summer; I need a break."

During our senior year, Shel was selected to attend the University of Michigan on an accelerated scholarship which meant she started her college classes during our last semester of high school. She's been attending college longer than anyone I know. It doesn't help that she wants to be an M.D.; she'll never be done with school.

"I talked to Matt yesterday," she says. "He told me to tell you he's thinking about you. He tried to catch up with you the other day, but ... you know ..."

I pull my knees to my chest and rest my chin on them. "Tell him I said hi."

She nods. "You know you do have to eat, right?"

Obviously, my mother has mentioned my lack of appetite. "I know."

"I was told your dinner would be ready in an hour."

We sit in silence and watch the sun fade. The small family packs their blanket and leaves, the friends say goodbye and leave the picnic table. The jogger has long since run off.

"Em?"

"Hmm?"

"Are you going to be okay?" Shel asks quietly.

I can't answer her.

~

RUBBING the sleep from my eyes, I check the alarm clock. 10:42 a.m. Yawning, I stretch and then change position, snuggling into my old bed and familiar smelling sheets. I don't think my mom has used a different detergent since I was born. The smell is comforting.

"Knock, knock," my dad says as he cracks open my bedroom door.

I pick up my head. "Hey, Dad."

"Mornin'," he says as he opens the door wide. "Just checking to see if you're awake. Hungry?"

I'm not, but I don't want to admit it. For the first time since I've been home I notice a significant amount of gray now peppers my father's brown hair. Positive I am the cause, I answer, "Sure," even though hunger is a need I haven't felt in a long time.

His slate blue eyes light up. "What'll it be?"

"Cereal is fine."

"You sure? I can make pancakes."

Pancakes are somewhat of my dad's specialty. This is how I know he's hurting for me but can't express it. Dad's pancakes usually only get made for special occasions, like birthdays. "I guess so, if you want to."

A smile breaks across his face. "Coming right up."

As he closes the door, I sit up slowly and catch a look at myself in the dresser mirror. I can see why everyone is concerned; I look like shit. No amount of makeup is going to cover my eye bags. The puffy, dark shadows look painted on my light skin. Peeling myself out of bed, I brush my teeth, attempt to tame my hair into a messy ponytail, and then head downstairs to the familiar smell of pancakes. Unfortunately, the buttery aroma does nothing for my appetite.

"There she is." My dad smiles at me, spatula in hand. "Just in time."

I take a seat at the kitchen island as he slides an "E" shaped pancake onto a waiting plate. "For you, madam."

I give him a small smile. "Where's the syrup?"

"In the fridge."

I stand and walk over to the refrigerator, reaching for the handle.

Something catches my eye, and I freeze. I can see the corner of a picture peeking out from behind a calendar. I slowly lift the paper, preparing myself to be confronted with a stinging memory. Instead, I see Michael and Kate, my older brother and his girlfriend, staring back at me, smiling with their new puppy, Jake.

I open the fridge, grab the syrup, and go back to my "E."

"Good morning," I hear my mom come through the door after her morning run. She smiles at me as she takes off her shoes. "How'd you sleep?"

"Okay."

"Good," she says. She walks over and plants a kiss on the top of my head. "I'm happy you're eating something."

I nod and take a bite. I don't have the heart to tell her it's more for my dad's benefit than mine.

"Michael will be over in about half an hour so we can head out," she tells my dad. Turning to me she adds, "Are you sure you don't want to come?"

I nod. My parents and brother are heading to my dorm room at Western Michigan to gather my things, since I won't be returning to the campus until next fall. "I think it'll be better if I stay here."

My mom's face crinkles, and her caramel-colored eyes soften into her worried/I'm-so-sorry/I-don't-know-what-to-do-look I've seen a million times over the last week and a half. I can't bear to tell her I'm afraid I will start screaming again if I see all of my memories from the past three years in one place, let alone try to pack them away in a box.

"Well, what will you do all day?" she asks, worried.

I want to tell her I won't off myself, but instead I say, "I'll be catching up on some reading. Once I get my laptop back I can start submitting my late assignments."

This appears to ease her worry. "All right. You have our numbers if you need us. And Mrs. Miller is next door, too."

I nod.

She releases her auburn hair from her low pony, and it falls to her shoulders, thick and mop-like. "I'm going to shower. Dale, did you put gas in the truck?"

"Yes, ma'am." My dad salutes her with the spatula.

I look down at my plate. I've only managed to eat my "E" into an "L." I poke at my alphabetical pancake, not wanting the rest of it.

"Here's a stack for Michael," my dad says, setting a plate of pancakes down by me. My brother is always hungry. "Coffee's kicking in." He winks as he heads to the bathroom.

Now my appetite is really gone. I sit and stare at my breakfast for a few more minutes before deciding that now is the time to throw it away without anyone seeing me. I head over to the wastebasket and toss it in. Even better, I return to the island with the empty plate in an effort to reassure my parents I've eaten and I'm feeling less depressed.

I hear the back door creak open and slam shut. A moment later, a taller version of my father appears in the kitchen. "Hey Ems." My brother walks over and gives me a lopsided one-armed hug. "Feeling okay today?"

I nod and lean in to his awkward hug. That's the extent of his inquiry. What else can he say? What do you say to someone who, just days ago, you had to pull off a casket screaming? He releases me and digs into the stack of pancakes, instinctively knowing they are for him.

"Hey, Mike," my dad says as he reenters the kitchen. My brother waves his fork at him, mouth full. Dad eyes my empty plate. "Want another? I'll make you another." His hands are busy whisking before I can tell him no.

Soon they are all ready to head out the door to bring my college life back to me in boxes. I follow my mother and brother to the door, so I can watch them leave. My dad turns off the stove and pauses to place more breakfast on my plate. He gives me a quick hug as he passes me.

I make my way back to my seat at the island and look down. A pancake in the shape of the letter "J" awaits me. I suck in my breath and turn quickly to look at my father with wide eyes before he steps out the door. Our gazes lock.

"I miss him, too," he says quietly, closing the door behind him.

CHAPTER 2

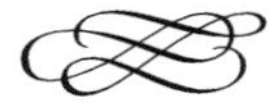

Tears stream down my face too fast for me to keep up with wiping them away. I just let them fall and drip off my chin into the sink as I attempt to wash the dishes from breakfast; the "J" discarded in the trash with the leftover pancake batter and coffee grounds.

Back in my room, I let the sobs loose into my pillow. Sleep takes me even though I've already slept away half the morning. Memories that I try to suppress while I'm awake keep making appearances in my dreams. This afternoon is no exception. My subconscious takes me back in time.

I'm looking in the mirror and I have to admit, for a change, I like what I see. The iridescent emerald fabric, which weaves through my black dress, complements my eyes; usually, they are such a freaky shade of green people think I wear contacts. Tonight, my eyes don't look out of place against my wavy up-do, formal attire, and made-up face. I actually went to the salon and had red highlights put in my brown hair to bring out the light auburn that was already there. It was a very girly act for me; normally, I just stick to the wake up, throw on some jeans, apply a little lip gloss, and go routine. My reflection turns in the mirror as I study myself. I'm impressed that my dress makes me look like I actually have a waist and a chest, a far cry from my everyday tomboyish appearance.

James and I are going to the junior prom. He couldn't find a date, which I think was a lie, and suggested we go together because we're best friends and we shouldn't miss out on a fun night. At first I rejected the idea because it would be too weird. James and I have been friends since elementary school; he, Shel, Matt and I have been inseparable since the fifth grade. But he wouldn't let the idea go and I conceded, just as I'm sure he knew I would. Shel was beyond ecstatic when I told her. She's been trying to convince me he's interested for a while, but I keep telling her she's crazy. He's James. I'm me. We're friends. We hang out. He's never said anything or acted any differently around me. In the weeks leading up to the dance, I reminded her at every opportunity this wasn't a real date.

I hear a car pull into the driveway and the door slam. My stomach leaps into my throat unexpectedly, my nerves taking me by surprise. To calm myself, I rationalize it's just another night out with James. Just like the countless other times we've been to the movies together or done homework or met up after his hockey games …

Sounds like dating to me, my subconscious chimes. Crap.

"Hey," I hear my mom at my bedroom door. "James is here."

"O-okay," I say nervously. "I'll be right down." Checking the mirror one last time, I suddenly feel small despite my 5'6 inch height made two inches taller with heels. The full skirt of my dress falls just above my knees making my skinny legs look like twigs. I'm feeling a lot of pressure surrounding this night. Will my flimsy legs support me? I play with a few loose strands of hair at my temple and reassure myself I can do this. Everything will be back to normal tomorrow.

I head for the stairs and when I make it to the landing before the second set of steps, I peek around the corner. Everyone is in the living room, including my brother. The boys are in a discussion, probably sports related. My mom is playing with the camera. I'm feeling self-conscious. I take a deep breath before heading down and catch a good look at my "date."

Okay, wow.

Is it the tux? A realization hits me of how good-looking he is. It's the same James. Sandy brown hair, blue eyes, athletic build. But he looks *different* somehow. Have his eyes always been that vivid shade of cerulean blue? Has his hair always fallen over his forehead that way? Have his shoulders broadened in the last 24 hours?

My mom catches me peeking at the scene below. "There she is!" she announces with excitement. "Come on down; I need pictures!"

In slow, careful steps, I make it to the bottom of the stairs. My dad comes over to me and smiles, holding me at arm's length. "You look beautiful," he says.

I make a face. "You're just happy I'm not in jeans."

"Go stand by the fireplace with James," my mom tells me.

My date and I meet in front of her designated picture spot, and our eyes lock for the first time. "Hi," he says with a shy smile.

I find myself distracted by the perfect curve of his lips, and all I can manage is a quiet "Hi" in return. Flashes ensue, lighting up the living room and pulling my attention away from his mouth. Is it getting hot in here or is it just me?

"'Kay, James put the corsage on Em," my mom directs.

James fumbles to open the plastic box that contains the flowers, and it slips from his fingers. I lunge forward to catch it, and we laugh at the awkwardness of the moment. I relax a bit as I hand the box back to him. This type of interaction between us is what I'm used to.

Once James pops the box top he sets it aside and slides the corsage over my hand. The flowers are striking. "What are these?" I ask, lifting my wrist to smell them. Three fuchsia blossoms with white centers are complemented by a black ribbon. They look exotic, almost tropical.

"Um, I don't know." He leans in to me and whispers, "My mother picked them out." He looks embarrassed, and I suppress a laugh.

"Look at me, you two," my mom says. "Smile. Put your arm around ... okay good."

More flashes. I think she's taking more pictures than necessary just in case my going to a dance never happens again.

As we stand there posing as a real couple, my body becomes

hyperaware of his proximity. The pressure of his hand feels warm at the small of my back, and I try to ignore it. Whatever cologne he's wearing isn't helping matters, and I feel the distinct need to put some distance between us. My senses have turned against me. This is my friend, James. That's it. That's all. He hasn't even told me I look nice. I make a mental note to berate Shel later for planting unwelcome thoughts in my head.

After what feels like an eternity, we are allowed to leave. "Have fun!" my parents wave from the back porch as James helps me into his older model Jeep Wrangler. It's cherry red with a black soft top, and he keeps it in pristine condition. Every time I ride in it, I'm impressed by how new it looks.

As we make our way to the high school, free of an audience, I apologize. "Sorry about all the pictures back there."

James shakes his head. "Don't be. This is a big moment."

I roll my eyes. "How so? I'm pretty sure dances happen every day."

"No," he smiles. "You look amazing."

Whoa. He actually complimented me. Maybe …? I push the thought aside and shrug off his words with sarcasm. "Are you saying I don't look amazing every day?"

"Basically," he winks.

And regular, non-complimentary, James returns. Jerk.

I can't come up with a witty comeback, so I stare out the window as he drives. My nervousness seems to have subsided somewhat since he seems to be acting like his normal self. It's not that long of a ride to the school and we manage to fill the silence with everyday conversation. Soon we are headed into the gym decked out for our "Evening of Elegance." Seriously, who comes up with these cheesy themes?

Once inside, Shel finds us among the crowd. "Hey! You look awesome," I say.

"Where's your man?" James asks, scanning the room for her date.

"He went to the bathroom. I swear he's got some sort of problem; he already went twice when he picked me up at my house."

I laugh. "He's probably just nervous. Besides, I told you it was weird to come with Zach. You barely know him."

Shel shrugs and smiles. "I thought 'why not?' Even if I don't have fun, at least I got to buy a new dress." She twirls in her most recent purchase, a graceful, floor-length gray and white sparkly number.

"Ah, it's all about the dress, is it?" James asks. He looks at me, kidding. "Is that why you agreed to come with me?"

"Of course." I smile sarcastically. "You know what a slave to fashion I am."

After some comments from the principal about the fundraising for tonight's event and thanking all the staff and students for their hard work, as well as some overly spastic comments from our overly perky student council president, we are allowed to enjoy ourselves. Shel and I leave the boys so we can dance; this is the fun part that we have been waiting for. After a few fast songs, at the end of the forever classic "I Will Survive," the music changes to something slow.

"Aw man," Shel whines as we leave the dance floor. "I guess I'll have to dance with Zach."

"And you thought you wouldn't have to?" I ask, surprised.

"I don't see you running to find James," she accuses.

"I told you. We're just friends."

"Emma," she says, stopping half-way back to the table. "I'm just going to say it. You're delusional."

"What? That's a mean thing to say. I am not," I defend myself.

"Whatever," she says in her snarky tone and rolls her eyes at me.

I follow her over to the table where she grabs Zach for a dance. Across the room, I notice James hanging out with Matt and some other friends. Left alone, I decide to sit and wait until the music changes. I think to myself about Shel and how wrong she is about James being interested in me. Apparently he doesn't want to dance or hang out with me. As I play with the decorations on the table, I admit to myself the thought makes me sad even though it shouldn't. Eventually, a couple of friends make their way over and their arrival interrupts my confetti art.

"Can we sit with you?" Olivia asks.

"Of course," I smile. "You guys having fun?"

"We were except now our dates have disappeared. Where's yours?" Taylor asks me.

I nod over my shoulder. "Over there somewhere."

"Ours are probably, too," Olivia sighs then frowns. "I don't get it. What's the point of coming to a dance if you're not going to dance?"

"The hope that they'll get lucky on the way home," Taylor laughs.

We all smirk and exchange knowing glances. Somehow the topic of our biology test comes up, so the conversation turns to a speculative debate about which essay option will be the easiest. In the middle of the discussion, Shel and Zach return to the table.

"What'd I miss?" Shel asks.

"A riveting discussion about the biology test."

"That's boring. C'mon!" she grabs my arm and tows me to the dance floor.

I spend half of the night dancing with Shel, Olivia, and Taylor. Olivia and Taylor's dates eventually reappear, but the girls are so mad at their abandonment that they mostly hang out with Shel and me, and take turns dancing with Zach during the slow songs. Shel doesn't mind sharing.

"It's your turn," Shel says to me.

"My turn for what?"

"To dance with my date."

I laugh nervously. "I don't want to dance with your date."

"Why not? He's enjoying it and it saves me. Besides, you haven't danced with anyone tonight other than me."

"It's okay, really."

"No, it's not okay. I'm starting to get a little pissed at your *friend*," her snarky tone returns.

I know that tone and reassure her. "Don't worry about it. I'm fine. I'm having fun. Really."

She makes a face. "I'm going to get Zach."

"No, don't!"

"You are going to dance at the *prom* with a *boy*," she states defiantly.

"Ugh. You're impossible."

Shel leaves me in the middle of the dance floor, surrounded by couples. I feel uncomfortable and out of place. After a minute, Zach appears from the sea of well-dressed horny teenagers.

"I'm sorry," I say as he puts his hands around my waist and I put my hands on his shoulders.

"It's not a problem," he smiles. "This night is turning out to be pretty good for me."

"I bet." We laugh.

"James isn't going to be mad, is he?" he asks.

"For dancing with me? Doubtful."

"He looks a little upset," Zach nods over my shoulder.

As we turn I catch a glimpse of James standing to the side of the dance floor. Yeah, his eyes are burning a hole straight through us. Great.

We spend the rest of the song in silence looking everywhere but at each other. It's incredibly uncomfortable. Shel is going to get it for putting me in this situation.

"Thanks," I say to Zach when the song ends.

"No problem."

We're headed back to the table when Olivia passes us and swoops up Zach. I find Shel. "You are in so much trouble."

Something grabs Shel's attention behind me for a moment. She refocuses on my eyes, whispers "Not now," and turns away.

"Hey! I need to ..."

I'm cut off by someone grabbing me from behind by my waist, encircling it with a strong arm, and pulling me tight against a body.

"Will you dance with me?" James whispers in my ear.

It takes a moment for me to respond. This is unexpected, and in response, my heart flutters. "S-sure."

He lets me go, so I can turn around, and then takes my hand. I look up at him and he's staring at me intently with his brilliant blue eyes.

When we reach the dance floor, I turn to face him and start to put my hands on his shoulders, but he grabs me tight around my waist, pressing me to him. I have no choice but to reach up and wrap my arms around his neck. Even though I'm wearing heels, he's still taller than me.

"Is this okay?" he asks softly as we start to move in a slow circle.

I turn my head to look at him, our faces only inches apart. I can't find any words.

"You look confused," he says, a small smile playing on his lips.

I nod.

"About this?" he guesses, amused.

I let out a sigh. "Are you going to tell me what's going on?"

"See that girl over there?" he nods in the direction behind me.

I crane my neck to the right to see who he's talking about, but he's holding me so tightly I can't move my head much. All I see is the edge of the mirrored wall behind the dance floor and some random people at tables. I don't want to look like an idiot, so I nod yes.

"I'm trying to make her jealous."

I turn to face him. "What?"

Before I realize what is happening, his lips are on mine. I completely tense up. All kinds of thoughts race through my head – What the hell? Who is this other girl? Wait. James is kissing me?! Suddenly, my mind registers the actual kiss. Soft, sweet, and … over.

"Did it work?" I ask quietly.

"Did what work?"

"Does she look jealous?"

"Who?"

"The girl."

James laughs. "It's hard to tell. She looks like she might be angry. Maybe I should kiss her again."

"Wait … what?" I'm so confused. I take a step back from him. "Would you just stop it? Tell me what's going on."

He laughs and turns me around by my shoulders to face the wall behind us. It's the mirrored wall behind the dance floor and I stare at our reflections. "You," he says, his breath warm on my ear. "I was talking about you. You're the girl."

Oh. *Oh.*

His hands circle my waist, and he turns me around. My stomach flips beneath his touch as I rest my hands on his arms, noting for the first time how toned they feel through the thin sleeves of his tuxedo shirt. All that time on the ice must pay off.

"Tell me what you're thinking," he asks quietly as we start to move again.

Questions race through my mind, and I can't pick just one. "I'm thinking I have a lot of questions."

"Fire away."

"Are you going to tell me the truth?"

"Why wouldn't I?"

"Because I'm not feeling a whole lot of honesty right now. You've barely spoken to me all night."

James releases a defeated sigh. "I know. I'm sorry. My nerves got the best of me."

"Nerves?" I ask.

"It's not every day that you decide to tell your best friend you have feelings for her."

I swallow.

"I should have done this sooner. Much sooner." He shakes his head. "Like years ago."

"Years?" I squeak.

He gives me an incredulous look. "Really? How is it possible that you could not know how I feel about you by now?"

I pause to think as we continue to move in a circle. "You're my best friend."

"So? I can't be anything else?"

"You've always been in my life. I never considered anything else. And you never said anything."

He frowns. "It never once crossed your mind that I might have feelings for you other than friendship? You've never thought of me in any other way?"

I bite my lip, embarrassed.

"What?"

A blush creeps over my cheeks. "Tonight. Getting ready. It crossed my mind."

His expression lights up like Times Square. "Really?"

"Really," I smile.

He looks relieved. I think I am too, but inside I feel strange. I'm excited and worried at the same time. I've never had a serious boyfriend before. I've always known he's a great guy, but I literally noticed how cute he was only hours ago. Is it possible I knew how he felt all along but wouldn't allow myself to process it because we were friends?

As he pulls me close, I decide to dwell on that thought later. I tuck my head beneath his chin and relax into him. His body feels strong and warm against mine, and I admit it feels really good to be where I am right now.

Eventually the song ends and another fast song starts. We separate and look at each other. It's a little awkward, like we've been caught doing something we shouldn't have done or like we're seeing each other for the first time. Thankfully Shel is by my side in seconds, pulling me away to dance with her again. I wave to James as I'm towed away. He smiles and waves back.

"Tell me!" Shel demands as we dance out of his line of sight.

"You knew about this all along!" I accuse her over the music.

"Knew what? That he was going to kiss you? No," she says matter-of-factly. "Heck, I didn't know if you two had been together all along anyway and were just keeping it a secret."

I lean into her ear. "You saw that?"

"Heck yes! I think everyone *saw that*."

I am horrified. My first kiss with James and it was on public display?

"So, what's going on?" she asks impatiently.

"He said he has feelings for me."

"Well, duh. I think everyone knew that but you."

My face twists in confusion.

"You never listen to me. How long have I been telling you this?" She spins around. "Like I said earlier, you're delusional."

Suddenly nervous, I ask, "What do I do?"

Shel leans in toward me on one of her dance moves and laughs. "Enjoy it!"

I try to concentrate on dancing with Shel, but my attention keeps wandering back to James. I catch his eye from across the room, and he gives me an amazing smile that makes my heart beat double time. I can't help myself and grin back. I think about all the years we've known each other and what this could mean.

Suddenly, my subconscious propels me forward in time, to about two weeks ago. It picks up a memory of our argument, at the moment where I yelled, "What does that mean?"

James pins me with hard eyes. "I'm trying to tell you nothing happened and you won't accept it!" He's pissed.

I'm so angry with him right now. It's an unfamiliar emotion around James; we hardly ever fight. I'm a terrible fighter; instead of yelling I usually end up crying, but on this particular day I was on a roll. Aggressively, I snap, "You expect me to believe that?"

"Yes." He looks at me exasperated. "When have I ever lied to you?"

I give him a wary look that questions his statement.

"So, now you think I lie to you?"

I don't answer. Instead, I continue to glare at him with my arms crossed.

"Fine!" He heads for the door, then turns around, changing his mind. "Might I remind you of all I gave up for you? For us?"

Not this again. I let out an irritated huff. "Listen, you know why you came here."

"Whatever." He makes it to the door this time. He leaves, slamming it behind him.

The door slam sounds so real that it startles me awake. My eyes instantly blur with fresh tears. I never should have let him leave.

CHAPTER 3

When my parents returned home with my things, I unpacked all the essentials – clothes, laptop, headphones – and left one box sealed up tight. My mother thought it would be best to pack all my pictures and other personal memory-type stuff separately. I love her for that.

Days later, I stare at the blinking cursor on my laptop screen. What else is there to say about the law and how it pertains to S corporations? This assignment is about as dry and boring as they come. But I continue to plug away at it. I only have a few remaining course assignments. It really doesn't bother me. The work keeps my hands and my mind busy when I'm awake; my memory, dreams, and tears keep me occupied while I'm asleep.

I hear the back door open and close, and voices start to carry up the stairs. Thinking it is my brother and Kate, I hit save on my laptop and start to make my way down the stairs so I can pretend to be social. About two steps down I overhear my mother say "It's so good to see you," her tone suggesting that company has stopped by, not family.

"You too, Marlene," I hear the voice of James' father.

My stomach instantly turns into knots. I'm not ready for this. My pulse starts to pound behind my ears.

"Eric, Carol," my dad greets James' parents as their voices grow louder. "What can we do for you?"

"Is Emma here?" Mrs. Davis asks, her tone a bit harsh.

My mother responds cautiously. "She's upstairs. Would you like me to get her?"

I know I cannot go downstairs. My heart is racing, and I can feel my face starting to get hot.

"Oh no, no," James' dad says nervously. "We've just been ..." he hesitates as he searches for the right words, "concerned about her since the service."

"The service was beautiful," my mother says. I can picture her extending her hand, offering the Davis' a seat. "So many people were there. Your son was very loved."

Mrs. Davis unexpectedly snaps, "We know."

I can feel the electricity in the room change even though I'm on the landing.

Mrs. Davis' voice is livid. "Your daughter nearly ruined our son's memorial!" she hisses.

"Carol. You said you wouldn't do this," Eric pleads with his wife.

An image of my parents regarding each other nervously pops into my head. "You do know she is devastated, right?" my mother asks, flustered. I can visualize her wide, surprised eyes.

"Of course she is. We all are." Mr. Davis' tone insinuates he is trying to diffuse the situation and apologize for his wife's demeanor.

"What my wife is trying to say is if Emma could have prevented her outburst, she most certainly would have," my dad explains.

Mrs. Davis doesn't care. "Your daughter's actions disturbed a lot of people," she spits her words. "Our family will forever carry that image in their minds. We are all grieving, and witnessing that outburst on top of what's already happened didn't help. My son's last moments on this earth are now forever tied to your daughter's lack of decency!"

I am mortified. Half of me wants to run away and hide; the other half wants to run downstairs and apologize. To make it right. But I can't do either. Instead I lean against the wall for support.

"Why exactly are you here?" my mother demands. "Are you looking for an apology? Because you're not going to get one. You can't tell my daughter how to grieve!"

"Okay," my dad intervenes. I'm sure he's placed his hands protectively on my mom's shoulders by now. "I think we can all agree that everyone is on edge. Let's not make things worse by arguing."

Mrs. Davis is brusque. "We want to know what happened."

"Details," James' father adds quietly.

"Details? Of the accident?" my mother asks, shocked.

I feel my body sliding against the wall until I hit the floor. I pull my knees to my chest.

"Yes. We assume you've discussed this with Emma."

"No. She hasn't said a word about that night."

"You haven't asked her?"

"Whatever for? So she can relive the pain? She's barely eating and speaking as it is."

I hear Mrs. Davis huff. "She has to know something; some detail that would let us know what led to this."

"Carol," my dad says softly. "Would any minute detail change reality? Emma wasn't even with James that night. She was in her room. How could she possibly know much more than us?"

Mrs. Davis' voice wavers, as if she cannot control her emotions. "I know that my son is gone. I know he spent more time with your daughter than anyone else on this planet. And I know she knows something we don't."

"That's impossible," my mother says with disbelief.

No one says anything for a moment. Tension hangs heavy in the air; I can feel it all the way up on the landing. My parents may be retired and in their mid-fifties, but they're active. They could take the uppity Davis'. Eric and Carol are soft. They play tennis and have a lawn service.

Mr. Davis breaks the silence in a kinder tone. "We came here to ask you if you would let us know if she mentions anything. For our peace of mind."

"Of course," my dad replies. "But I'm sure you can understand why we won't push her."

My mother has had enough. "Are you finished?" she snaps. An image of her standing with her hands on her hips floats up to me, just like she would do when I was in trouble as a child.

Footsteps head toward the door; one set marches with determination. I can only assume its James' mother by the clicking of the heels. I hear Mr. Davis quietly apologize as he leaves. "I'm sorry. Things have been ... difficult."

Tears stream down my face in silence. *"I'm so sorry!"* my brain screams at them, hoping they will hear it telepathically. I want to go back to my room and hide but it's as if my arms and legs have forgotten how to move. I am a statue, sitting on the floor, hugging my knees to my chest.

I don't know how long it takes my mother to find me frozen on the landing.

"Oh! Emma! What's wrong? Are you okay?" she asks panicked, kneeling down to take my face in her hands.

I look through her. I can barely speak. "It's my fault."

"What? What's your fault?"

Silence.

"Honey? Did you hear our conversation with the Davis'?"

Silence.

"You did, didn't you? Damn them." She's angry. "Listen to me, Emma, they didn't mean what they said. They are mourning. People say things they normally wouldn't when they are hurting. They are trying to make sense of something that doesn't make sense."

"It's my fault."

"No, sweetie, believe me it's not."

My eyes focus on hers. I find my voice, stronger now, determined. "It's my fault."

"What is? What is your fault?"

I snap. "The accident!" I yell. I yank my head free of her grasp. "The accident is my fault!"

~

I LAND ON MY STOMACH, arms in front of me from my attempt to catch myself. I open my eyes and look around, letting my eyes adjust and trying to catch my breath. It's dark. Night-time. I can feel frost on the grass beneath my fingertips; the cool spring air bites my skin. I can hear the sounds of passing cars. I am outside.

I glance around to get my bearings and see it. The Jeep is off to my right, upside down, the front end crushed against a tree. The radiator hisses and one back tire spins. Just beyond the truck is a small embankment; beyond that a two lane highway. I immediately know where I am.

I start running. *I have to get him out!* But no matter how fast I run, no matter how much adrenaline pumps through my veins, the further the vehicle seems to get. I can feel my lungs burning as I push my body to move faster. I start to panic. *Get him out!* My legs are starting to wobble beneath me, turning into Jello.

"No!" I scream as I fall to the ground, unable to run any farther. My legs will not cooperate anymore. I stare at the ground as I grab handful after handful of grass, grabbing and then pulling, grabbing and pulling, my legs dead behind me. Mercifully, I reach out again and see the Jeep just beyond my reach. My adrenaline soars as I realize I'm close. I manage to get up on my hands and knees and crawl the rest of the way to the truck.

"JAMES!" I scream his name.

I make it to the side of the vehicle and look through the jagged glass where the window used to be. I see blood. Gallons of blood. All over the seats, on the dash, on the windshield, the floorboards – it's as if the entire inside of the car is made of blood. I gag at the sight and the smell and cover my nose with my wrist. James is not inside. Why can't I see him? Where is he? I know he's here!

Panicked, I half-walk, half-crawl my way around the Jeep

searching for him. I step in something wet. Blood is starting to seep out of the truck on to the grass. It's as if the truck itself is bleeding.

"JAMES!" I scream over and over, my throat growing raw. I circle the Jeep again and again, searching. I cannot find him. Exhausted, my body threatens to give out on me entirely.

Eventually I collapse, sobbing, next to the bleeding truck. I cover my face with my hands and realize they are sticky, covered in blood.

"You!" I hear a female voice snarl at me.

I look up and see Mrs. Davis coming from the embankment by the road. She's headed straight for me; her face is twisted into a murderous expression. In accusation. I am terrified of her, but my body will not move.

When she reaches me, she growls, "This is your fault!"

I can only cower.

Her hands wrap around my neck, squeezing and cutting off my air supply. I choke and sputter and try to rip her hands away, but my hands are slippery from the blood and I can't get a good hold.

"This is your fault!" she continues to yell at me.

"Your fault!" My lungs are burning.

"Your fault!" My eyes close.

"Your fault!" I scratch at her hands as they grow tighter.

"Your ...!"

"EMMA!" I continue to scratch and claw.

"EMMA! Stop!"

I think I hear my mother's voice, but it can't be. Mrs. Davis is trying to kill me, and the Jeep is bleeding!

"Stop! It's me! It's me!"

I open my eyes and see my mother holding my arms by my wrists trying to stop me from clawing and scratching her.

"It's me."

I stop wrestling her, confused. I press my eyes together tightly and reopen them. "Mom?" I ask in a scratchy voice.

"Shhh. It's me." She releases my arms and feels around my forehead. Worriedly she asks, "Nightmare?"

I feel the pillow beneath my head when I nod and realize I am in bed.

"Here." She hands me a glass of water from the bedside table, then sets a small pill in my other palm. "This will help."

I put the pill in my mouth, and she helps me swallow a few sips of water. I lay my head down and close my eyes. As I stare into blackness, I try to think of absolutely nothing. The nightmare felt so *real.* I could feel everything, smell everything. A chill goes through my body as Mrs. Davis' face reappears in my mind. *Please,* I beg myself. *If I dream anymore, don't make it a nightmare.*

"I love you, Em," I hear my mom say as the door closes.

My body starts to relax, and I wonder what type of pill she gave me. My mind starts to drift. *No nightmares. Please.*

My subconscious listens to my silent plea and rewards me with a perfect rendition of James' voice.

CHAPTER 4

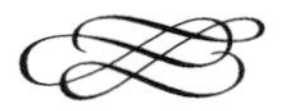

"I love you."

"What?" I look up at him, confused.

"You heard me."

James and I are lying together on the couch in his living room. We were supposed to go out but decided watching a movie was better than riding mountain bikes in the rain, even if it is August and the light shower will cool the mugginess.

I turn my attention back to the movie. Did he just say what I think he said?

"So?" he prompts.

I manage the lamest response possible. "So … what?"

"Really?"

I stare up at him stupidly.

He frowns and looks away.

Damn. I've hurt his feelings, and I didn't mean to. I straighten up so I'm sitting by his side, facing him. "Hey."

He's focused on the movie now, his mouth set in a hard line.

"I'm sorry."

No response.

"I really am."

He says nothing.

How do I fix this? "I just didn't expect, you know … so soon …" I can't form a sentence.

He still says nothing.

We sit in silence for countless minutes. His focus is on the television, mine on my hands that are clenched together in my lap. There's an uncomfortable tension between us. I don't know what to say, and I don't want him to be angry with me. Maybe I should just go.

I unfold my legs and start to leave when, suddenly, he pounces at me, grabbing both of my shoulders and pushing me on my back against the couch. My breath comes out in a whoosh. "Hey!"

He hovers over me on his knees, his hands holding my shoulders against the furniture, pinning me. I look up at him, and he's smiling like this is the funniest thing ever.

"Caught ya." He smirks.

"Oh, now you're speaking to me?"

He laughs.

"It's not funny!"

He rearranges his face to be serious, but his eyes are still laughing. "You're right. It's not."

I struggle against the pressure of his hands. "Let me up."

"No."

"Why?"

"Not until you say it."

"Say what?"

He raises his eyebrows at me. "Like you don't know."

He wants me to say I love him? I buy time. "And if I don't?"

His blue eyes light up at the challenge. His hands leave my shoulders for a split second and he collects my wrists in one hand, leans over, and pins my arms above my head. "I'll make you talk," he says and goes for the most ticklish spot on my body with his free hand – my ribs.

"Stop! Don't!" I yelp. I try to squirm away by twisting my body from my waist, but it just gives him easier access to my side.

"Give up?"

"No!" I laugh and try to move in the other direction.

He continues my torture, and I can't speak through my laughing fit. I'm laughing so hard I can't breathe.

"Give up yet?"

"No!" Tears start to stream down my face.

"How about now?"

"Can't … breathe …" I gasp.

"I can do this all day," he teases me.

I feel like I'm going to pee my pants. "Okay! Okay! Stop! I'll talk."

He stops tickling me but doesn't let go of my wrists. He leans in so we are nearly nose to nose. "Well?"

My breath catches. At first I think it's because I'm recovering from my hysterics, but the tingles that float over my skin tell me it's for other reasons. "Um …"

"Um what?" He grins.

I can't help it. That lopsided smile gets me every time. In one quick motion I lift my head and catch his mouth with mine. It takes him off guard and, lost in the kiss, he releases my wrists. The thought crosses my mind to use my freed hands to push him away and escape, but my body has other ideas. One hand wraps around his neck while the other tangles in his hair, holding him in place. Our kiss deepens and I pull him close, deciding I want to stay here indefinitely.

After a few moments James rests his forehead against mine. "Nice try."

"I thought it was nice."

"Stop trying to distract me."

"Is it working?" I joke.

He lifts his head to look at me, and his face is serious but not angry. He pushes himself back so he's sitting at the opposite end of the couch. He offers his hands and I take them. He pulls me up so we're sitting facing each other.

"Maybe I did this the wrong way," he says, nervously running a hand through his disheveled hair. His sandy brown locks have turned a little blonde from the summer sun.

I shake my head. "No, you're fine. It's me. You just caught me by surprise, that's all."

He sighs and looks down. Neither of us knows what to say; it's uncomfortable for both of us.

I suddenly become interested in picking at my cuticles while my mind races. I know he loves me; he didn't have to say it. But he did. And I know I love him. So why can't I just say it? Is it because we've only been a couple for a few months? He's been my best friend since forever. If I didn't love him as a boyfriend I would most certainly still love him as a friend, but then you don't randomly tell your friends you love them …

The rambling in my head is cut off when James reaches out and gently lifts my chin so we're looking at each other. Staring me straight in the eyes, he says, "I love you. I'm about 99% sure you love me, too. So, you don't have to say it right now. No pressure."

Now I want to say it. To make him feel better. To make things easier.

"I …"

"Don't say it just to say it."

"But I …"

"Emma."

"Listen! I ..."

"Emma. Seriously."

"I am being serious." I slap both my hands down on his hard chest in exasperation and lean in to get in his face. "Listen. You know it takes me a minute to process things. I'll admit I choked earlier. But I want to say it. I want you to be 100% sure. I. Love. You." I enunciate each word.

He considers this for a moment. "You're not just saying it?"

"No. I mean it."

His face relaxes.

"You really had doubts?" I ask.

"Well …"

I frown. "I would think that kiss would've made things clear."

James gives me a sly smile. "Maybe you should kiss me again, just to make sure I get it."

My eyebrows jump. "Really? You think so?"

"I do."

I pretend to mull it over for a moment, and then I smile. "Nope. I think you get it just fine."

He shakes his head. "I don't."

"You do." I try to lean away, but he wraps his arms around me before I can get very far.

"Honestly, I don't get it," he says as he attempts a sad puppy dog pout.

I laugh. "If you keep that up, I may never kiss you again."

"You will," he says, leaning in to me.

And I do.

"Em, wake up."

I try to open my eyes, but they feel like weights have been tied to them.

"You've got to get up."

I turn my head in the direction of my father's voice and try to speak, but my mouth won't move. I want to tell him I'm tired and I can't open my eyes and he needs to leave me alone.

I feel him sit on the bed and gently shake my shoulders. "Emma?"

I try to open my eyes again. *Why won't they open?*

"She's been sleeping for hours," he says to someone. I can hear the worry in his voice.

"It's okay, Dad," I want to say. "I like this sleep. There are good memories here."

"She'll wake up when she's ready," my mom says.

"Are you sure you didn't give her too much?" he asks.

"I only gave her one of the sedatives Dr. Morris prescribed for my insomnia."

My dad sighs. "If she doesn't wake up soon, I'm calling the doctor. I feel like we're not doing a very good job. Maybe we should call a professional."

"Dale, we need to give her some time to work through this."

"Do you think she needs some friends around? You know, people she can talk to?"

I think I hear my mom move closer. "I'll give Shel a call in a few hours. Maybe she can pay Emma a visit."

Ah, Shel, I think. *I miss her.*

"Come on, let's leave her be."

My dad leans over, kisses my forehead, and the smell of Irish Spring soap lingers in the air. I feel the bed move as he stands, and I hear them leave. My eyes still feel heavy. *Will I ever open them again?* Whatever that sedative was, it's powerful. Since I can't open my eyes and fully wake, my thoughts turn to Shel. Shelby. The only best friend I have left.

An image pops into my mind, and I try to smile at the memory, but my mouth won't cooperate. Shel and I are crouched at the end of James' driveway in the weeds. It's hard to contain our giggling. We're holding rolls of toilet paper, cans of shaving cream, and a couple bars of soap. Devil's Night is a beautiful thing.

"Okay," she whispers. "You start on the trees down here. I'll head up to the cars and start with the cream and the soap."

I nod and watch her creep up the driveway, looking like a mugger. Her black sweatpants and sweater conceal her enviable curves; her ski cap hides her straight brown hair and bangs. I try to be stealthy in my identical ensemble and crouch low. I make it over to the side yard where I throw a roll of toilet paper into a nearly leafless maple tree. It catches on a branch and unravels as it falls to the ground. I grab it and toss it back up, grab it and toss it, trying to be speedy. Once this tree looks full, I move to another one a little farther up the drive and get started.

I can hear Shel pressing the shaving cream out of the cans in between the crunch of fallen leaves beneath my feet. I glance up the drive and see her methodically covering James' windshield with shaving cream. I laugh to myself. That will serve him right. Two can play at this game.

Earlier in the day, Shel and I got wind from Zach during school that James and Matt were planning an epic tp-ing event at my house around midnight. We decided it would be fun to beat them to it and devised a plan: we'd leave earlier and wreak havoc at James' house first. If the boys still carried out their scheme after seeing what we had done, we'd be waiting in the darkness back at my place ready to bust them before they could do any real damage.

I've finished with about three trees when I run out of paper. "Shel!" I whisper-yell to her.

She looks my way. She's finished with James' Jeep and is busy soaping Matt's pickup.

"I'm out. I'm going back to the car for more supplies."

I see her nod. I creep back down the driveway to Shel's car, her grandmother's old tan Lumina, which we've parked a little way down the road from the house. I make it to the car and open the squeaky rear door. I grab as many rolls of toilet paper as I can and try to shut the door as quietly as possible, although I'm not sure who would hear me out here.

I concentrate on keeping a hold of all the rolls as I creep back up the driveway. I shouldn't have grabbed so much. Back where I left off, I let the rolls fall to the ground except for one and get ready to heave it into the tree. I take a second and glance over at Shel to see how she's coming along, but she's not by Matt's truck anymore. Confused, I start looking around the yard to find her.

"Shel!" I whisper as loud as I dare.

No answer.

"Shel! Where are you?"

Again no answer. Where could she have gone? Did I pass her on my way back from the car? Impossible. I start to walk toward where I last saw her. "Shel!"

SMACK!! Something hits me dead center in the middle of my back. I whip around to see a tall, wiry blonde running away from me, laughing. Matt! I look down and see a cracked egg shell and yolk on the ground. He's throwing eggs.

Crap! We've been found out. I run around James' truck to duck down and hide. When I come around the side, I get a good look at the front porch and see three cartons of eggs sitting on the ground. I run over to them, grab as many eggs as I can hold, and run back, ducking low. Hearing footsteps approaching on the other side, I stand up quickly, turn, and launch an egg. It connects with my target perfectly – except my target is Shel.

I can't help but burst out laughing. "I'm so sorry," I tell her as she stands there dripping with egg. I notice she's holding a couple of eggs, too. She must have found them while soaping.

She starts laughing. "Come on. I think they ran around back."

We pass by the porch, and Shel picks up a few more eggs. "Stupid of them to leave them out like this."

We head around the back of the house and crouch by the deck.

"Shhh," I whisper to Shel.

We hear the patio door slide open. "They've got to be out front," I hear James whisper. "You head around that way, and I'll go around the other way," he says.

Shel and I look at each other. The boys have to come off the deck to go around the house; they will walk right past us. Shel nods at me and mouths "1 … 2 ... 3!"

We jump up at the same time and start throwing our eggs.

"Take that!" Shel yells.

"Hey! Ahhh!"

"Split up!"

James and Matt take off in different directions while trying to block our shots. James leaps over the railing of the deck and takes off toward the side yard; Matt has no choice but to take the steps and run right past us.

One of my eggs makes perfect contact with his temple. I bust out into hysterical laughter and shout, "Payback!" then take off running in the opposite direction.

Shel must have followed me because we end up together behind the shed. "Now what?" I ask her. "We're out of ammo."

"Temporarily," she says. She nods to the left, and I see the hose reel connected to the side of the house. "You go and man the hose. I'll flush them out." She flashes an evil smile.

Nodding, I take off. When I reach the hose, I unroll it a bit so I have some slack to work with. I turn on the faucet, grip the nozzle, and stand pressing my back against the siding. I whisper to Shel, "Ready!"

Shel takes off around the front of the house. It's not long before I hear "There she is! Get her!" Running and laughter ensue, headed in my direction. Shel runs past me and shouts, "Now!"

I step away from the house and squeeze the nozzle of the hose as far as it will go. A concentrated stream of water sprays out and nails James right in the face as he runs up on me.

"Arrggh!"

"Gotcha!" I yell as he sputters and tries to block my shot. I drop the hose and take off running. I catch a glimpse of Matt chasing Shel around the side of the house again, so I decide to take off deeper into the backyard. I hear footsteps behind me, chasing me. I can't see any good place to hide, and I'm started to get winded. He's going to catch me. I have no idea how far behind he is, so I make a wide turn and attempt to head back near the house when I feel a hand brush against my shoulder, trying to grab my shirt. "AHH!" I scream.

"Come here!" James shouts, laughing.

I keep running toward the house. Maybe I can make it around the front and hide by the porch to grab more eggs. I can't hear James behind me anymore, but it's highly unlikely he's given up. I'm almost there. I round the corner of the house to the front yard when, out of nowhere, I'm met with a handful of shaving cream to my face.

"Ahhh!" I yell as I'm knocked off balance. I recover nicely, though, and wipe away enough of the foam to see Matt standing there, covered nearly head to toe with the stuff. Shel's standing next to him, just as covered. Both of them are laughing hysterically, gripping their sides. They must have had one heck of a shaving cream fight with the cream Shel used on James' windshield.

"Gotcha!" James runs up and surprises me from behind. He swoops me up with one arm around my waist. I struggle against him. "Now what are you going to do?" he laughs.

"Get you with the hose again!"

"Oh no you're not."

"Once I get out of here, you're done," I tease.

"Not gonna happen."

I continue to push against his arm, trying to break free. "Put me down."

He laughs.

"Hey guys," Shel calls to us. "I'm sticky. And hungry."

"Same here," Matt says, shaking shaving cream off his fingers. "Let's clean up and get something to eat."

"Will you behave if I put you down?" James asks me.

"Of course," I say sweetly. "But I win."

"What? You so did not win."

"I did too. You have to admit that was an excellent shot with the hose."

"I will give you that," he says as he releases me. "But you fell right into my trap. Who do you think told us you'd be coming here tonight?"

"Zach."

He grins. "Matt and I were prepared for you all along. You should have just waited to jump us at your house later."

"Ugh!" I punch him in the arm.

He looks up at my handiwork with the toilet paper in the trees. "What a waste of perfectly good toilet paper," he snickers.

I pull a glop of egg off his shirt. "What a waste of perfectly good eggs," I mimic him and smash the yolk on his cheek, dragging my hand down the side of his face and rubbing it in.

"You are going to pay for that," he says angrily, but his eyes light up.

I start to giggle as I back away from him with my hands held out in front of me. "What are you going to do?"

"You'd better run," he threatens.

"I'm not scared of you," I boast.

In one quick movement, he charges at me, grabs the top of my legs, and throws me over his shoulder like a sack of potatoes. "I warned you."

"Shelby! Matt! Help!" I yell at the ground and kick my legs as he starts to carry me behind the house. I look over near the porch where they had been standing, but they're gone. They must have gone inside while we debated who the winner was.

"Where are you taking me?"

"You'll see."

We're coming up on the hose. "Oh no. Not the hose. I'm already enough of a mess as it is," I yelp.

With me still hoisted over his shoulder, he bends down to make sure the hose is still turned on. He grabs the nozzle. "I think you have something on your face," he laughs. "Looks like shaving cream. Let me get that for you."

"No! No! Okay! You win," I protest.

"Um, I think it's too late for that." He reaches behind his back with the hand that holds the hose and points it directly at my inverted head.

"Please don't!" I shield my face with my hands. This is going to be cold. I let out a small "eeek."

He laughs and drops the hose, then puts me down so I'm standing in front of him. "Do you really think I'd shoot you in the face with a hose?"

I look up at him and shrug. "Why not? I shot you in the face with it."

He grins. "I can take it."

"You're not so tough." I wrap my arms around his waist. "All talk and no action."

"No action, eh?" He raises his eyebrows. He leans down and plants a kiss on me that makes my head spin, then pulls away. "You taste like shaving cream. It's gross."

"Oh, well, thank you. You have egg all over your face, and it's gross," I laugh.

Shel's voice comes from behind us. "You're both gross. Would you get your hands off each other for a second? What do you want on your pizza?"

CHAPTER 5

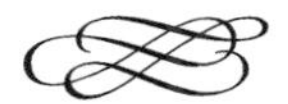

When the sedative wears off enough for me to open my eyes again, it is late afternoon the next day. I stretch out my body, and my muscles protest. I must have stayed in the same position the whole time. Ouch.

As I wait for the blood to return to my limbs, I replay the Davis' visit and how angry they are with me. My heart hurts. I wish I was strong enough to have talked to them, to apologize for temporarily losing my sanity. I didn't plan for it to happen; I was doing pretty well until I lost my concentration on that blasted plant. The orchid. I realize now why I was drawn to it. The same fuchsia flowers were in my prom corsage.

I get out of bed and shuffle my way to the bathroom.

"Em? Is that you?" I hear my mom shout up the stairs.

"Yes!"

"Everything okay?"

"Yes! I'll be down in a sec." I look in the bathroom mirror. Yikes. I brush my teeth and then try to comb through the snarls in my hair. It's not working very well. I then realize I'm in the same clothes I wore yesterday and decide a shower is in order.

The hot water feels amazing. I soap up my hair, pile it on top of my head, and let the water pound on the back of my neck. It relaxes my muscles and reminds me of when James would rub my shoulders when I was stressed. I could sure use a massage right now. I try to remove the tension from my shoulders myself, but it's a lame attempt and does nothing.

"I wish I could do that for you."

My head snaps up, and I jump as if I've been electrocuted. James' voice is clear as day.

Startled, I glance around the shower. I swear it sounded like he was *right here.* My heart starts to beat faster as I push aside the floral shower curtain, expecting to see him standing there. I look around the bathroom. He's not here, of course. I pull the curtain back and wrap my arms around myself. In my drug induced state, my mind is playing tricks on me.

Deciding that human interaction is what I need right now, I quickly finish the shower, throw on some cut-off jean shorts and an old WMU tee, and head downstairs. As I do, I twist my wet hair into a low knot.

I find my mom curled on our suede beige couch reading. She looks up from *The Flint Journal.* "Feeling better?"

"I think I'm still a little groggy," I tell her. *And I'm hearing voices,* my mind adds.

She frowns. "Apparently you needed some extra rest."

I shrug. "Maybe. I'm going to get something to eat. That will probably help."

"There's Chinese in the refrigerator. Your dad got take out."

I nod and head to the kitchen. Inside the fridge I find a carton of almond chicken and a carton of fried rice. I set about plating it, then place it in the microwave.

My mom enters the kitchen. "So ..."

I look at her. "So?"

"We need to talk." She takes a seat on a stool at the island.

I return my attention to the microwave, enter the time, and press start. "About?"

"Well, for starters, I talked to Shel."

I turn around and lean against the stove.

"Your dad and I think you need someone around who you can talk to, a friend to hang out with," she says. "It might make you feel better."

"Haven't I released enough emotion?" I ask sarcastically, referring to my recent meltdown. I never thought I was capable of screaming the way I did at the funeral home.

She shrugs. "Maybe, maybe not."

I take in her pensive expression. "Listen, I'm sorry. I'm sorry for breaking down at the funeral and for yelling at you the other night. I didn't mean it."

"You don't have to apologize." She leans one arm against the granite countertop. "I can't tell you how angry I am with that witch Carol Davis for making you feel like you should be ashamed. What she said was uncalled for. You can erupt anyway you please."

Am I a volcano? I could be Mt. Vesuvius. I think of my bloody dream and fighting off my mother. Nothing like that has ever happened before.

"You need to release your feelings; it's not healthy to keep them trapped inside," my mom says. "I've only seen you cry twice since this happened."

I study the floor next to the stove and direct my words to the wood instead of her compassionate face. "I've cried more than you know."

My mom sighs. "Your father and I don't want you to feel like you can't express your feelings. You don't have to hide them. That might be why you had that nightmare. Shel agrees with me."

"So Shel is a psychologist now?" I smirk. "What happened to becoming an M.D.?"

"Look." My mother sets her palms against the counter. "Your father and I are worried. We know things will get better with time, but recent events …" she trails off. "We're concerned as any parents would be. You sleep all the time. You haven't left the house. You haven't talked to your friends. You're not eating …"

I point toward the microwave. "I'm eating."

Her eyes soften. "Not regularly." She hesitates. "You haven't unpacked anything we brought home from school except your computer. Em, when's the last time you said James' name?"

Where is she going with this? "It's only been two weeks," I whisper.

"Honey, it's been a month."

The realization startles me. The microwave beeps, but I don't move to collect my food. What little appetite I had is gone. Has that much time really passed?

"You're becoming a shell of yourself," she says and stands. She walks around the island and stops in front of me. "That's why Shel is coming to stay for a few weeks. Longer if necessary."

I snap to. "No. Mom. I think she's taking spring classes. I don't want to inconvenience her."

"It's been worked out," she says and rubs my arm. "There is no inconvenience. Besides, Shel wants to help."

I stare at her. The last thing I want to do is expose Shel to my depression, if that's what this is. Am I depressed? Or going nuts? A month of my life has disappeared, and I just heard James' voice in the shower.

My mother places her hands on my shoulders. "I want you to know this is the first step. If we don't see some of the old Emma back by the end of the summer, your dad and I will look into therapy."

It's one thing to question my own sanity. It's quite another to have my parents and best friend do so behind my back. "Why?" My expression twists. "I'm not losing it. I'm not crazy."

I think.

"I didn't say you were." My mom remains calm. "But, we need to find a way to cope with this. James was part of our family. He's been hanging around this house since you two were ten. It would help us all ... your dad, me, even Mike, to talk about him."

"So what's stopping you? Reminisce all you want." I need to check my harsh tone. I know my parents only want what's best for me.

"The last time anyone mentioned James, other than right now in this moment, you went into some sort of trance." Her kind eyes narrow. "Do you remember what happened after the Davis' left?"

I look away from her as I think back. Things are blurry, probably due to the pill she gave me after my nightmare. "You found me on the stairs. Then I went to bed."

Her voice wavers. "Dad had to carry you to bed. You wouldn't move; it was like your muscles were locked. Sweetie, you kept saying the accident was your fault. Why would you say that? How could you think that? You cried yourself to sleep."

My eyes sting, and I slam them shut to prevent the tears from falling. It doesn't work, and a few drops tumble down my cheek. I can't tell her why I'm the reason James is no longer with us. It's too painful.

Her fingers leave my shoulders, brush beneath my eyes, and smear my tears. There's no way she can catch them all, and they continue to fall and roll down my face. She gives up and wraps me in a warm hug instead.

"James fell asleep at the wheel," she says softly, yet holds me tight. "There's nothing you could have done."

That's not true. There's one thing I could have done. One thing I should have done.

My mom allows me to cry against her. She doesn't ask questions. She doesn't press the therapy issue or talk about Shel's upcoming stay. She just holds me and strokes my hair like I'm a little girl again.

ONCE I CALMED DOWN and took two, maybe three, bites of almond chicken, I spent the rest of the evening watching television with my parents. We started with the six o'clock news then changed to the History Channel, where we were sucked into a marathon of *Pawn Stars*. Chumlee cracks me up. Well, he typically does. Due to my somber mood, he just made me smirk a lot.

My dad yawns. "Well, I'm ready for bed." We lost mom for the night about an hour ago. He turns to me, his body half hanging off the recliner. "Are you heading up?"

I don't feel sleepy at all. "No, I think I'll stay and watch something else."

"Not tired?"

I shake my head.

My dad's mouth quirks up. "Imagine that. A good doping will do that to you."

I roll my eyes. He doesn't like that my mom gave me a sedative that knocked me out for half a day. The two of them ended up having breakfast for dinner and before he cracked each egg he'd hold it up and say, "This is your brain." Then he'd crack the egg into the pan and say, "This is your brain on drugs," as it sizzled. Then he'd leer at mom. "Any questions?" I guess it's an old '80s commercial. After the sixth time he said the slogan, she snapped him with the dish towel.

My dad pats my head as he passes me. "Good night, Em Bug."

I stare after him in surprise. I can't remember that last time he called me that. "'Night."

When he disappears up the stairs, I start to flip through the channels. Infomercial, infomercial, *Jersey Shore, HGTV,* infomercial. As I continue, there's really nothing on I want to watch. I mute the TV and stretch. What to do? There's a book I was in the middle of reading before I came home. I head upstairs and grab it, along with my pillow to make me a cozy reading space on the couch. I get a bottle of water from the fridge and settle into my little nest to pick up in the middle of *The Girl with the Dragon Tattoo.* I've missed Lisbeth Salander; she's definitely kick-ass, something I am completely unfamiliar with.

I find my bookmark, open the book, and start scanning the paragraphs to figure out where I left off. I bend the spine back and forth and settle in to read when a piece of folded notebook paper falls out from between the front cover and first page.

What's this? I close the book and unfold the paper.

Em –

Things have been crazy busy lately so I wanted to go old school and put it on paper (this way you can keep it forever) and tell you I love you more than you know.

More than the sun

More than the stars

More than breathing

More than life itself.

Until the end of forever,

James

My throat tightens, and my chest feels hollow.

I wish I had found his note sooner, when I could have told him I felt the same. I would give anything just to be able to tell him again that I love him. To hold him in my arms, kiss his crooked smile, and run my fingers through his hair. To tease him about drinking too much Red Bull because he stayed up late watching a game or admonish him for not doing his laundry. Lately we'd been making plans for our senior year and beyond; we'd requested an off-campus apartment for housing in the fall. The goal was to live together, graduate together, and start our future together.

I lay my head down in my reading nest and hold the paper close to my heart. You would think there wouldn't be any tears left, but they spill silently down my face. With my book forgotten and my pillow soaked, I clutch the note to my chest and repeat the same thing over and over in my head, trying to lure sleep into taking me.

I love you. I miss you. Until the end of forever.

I OPEN my eyes and groan. "Oh, man."

"Nice to see you, too."

Shel is sitting across from me in a chair with her arms and legs crossed, her big brown eyes trained on me. I imagine she has been impatiently waiting for me to wake up. The ends of her light brown hair have been colored a fiery red, and her blunt-cut bangs remind me of Zooey Deschanel. She uncrosses her arms and leans forward, resting her chin on her hands.

"How long have you been here?" I ask, burying my face back in the pillow.

"About an hour."

I pick up my head and look at her. "I planned to be dressed when you got here, so you wouldn't think I was totally crazy."

"I don't think you're totally crazy." She smiles. "I think you're just a little crazy."

I sit up and roll my eyes. "Thanks." Looking around the room, I ask, "Where is everybody?"

"Your parents went to Home Depot. I guess they have some big yard work plans today."

"Yeah, they've been itching to get the garden in. Where's your stuff?"

"Your mom got me settled in Mike's old room pretty quickly." She chuckles. "Your parents seem excited I'm here."

"They are," I agree.

"Are you okay with my being here?"

I pause for a second and give her a small smile. "Of course I am, but it is a little embarrassing. I wish they'd waited until the summer to bother you, when you had planned to be home. I don't want this to screw with your classes ..."

"It's not a bother. My school won't be screwed up. You do remember who you're talking to right? Captain OCD?"

I laugh and nod. "Yeah, you are a little overly organized." I stretch. "I guess I should get dressed." I pull off the blanket that someone put over me and stand. The note I found the night before falls to the floor. I bend down quickly and pick it up.

"What's that?" Shel asks.

I want to say it's nothing because that would be easiest. Instead, I look down at the note in my hands and hold it out to her. If she's here to help me get through this, why not start now?

Shel gives me a confused look as she stands and takes the paper. As she reads it, her eyes get wide and then she looks at me.

"It was in my book," I explain as I gesture to *Dragon Tattoo* on the coffee table. "He must have put it there sometime ... anyway, I just found it last night."

Shel looks hurt for me. Her face crumples and she takes a few steps, wrapping me in a hug. I'm surprised by her action; she's not usually one for anything touchy-feely. It takes me a minute to pat her on the back reassuringly.

"It's okay. I don't typically sleep with things from my dead boyfriend. I just happened to find it last night," I try to explain, so she doesn't think I've completely lost it.

She abruptly lets me go and steps back. She hands me the note and says, "You keep this in a safe place. So you can look at it whenever you feel the need. Sleep with it if you have to. Do you want me to laminate it?"

"What?"

"Laminate it. So it stays nice and doesn't tear."

"No." I shake my head. "You think I should continue to sleep with this?" I was going to slide it under the flap of the still-sealed box of pictures and memory-type stuff from my dorm.

"If it makes you feel better. If it makes you feel closer to James."

I hadn't thought about that.

"What does make you feel better? Anything?" she asks.

There is one thing. "Not talking about it," I say matter-of-factly.

She makes a face. "You mean not dealing with it." She crosses her arms.

"Shel, I can't sit here all day and just bring up random–"

She shakes her head adamantly, cutting me off. "That's not what I meant. You don't have to talk about him all day, every day. But think about what he would want. Would he want to see you sink into a depression? Seclude yourself? Starve?"

Of course he wouldn't want that. "I don't think that's what is happening. I don't think I'm depressed. I'm just ... really sad."

"Hmm." She pauses for a moment, squints her eyes, and tilts her head as if evaluating me. "I think you'll be all right."

"Gee, thanks doctor."

She smiles. "Sorry. I was thinking about what your mom told me when she called."

"What did she say to make you drop everything and come to my rescue? I'm starting to worry."

Shel reaches for my elbow. "I'll tell you while you get dressed. I don't want your parents to come home and find you in your pink pj's and fuzzy socks. It's noon. They'll fire me."

My best friend leads me upstairs where she sits on the bed as I go to my dresser and place James' note in my top drawer, tucking it under my socks. "Be right back," I tell her and head to the bathroom. I quickly brush my teeth and almost expect to hear James' voice. But I don't.

"So," I ask Shel when I return to my room. "What'd my mom tell you?"

She sighs. "Don't be mad. I think your parents are just really worried."

"Dude, you're scaring me." I take a cue from Shel's attire and pull some jeans and a black tank top from my dresser.

"She said you were sleeping all the time. That it was next to impossible to wake you up. She told me that when you are awake, you're robotic, like not really there."

I concede that evaluation and nod as I dress.

"You're still not eating ..."

Again with the food? I pull my top over my head. "I eat! I mean, not like normal, but more than the last time I saw you."

"Okay." Shel lets that one slide. "She said you have bad dreams. Nightmares. She said you attacked her."

My face flushes red in embarrassment.

"What was the nightmare?" she asks, concerned. "I don't remember you ever having those, even as a kid."

I take a deep breath and sit next to her on the bed. "I dreamt of the accident. I was there but couldn't find ... him. I saw the Jeep and tons of blood; it felt so real. I could sense everything, even smell it. I was screaming for him, and I was so weak and tired. Then his mother was there, strangling me, choking me, and yelling that it was my fault. I was fighting her off when in reality it was my mom trying to wake me from the dream."

Shel's eyes are wide. "What do you think brought that on?"

"The Davis' paid my parents a visit. I overheard their conversation."

"And?"

"They are upset with me and the way I acted at the funeral. Their family was offended."

Shel's face twists in disbelief. "Are you serious?"

I look down, ashamed.

"What did they want you to do? Sing and dance like everything is fine?"

My eyes burn with tears as I remember my breakdown. I try to blink them away.

"Em, you shouldn't feel bad about what happened. That's what funerals are for, for people to grieve and say goodbye and get upset …"

"Shel." I stop her and close my eyes. "You were there," my voice shakes. "You heard me screaming … saw me crying ..."

My chest tightens. I remember the feel of plastic against my back as I slid from the chair. I remember how rough the carpet felt as I crawled across the floor on my hands and knees. I remember trying to stand and my legs failing me, my hands reaching to grasp the casket but sliding off the varnished wood. I remember trying again and again only to have my father and brother grab ahold of me to pull me back. I struggled with them, pushed them away as my fingers finally found purchase on the shiny wood. I remember gripping it as tight as humanly possible and feeling my brother try to pry my fingers off as my father held me around my waist and pulled me back. All the while I was screaming, "No! Let me be with him!"

Tears run freely down my face as I open my eyes and look at Shel as I choke out, "I wanted to be … I tried to crawl in … I wanted to be inside with him." I cover my face and sob into my hands. "How sick is that?"

After a moment, Shel gently pulls my hands from my face. Tears make silent tracks down her cheeks, too. She smiles weakly. "I don't think that's sick at all. Now, eating strawberries dipped in ketchup, that's sick."

I stare at her stupidly for a moment and then a laugh escapes. I quickly slap my hand over my mouth, and she starts to laugh, too. The laughter is contagious and, before we know it, we can't stop. We lay on the bed convulsing in a fit of hysterical giggles and grief.

"I'd forgotten about that," I tell her when my laughter subsides enough so I can breathe.

"It was so gross. But it won me ten dollars, didn't it?" Shel says, wiping the tears from her face. "I still have to repay Matt for that dare."

"How many years has it been? Like five?"

"Probably. But some things you never forget."

We lie on the bed and stare at the ceiling while our breathing returns to normal. As I wipe away my tears, I turn my head to face her. As much as I don't want to admit it, it feels good to laugh. "I'm glad you're here." I smile.

"Me, too." She smiles back at me.

CHAPTER 6

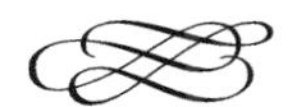

James makes an appearance in my dreams again. I'm starting to get used to this. In fact, it's becoming a comfort. I can count on my subconscious to replay memories I haven't thought of in years, almost as if there is a movie library in my head and my mind selects which film to play each time I sleep.

"I love you," James says to me.

"I love you, too."

"No, like really love you."

"I know."

"No. Like seriously forever love you."

I look up from my book and stare at him. We're supposed to be studying for our world history final. Two more weeks of high school and then we're done. Officially graduated. I smile and lean forward to kiss him.

"I know."

He kisses me back, but something feels off.

"Okay." I close my book and scoot closer to him on the floor. "What's up?"

"What do you mean?"

"Something's bothering you."

"Nothing's bothering–"

I give him my don't-lie-to-me look.

He rolls from his side to his back and covers his face with his hands. "I can't tell you."

"Of course you can."

"I can't."

"You can."

He shakes his head.

What could it be? I start to get nervous. "So, you're just going to lie there?"

He sighs, moves his hands to rest on his stomach, and turns his head toward me. "I got the letter from Ferris."

"And?"

"They offered me a full ride to play on the team."

I zone out for a minute, then shake my head to clear it. "That's amazing!"

"No, it's not."

"It is."

James props himself up on his elbow. "This wasn't the plan."

"Well, no," I say. "But you can't turn it down. It's an opportunity of a lifetime."

He reaches out and pulls me against him, so I'm lying beside him with my head resting on his chest. He wraps his arms around me. "We won't be together."

Ferris State University had expressed interest in James this past hockey season, and we've been anxiously awaiting this news. In the meantime, we applied to other schools and Western Michigan accepted us both. I received a partial scholarship as well, which made WMU a permanent part of my future. Since it appeared Ferris was dragging their feet, James was making plans to become a Bronco in the fall with me.

"But we'll be close," I say. "It's just under a two hour drive from Kalamazoo to Big Rapids."

"Been doing some research, have we?"

I shrug. "Maybe. Just in case." I lift my head to look at him. "Your parents must be ecstatic."

"That's an understatement." He crookedly smiles.

"I'm proud of you."

He lifts his head and kisses me. "I'm going to miss you."

I sigh. "I guess we'll have to make the most of our summer."

His smile fades, and my eyes search his face. "What is it?"

"They want me to help with the kid's summer hockey camp. I have to leave in three weeks."

I can't hide my disappointment, and my expression wilts. "Really?"

He nods.

I place my head on his chest again, so he can't see my face if my emotions decide to betray me.

"I'm sorry," he murmurs.

"Don't be," I tell him, but my voice wavers. "It is what it is."

"You know I hate that saying."

I chuckle. "I know."

"Listen." He sits upright and takes me with him, so we're sitting facing each other. "I don't have to do this. We have everything worked out for Western."

Inside I want that. Bad. I want to be selfish and tell him 'Okay! Tell Ferris they can kiss it.' But my rational side wins out. "Don't be ridiculous. Your parents would murder you if you turned this down. No way. You're going to Ferris."

He takes my hand and stares at it, then runs his thumb lightly across my knuckles. "I feel bad."

I shake my head. "Don't. We'll work it out. I have a car, you have a car, there's this modern technology called a phone. We'll be fine."

He gives me a worried look and reaches out to push my hair behind my ear. "What if you find someone else?"

His question takes me by surprise. That's what he's worried about? "That won't happen." I squeeze his hand in reassurance. "What about you? What if you find someone else?"

"Not possible," he says without hesitation.

"How can you be so sure?" I ask him playfully. "There must be plenty of sexy blonde coeds throwing themselves at the star athletes."

He grins. "Well, if you put it *that* way ..."

"Ugh!" I drop his hand in mock disgust.

He laughs, reaching for me. "You know I prefer brunettes. Come here."

I cross my arms defiantly. "Why?"

"Just come here."

I eye him warily and take his hands. He pulls me into his lap and presses me to him, my head resting on his shoulder.

"You know I love only you," he says. His voice is low, like it's caught in his throat.

I think about that for a second. "Why?" I ask. "Why do you love me?"

I can feel his breath catch. "Because you're mine," he replies softly.

A warm feeling spreads through my chest. I love being his. "That's all?" I tease.

He lets out a nervous laugh. "No. It's just hard to put into words."

"Try," I say, curious. I've never asked for a detailed list of why he loves Emma Donohue before.

He squeezes me tighter to him. "I feel ... I don't know ... *better* when I'm with you. If we're apart, I can barely wait to be with you again. When we're together it feels right. It doesn't matter what we're doing, it feels natural ... like I'm exactly where I'm supposed to be. There's nothing false about us or between us. Does that make any sense?"

I nod into his chest. It makes complete sense. "Thank you," I whisper.

"Are you upset?" He sounds worried. "Did I say something wrong?"

"No; your words were perfect." In fact, I'm trying not to cry. His feelings mirror my own.

"Are you sure?" He lifts my chin, so he can look me in the eye.

A tear escapes, and I quickly wipe it away. "Yes. I think you may have melted my heart."

He gives me a soft smile. "I'd like to tell you one more thing, if your heart can take it."

"What's that?"

He stares at me intently, as if his eyes can see right through me. "You are absolutely beautiful."

The intensity in his stare makes me forget how to breathe. His hand, still lifting my chin, pulls my face toward his, and his mouth literally crushes mine. I let out a squeak of surprise. This is not his typical kiss.

My reaction makes him smile against my lips, but it doesn't stop him from kissing me. Instead, his hand leaves my chin and finds its way to the nape of my neck, sliding up into my hair to hold me in place. As his mouth molds to mine, I set my hands flat against his chest; I can feel his heart pounding through his shirt. His lips move and trail along my jaw as his free hand glides around my waist and finds the exposed skin at the small of my back. He flexes his fingers, pressing them into me, and a wave of electricity slides up my spine. His other hand moves from my hair and gathers it, pulling it to the side. A moment later I feel his breath under my ear, and I flinch. He laughs as he kisses me, knowing that sensitive spot. He always teases me there, on purpose, to make me jump.

Despite the fact I'm sitting sideways in his lap, I want to be closer. I grip his shoulders and pull myself forward, freeing a leg to adjust my position. His lips disappear from my skin.

"What are you doing?" he whispers.

"Moving." I smile and face him head on, wrapping one leg around his waist and then the other. He curls his hands under my knees and pulls me forward so our bodies meet. I wind my fingers into his hair and pull his mouth to mine again. His grip tightens around my knees then skims up my legs to slide beneath my backside. He pulls his mouth away from mine and finds my ear.

"We have to stop hanging out when your parents are home."

His kisses sear down my neck, and I lean into him. "That's kind of impossible. We'd never see each other."

We both hear the door knob rattle at the same time. It's like we've been stung, and we spring apart. I scramble to pick up my history book and open it to bury my face in any page.

"Um ... hey guys," my mother says cautiously from the doorway.

I barely look up over the top of my book. My face feels like it's on fire; I know its flaming red.

"Hey, Mrs. Donohue," James says nonchalantly. I steal a sideways glance; he's lying on the floor, propped up on his elbow, a notebook in front of him. He flashes her an innocent smile.

"Just putting laundry away," she says as she enters my room with the basket. She heads to the bed and sets down a stack of folded clothes. I keep my face buried in my book.

As she leaves, she stops just outside the door and turns. "It's stuffy in here, don't you think? This door should probably stay open," she says as she swings it wide.

I glance up at her again. She gives me a knowing look with her eyebrows raised. My ears feel hot, and I quickly look back down.

"Whatever you say, Mrs. D," James says. It sounds like he's smiling.

After she walks away, I slam the book shut and look at him. "You know there's a parental talk in my future, right?"

He bursts out laughing.

"It's not funny!"

He grins. "Your face is fifty shades of red." He sits up and starts to move over to sit next to me. I give him a dirty look.

"What?" he asks innocently.

"You can't sit next to me if you won't keep your hands to yourself."

He cocks an eyebrow. "As I recall, you're the one who wrapped yourself around me."

I roll my eyes. "You started it."

He smiles and settles next to my side. I open my book again and attempt to find where I left off. After a minute or two James says, "Well, there's one good thing about my leaving for college so soon."

I look up at him. "What's that?"

He winks at me. "My dorm room."

~

"We need summer jobs," Shel says as she leans over the paper, perusing the want ads. "You need a routine and the money wouldn't hurt."

"Anything look good?" I ask while trying to show interest in my scrambled eggs. I'm exhausted. The memory from last night woke me, and I couldn't go back to sleep for hours. I try to hide my smirk behind a fork full of eggs as I recall the dream and the "talk" that took place after James left that day. My mother insisted I get on birth control pills. I didn't refuse.

"Not really. We should look online after breakfast," she suggests.

"Mornin' ladies," my dad greets us as he enters the kitchen. "Got any plans for today?" He pours himself some coffee.

Shel says, "Job hunting," as I say, "Not really."

He smiles. "I see." He takes a sip from the mug. "Whip her into shape, would ya, Shel?"

"I'm on it," she says and gives him a conspiratorial look.

He starts to leave the kitchen, then stops and turns back. "You know, when your mom and I were in town yesterday I saw a flyer at the grocery store. Bay Woods is looking for summer help."

"What's Bay Woods?" Shel asks.

"Golf course," I respond.

"Hmm. We'll have to check that out," Shel says. "Thanks Mr. Donohue."

He tips an invisible hat to us and leaves through the back door.

"All right." Shel finishes her orange juice. "We should head out by ten."

I look at the clock. It's 9:30. "Geez. Why are you in such a rush?"

"Speed of business. Finish up." She gestures to my uneaten eggs. "I'm going upstairs to get ready." She walks to the sink, rinses her dishes, and puts them in the dishwasher. She glances back at me. I haven't budged.

"Make a move," she chastises me. As she heads upstairs she yells back, "Today is a new day!"

Ugh. I have never been a morning person. When she came in and woke me up this morning around nine, I about slugged her.

I take a bite and swallow it down. The eggs have gone cold. Ew. I get up and scrape them into the garbage, rinse my plate, and stow it in the dishwasher. I take a moment and stare out the window over the sink. The sun is shining, and I notice two white butterflies dancing around the lilacs. My gaze moves to the birdfeeder, where a Blue Jay and a sparrow are vying for seeds. Our neighbor, Mr. Miller, is already out and working in his garden. I notice our flower beds need weeding; maybe I'll offer to help my mom after we get back.

"EMMA!" Shel yells down the stairs. "COME ON!"

I close my eyes and beg karma for forgiveness as I silently curse Shel's name. Would it kill her to chill for a second? I slowly turn and shuffle toward the stairs.

CHAPTER 7

After my dad's suggestion of the golf course, Shel decided to skip the online job search for now and head there first. After we investigate that lead, her plan is to go back through town and see what jobs might be available there.

"As long as we agree not to apply at McDonald's," I say when we're in the car. "I would like to avoid fast food if at all possible."

"Agreed." She adjusts the rearview mirror of my white Grand Am. "Why am I driving your car again?"

"My dad says it needs to be driven. It's been sitting in the driveway since I came home last month." It feels odd to sit in my car. It almost smells musty from lack of use.

"Ah." Shel nods in understanding.

I direct her to the golf course, which isn't too far outside of town. We follow the long, tree lined drive until we spot the sign for the main office. "Didn't this place used to be something else?" she asks as we park outside the pro shop.

"No, I think they just changed the name. New owners or something."

We walk into the pro shop, and I glance around. Polo shirts hang precisely on racks, golf shoes line the back wall, and hats are stacked neatly for sale with the Bay Woods logo. The front counter is glass and holds tees, gloves, and boxes of golf balls. The woman behind the counter greets us. "Good morning! How may I help you today?"

"We heard you were hiring." Shel smiles as we step to the counter.

"We are. We're looking for rangers, cart, and concession staff. You need to be at least twenty-one to work the beverage carts and main concession."

"You're in luck because we're both twenty-one," Shel says.

"Great!" She opens a drawer and pulls out two applications. "Fill these out and return them to me. You can have a seat at the tables in the main concession area, if you like." She nods to the left.

"Thanks," Shel says and takes the two pens the woman offers.

We head to a table and start to complete the apps. The area is relatively cozy and has a sports bar feel with two large flat screens in opposite corners of the room. The walls are decorated with autographed golf paraphernalia and some trendy signs that read "Who's Your Caddy?" and "How Am I Driving?" Three men sit at a table across from us; they look like business associates. Shel pauses for a minute and looks around. "I bet we could run into some pretty cute guys working here," she muses.

I look at her annoyed. "Really?"

"Sorry," she says regretfully. "I meant for me, not for you."

We go back to the applications. "I need a third reference. Can I use your mom?" she asks me.

"Yeah. You use mine and I'll use yours."

We complete the apps and turn them in to the lady at the front counter. She tells us someone will be in touch within the week.

"Where to next?" I ask as we get back in the car.

"Let's try the bookstore in town," she says. "You still like to read, right?"

"Sure."

It turns out to be slim pickings when we get into town; not many places are hiring. We manage to successfully apply at two more places – the "Book Nook" and a new consignment shop.

"Well, I'd say this afternoon was a success," Shel says as we leave the resale store. "Hungry?"

"Not really."

She eyes me suspiciously.

"Seriously. I'm not."

"Well I am." She looks around. "Let's hit the Subway."

We walk across the street to the restaurant, and I wait in line with Shel. The tiny place is busy and crowded. As my eyes jump around the lobby between the people, the menu, and the fresh sandwich ingredients, my skin prickles. This is the first time I've been out in public in a month. It feels off, like everyone is staring at me even though I know they're not. Maybe it's just the tight space; these people are only getting lunch like any other day. I feel strangely out of place and out of sync.

"And what would you like?" the sandwich artist asks as she pulls on her plastic gloves.

"Uh ..." I stutter. I cave in and get myself a small turkey sub and a bottle of water. I'm truly not hungry, but I don't want to look weird watching my best friend eat.

"Hungrier than you thought?" Shel asks after adding a cookie to her order.

"Guess so." I shrug.

Once we find a table, she polishes off her foot-long Cold Cut Combo in half the time it takes me to eat a portion of my small meal. I have to admit my head does feel clearer with something in my stomach, and I take my time to finish. I feel calmer than I did standing in line. I even manage to tease Shel about her metabolism. "A sub and a cookie and chips? Where do you put it all?"

She looks down at her curves. "These hips don't lie."

I scoff. "Okay, Shakira."

Shel really does look great. She always has had that perfect 36-24-36 thing going on. I, on the other hand, was hard pressed to fill a B cup until a few years ago. While I'm thin, I still can't find my waist. Or my hips. It's like one straight line. James used to tell me I looked athletic. I would laugh because I'm no athlete.

Back in the car, headed home, I think about our time in town. I feel like I've overcome a small hurdle, like I accomplished something. My eyes land on Shel. "Thanks for getting me out of the house."

She smiles. "You're welcome." The car slows and she makes a right turn.

"Where are you going?" I ask, confused. She should be turning left up ahead.

"There's something I think you need to do."

I look out the window puzzled. There's not much down this road except … Panic grips my heart. "Shel. No."

"Yes."

I shoot her a stern look. "Turn around right now."

"No."

"I'm not kidding. Stop the car."

She stares calmly out the windshield. "You forfeited your rights when you gave me the keys."

I want to grab the wheel, but I squeeze my eyes shut instead. This is one hurdle I cannot overcome. Not today. "I can't do this," I beg.

"Yes, you can." The car slows again, and Shel makes another right turn. The car creeps around a curve and comes to a stop. She turns off the engine.

"C'mon. Let's go," she says in a soft voice.

I shake my head no, eyes still closed.

"I'll be with you the whole time."

I set my mouth in a hard line and don't move.

"Okay," she says. I hear her open the door and get out of the car.

I sit with my eyes closed and concentrate on breathing. I don't know if my hyperventilation is out of fear or anger, but it's getting worse. How dare she? Who does she think she is anyway? Where does she get off thinking she knows what's best for me? This is my life, my heart! How can this possibly help anything?

I try to slow my breathing by forming a speech of verbal abuse I will unleash on her when she gets back in the car. I need to make it clear – if she's going to continue to stay with me, we need to set some boundaries. I'm all for trying to heal and move forward, but this, this seems way too soon.

When I open my eyes, I find Shel leaning against the hood of the car with her back to the windshield. I take a few minutes and seriously contemplate wrestling my keys away from her. It'd be a tough fight, and on a normal day I could probably take her. But not today. I don't have the energy.

With a defeated sigh, I slowly push open the door with shaky hands. I walk over and lean against the hood next to her and stare out over a place I never thought I'd be. Not now and certainly not in the near future.

Whispering Oaks Cemetery.

"Ready?" she asks quietly and holds out her hand.

I try to be angry, but my voice catches in my throat. "You tricked me."

"He'd want you to visit," she says softly.

I give her a pained look and slowly grasp her fingers.

We walk hand in hand along the dirt drive that circles the cemetery in silence. It really is a beautiful place with tall maple and pine trees that are hundreds of years old. It is meticulously landscaped; early wildflowers bloom along the sides of the drive, and the grass smells freshly mowed. Birds sing and chirp as they fly from tree to tree. Older headstones and regal mausoleums stand in the front of the cemetery. As we walk closer to the back, sunlight reflects off the newer, shiny headstones.

We make it to the far end of the cemetery where an open area of neatly mowed grass lies empty, patiently waiting for its future inhabitants. Shel veers slightly to the left, and I follow behind her, never releasing her hand. I know we're close when her walk slows. She was here following the service, while I was having my break down in that little room in the funeral home.

"We're here," she says quietly.

I'm scared to look. Shel steps to my side, so she's beside me instead of in front of me, and reveals a perfectly domed mound of dirt adorned with floral arrangements that have long since dried and shriveled, their bright bows the only color left against the brown dirt.

My throat constricts, and my chest tightens.

Shel squeezes my hand. I squeeze her hand back, and we just stand there, together, staring at the ground.

I'm not sure how much time has passed when she asks, "Do you want some privacy?"

I think I do. I nod and whisper, "Don't go too far."

"I'll be right over there." She points to a bench that sits off to the side of the drive. She lets go of my hand and walks away.

Left alone, I'm not sure what to do. I kneel down beside the gravesite and rest on my heels. I reach out and feel one of the bows, the navy blue one. When I turn it over, the word "Son" is imprinted on it in fancy gold lettering. Tears prick my eyes.

The wind rustles the leaves on the trees and blows the ribbon out of my fingers. I stare at the withered flowers for a moment, then tilt my head and look at the top of the dirt mound where I imagine James' head would be.

"Hey." My voice is barely there. "I'm sorry it took me so long to get here."

I close my eyes and listen to the sounds around me. The wind, the birds, and the silence in between. There's no sobbing or screaming like I feared, just a few stray tears wind down my face.

"I miss you. So much."

A warm breeze swirls around me, and I wrap my arms around myself as if to hug the air back. After a few minutes I realize I feel very calm, peaceful even. I open my eyes. "I won't stay away," I whisper. I reach out tentatively, placing my hand on the dirt. It feels soft under my palm.

My heart aches. I silently wish that he is safe. Somewhere warm and somewhere free of pain. Somewhere happy. I smile as his grin flashes across my memory. "I love you," I say quietly.

"Until the end of forever," my mind answers in his voice, making me smile again.

I press my palm into the dirt, so when I remove it, an imprint remains. I start to make little swirls in the soil around my handprint. I imagine him looking over my shoulder, watching me. I can sense his amused face as I imagine our conversation:

"Why are you playing in the dirt?" he asks with lopsided smirk.

"Because I'm trying to touch you."

"Why?"

"Because you're gone."

"I am not gone."

"Yes, you are."

"I'm not."

"Are you trying to pick a fight with me?"

He laughs. "Why would I do that? I never win."

"That's true."

"So why do you think I'm gone? I'm right here."

"You died."

He frowns. "I know; I was there."

"And I wasn't," I sadly sigh. "Promise me you'll never leave me."

He smiles. "That's kind of creepy."

"I see you haven't lost your sense of humor."

"You know I'll always be with you."

"In my heart, right?"

"Of course."

"That's not good enough."

"Being stubborn, are we?"

"I'm not trying to be. I just know what I want."

"I guess I'll have to work on that."

"Please do."

My imaginary conversation with James ends when I run out of space around my handprint to continue my art. I've managed to create a handprint that looks like its radiating heat with swirls coming from the fingertips and out around the palm. I smile weakly at my creation.

I push against the ground and stand. I press my dirty fingertip to my lips and then hold it out to send James a silent kiss. I allow my heart to wrap around the fact that here is where I can go to be near him. "I love you, and I'll be back soon," I say.

As hard as it was for me to get out of the car and walk here, it is even harder for me to walk away. I force myself to turn. I make it to the bench and sit down.

"Everything okay?" Shel asks.

Surprising myself, I say, "It will be."

She nods and then stands. She extends her hand and helps me off the bench. "Then mission accomplished. Do you forgive me?" she asks sheepishly.

"For now," I say. Then I throw my arms around her. "Thank you."

CHAPTER 8

As luck would have it, two days later, Bay Woods called to ask us both for interviews. Apparently we were the only two who applied who weren't still in high school. I think the interview itself was more for protocol than anything; it basically consisted of two questions: what days of the week can you work, and when can you start?

Our training began that Friday. We were shown how to work both the main concession and the beverage carts, since we are old enough to serve alcohol. At first I was worried about bartending, but thankfully the drinks offered are no more complicated than a gin and tonic. At the end of our training day, we were each given three teal blue "Bay Woods Golf Course" polo shirts. Official employment would begin on Monday.

"We should celebrate," Shel says on our way home after training.

I make a face. "I don't feel like going out."

"You never feel like going out," she huffs.

I roll my eyes at her. "You can go. Have fun."

"Who am I going to go with? Myself?"

I sigh. I can tell from her tone this is one of her I'm-going-to-get-my-way moments. "What did you have in mind?"

"Let's get some dinner," she suggests. "What about that place in town? The one that has the live band on weekends?"

"Louie's Roadhouse?"

"That's the one. Don't they have awesome breadsticks?"

"Yeah. And the portions are huge."

"So, is that a yes?" She looks hopeful.

"Fine. Yes."

She claps like a perky cheerleader. I make a turn on the next street to take us through town instead of around it.

Pulling into the restaurant, it's hard to find a parking space. Friday night is a busy night for Louie's. I manage to find one on the outside of the lot and squeeze my car into it. Inside, the place is packed. A classic rock band plays loudly in the corner under neon bar signs while people dance. It feels a little claustrophobic to me, but Shel's eyes light up.

"How many?" a waitress asks loudly over the music.

"Just two!"

We get stuck at a small table in the back, right outside the restrooms. Shel speaks with the waitress briefly who disappears, only to reappear moments later with two huge strawberry daiquiris. She places one in front of each of us.

"I can't drink all of this," I protest to Shel. "Besides, I'm driving."

"I think you'll be okay," she yells across the table. "I know you won't finish it and besides, we're supposed to be celebrating."

I take a drink, and it does taste good. We turn our attention to the band and the dance floor. I have to admit that people watching is one of my favorite activities.

Eventually we order. When our food arrives, my chef salad is monstrous. As I'm cramming another bite into my mouth – why can't they ever cut the lettuce in small pieces? – I hear a male voice say, "Well look at what the cat dragged in."

I look up just as Shel is jumping out of her seat to hug some big guy. He wraps his arms around her. What the heck?

She steps back from him, excited. "When did you get into town? What are you doing here?"

"Last night, actually. My buddy plays guitar." He nods toward the band. Then he seems to notice me. With a soft expression he yells over the music, "Hey, Em. How've you been?"

Who is this person? How does he know me? I stare at him stupidly.

"Emma," Shel scolds me. "Say hello to Matt."

Matt? Holy crap, I wouldn't have recognized him in a million years. He still sports his textured blonde hairstyle, but he's bigger than I remember. More muscular. I smile, embarrassed. "I'm sorry!" I yell. "I so did not recognize you." I stand up, and he gives me an awkward hug.

He smiles and looks around. "Listen, I'll come back when the band breaks. I can hardly hear."

"Okay!"

Matt waves and makes his way to the restroom.

"I didn't think he was coming home until next month," Shel says between bites.

I try to remember the last time I saw Matt. An image springs to mind of him stopping by James' house the summer after high school while we were washing the Jeep. I smile as I remember trying to stay out of the water fight that ensued only to end up drenched anyway. Wow, that was almost three years ago.

After we finish our dinner, the band takes a break. A DJ fills the silence, but he's nowhere near as loud. Matt reappears, pulls a chair over from another table, and takes a seat. He's tall, over six foot, and his knees bump the bottom of the tabletop when he sits. I chastise myself for wondering if he's on steroids. The last time I saw him he was still wiry Matt; he played baseball in high school. Now, his white Old Navy ringer tee barely stretches across his chest.

"So," he looks at our drinks, "what can I get you ladies?"

"Oh, nothing for me, thanks," I say.

"Another daiquiri, please," Shel requests.

Matt calls a nearby waitress over and orders the daiquiri and a beer. Turning his attention back to us he asks, "What brings you guys out?"

"We're celebrating." Shel looks at me. "We are officially employees at Bay Woods starting Monday."

"That's a nice course," Matt comments. "I golf out there quite a bit, when I'm home."

Shel and Matt delve into conversation, as if they see each other every day. I basically observe and nod once in a while.

Someone taps me on my shoulder. I turn and come face to face with some random stranger with greasy hair and bad skin. His rancid beer breath is right in my face. I lean away from him.

"You wanna dance?" the guy slurs.

Dear God, no. "Um. N–no thanks," I say politely and turn back around.

"Wahs your problem?" He peers around my shoulder. "Yous think you're too good or somethin'?" He grabs my arm.

"Hey!" My skin crawls where he touches me. I try to pull away and lean back at the same time.

Matt stands abruptly, knocking his chair over. "I wouldn't do that if I were you," he growls and takes a step forward.

Drunk guy lets go of my arm. "What's it to you?" he says angrily and stands up tall. With the two of them facing off like this, it's clear Matt has the advantage. He is much taller and more muscular than drunk guy.

Matt's brown eyes go dark. "It would be best if you left. Now."

Drunk guy puts on a tough face but sways a little when he takes a step. He regains his balance and stares at Matt. Then he looks at me. "Forget it. You're not worth it," he sneers. He turns and stumbles away.

Matt stares him down until he's back on the other side of the bar. He picks up his chair and takes a seat.

"Thank you so much," I say gratefully.

He takes a drink of his beer, then smiles at me. "Any time."

Shel picks up the conversation where they left off as I sit there waiting for my adrenaline to return to normal levels. I check my phone. It's only nine, but I'm ready to go home.

I manage to make it only fifteen more minutes until I bring it up. "Shel, you ready to go?"

She frowns at me. Guess that's a no.

As their conversation continues, I decide to make a trip to the restroom. When I get back, the band has started again and both Matt and Shel are standing.

"What's up?" I yell over the music.

"I thought you were ready to go?" Shel asks.

"Yes!" I answer, probably too enthusiastically.

We make our way outside, and I inhale the night air. It was really stuffy inside Louie's. Matt follows us out. "Where are you parked?" he asks.

"Way over there," I gesture ahead of us.

We start to walk toward my car. "Thanks again for your help back there," I tell him. "I really appreciate it."

"Yeah, I'm glad I didn't have to pull out my mad ninja skills," Shel teases.

Matt laughs. Little does he know Shel really does have mad ninja skills. Well, karate skills from an elective she took last year.

We're just about to the car when I hear scuffling behind us. Shel and I turn around and see two people. I recognize drunk guy immediately. Suddenly, his buddy has Matt in a headlock.

I never figured Shel for a scared screamer. As Matt wrestles with the guy to get out of his hold, Shel lets out one of the loudest shrieks I've ever heard. Drunk guy actually takes a step back at the sound.

I start to panic as I back away and attempt to wrestle my cell phone from my purse. I keep my eyes locked on Matt. Why are these guys attacking him? *Call the police!* my brain silently screams.

"Let go of me, asshole!" Matt grunts as he maneuvers his way out from under the guy's arms and tries to pin them behind his back. The guy is too fast and ends up escaping Matt's grasp. They separate, a few feet apart, and start to circle one another.

"Knock it off!" Shel yells at them.

Matt lunges at the guy, and he jumps out of the way.

I'm still trying to get my damn phone out of my purse.

Drunk guy decides to step in. His hands grab Matt's shirt, but he's not strong enough, or maybe he's too inebriated, to hang on. Matt takes his arm and easily knocks the guy free. Drunk guy falls to the ground right in front of me, and I jump back. I scramble out of the way and run to Shel's side.

"Don't you know karate?" I ask her frantically.

"Like two moves," she snaps at me. "And this isn't the most controlled environment!"

Distracted by shaking off drunk guy, Matt is caught around the waist from behind, his arms pinned to his sides by his original assailant. He struggles to break free.

"What do you want?" Shel screams at them.

I have gone mute as the sense of déjà vu settles over me. The same scene flashes before my eyes, but it's at school, at Western. James is fighting off Patrick, a lab partner of mine who became overly friendly and turned into somewhat of a stalker. It started with a few notes that went from innocent to threatening. Then, he seemed to show up everywhere I went. When I discovered he had registered for all the same classes as me for the next semester, James came to campus to take care of the situation. He only meant to talk to him, maybe scare him into leaving me alone, but the talk quickly escalated into a fight. Patrick had James pinned, just as this guy has Matt.

"Please don't hurt him," I beg Patrick.

"Stay back, Em!" James warns me.

Patrick grunts. "Call off your boyfriend!"

"James! Stop! Both of you! Stop!" I yell.

"Tell him we're friends," Patrick demands as James continues to struggle. "Tell him!"

"Okay! Okay! We're just friends!" I say to James. "Let him go!"

Patrick actually released his hold on James, after which James quickly turned and punched him in the face. Blood spurted everywhere as he fell backward. Patrick lay on the ground for a few minutes, then recovered from his fall and took off across the parking lot, holding his nose. I never saw or heard from him again, but I was always looking over my shoulder, afraid he would reappear at any moment. That's when James quit the hockey team and left Ferris. He immediately transferred to Western to make sure I was safe.

The memory takes only a second to play out behind my eyes, and in that time, drunk guy has recovered from his fall and staggers toward Matt. "This is for tryin' to be tough," he taunts and closes his hand in a fist. "This'll ruin that pretty boy face of yours," he sneers as he winds up to punch.

"No!" I find my voice.

Thankfully drunk guy is pretty drunk because the punch he throws knocks him off balance and his fist heads for Matt's stomach, not his nose. Matt kicks drunk guy in the gut, sending him sprawling. The force must have worked in Matt's favor, because he finally breaks the hold around his arms.

Matt turns on the guy who was holding him and lands two solid punches, one in his stomach and one on the side of his jaw. I cringe at the sound they make. The guy stumbles backward.

I hear voices and realize some people in the parking lot are making their way over to see what's going on. "Matt!" I yell as Shel and I run for the car. He glances at me for a moment and then turns his attention back to his attackers. I yank open the car door, crawl in, and start the ignition.

The guy Matt punched is recovering and takes a few steps toward him. Matt turns and makes a beeline for the car. He throws open the passenger side door and falls in. "Go!"

I leave the parking lot quickly and drive back through town. I concentrate on going the speed limit. My knuckles are white with tension as I grip the steering wheel.

Shel erupts from the backseat. "What was THAT?"

Matt flexes his hand. Even in this poor light it looks swollen. "I think our buddy doesn't like me too much."

Shel snorts. "What idiots!"

"Guess I won't be going back there for a little while," Matt chuckles.

Shel reaches through the seats. "They didn't even land a punch. High five." Matt smiles and slaps her hand with his good one.

I'm still tense, and I feel awful for doing absolutely nothing to help him during the fight. "I'm going to take you to my house so we can get some ice on that hand," I say.

"Nah," Matt says. "I've had worse."

"Do you make a habit of this?" I ask with wide eyes.

He shakes his head. "Fighting random strangers? No." He pauses. "But I do help my dad out from time to time, and I've gotten some pretty nasty bites."

I forgot Matt's family owns the veterinary clinic in town.

"Regardless, let me help you. I feel bad after standing there and doing nothing."

He doesn't protest, and I make my way through town toward home. Shel and Matt rehash the fight, play by play, like it was the WWE.

We make it home and walk through the back door and into the kitchen. "Sit there," I direct Matt to the island. I go to the freezer, pull out a cold pack, and then wrap it in a dish towel. I take his hand and look at his knuckles. They're red and swollen. "Here." I place the wrapped cold pack on his hand. He grimaces.

"See, you are hurt," I say. "Don't move." I leave the kitchen and head to the bathroom to retrieve some ibuprofen. I run into my mom in the hallway.

"Hi," she says. "Where have you been?"

"Long story." I step past her into the bathroom and turn on the light. "Matt and Shel are in the kitchen."

She looks surprised. "Matt Randall?"

I nod and grab the Motrin bottle from the drawer. She heads to the kitchen, and I follow her.

"Well, hey there," my mom greets him affectionately. "It's good to see you."

Matt smiles at my mom. "You too, Mrs. D."

The way he says "Mrs. D" stops me short and pulls at my heart.

"What happened to you?" she asks, concerned.

Shel launches into an animated play by play of the night's events. Matt is barely allowed to speak. I head to the sink to fill a glass with water. I bring it over to him along with the bottle of Motrin and shake out some pills.

"Thanks," he says as I dump the pills in his hand. He pops them in his mouth and then takes the glass.

"It's the least I can do," I say, still feeling guilty. If it wasn't for me he wouldn't have been jumped.

My dad hears all the commotion from the kitchen and comes downstairs in his pajamas to see what's going on. He didn't expect our guest either, yet they all break into conversation which easily moves into the living room. Honestly, I'm tired, and I really would like to take Matt home or back to get his car or wherever now that he has ice on his hand.

Matt sits at one end of the couch in order to lay his hand on the arm rest. Shel takes the other end, so I plop down in between them. My parents sit in the chairs across from us and continue talking. I don't care to contribute to the stroll down memory lane right now, and I feel my eyelids getting heavy. Damn daiquiri.

When I open my eyes, I'm curled up on my side underneath someone's arm. My parents are no longer sitting across from me, but Shel is, her feet tucked up into one of the chairs. She's flipping through a magazine. I blink to clear my vision and realize my head is resting against someone's side. I look up and see Matt, his head resting back against the couch. He's asleep with his arm wrapped protectively around me.

I jump up and away from him, throwing his arm off me in the process.

He wakes, startled. "Wha–"

"I'm sorry," I apologize. "I didn't mean to wake you. I just … you there …"

He rubs his face with his good hand to clear his eyes. He smiles tiredly.

Confused, I look at Shel. "You're quite the partier," she says as she tosses the magazine aside and stands. "C'mon Matt. I'll drive you home."

He pushes himself off the couch and looks at me. He can tell I'm embarrassed. "Don't worry about it," he says. "I'll see you around." He starts to leave the room and then pauses. "Thanks for fixing my hand."

I give him a small wave. "Yeah, I'll see you."

As they leave, I put my head in my hands. I feel ridiculous for falling asleep on somebody I barely know. Well, barely know anymore.

On my way up to bed, I turn off all the lights but one, so Shel can make her way upstairs when she returns. I walk with heavy feet to my room and turn on my bedside lamp. The red numbers on my alarm clock seem to shout the time at me. It's after one in the morning. Yawning, I lean over to grab my pajamas when I notice something laying on top of my dresser. I walk over to see what it is.

Laying there, unfolded, is the letter from James I found the other night. I thought I'd put it away in my drawer? I fold it up, open the top drawer, and tuck it under my socks again. Maybe my mom found it when putting laundry away. I'll ask her about it tomorrow.

Walking back over to the bed, I pick up my pajamas and put them on, then head to the bathroom to brush my teeth. When I turn on the light, I almost scream.

There, on the counter, is a fuchsia orchid.

CHAPTER 9

I stare at the potted plant. Afraid it's a hallucination, I decide not to try and touch it. If it is imaginary, my hand would pass right through it, and then I'll know for sure I've lost my mind entirely. Instead I close my eyes, feel around for the light switch, and return to my room. I'll deal with it tomorrow. If it's still there.

Lord, I need sleep. I crawl under my covers and close my eyes, but sleep avoids me. My muscles feel tense so I try to relax my body one part at a time, starting with my neck and working my way down. I feel better, but I'm still awake. I try the proverbial counting sheep, which morphs into another vision, and I end up counting the punches Matt landed on that guy earlier – one, two, one, two, one, two. I grimace and roll over, trying a new position. After a while, I hear Shel return, and then the door closes to Mike's old bedroom. I flip over again. This is unusual; my power nap on Matt must have screwed me up.

I can't turn my brain off. I go over the things I learned today at Bay Woods. I'll have to remember to get my work shirts out of the car tomorrow. I'm sure they are a wrinkled mess. The car. I'm going to need to get gas before Monday. I wonder about the oil. When's the last time that was changed? James usually kept on me about that. I'll have to check the sticker. It's dirty too; James will be sure to bring that up.

He keeps his ride meticulous. I, on the other hand, prefer to use my time to clean other things. My dorm room, for example. His room is an absolute disaster, yet he manages to keep his car like new.

"I know you have the ability to clean!" I chastise him as I'm picking up. I hold up a glass where milk has congealed to the bottom. "This is just gross."

"Oh, you love it," he teases me.

"Stale milk?"

"No, coming over here and taking care of me." He winks.

It's the same conversation every time.

It's then that my brain stops, and I realize I won't have that conversation again. It's impossible to have that conversation again. The familiar squeeze returns to my chest, and I'm overwhelmed by sadness. Why can't I fall asleep already?

Unwillingly, my thoughts turn to the last time I saw James. We were fighting. I'd accused him of lying to me, lying about leaving. He had been with me at Western for nearly two years after the Patrick incident. I knew he missed being at Ferris. In the year he had been there he'd established himself as one of the top players on the team; the coaches knew him, relied on him. The same situation didn't apply to WMU. And Ferris was calling again. His old coach was on him about transferring back, but, of course, I didn't want him to leave. The coach was persistent. James finally agreed to meet with him, promising me he was staying put and would be telling the coach just as much. But I was worried; I knew how much happier he would be there. I was so selfish. When he came back from the meeting, I'd accused him of changing his mind. I should never have done that.

"Why would you think I'd leave?" James looked hurt.

"Because I know you're unhappy."

"What? That's not true."

"You wouldn't be happier? Your parents would be."

"This isn't about them."

I crossed my arms. "Then what did you tell Coach?"

"It's not that easy. I didn't want to let him down so ..."

"So, you're going back," I snapped.

"I didn't say that. Would you let me finish? Nothing happened that you and I didn't discuss."

"What does that mean?!"

"I'm trying to tell you nothing happened, and you won't accept it!" He was pissed.

"You expect me to believe that?"

"Yes. When have I ever lied to you?" He paused when I didn't answer. "So, now you think I lie to you?" he asked bitterly.

Again, I didn't answer him.

"Fine!" He made his way to the door and then turned. "Might I remind you of all I gave up for you? For us?"

I roll my eyes at being reminded about what he gave up yet again. "Listen, you know why you came here."

"Whatever."

That's when he stormed out.

A couple of hours later, James called to ask me to go out that night, to get something to eat. But I was still upset, still suspicious, and there wasn't a hint of an apology in our conversation. Don't ask me why I felt I was the one who was owed an apology; it should have been the other way around. I remember thinking we had bigger issues than dinner and, feeling annoyed, I told him no, I didn't want to go out, I had studying to do. He hung up the phone with a huff.

As I spent the rest of the night replaying our argument, the guilt started to creep in, eventually overtaking me. I called James, but he didn't answer. I left a message. After midnight, when I hadn't heard from him, I started to get really concerned. Could he still be upset with me? I'd really done it this time. I started to feel sick to my stomach. I decided to call again, regardless of the time.

"Hey." Thank God he answered.

"I'm sorry," I said.

"Me, too."

"Where are you? The phone sounds weird."

"Driving."

"Where?"

"Some of the guys and I went out." I could hear him yawn.

"Well, about earlier ..."

"Hang on. I'm about five minutes from being outside your door."

"Oh, okay."

"See you in a sec."

He hung up the phone.

And never arrived.

The tears are back. I cry silently and wipe them away as fast as they come. Pretty soon my cheeks feel raw from the wiping, and I give up. It's like my whole body wants to torture me; my mind won't let me sleep or think of anything else, and my body feels so weak I don't have the will to stop the tears.

I don't know how many times I called James' cell when he didn't show up. Twenty? Fifty? Two hours later, sick with worry, I called that last time. Someone answered the phone.

"Hello?" a strange male voice answered. I could hear commotion in the background.

"Hello? Who's this?" I asked, confused.

"Who are you looking for?"

"James. James Davis."

"And who are you, ma'am?"

"Did I dial the wrong number?" I ask.

"No, ma'am. Who are you again?"

"Emma."

"Emma? How do you know James?"

"He's ... he's my boyfriend."

The man pauses. "Emma, does James have parents?"

Who is this guy? I remember thinking. "Yes, of course he has parents! Why are you asking me this?"

"This is Sergeant Earnest with the Kalamazoo Police Department. Emma, I'm going to need James' parent's phone number."

"Why?" I remember my hand starting to shake violently.

"Emma, there's been an accident."

The official police report states James fell asleep and swerved off the road. A small embankment caused his Jeep to flip into a tree. He laid there, alone, for at least two hours before a passing motorist thought to call the police. Two hours. Alone. Dying.

I can't help it and horrible sobs rip through my chest. If I had gone with him when he asked, he wouldn't have been out so late, wouldn't have fallen asleep, wouldn't have *died*.

That is why the accident is my fault.

Because we were supposed to be together and we weren't.

I will never forgive myself.

The loud sobs continue and Shel is in my room in a matter of seconds, holding me. I can hear my parents enter the room, and Shel passes me off to my mother.

"Shhhh," she says as she rubs my back. "Another nightmare?" she asks.

I shake my head no. I only wish it were a nightmare.

"Whatever it is, it'll be okay," she tries to console me.

I shake my head violently.

"I'm right here. I won't let you go."

She holds me and rocks me like a baby. Eventually the sobs subside, leaving me drained. I disentangle myself from her and lie down. She lies beside me, and Shel crawls in on my other side. I fall asleep tucked between the two of them, like an infant, my tears still tacky on my cheeks.

CHAPTER 10

Over the next few days, my parents and Shel give me plenty of space. No one brings up my sobbing episode and neither do I. I do manage to ask my mother about the plant in the bathroom, since it was still there and, thankfully, not a figment of my imagination. She said it was delivered to the house the day Shel and I were at training, but there was no card to say who it was from. She assumed it was sent by someone with condolences, and she meant to call the flower shop to ask about it. She put it in the bathroom since orchids like a humid climate, but quickly forgot about calling after Matt's visit and then my late night disruption. I really don't care who it's from as long as it's real. But aren't there any other kinds of flowers in the area besides those that match what James used to give me?

Our first day at Bay Woods was a little hectic, but as the week went on, Shel and I fell into a steady rhythm. The environment was friendly, our manager easy-going, and driving the beverage cart around outside in the sun was an added bonus. It was exhausting work, however, with all the stocking and lifting. I was using muscles I never knew I had. Shel's hope is that, by the end of the summer, we will have built up some core strength and have amazing tans.

"This routine agrees with you," Shel comments at the end of the week.

I add more hot dogs to the roller. "How do you mean?"

"You look rested; your eye bags look smaller."

I grimace. "Thanks for noticing."

"You're welcome." She smiles.

"I have been sleeping really hard. I'm so tired by the time we get home."

"Tell me about it." She stretches her back.

That's when I realize I haven't had any more memory dreams. Not one. I try to think back to the last one I had. My face falls.

"What's wrong?"

Before I can stop myself, I say "I've stopped dreaming."

Shel looks confused.

"Never mind," I say quickly, shaking my head.

A customer approaches the counter and needs Shel's attention. I go back to the hot dogs. Have I thought about James every day? Yes. But my dreams have stopped, and it makes me sad. I enjoyed the memories my subconscious found and shared with me again. Silently, I pray that the dreams will return; I don't want to forget anything. Ever.

"I hate it when you're sad."

James' voice rings loud and clear in my head. A perfect rendition, just like when I was in the shower. My head snaps up.

"I'm right here with you."

Shel nudges me. "We're out of napkins. I'll go get some more from the back."

I nod at her and move to the front to take over the register.

What was that? Hearing his voice again? Maybe my mind is compensating for the lack of dreams by recalling his voice. I smile. That's okay with me.

I busy myself checking the condiments to make sure they are full and notice the salt shakers are low. I crouch down and start to rummage around under the counter for the funnel to fill them.

"Man, the service in this place sucks."

Seriously? I pop up from behind the counter to see Matt standing there, pulling on the fingers of his golf glove. I sigh in relief. "I was ready to let you have it."

He smiles at me. "How's the job going?"

"Pretty good. How'd the course treat you today?"

"Not too bad." He turns slightly and tilts his head to his left. "My old man still beat me, though."

"Hey, Matt!" Shel says as she returns with the napkins.

He waves to her.

"So," I ask him, "what can I get you?"

"Well, I owe my dad a beer for beating me, so two Miller's please."

I nod and walk to the cooler.

"What have you been up to?" I hear Shel ask him as I pull out the cans.

"Not much. Visiting with family, mostly," he replies. "Helping out at the clinic when Sheila calls in."

Shel laughs. "I can't imagine you as a receptionist."

Matt pretends to be offended. "I'm pretty good at it if I do say so myself."

"Here you go." I put the cans on the counter, and he hands me some bills.

"So, it's Friday night. What are you up to?" he asks.

"Nothing," Shel is quick to respond. Too quick. I give her a wary look out of the corner of my eye.

"Great," Matt says. "We're having a barbeque at our house tonight, to kick off Memorial Day weekend. You down?"

No, I think. The last thing I want to do is pretend to mingle with people I don't know.

"Sure!" Shel responds.

"What about you Emma?" Matt asks.

"Oh, I don't think …"

"We'll be there," Shel cuts me off with an elbow to the side.

"Invite your parents, too," Matt tells me. "We'll be starting around seven," he adds as he starts to walk away.

"Should we bring anything?" Shel asks.

"No, just yourselves." He smiles and walks toward his father to hand him his prize for winning today.

I glare at Shel.

"What?"

"I don't feel like ..."

She cuts me off again with a pout. "You never feel like it."

I huff and go back to looking for the funnel to fill the salt shakers.

"You need to get out," she presses.

I find the funnel and stand. "Do you remember the last time we went out?" My question comes out harsher than I intended.

She blinks and then narrows her eyes. "Yes. I do."

"And?"

"It will be fun. We won't stay late; we have to be back here at eight a.m. anyway."

All I can do is sigh.

When Shel tells my parents about the barbeque, they are just as excited as she is to have something to do this evening. Saying "You can't just show up *empty-handed,*" my mother goes about preparing a potato salad as Shel and I change out of our sweaty work clothes. We decide to drive separately to Matt's house; my parents may not want to stay as late as Shel and I. This works for me. If Shel wants to stay later, I'll hitch a ride back home with my mom and dad.

When we arrive at the Randall's, I try to remember the last time I was here. It had to be sometime in high school. When I was little, I always thought Matt had the coolest house because they had a big yard and a pool. Arriving here now, I can see his parents have done a lot of landscaping work over the last few years. When we walk around to the back of the house, the yard looks amazing. A huge tent is set up near a fancy stone fire pit with matching stone benches. The tent has been outfitted with tables and chairs and little outdoor lanterns hang underneath. The pool still stands in the center of the yard, but it is now surrounded by an elaborate deck, which has stairs that lead to an ornately designed paver patio complete with outdoor bar. Next to the bar stands the largest grill I've ever seen. Their backyard looks like an outdoor kitchen. Tiki torches are lit to fend off mosquitoes, comfy patio furniture is set throughout the yard, and Mrs. Randall's flower beds are overflowing with colorful perennials. Music fills the air, coming from speakers that are hidden in the gardens to look like rocks. Several people mill about with drinks and several more are lounging in the chairs and under the tent. The whole scene is impressive.

"I'm so glad you could make it." Mrs. Randall appears, wearing an apron. She hugs my mother and then me, taking me by surprise. "I was thrilled when Matt told me he had run into you at the golf course."

"Thanks for having us." My mother smiles at her. "Where would you like the food?"

"Oh, I'll take it," Mrs. Randall says, taking the salad. "Go ahead and make yourselves comfortable. Dan's firing up the grill as we speak. There are drinks at the bar." She nods toward the patio.

"Thanks," we all say.

Mrs. Randall gets distracted as more guests arrive, and she starts to walk away. "I'll be busy until the food's ready, but I hope we get a chance to catch up!" she says over her shoulder.

We head to the bar. I make things easy and grab a bottle of lemonade. I spy a grouping of empty chairs and head that way. "I'll be over there," I tell Shel.

I plop down in one of the lounges and prop my feet up. The sun is shining, and it warms me. I take a drink of lemonade and close my eyes. I could get used to this minus all these people.

I sense Shel arrive and sit down on the lounge next to me. I open my eyes and squint at her. "What'd you get?"

"Margarita."

We sit in the sun, sipping our drinks. It's a fun and friendly atmosphere, although I don't recognize many people. I notice my parents talking with someone across the yard by the fire pit. Soon I start to smell meat cooking on the grill, and my stomach growls.

"Whoa! Was that you?" Shel asks.

I pat my belly. "Yep."

Within minutes Shel's stomach growls just as loud. We burst out laughing.

"What's so funny?" Matt asks as he walks up behind us.

"Our stomachs are talking to each other," Shel explains and swings her feet off the lounge so he can sit.

"That looks good," he says to Shel and takes her drink from her hand. "What is it?" he asks as he tastes it.

"Margarita. A strong one. Who's your bartender?"

Matt laughs. "My uncle Al. You might want to take it easy with those." He hands Shel's drink back to her and looks at me. "What have you got?"

I hold up my bottle. "Lemonade, straight up."

"Ah. Living on the edge, I see." He smiles.

I notice people making their way toward the tent with plates. "Must be time to eat," I say and stand. "I'm starving."

Shel looks at me with wide eyes. "Really?"

I give her an exasperated look. "Yes, really."

"I'm starving, too," Matt says. "Let's go before everything's gone."

We make our way to the buffet table and fill our plates. We return to the lounges to eat instead of heading to the crowded tent. Shel and Matt carry on effortless conversation as usual; I concentrate on my barbeque ribs. They're delicious.

After we finish, Shel gets another margarita. She and Matt decide to play a game of horseshoes with a couple of Matt's cousins while I watch from a nearby hammock. Everyone is so carefree; it feels nice to be taking part in it, albeit a small part. I think of James and how much fun we would have had here. At first I smile, but then my face falls. I try to stop it, but I miss him so much.

As dusk falls, a fire is lit in the fire pit. I wander over to make a quick s'more. Sitting down on one of the benches, I skewer my marshmallow and hold it over the fire. Once it's good and crispy, I pull it off the stick by squashing it between two graham crackers and pulling. I keep the chocolate separate, taking a bite of it and then a bite of the marshmallow/graham cracker combo. The chocolate doesn't melt all over your fingers this way.

"I thought I was the only one who did that," someone says as he takes a seat beside me. I look over to see some guy I don't know.

I scoot over to give him some room. "It's less messy." I shrug.

He skewers his marshmallow and begins the same process. "I'm Dane," he introduces himself and shifts his marshmallow stick to his left hand to offer me a handshake. "You are?"

"Emma." I shake his hand tentatively.

"How do you know the Randall's?" he asks.

"Matt invited me. I've known him since we were little." I pause. I really don't want to talk to this guy, but my conscience tells me to be polite. "You?"

"Old family friend." He smiles at me. "My dad and Dr. Randall are long-time fishing buddies."

I nod while I finish my s'more, then stare at the fire. I have nothing to say to Dane, but it feels rude to just get up and leave. I assess him out of the corner of my eye. He sits taller than me and he's about my age, maybe slightly older. In this light, he looks like he has dark hair and eyes, and he's wearing a black fitted t-shirt and jeans. If I wasn't so melancholy, I would say he was cute. We sit in silence as he assembles his graham crackers and marshmallow.

He clears his throat. "I couldn't help but notice you're looking kind of sad. Anything wrong?" He takes a bite.

I wasn't expecting that question. I stare at the fire as my mind answers him. *Yes, something is very, very wrong. James is gone, and I am alone. I've stopped dreaming about him, but sometimes I hear his voice. I may be going crazy. It's hard for me to do anything but what my friend tells me to do. I'm pretty messed up and not much fun. You can go now, it's okay.*

But I say nothing.

I continue to look at the fire as he finishes his s'more. Dane shifts his weight, like he's uncomfortable. "So …" he trails off awkwardly.

I give him a small apologetic smile. I wish I was better at this, better at putting up a good front.

"You're not trying very hard."

James' voice sounds crystal clear. My smile disappears, and my body tenses in surprise.

"But then again, you never were a very good liar."

I turn abruptly and start to look around behind me.

"Is something wrong?" Dane asks, trying to find what I'm looking for.

"Oh, no." I face him, trying to act casual. "I thought I heard my name."

"Oh." His expression tells me he's rethinking his decision to come and talk to me.

"Yep, still a horrible liar," I hear James snicker.

"Is this thing on?"

I jump as someone taps a microphone. I turn toward the patio and see a group of people gathered around. "It's time for some karaoke! Who's first?" People laugh and a few hands shoot up.

"Do you want to go and watch?" Dane asks me.

I turn back to face him. "I … um …" My brain is completely scattered by James' voice.

"Do you want to watch or don't you?"

I'm still trying to process my thoughts. "Uh … well …"

"I'll make this easy for you," Dane says, shaking his head. "I'm going to go watch people make fools out of themselves. If you want to join me, you can." He stands. "It was nice … er … talking to you," he says and walks away.

I sigh and close my eyes. Could I have acted any more idiotic?

I can hear James laugh. *"That was smooth."*

With my eyes still closed, I smile and wait for James to say something else.

Instead, I hear the karaoke music start and a girl start to warble Brittany Spears' "Baby One More Time." I will James' voice to come back.

When I don't hear him by the end of the song, I open my eyes, disappointed. Another guest takes the mic, and I realize I haven't seen Shel, or my parents, in a while. I decide to head over to the karaoke concert to find them.

I take my time walking back to the patio, thinking about James' voice. It's right. I haven't been trying very hard. I attempt to rearrange my face to look somewhat interested in the entertainment. As I approach the patio, Dr. and Mrs. Randall are beginning a hilarious rendition of Sonny and Cher's "I've Got You Babe." I can't help but laugh as I watch them. At the end of the song everyone claps and cheers as they take exaggerated bows.

As the next person to sing is decided, my eyes scan the patio looking for Shel or my parents. Something catches my eye.

And what I see infuriates me.

CHAPTER 11

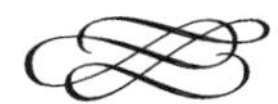

Off to the side of the patio, tucked behind the group of spectators, is where I find them. Matt is sitting in one of the patio chairs and Shel is sitting on his lap, facing him, and they are kissing. There is no logical explanation for it, but anger constricts my chest. I move out of the group of people and slowly walk behind them to the other side of the patio to make sure what I'm seeing is real.

I stop and blend into the guests when I get as close as I dare. I was wrong; they are not just kissing. They are full on *consuming* one another. I see Matt's hands wrap around Shel's waist and then move up her back. I look down at the ground and clench my hands into fists as I try to calm myself.

My mind seethes. The reason she drug me out here tonight was this? Why? Why not just let me stay home?

I hear Shel giggle, and I glance back at them through narrowed eyes. I can see Matt raise his finger to his lips. He tells her to "shhhh" while laughing himself. He starts to kiss her neck. That's when I decide I can't take anymore. I'm leaving.

I wrap my arms around myself and walk quickly through the backyard, around the house, and back to the street. The spot is empty where my parents had parked. "Thanks for telling me you were leaving," I mutter under my breath.

I pull out the keys, get into my car, and slam the door shut behind me. I start the engine and grip the steering wheel, pausing to glare back at the Randall's house. I shake my head in disgust and throw the car into reverse.

"How will Shel get back?" James' voice rings clear.

I'm so upset I don't even flinch. "She's in good hands," I snap out loud to the empty car.

I make sure to back out carefully, but when I throw the car into drive, the tires squeal as I hit the gas.

THE NEXT MORNING I rise with the alarm clock, surprised I slept without tossing and turning. My thoughts return to last night, and I groan. My anger with Shel and Matt may have subsided, but I still feel annoyed. I drag myself out of bed to get ready for work. Memorial Day weekend is supposed to be huge for golf; I'm sure the course will be packed.

After showering, I head downstairs to grab something quick to eat. When I pass Shel's door, I notice it's been left slightly open. I can hear her alarm going off. I peek in and see her passed out in the bed, dead to the world, still dressed in what she was wearing last night.

Really?! My anger returns in full force. Today is supposed to be extremely busy; I'm going to need her help and she's going to make us late! Instead of doing the right thing, which would be to wake her, I storm down the stairs.

"Mornin'," my dad says over a bowl of cereal.

I throw open the pantry door and grab a couple granola bars.

"Have a good time last night?" he asks me.

I grab my keys off the counter and head for the back door, not even bothering to wait and see if Shel decides to wake up for work. "Terrific," I grumble to him over my shoulder as I leave the house.

Bay Woods is packed when I arrive. I walk into the pro shop to clock in and check the schedule. I'll be on the beverage cart for most of the day. Thankfully Shel is assigned to the main concession – if she makes it in. I say a quick hello to Kris, my manager, and head out to the cart area to check my cart and see what needs restocking.

I'm in the middle of unpacking a case of water and burying it in ice when I hear a voice hiss from behind me. "Why did you leave me?"

I look up to see a disheveled Shel, her hair pulled up in a hasty ponytail, shirt wrinkled, half tucked in and half hanging out. Two mismatched socks, no makeup.

"It wasn't my day to babysit you." There's an edge to my tone that comes out sharper than I intended.

She blinks and her mouth falls open in surprise at my response. She quickly shuts it and looks confused. "What did I do to you?"

I finish burying the water bottles and slam the cooler door shut. I gather the plastic from the case of water off the ground and crumple it into a ball, then start to walk to the dumpster.

"Hey!" she yells at me. "I'm talking to you!"

I pause, my back to her. I look down at the crumpled plastic in my hands and then over my shoulder at her. "Have a good time last night?" I ask in a nasty tone.

Shel shakes her head and looks at me like I'm insane. "What?"

I turn and face her. "Last night. Did you have a good time?"

Her face is still twisted in confusion. "Why?"

"As if you don't know," I accuse her.

"You're mad at me because I got drunk? I only had three drinks! I can't help it Uncle Al doesn't know what a shot is," she defends herself, growing angry.

"And?"

"And what? I'm the one who's supposed to be mad here! You took off last night without warning; I had to find a ride home. I get a little hung over and you abandon me again this morning."

"Like you really had a hard time finding a ride home! If you would have taken your tongue out of Matt's mouth for two seconds you might have realized I was ready to leave!" I know I'm being loud, but I really don't care. I know my anger is irrational, but I can't help it.

Shel's face goes slack. "What?"

I lose it entirely. "Stop it!" I'm yelling now. "If you wanted to hook up with Matt, why did you have to drag me along? Couldn't you have just left me at home? Where I don't have to pretend that everything's okay? Where I won't embarrass myself in front of strangers? Where I won't be reminded of what I don't have?" Angry tears are running down my face. I realize now the root of my anger. *I don't have that anymore.*

Shel looks shocked, as if I've physically hit her. After a moment she rearranges her face and walks toward me. "Look ..." she says quietly.

I back away from her and put my hands out to stop her. "Just ... don't." I turn back to head for the dumpster, hastily wiping the tears from my face. As I walk, I check my phone. I have only ten minutes to compose myself before I'm supposed to be out on the course.

The day goes by quickly due to how busy we are. I'm grateful for two reasons: it keeps my mind occupied, and it's easy to avoid Shel. I know we're going to have to talk this through, but I need some time to think about what I'm going to say. She's done nothing but support me over the last two weeks. The apology I owe her is huge.

Around six, I return to the pro shop and hand my cart over to Katie, a new hire, for the next shift. I wander inside to clock out and then take a quick glance into the main concession. Shel isn't there. It's probably better if we talk at home anyway.

When I pull up the driveway, Shel is sitting on the back step. I slowly get out of the car, walk up, and stand before her. I twist my fingers together nervously and stare at the ground like a child who is about to be punished. I'm unsure of where to start.

She beats me to it. "Do you want me to leave?" she asks pointedly.

I look up at her. "No. Absolutely not."

She sighs and pats the spot next to her on the step. I take a seat and ask her quietly, "You know how sorry I am, right?"

She nods. "I'm sorry, too."

"You have nothing to apologize for."

"No, I do." She meets my eyes. "I was careless."

"No, you're normal. I'm the one with the crazy emotions."

Shel snorts. "I may have some crazy emotions myself."

We pause for a moment and stare out across the yard.

"Look," I say. "What you do is none of my business. If you and Matt are together, that's actually really great."

"Except we're not," she sighs.

I look at her in disbelief. "Excuse me?"

She gives me a guilty look. "It appears I owe someone else an apology, too."

I'm confused. "So, what happened?"

"Long story short, margaritas happened," she says, embarrassed.

"Oh no."

"Oh yes."

"Do you think he thinks you two are ..."

"I'm not sure what he thinks." She shrugs. "He was out of it, so some friend of his drove me back here. David? Don?"

"Dane." I groan, remembering my idiotic stuttering.

"You know him?"

I make a face. "He's the one I embarrassed myself in front of."

"Yikes."

"Yeah. I wouldn't be surprised if he thinks I'm ... what's a good word? Special."

Shel laughs. "Well, that makes two of us."

I lean my head against my best friend's shoulder and smile with her. Lately, we're two peas in a pod when it comes to social awkwardness.

"Seriously though," Shel says when her laughter fades. "I am sorry. I have been pushing you. The cemetery, the job, the bar, this thing ..." She waves her hand absentmindedly. "I haven't been here that long. It's a lot. But my intentions are good."

"I know. I do appreciate it. Truly."

"Okay," she pauses and holds out her pinky finger. "From here on out I promise not to push so hard."

I loop my pinky around hers. "And I promise to remember that other people have lives and to try and keep my emotions in check."

We pinky swear like we did in elementary school, and after a moment, she grimaces. "I guess I should find Matt and sort that out, too."

"I don't envy you. Do you need me to go with?"

She shakes her head. "No. I'm a big girl. It's my mess."

"You're sure?"

"I'm sure." She stands and heads for her car. "Wish me luck?"

I give her a sympathetic look. "Good luck."

After Shel pulls out of the driveway, I head upstairs to clean up. I feel entirely gross physically, but mentally relieved she accepted my apology.

While changing clothes, I try to decide what to do with my time tonight. When nothing immediately jumps to mind, my thoughts turn to Shel. I hope Matt isn't too hard on her. Hopefully it won't be that bad; maybe what happened isn't a big deal to him or maybe he was too drunk to remember much. Or maybe he will be upset. I know if it were me, I would be upset. I can't imagine being intimate with someone so casually. I guess that's a result of being with the same guy – the only guy I've ever been with in my life – for four years.

That's when the thought pops into my mind. I know what I'm going to do tonight. I'm going to visit James.

I PULL into Whispering Oaks cautiously. I can't believe I'm doing this, but it feels like something I should do. I told him I would come back.

I feel nervous. As I pull to a stop and turn off the engine, I glance around at what I can see of the cemetery. I know it's a public place, but I would prefer to be here alone. Since I don't see anyone, I reach over and pick up the potted orchid from the seat beside me. I thought I could leave this here for him; it would have more meaning here than in my bathroom.

I start the slow walk along the dirt drive clutching the orchid. I guess I could have driven around to the back, but the walk will give me time to calm my racing heart. Why am I so nervous? It's only logical that I would come here. Maybe it's because I decided to do this on my own, without anyone making me. I concentrate on the sounds around me. It's only my second time here; is it always this serene?

Well, duh, I think to myself. Of course there's not much activity going on. This place is pretty dead, if you know what I mean.

Badabum tsch! Lame joke drums sound in my brain.

I make it to the rear of the cemetery and remember where to turn left. Unfortunately, I see a few new mounds of dirt ahead of me, or at least I didn't see them the last time I was here. I hope they haven't removed the flowers that were there; James' headstone wasn't in place yet and without the flowers I may not find the right spot. I decide on which location would most likely be his and walk there first. As I get closer, I'm relieved. I recognize the flowers; I see the blue "Son" bow. But something is different.

He has a headstone now.

My breath catches at the sight. It seals my reality, and I have a hard time filling my lungs.

Despite this, I make it to James and force myself to take in his gravesite's new addition. It's a square stone, polished black with white specks, which stands on a rectangular base of the same rock. It's very masculine but looks so smooth and soft. I'm drawn to it, and I take a step forward to kneel beside the headstone. I touch the black rock; it is as smooth as it looks. I trace the gray engraving with my finger:

James Henderson Davis
Beloved Son
June 11, 1990 – April 12, 2012

"They forgot to add 'Soul Mate' after 'Beloved Son,'" I whisper. I can't resist the smoothness of the rock, and I lean forward to place my cheek against the top of the stone, closing my eyes. It feels cool against my skin. Again, I listen to the wind and the birds as I kneel there. My heart is no longer racing.

After a few moments, I open my eyes and present the orchid.

"I brought you this," I say aloud and place it in front of the headstone. "I thought you might like it." I position it so it sits straight on the uneven ground. I notice the contrast between the black stone and the fuchsia petals. "It looks much better here."

Sitting on the ground, I hug my knees to my chest. Absentmindedly, I look down and see my hand print is still visible in the dirt, but it's now partially marred by someone's boot print. They must have stepped on it when they set the stone. I get to work recreating it; pressing my palm into the ground and taking my time drawing the dirt swirls. I decide one print isn't enough and create another with my other hand, swirling the soil with my finger.

"I hear your voice sometimes," I tell him and smile. "I like it. Could you talk to me more often please?"

Silence.

"I'm waiting."

The James voice does not come. I frown. "And you always said I was the stubborn one."

I finish my swirls then wrap my arms around my knees again. I look up at the towering trees and the blue sky. "It's hard without you here." I pause. "Shel's staying with me. She's been trying to help, but I'm sure you've seen that." I take a deep breath. "I hope you've seen that."

I sit in silence a while longer. My legs start to fall asleep in the position I have them in, so I adjust and sit cross-legged on the ground. "We went to Matt's house last night, but you probably know that, too. I bet you think what happened between Shel and Matt is pretty funny. She feels terrible about it, though."

I don't know exactly how long I sit there dividing my stares between the sky, his headstone, my handprints, and the ground. The sun drops low in the sky and I guess, for now, there's nothing more to say. I reach out and run my fingers across the smooth stone again.

"I love you so much."

I stand and brush dirt from my shorts. "Take care of my flower. It was sent by some unknown admirer. Was it you?" I shake my head because that could never be true. I kiss my fingers and press them to the top of the stone. "It's getting late. I'll be back to visit you soon."

My legs are stiff from sitting on the hard ground, making the walk back to my car a slow one. I concentrate on my toes as I shuffle along, pondering the idea of bringing a camping chair with me the next time I visit. I wonder if anyone has done that before. Some gravesites have permanent benches. Would a lawn chair be much different?

As I approach the spot where I parked, I pull my keys from my pocket and look up. All of my muscles instantly lock. My heart stops beating.

There, leaning casually against the side of my car, is James.

CHAPTER 12

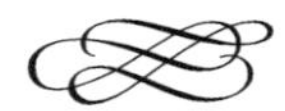

I blink. Once, twice, three times. When he doesn't disappear, I slam my eyes shut.

He's not real. He's not real. He's not real. He's not real.

My heart must have started again because it's pounding blood through my ears.

He's not really here.

Now I'm having visions?

Why am I having visions?

I'm having a psychotic breakdown.

Yes, that's why. That's why I'm seeing my dead boyfriend leaning against my car.

What if I can't open my eyes?

What if I can't get home?

Why didn't I tell anyone I was coming here?

"Breathe, Emma."

My frozen body jerks at the sound of his voice. It's like he's standing directly in front of me now. I smash my eyes together tighter and cringe.

"Emma, please breathe."

You're not real!

"Em, you're scaring me. Please breathe," he pleads.

I'm scaring you?

"If you pass out, I'm not going to be able to help you!" he begs.

I'm pretty sure I'm beyond help now.

"Emma! Damn it! Open your eyes and breathe!"

Make me.

And then my legs do give out. My body meets the gravel, and I am lost.

I OPEN my eyes to darkness. I blink a couple of times to make sure my eyes are actually open. I can see the faint shadow of my car several feet ahead of me, but it's sideways. My cheek feels rough, and I realize I'm lying on the ground. I spring to a sitting position, and my head immediately begins to spin. I hold my head in my hands until my equilibrium returns. How long have I been here?

The realization hits that I have been passed out on a dark cemetery drive, and I am instantly fearful. I stand as quickly as I dare and stumble my way to the car. I wrench the door open and fall inside, locking the doors. I feel safer inside the vehicle. I sit for a few moments, resting my head on the steering wheel, collecting myself.

That's it, I tell myself as I turn the ignition. *I cannot come here alone again.*

I concentrate exceptionally hard on driving as I make my way home. I feel completely exhausted, but it isn't even ten o'clock. I reflect on what happened at the cemetery. What was that? Obviously all the emotions from today have taken their toll.

"Where have you been?" Shel demands as I enter the kitchen. She's sitting at the island, clutching her cell phone. "I've been blowing up your phone for over an hour!"

I toss my purse on the counter and take out my phone. Yep, fourteen missed calls and five voice mail messages. "I'm sorry," I mumble to her sleepily.

She stands and comes around to stand in front of me. "Are you all right?" she asks, concern etched on her face.

What do I tell her? I struggle for a minute and then decide on a half-truth. "I went to visit James."

She looks at me warily. "And?"

"Believe it or not, I fell asleep."

Her mouth falls open in awe. "In the cemetery?"

I shake my head. "Trust me; I'm just as shocked as you and completely creeped out."

For more reasons than one.

I wrap my arms around myself and change topics. "How was your um … visit … with Matt?"

She looks troubled and bites her lower lip. "It went okay."

"Just okay?"

"I think he's a little upset with me."

"Really? What did he say?"

"He said everything is okay between us, but he still seemed a little peeved about the whole thing. He wouldn't make eye contact with me. I got the feeling he just wanted me to go away."

"I bet he's more embarrassed than anything," I encourage her. "Give it some time. He'll come around."

"I really hope so. I feel so guilty. I would hate for this to ruin our friendship."

I scowl at her. "Why is it all your fault? As I recall, it takes two to tango."

She lets out a small laugh. "This is true."

I yawn. "Are you heading up?"

"Right behind you."

We make our way upstairs. Outside Mike's room, Shel stops. "I'm impressed that you went to the cemetery alone."

I give her a small smile. "Thanks." Little does she know that won't be happening again anytime soon.

"Good night," she says as she disappears through the door.

"'Night."

When I get to my room, I close the door and lean against it in the darkness. I feel drained; physically and mentally.

"Don't be scared."

All my muscles tense. The James voice has returned. Moving just my eyes, I look around the room frantically.

"Please don't be afraid," it says softly.

I can't tell where the voice is coming from. Is it only in my head again? Scared to move, I fumble for the light switch.

"Don't turn on the light," the voice says. "Talk to me first."

Talk to you? About what?

"Please, Emma. This is so hard. Say something."

I swallow. What do I say? If I cooperate with my psychosis, will it leave me alone?

My voice catches in my throat and comes out in a raspy whisper. "Wh–what do you want?"

I hear a sigh of relief. "To be near you, always."

I hesitate. Now what?

"C'mon, Em. I know you have to have more questions than that."

I go for the obvious. "Um … are you in my head?"

The voice pauses to consider. "Sometimes."

"What about now?"

"No, I'm not in your head now."

Panicked, I start to look around the room again. "If you're not in my head, where are you?"

"Across from you. By the window."

My eyes immediately zero in on that spot, but I see nothing but darkness.

"I can hear your heart pounding," the voice says. "I'm not going to hurt you; you know I would never hurt you."

Uncertain, I whisper nervously, "I–I know."

"This is … it's … there are no words to describe this. But I am here. I want to stay with you."

This can't be happening. "How is that possible?" I ask the darkness.

"I will do everything I can to make it so," the voice sounds determined, almost aggressive. Then it softens. "I've missed you so much."

My fear lessens a little with those five words. "I've missed you, too."

"I'm sorry … for everything," it whispers, broken. "I will never forgive myself for what I've put you through. To see you in pain … it … it devastates me."

My heart breaks, and my arms ache to hold James. The voice sounds so real, as if he really is here in my room with me. My chest constricts in that all-too-familiar way. "Hearing you helps me," I say. "I wish I could hear you more often."

"I'm working on that," the voice sighs tiredly. "There is so much I have to learn. It's frustrating; I'm not very good at being patient."

I shake my head, confused. "I don't understand."

The James voice chuckles softly. "No, you wouldn't understand." It pauses and sighs again. "I have so much to tell you."

My heart has slowed to its regular rhythm. I am no longer afraid. Still searching the darkness, I say, "I want you to tell me."

"Slowly. I need to take things slowly. I was in such a hurry earlier …" The voice chastises itself. "Are you okay? Are you hurt?"

"From falling? No, I'm fine."

"That was so stupid of me. I tried to wake you, but I couldn't … I couldn't touch you. I kept trying … I felt so helpless with you lying there. But I stayed with you," the voice hastily adds. "I stayed with you until you woke up; I was with you the whole way home."

"Of course you were," I placate the voice, not wanting it to be upset. "You are always in my head, in my heart."

"No, no. I was literally there."

"How?" I ask, my doubt evident. "How is that possible?"

"I want to show you, but I don't know if it's wise. Maybe later, after you're used to speaking with me more …"

Suddenly, the urge to know overwhelms me. What if this isn't psychosis? Honestly, I'm not this creative.

"I want to know," I blurt out. "I need to know."

The voice hesitates, doubtful. "I don't know. What if you're not ready? I can't bear to hurt you again."

Confidence surges through me unexpectedly. "I'm ready."

"If anything happened ..."

I know it's wrong, but I say it anyway. "I think you owe it to me."

The voice sighs, resigned. "I owe you so much more."

After a few moments of silence, just when I think I've lost the battle, I hear, "Turn on the light."

I turn to the right and feel along the wall for the switch. I flip it on and turn slowly to face the room. What I see makes my chest want to explode with happiness.

James is here. Literally *here.* Standing across the room by the window, dressed in jeans and a polo shirt. He looks a little pale, but otherwise he looks like my James. My heart threatens to burst, and I swallow a sob.

"You're here," I whisper in disbelief.

"Like I said." His blue eyes light up, and he gives me a crooked smile.

Oh, that smile! I want to run to him and wrap myself around him and never let go. I take a tentative step forward. "Can I ...?" I ask permission.

"Absolutely."

I want to launch myself at him, but I force myself to walk slowly, around the bed, until I'm standing in front of him. Looking up into his face, overwhelmed and in awe, all I can manage is "Hi."

"Hello." He grins down at me. "Are you feeling faint?"

I shake my head. "Not this time."

"Good," he says.

"I ... I ..." I can't seem to form a sentence anymore.

"What?"

"Can I touch you?"

His face falls.

"What's wrong?"

"That is what I have to show you." He frowns. "You're still sure?"

I nod quickly.

He closes his eyes and opens them slowly. "Hold out your hand," he says.

I raise my hand and hold it out to him, palm up.

Slowly, he raises his hand, and moves to set it on top of mine, as if to grasp it. When his hand touches my skin, I feel a chill run through me. His hand closes around my fingers.

And it passes right through, as if I weren't even there.

CHAPTER 13

I gasp and pull away quickly, clutching my hands together and holding them to my stomach. I try not to appear frightened, but when I look up at him, I know I failed.

He closes his eyes and his face falls. "I'm sorry," he whispers.

Words escape me. "I–no–I'm okay," I stutter. When he doesn't open his eyes, I start to panic. What if he thinks it's too much for me to handle and he leaves? "Please look at me," I plead. "I'm not afraid. I'm not."

He opens his eyes, and they reflect his worry. "Are you sure?"

"I'm not sure exactly what I feel," I say. "But I know it's not fear."

James gives me a tiny smile and appears to relax a little.

I want to touch him so badly. I start to reach out toward him slowly. I can see him tense up. "What are you doing?" he asks.

I freeze mid-reach. "Can't I touch you? Now that I know?"

He looks surprised. "I ... I didn't think you would want to."

I smile at him, to reassure him, and continue my reach. I lay my hand against his face, and he closes his eyes, pressing his cheek against my palm. I feel nothing, but a chill runs through my arm, like a cool breeze.

"You feel so warm," he sighs against my skin.

"You can feel me?"

"Just warmth," he answers and opens his eyes, smiling.

"How does this work?" I ask him, bewildered.

James shakes his head. "I wish I could explain it to you. I'm still learning myself."

"Learning what, exactly?"

"How to be a Guardian."

I gaze at him, stupefied. "A what?"

He smiles at me. "There's so much I want to tell you."

"So tell me."

"It's a lot."

"I can handle it." I nod enthusiastically.

"I have a better idea, for tonight anyway." He steps closer to my bed. "You should get to sleep. You have to be at work in the morning, right?"

I give him an incredulous look. "Really? You've returned from the dead and you want me to go to sleep?"

He nods.

"So I won't be late for work?"

He nods again.

"That's not going to happen." I cross my arms in defiance. I'm finding it incredibly easy to fall into our old routine.

"Just get in the bed," James scolds.

I roll my eyes at him. "Am I allowed to change? Or must I 'pretend sleep' in my clothes?"

He laughs. "I've missed your stubbornness."

Annoyed, I march to my dresser and pull some pajamas from the drawer. "Turn around," I order him.

"Why?"

"So I can change."

His eyes blatantly travel from my head to my toes. "It's not like I haven't seen it before."

My face flushes. "You weren't a ghost before."

"Guardian," he corrects me.

"Whatever. Whatever you are now, you weren't that then."

"I was the other day in the shower." He winks at me.

My mouth falls open in disbelief. That was the first time I'd heard his voice. "You were really there?"

He nods, a big grin on his face.

The realization hits, and my mouth snaps shut. "You. Were. There." I growl at him.

"What?" He looks confused.

"You should use your powers for good, not evil," I say sarcastically. "Spying on naked women. You should be ashamed of yourself."

"Naked woman," he corrects me again. "Singular."

I give him a dirty look and turn my back to him. As I change clothes, a huge smile breaks across my face. I want to hug myself. He was really there.

"Okay." I turn back around, now in my sleep shorts and t-shirt.

"Turn off the light," he tells me.

Instantly, I pout. "I won't be able to see you."

"I'm not going anywhere, I promise."

I sigh and walk over to flip the switch. When I turn around, I see nothing but darkness. I start to walk around to the side of the bed where James was standing, arms outstretched. "Where are you?"

"I'm right here."

His voice is closer than I anticipated, and it startles me. "Geez!"

"Sorry," he immediately apologizes. "Now, get in the bed."

I pull the covers back and crawl in, lying in the middle, on my side, like always. "Now what?"

"Don't jump," he says calmly.

What's he going to do?

Slowly, creeping from the top of my head, over my shoulders, along my back, and down my legs, I feel the chill. It stays there, and a branch of the chill spreads across my stomach, over my arms. It feels cold but also heavenly.

"What are you doing?" I'm barely able to whisper.

"Are you all right?" he asks softly.

I nod into the pillow.

"I thought I would stay with you tonight, if that's okay?"

A tear escapes my eye and runs down my cheek. "It's more than okay."

"You'll probably want to pull the covers over you," he whispers in my ear. "You might end up shivering if I keep holding you like this."

I do as I'm told. The warmth of the blankets and the chill of his body are the perfect balance. My entire body wants to sing; I feel so peaceful.

"How can you do this?" I ask quietly.

"What? Lie here?"

I nod.

"Right now, for me, it takes a great deal of concentration. Most of my energy has to stay focused on remaining in this exact spot."

"What do you mean 'right now'?"

"Certain things will get easier, as time goes on." The chill against my arm starts to move. I visualize James running his fingers to my elbow and back down to my wrist.

"Why didn't you reveal yourself to me sooner?"

"I wanted to, but I had to be taught how. In the beginning, all I could do was watch you. I wanted to show you I was still around so badly, but I had to learn to speak to you first," he pauses then snickers. "Your reaction in the shower was priceless."

I try to elbow him in the gut, but my elbow hits only cool air behind me. "I'm glad my thinking I was going insane entertained you," I hiss quietly.

"Aw, don't be upset. Besides, you could only be one kind of crazy," he teases.

"And what's that?"

"Crazy about me, of course."

"Oh, *of course*," I say sarcastically, but I can't help it and let out a quiet giggle.

"Talking to you is still hit or miss; I don't know how I've managed to speak with you this long tonight. It has to be tied to the manifest in some way ..." his voice fades in thought.

What? It's hard to wrap my mind around what he's telling me, but

I'm trying to keep up. "If things are hit or miss, how do you know you'll be here tomorrow?"

"I'll still be here," he promises. "I'm always here. You just can't see or hear me all the time. Maybe it will be easier for me, now that I've had a successful manifest. Obviously tonight's attempt has gone very well," he says, his voice full of pride. "Garrett will be pleased, although he probably won't be happy with how long I've stayed with you."

"Who's Garrett?" I ask, confused.

"My Guardian."

I think I understand. "Your teacher?"

"Both."

"He will be angry with you?" I can't help myself and a yawn escapes.

"He only gave me permission to try and show myself – manifest – at the cemetery," he sighs. "I had to talk him into letting me; it's still very early in my learning for that big of a step."

"Why did he allow it then?"

James laughs softly. "I haven't shut up about you since I ..." his voice trails off. "I think he got sick of my nagging and caved in. And then, after you fainted, I couldn't leave you without trying again. I had to make sure you were all right."

"Well, when you see him, you can tell him it's my fault. Thank him for me, too."

"Will do," he says quietly. "Now, try to go to sleep."

My eyes pop open. "To see him again means you have to leave?"

I feel the chill along my body grow more intense and then release, as if James hugged me and then let go a little. "Yes, I will have to return to Garrett and my Guardian study because I'm bound to the option I chose. But I can always find you. As time goes on, it'll be easier to understand. I hope."

I try to make sense of everything, but my mind is overwhelmed. Option he chose? "I think you're going to have to write this down for me. But I trust you."

"Good. Now, go to sleep."

"No. I just got you back."

"Yes." I feel the chill intensify in a concentrated spot on my cheek and then disappear.

"Did you just kiss me?"

"Yes."

The cool air moves against my neck, and I picture him nuzzling me there. I lean toward the chill and smile. "Kiss me again, please."

He complies with my request but on my temple this time. And then again, under my ear.

"You came back to me," I murmur.

"We aim to please," I can hear his smile. "I love you," he whispers.

"I love you, too."

"Go to sleep."

"So demanding," I mumble.

The chill intensifies along my body again, and eventually I allow sleep to overcome me.

CHAPTER 14

I'm too hot. I break free of the blankets that are wrapped around me like a burrito. The air outside my bed feels cooler. A lazy smile spreads across my face as I remember last night.

My eyes fly open, and I spring upright, realizing the chill of James is gone. I look around the room, searching.

"James?" I ask quietly. "Are you here?"

Silence.

"James?"

Nothing.

"Say something."

My heart sinks as I hug my knees to my chest. A heavy feeling of loneliness settles over me. Last night wasn't real, was it?

Of course it was, my mind taunts me. *Your dead boyfriend returned to you as a ghost – NOT! You've been Punk'd by your broken heart!*

Defeated, I close my eyes and rest my forehead against my knees. I expect the few tears that escape. I remember the feeling of him lying next to me, his voice, his smile. It was a wonderful delusion while it lasted. I know I shouldn't, but I wonder how to make it happen again.

I pick my head up and wipe away the tears. I glance at the clock. I need to start getting ready for work, but I remain tied to my bed.

"What's with all the drama?"

I quickly scan the room. "James? What … where are you?" I whisper, panicked, when I can't find him.

"Don't worry; I'm here."

"Where?"

"You can't see me right now. Seriously Em, calm down, you're going to give yourself a stroke."

I take a deep breath. "When did you leave? Why did you leave?"

"I had to go this morning. Listen," he sounds distracted. "I'd love to stay and talk right now, but I can't. I'll find you later tonight, okay?"

"You promise?"

"I swear."

"Okay," I say quietly to the air. "Love you."

"Love you t–" It sounds like he's cut off.

I finish wiping the last of my tears and think about what he said. I pry myself out of the bed and begin to get ready for the day. As I do, a grin slowly spreads across my face.

Last night really happened.

"ALL RIGHT!" Shel says, slamming her hand down on the counter. "What's going on?"

I look at her innocently. "What do you mean?"

"Something's up. You've had this loopy smile on your face all day and now you're *humming,*" she winces. "It's annoying."

I can't help but smile at her some more. "So, now I'm too happy for you? Make up your mind. Happy or depressed, I can't be both."

She eyes me suspiciously. "I'm forced to choose happy." She crosses her arms. "So what gives?"

I want to shout from the rooftops that James has returned, but I force myself to respond in measured words. "I'm just feeling … you know … better." I shrug.

"Better?" she asks. "Just like that?"

I try to act casual, like it's no big deal. "Just like that."

"I guess that's a good thing." She narrows her eyes and goes back to cleaning the counter top. "But could you stop with the humming?"

"Whoa. Somebody's in a bad mood."

Shel stops wiping and sighs. "This Matt thing has me really messed up. I can't stop thinking about it. I need to be sure he's not mad at me."

Just then, two people walk in to the main concession area. I look past Shel and mutter, "Ask and you shall receive," nodding toward the entrance. Matt and his friend Dane have arrived. My eyes catch Dane's for a split second, and I quickly look away. Hopefully, I can refrain from acting like an idiot today.

Shel catches my drift and looks a little surprised. She rearranges her face to look nonchalant, then turns around.

"Hey there!" she greets the guys. Matt stands off to the side, his hands stuffed in the pockets of his cargo shorts, pretending to be interested in the posted menu. He says nothing.

Dane gives a small wave and leans over the register slightly. "I'm glad to see you're feeling better." He smiles at Shel conspiratorially.

Matt nervously clears his throat and shoots him a look out of the corner of his eye. Dane appears to understand his unspoken message. "We'll have two hot dogs, please," he orders. "I'll have a Coke, and, what did you want?" he asks Matt.

Matt looks up, irritated, like Dane should know better. "The same."

"Oh, yeah, two Cokes." Dane smiles, and his eyes light up. I was right the other night by the fire. His perfectly tousled hair is dark brown, and his eyes are a rich hazel.

Shel rings up the order. "That will be $8.50," she says politely, but when she turns to me, her smile fades and her eyes widen. "You got the dogs?" she asks as she heads to the cooler.

"Yep," I say and turn to grab the buns.

"Hey, Emma."

I turn and give Dane an embarrassed nod. "Hey. Golfing today?"

James laughs sarcastically in my ear. "No, they stopped by because this is the best restaurant in town."

I try not to appear stunned in front of Dane *again* and relax my face. I glance out of the corner of my eye to make sure James isn't standing next to me. He's not.

"Yeah, figured I'd drag Matt out for the afternoon." Dane smirks.

I finish up with the hot dogs and bring them to the counter. "Here you go." I hand him the food.

"Thanks." He takes one and hands the other to Matt, who has yet to say anything to us.

Shel returns with the Cokes and sets them on the counter to take Dane's cash.

"So," Dane says as he collects his change from her. "Since you're both here, I might as well ask. What are you two lovely ladies doing tonight? Care to double?" He glances at Matt with a wicked grin. "I have some lawn furniture at my house that needs christening."

Matt nails Dane with a murderous expression. "Dude."

Dane holds out his hands, "What?"

"This lovely lady already has plans tonight," James growls over my shoulder.

Shel quickly turns to me and mouths, "What's going on?"

I shake my head and shrug.

Matt lets out an exasperated sigh and his shoulders sag. "Shel, can I talk to you outside for a minute?"

She rounds the counter, and Matt hands his hot dog to Dane before following her outside. Dane chuckles and takes a bite.

"What's so funny?" I ask.

He chews, then answers me. "I'm just giving him a hard time. Whether he wants to or not, he needs to talk with her. He's been sulking since Friday."

"Really?"

Dane nods emphatically. "He just needed a little push, that's all."

"That was a little push?" I smile. "Looked more like a shove to me."

He laughs. "I knew he wouldn't just stand there and do nothing if I said what I did."

"Sneaky."

Dane smiles, but then his look turns serious. "Listen, I want you to know I wasn't asking you out for real. I would never do that."

I can't help it and my face falls, hurt. Not that I care, but that was kind of mean.

"Wait. That came out wrong." His face turns red. "Of course, I want to take you out. No! What I mean is …"

"It's okay," I mutter and start to walk away.

"No. Wait." He reaches across the counter and grabs my arm.

James growls in my ear.

"What I meant to say was that I'm sorry about your loss," he says in a rush. "Matt let me know about his friend ... your … James," he finishes. "I'm sorry." He looks sincere.

"It's okay." I give him a weak smile, and he lets go of my arm.

"Damn right," James snaps.

Worry clouds Dane's model-like features. "I'm not that big of a jerk, I swear."

"That's debatable," James mutters.

I shake my head at both James' and Dane's comments. "I don't think that."

"You're sure?" Dane asks.

"I'm positive."

His face relaxes. "Good."

"Excuse me?" Another golfer has arrived at the counter. Dane grabs his food and drinks as he moves out of the way.

It seems like I serve quite a few more customers while Dane stands at the end of the counter, finishing off both his and Matt's lunch. I find it uncomfortable trying to work while he stands there looking at the TV, looking at me, back to the TV, back to me. I glance at the clock. Where are Matt and Shel?

Dane notices my observance of the time. "Taking a while, aren't they?"

"Should we be worried?"

"Nah," he replies shakes his head.

The minutes pass. I look at the clock again. Our shift ends in fifteen minutes. I decide to close out my drawer and get things ready for the next employee.

"You're off at five?" Dane absentmindedly asks.

"Yep." I'm anxious to get home. A shiver of excitement runs through me at the thought of seeing James again.

Dane hangs out at the end of the counter for the next fifteen minutes until Katie shows up for the evening shift. Doesn't he have anything better to do? Where the hell is Shel?

"Hey, Emma," Katie says as she comes around the corner. "Busy today?"

"Not too bad." I smile as I grab my bag and Shel's things. "Everything's all restocked." I walk out from behind the counter. "Have a good night."

"You, too," she says and her eye catches Dane walking up to me. She shoots me a questioning look.

"I'll walk you out," he says.

James' voice sounds menacing over my shoulder. "The hell you will."

"Uh … that's okay," I stammer. "I need to find Shel anyway; she's my ride."

"Funny, Matt rode with me." He smiles. He reaches around me and holds the door open. "Let's find them together."

James snaps, "Persistent, isn't he?"

I have to fight to keep a straight face. Why is he acting like this? I take two steps toward the door and wave at Katie. "See you next week."

She subtly nods in Dane's direction and mouths, "He's hot!"

I roll my eyes at her as I walk out the door.

When we get outside the pro shop, I don't immediately see Matt or Shel. Dane follows me as I turn and head in the direction of the parking lot.

"Any idea where they might be?" I ask him. I really want to get home.

Dane looks around. "Nope. I figured they'd be right here." He frowns.

I continue around the pro shop to where they park the golf carts. The area is pretty empty this time of the day. There's no sign of them. "Maybe they're already by the cars?" I ask hopefully.

Dane shrugs. "Lead the way."

We pass the clubhouse on our way to the parking lot. I can see Shel's car amongst the others but no Shel or Matt. My heart sinks. Where are they?

I stop walking and cross my arms, looking around. "Where could they be?" I whine. "I really need to get home."

"If you need to get going right now, I'll take you," Dane volunteers.

"I bet you will," James seethes.

"Ah, no. That's okay." I look around. I wish James would knock it off. He's distracting me.

"Hey, look at it this way," Dane says. "Their talk must be going well. Maybe good enough for them to disappear, if you know what I mean." He winks.

A loud "Ew!" escapes me before I can stop it. Dane laughs, and I can't help but laugh along with him.

Suddenly, we hear a loud scream and our laughter is cut short. I look at Dane with panic because I've heard that scream before.

Outside Louie's Roadhouse.

It's Shel.

In a split second, Dane and I are running in the direction of the clubhouse. We hear Shel scream again and halt.

"This way!" Dane points to the right and takes off running.

I try to keep up with him as he runs along the side of the building, but I fall behind a few feet. He makes it to the corner before me, turns, and disappears. I kick it into high gear to catch up with him, and when I speed around the corner, I slam right into his back.

"OOOF." I lose my footing and fall to the ground.

"Emma." Dane turns around. "Are you okay?"

How embarrassing! I blink up at him and instantly try to stand. "Yeah, yeah, I'm fine."

"Here, let me help you." He reaches for my hand.

"No, I've got it."

As I'm standing, Dane grabs my elbow and steadies me anyway.

"So help me ..." I hear James in my ear.

I yank my arm out of Dane's grasp. "Thanks, I've got it," I say sharper than I intended.

He looks at me concerned. "You sure you're okay?"

I nod and start to wipe my shorts. "Yes, I'm fine. Thanks," I say softer. The sound of laughter and splashing registers in my brain. I look past Dane.

"Oh yeah, I found Matt and Shel," he says and gestures over his shoulder.

Behind the clubhouse sits a large decorative pond with a waterfall, and Matt and Shel appear to be wrestling each other in it. Shel lets out another shriek as Matt throws a lily pad in her face.

I march over to the edge of the pond and give them both a scathing look. "Do you have any idea what time it is?" I snap.

They hesitate mid-splash as they look up at me. "Sorry," Shel says, trying to stifle her laughter.

I sigh, crossing my arms. "Can we go?"

"Sure, you can go," Matt says, smiling sweetly as he walks toward me. "For a swim." He reaches out, grabs my ankles, and tries to pull me into the pond.

"No! Don't!" I shout as I try to back away, losing my balance.

"Gotcha!" Dane grabs me from behind, underneath my arms, to keep me from the water. I am now the rope in a tug-of-war.

"Let go!" I protest and try to twist out their hold. The last thing I want to do is end up in pond water. I see a mental image of how ridiculous we must look to everyone at the clubhouse. As I start to laugh, I yell, "No! Put me down."

Matt laughs as he reaches farther up my legs to get a better hold. Since his is hands are wet, his grip slips, and I manage to free one leg. I let out a victorious "Ha!" I go to work on trying to kick my other leg free, which he is now pulling on with both hands.

Thankfully, Dane has better leverage standing outside the pond and he yanks me free of Matt's hold. I end up on the grass on my butt – again – and Dane falls beside me. I lie back on the grass and hold my stomach as we convulse with laughter.

"Having fun?" James asks sadly in my ear.

I immediately feel guilty and try to compose myself. As I sit up I catch Kris, our manager, out of the corner of my eye. She's accompanied by the clubhouse director, and they don't look happy.

"Um, guys?" I try to get everyone's attention. "Guys!"

Matt is helping Shel out of the pond by the time they make it to us. "Just what exactly is going on here?" the clubhouse director, Jeff, asks sternly. "The guests are complaining!"

"Sorry," Shel says, dripping. "I … I fell in."

It's a lame explanation, and Jeff doesn't buy it. "Both of you work here, right?" he asks, pointing to Shel and me. We nod. He looks expectantly at Kris.

"Shel, Emma, you know this isn't professional. You have to know that playing *in* the water feature is not allowed," she scolds us. "People are trying to have a nice dinner over there." She nods towards the clubhouse patio.

We look down at the ground. Matt starts to defend us, "Listen, it's my …"

Jeff holds up a hand to silence him.

Kris continues. "Guys, I don't like this, but I'm going to have to take you off the schedule for a couple of days. I can't have the other staff thinking this is an okay thing to do with their friends."

Even though this is so totally not my fault, I nod and say, "I understand."

"Wait," Dane speaks up, coming around to the front of the group. "Wait until I speak with my dad first; no one needs to be suspended."

"And just who are you?" Jeff asks sarcastically.

Dane offers a hand to Jeff. "We haven't had a chance to meet. I'm Dane Walker."

Jeff loses the sarcastic expression and shakes Dane's hand slowly. "Mr. Walker's son?"

"The same." Dane smiles at him casually.

Shel and I look at each other, surprised. Mr. Walker's son? The same Mr. Walker who owns Bay Woods?

"Dane," Kris sighs. "I'm sorry the girls are your friends, but this is protocol."

"Just let me talk with my dad tonight. I'll have him call you," he promises.

Kris thinks it over. "Okay," she concedes and looks pointedly at us. "I'll call you after I talk to Mr. Walker."

We nod in understanding. Shel mutters, "Thanks" as I mutter, "Sorry."

"Nice to meet you," Jeff grumbles to Dane and turns to follow Kris.

When the managers disappear inside the clubhouse, Matt lets out a low whistle of relief. We all look at each other and, as giggles threaten, I walk over to pick up our things. "Let's go Shel, before you cause more trouble."

"Me cause trouble?" she says indigently. "I was pushed into the water!" She gives Matt a dirty look.

"It was a tap," Matt defends himself. "You're the one who lost her balance and pulled me in with you."

They rehash the incident as we head back to the parking lot. "See you later." She punches Matt good-naturedly as I hold out her purse.

"Yeah, see you." He smiles at her. "Bye, Em."

I wave. "Thanks for the save back there." I smile at Dane as I round Shel's car.

Once inside, I ask, "So, I take it everything is okay between you and Matt now?"

Shel pushes her wet bangs out of her eyes. "Yes. We can lay that monster to rest."

"Explanation please."

"He felt bad, and I felt guilty. I guess we needed some extra reassurance from each other that it was just a mistake." She laughs. "I also promised to never drink anything made by his uncle again."

"Good," I tell her as she backs out of the parking space. "By the way, you owe me. I had to do the cash out and restock by myself."

"Sorry. At least you had Dane to talk to." She smiles.

I give her my "oh please" look. "What's up with his dad owning the course? Did you know about that?"

"Nope."

I glance out the window as we head down the golf course drive.

"No wonder he was comfortable hanging out at the counter all afternoon."

"Maybe it was the company," she suggests.

I give her an annoyed look as I hear James in my ear. "We have to talk."

CHAPTER 15

Upstairs, I wait impatiently for James. I haven't heard him since his last comment, and it has me on edge. I faked a headache after dinner, so I could come up to my room and pretend to lie down. I wanted to be alone in case he decided to come early.

I pace back and forth at the foot of my bed. Why is he acting so jealous? Is he angry with me? If he's been watching me like he says, he has to know I've done nothing to provoke today's interaction with Dane.

I sigh as I flop down on the bed. I peek at the clock. It's almost ten. Where is he?

My cell phone rings, and I get up to answer it. It's Bay Woods.

"Hello?"

"Hi, Emma. It's Kris. Sorry to call so late."

"That's okay. What's up?"

"I've just talked to Mr. Walker. You and Shel are not on for tomorrow, but you will be allowed to work what we had scheduled for the rest of the week. Sound okay?"

I sigh in relief. "Thank you. I really appreciate it. And I'm sorry."

"I'm sorry too, kid. Honestly, none of this would have happened if it wasn't for that uppity Jeff. I would have just told you to quit it and not do it again. Seriously, I think he's trying to prove something because he's new."

I laugh.

"Anyway, would you save me another call and let Shel know?"

"Yes. I'll go tell her right now."

"Okay. Thanks, Emma. See you Tuesday."

"Yep, see you then."

I hang up and leave to find Shel. Turns out she's in the shower, so I shout the information to her through the cracked bathroom door. When I return to my room, I close the door behind me and sigh.

"Hi."

I jump and turn around. James is sitting on my bed.

"Hi!" I'm so excited to see him, I forget my earlier brooding. I skip over to stand in front of him. "Where have you been?"

He smiles. "Sorry to keep you waiting." He reaches for me, and I place my hands in his gently. The cool feeling spreads through my hands and up my arms. I smile then sit down next to him, still holding his hands.

"How was your day?" I whisper to him. The last thing I need is for my parents or Shel to hear me. They'll think I'm talking to myself.

He frowns. "Disturbing."

"How so?"

He cocks an eyebrow at me. "Who's your new friend?"

My face twists. "Who? Dane? He's Matt's friend, not mine."

He looks at me skeptically.

"What? You're seriously not jealous, are you?"

No answer.

"Listen, if you've been watching me you know I did nothing–"

James cuts me off. "I know." He releases one of my hands and rubs his eyes. "I know."

"Then what's the problem?"

"I don't like him ... touching you. Or Matt. Either one of them touching you makes me crazy." He looks at me and sighs.

"Why? You know I don't like it."

"Because I can't," he says softly. "I don't like it because I can't touch you."

His admission breaks my heart. To make him feel better, I place both of my hands on either side of his face. He closes his eyes as a small smile appears on his lips. "You really are warm."

"See, we can touch each other," I say quietly.

As he opens his eyes, he reaches up and circles my wrists. "It's not the same."

"Given our situation, I'll take it," I reassure him. I move my hands through his and place them against his chest. "I'll take whatever you're able to give."

His eyes soften, and he leans forward to kiss me. I feel the cool concentration on my lips and I kiss him back, focusing on moving my mouth with the cold air. Chills course through my body.

When the feeling disappears, I open my eyes to see him smirking at me.

"What? You kissed me."

"I'm just imagining what that would look like if someone walked in on us." He grins.

I laugh quietly. "Yeah, explaining that would be … hard."

After a moment, his expression turns serious. "I love you."

"I love you, too. Don't be jealous."

"Easier said than done," he says.

"Well, try not to be. I don't plan on spending any alone time with anyone other than you."

He looks at me longingly and reaches up to try and push a stray piece of hair from my face. It doesn't move. He frowns in frustration.

"Can you do that?" I ask. "Move things?"

"Not yet, apparently," he says. "Physical manipulation takes the longest to learn."

"Haven't you been practicing?"

"Not so much. Speaking and manifestation come first."

"Oh. Well, you're doing a really good job. I heard every comment you made today."

"No, you didn't." His eyes harden. "If you did, I doubt you'd be speaking to me right now."

My mouth falls open. "What did you say?"

"I just called your friend some choice words is all."

"James!" I hiss. "Be careful. It's hard for me to control my reaction when I hear you as it is."

His eyes light up. "I know. It's fun."

I playfully smack his arm, and my hand passes right through.

"You'll get used to it," he reassures me. "So," he looks into my eyes, "what do you want to do tonight?"

I tilt my head in curiosity. "What are my options?"

"Well, I already planned on staying with you, if that's okay."

"And we could practice the kissing thing," I suggest enthusiastically.

James shakes his head and smiles.

"What?"

"I didn't think you would take this so well. Most people would be scared to death."

"I'm not most people." I pause as my throat thickens. "We're soul mates."

James nods, but his smile falls as his eyes cloud over.

"What is it?" I ask.

"There are some things you need to know about being a Guardian." His tone is somber.

A million possibilities start to bloom in my mind. "Like what?" I ask, worried.

James looks pensive, like he regrets what he said. He moves away from me and stands. "You should get ready for bed."

"What? You're not changing the subject," I object and stand to face him. "Tell me."

"Don't you have to work tomorrow?"

"No. I have the day off courtesy of Matt and Shel turning the pond into a water park."

He shakes his head. "Get in the bed."

"And then you'll tell me?" I'm not dropping this.

"Yes."

Within seconds, I've changed my clothes. I turn off the light, jump into bed, and just like last night, James assumes the same position behind me, pressing his chest against my back. I wrap my comforter around us.

"Wow. When I said 'jump' you never said 'how high' before."

"Start talking."

I feel him kiss my cheek. "Pushy much?" he asks quietly.

Turning my head, I look at the darkness over my shoulder, where I know his face is. I softly ask him "Please" and hear a resigned sigh.

"What did you mean? Are we not soul mates?" I whisper, my voice breaking.

"We are." He holds me tighter. "Don't worry; we are."

"So what's with all the drama?" I ask, quoting him from this morning.

James is silent for a moment. "Em, this is all I can give you."

My response is immediate. "Like I said, I'll take whatever you can offer."

"How can you be sure this is what you want?"

I shift my body to lie on my back. "I'll always want you."

He counters. "I can't touch you."

"Yes, you can."

"I can't marry you."

"I don't care."

"We can't have kids."

"I'll adopt."

He lets out a heavy sigh. "I can't give you things."

"I've never been materialistic."

"We can't grow old together."

"Who's getting old?" I scowl.

I feel James pull away, and I imagine him propped on his elbow, looking down at me skeptically. "So you're telling me, at the age of twenty-one, you know without a doubt that you want to spend the rest of your life unmarried, celibate, and without children of your own? You want to be the crazy old cat lady who sits on her front porch talking to herself until I can be with you again?"

"I wouldn't be talking to myself," I dispute him. "I'd be talking to you, and ..." Something he said stops me. "Wait. What do you mean 'until I can be with you again'"?

James says nothing.

"It's when I die, isn't it?" I whisper, the finality of the thought sinking in. "We can be together when I'm dead."

James inhales sharply. "It's not that easy."

"Tell me how it works then."

Silence. Not being able to see his face to read his reactions is frustrating. I can't take it anymore and I lean through him, a cold chill passing through to my bones. I shiver and turn on the bedside lamp.

"What are you ...?" he starts.

I pass back through him to lie down on my back. There he is, just like I thought, propped on his elbow, looking down at me.

"I need to see you," I say quietly.

James gives me a sad, broken look. "I don't ever want to think of you dead."

I mirror his sad expression. "It happens to everyone, eventually," I say gently. Propping myself up to look him in the eye, I ask, "How does it work?"

James looks at me intently, seriously, then reaches out and touches my cheek, running two fingers from my temple to my chin. "When the time comes for you to pass," he closes his eyes and blanches at the thought, "I will be allowed to give up my Guardianship to be with you, if you so choose."

My mouth falls open in surprise. "Really?"

He opens his eyes as he nods. "You are my true love. Only a true love can release a Guardian."

"So, it's all up to me?"

"Well, yes; I mean it's a mutual decision, but ..."

"But ...?"

"It rarely ever happens."

"I will choose to be with you," I say, determined.

James shakes his head. "Not so fast." He pauses and sighs. "How do I put this?"

Impatiently awaiting his answer, I sit up and face him.

"I left you unexpectedly." He frowns. "I will never love again the way I was able to love you; you will be it for me."

Tears prick my eyes. I reach for his hand, and he sits upright, facing me, our fingers intertwined.

"You have a lot of life left to live," he says softly, looking at our hands. "You will find love again, as do most people who lose someone. You will build a life with this person; a life you can never have with me." He looks into my eyes. "It's very rare for a person to pass then choose to spend eternity with their first love, Guardian or not. People usually choose to spend eternity with the one they are the most tied to, the one they have the most memories with."

"I have the most memories with you," I reassure him.

"For now. But that's what I meant with the questions before. Do you think you're going to be able to live a long, full life alone? Unable to tie yourself to anyone else? No partner, no kids – waiting for me? I don't think so."

The idea of falling in love with someone else is absurd. "I'm not going to find anyone else."

James shakes his head, frustrated. "Emma, you can't know that."

"I'm not going to have this fight with you," I say calmly. "There is a way for us to be together one day." I lean forward, so we're nearly nose to nose. "I will choose you."

James' face softens slightly as he gives me a sad smile.

"What?"

"I'm not going to lie. I love hearing you say that."

"Get used to it." I smile and lean in to him.

I feel the cold concentrate on my lips. It stays there and moves against me for a few moments, then travels to the corner of my mouth, along my jaw, then trails down my neck. When he reaches my collarbone, a shiver runs through my entire body, making me jump.

James laughs. "Chilly?"

"Just the opposite," I admit, blushing.

James wraps me in his arms, kissing the top of my head. "What am I going to do with you?" he laughs softly against my hair.

"Stop doubting my love," I say against his chest.

He pulls away to look at me. "I don't doubt that you love me," he says sincerely. "I'm just not sure I'll be able to keep up with the competition."

I grimace as I let out an exasperated sigh. "There is no competition."

He gives me a wary look.

"Let's not talk about that anymore," I say as I move back and rest against the pillows. "Come here." I reach for him.

James relaxes and shifts to lie down with me, folding himself into my arms. He lays his head against my chest and holds me as our legs intertwine. I reach down to pull up my comforter again. I lie there, mindlessly running my fingers through his hair, amazed that I'm able to do this. My hand feels no texture, only cool air, but I wouldn't trade it for anything in the world.

After a few moments, James sighs contentedly. "I've missed this."

"Me, too." We used to spend hours wrapped like this while we watched television or just talked. It's so comfortable, I yawn. "Will you be able to visit me tomorrow?" I ask.

"I think I can arrange that."

A grin spreads across my face, and I can't help but sound excited. "We have the whole day."

"Does that make you happy?" he teases.

"Very."

"Do you want to turn off the light?" he asks, shifting to look up at me.

I gaze at him. The fact that I am able to look at him, look into those blue eyes again, astounds me. Without the light, I won't be able to see him. "No," I whisper.

He smiles and kisses my nose. "Good night."

"Good night."

James lays his head back down.

"I love you," I say.

"Until the end of forever," he murmurs against my chest.

CHAPTER 16

"I'm here."

I hear James' voice as soon as my eyes open. I look around the room, and it appears I'm alone.

"I didn't want you to freak out like yesterday morning," he teases.

"When can I see you?"

"Soon."

"Soon? Don't they tell time where you are?" I ask, annoyed.

James laughs. "Wake up on the wrong side of the bed?"

"No." I pout. "I woke up alone."

"I'll work on that," he promises. "I love you."

"I love you, too."

"Watch out for …"

Silence. "What?" No response. "James? Watch out for what?"

No answer. He must be gone for now. I sigh and roll out of bed.

AFTER BREAKFAST, I was recruited by my parents to help in the yard, which I didn't mind because it passed the time. Shel decided to spend our unpaid vacation day with her mother and attend a family Memorial Day get-together. By mid-afternoon, with the yard work done and Shel away, I was starting to get bored and impatient. Even with my brother and Kate stopping by for our small barbeque, I was still distracted, waiting for James.

I stare out over the backyard, thinking. Would we do more of the same today? What excuse could I use to abandon my family, so I could spend time with him? What if he doesn't show up until tonight? My heart sinks at the thought. I want to spend as much time with him as possible. This waiting is killing me. I need to know more about him, like what his limitations are, when he can come and go, things like that. I start to compile a mental list of questions.

"Hello? Earth to Emma."

I blink and refocus to see Kate waving her hand in front of my face. The movement makes her mousy brown ponytail bob.

"Are you finished?" she asks, reaching for my plate.

I look at the half-eaten hamburger. "Yeah, sure, thanks."

"Everything okay?" she asks as she stands.

Little does she know things are so much better than the last time I saw her. I smile. "Yes, things are great. Just a little bored, I guess."

Kate looks surprised by my response but smiles at me anyway. "If you want something to do, why don't you take Jake for a walk?" she suggests. "I think he's tired of being tied up."

I look over at Jake, Mike and Kate's yellow lab puppy, lying under the shade of our big maple tree. He's about three months old and so darn cute. "Yeah, I think I'll do that. Thanks," I say and head over to untie Jake. "I'll take him over to the park."

"'Kay. Make sure you take a poop bag," she says over her shoulder as she heads into the house with our plates.

"C'mon Jake." I bend down to meet him as he jumps up. I scratch behind his ears and ask him in a silly baby voice, "Who wants to go for a walk?" He licks my hand. I untie the leash, grab a plastic bag from Kate's purse, and head to the park.

Following Jake's wagging tail, we head up the road and across the street. When we get to the park, the main beach is crowded for the holiday. Every picnic table near a grill is occupied, the small play area is teeming with kids, and a line has formed outside the concession stand.

"Let's go this way, Jake." I steer him to the left. "You'll like the trail."

Jake and I start our walk on the main nature trail that circles the park. I laugh to myself as he investigates – and pees on – just about everything. He's excited and yanks my arm forward several times. There is no leisurely pace with him. "You're going to wear me out," I lightheartedly scold him. "But I forgive you because you're cute."

"You're pretty cute yourself."

I turn around to see James standing a few feet away, smiling at me. A huge grin breaks across my face.

"You're here," I say, my voice filled with relief, as he walks toward me. When he gets within reach, he wraps his cool arms around my waist and kisses my forehead.

"Hello."

"Hi," I breathe.

He smiles down at me. "Babysitting?"

"Just taking Jake for a walk to pass the time."

James takes a step back in order to kneel down. He reaches toward Jake. "Hey there, buddy," he says playfully.

Jake turns his head to look at James, and then trots over to where he's kneeling. To my amazement, he licks James' outstretched hand and jumps up slightly, begging to be scratched. James obliges, but it doesn't appear Jake feels it.

"He–you–he–" I stutter.

James grins up at me. "Yep," he answers my unasked question.

"How?"

James finishes petting Jake and stands. "Haven't you ever heard animals have a sixth sense?"

I give him a confused look.

"Let's walk," he suggests.

As Jake leads us down the trail, two older women pass us in the opposite direction. They smile at Jake and then at me, oblivious to James. Once the ladies are out of ear shot, I whisper, "Why can't they see you?"

His hand slides into mine, and the cool feeling radiates up my arm. "Because I only have permission to reveal myself to you."

I smile; his reason makes me feel special. "What have you been doing?" I ask.

"A little of this, a little of that."

"Can't you tell me?"

"What do you want to know?"

I give him an annoyed look. "Like only a million things."

"Just a million?" he teases.

We come up on a bench set to the side of the nature trail next to a sign about indigenous plants. I head to it and take a seat, then look at James expectantly. "If I ask you some questions, will you give me answers?"

"I've been waiting for an inquisition." He sits next to me and places his hand on my knee. "Fire away."

I watch Jake wind his leash around the bench leg as I retrieve my mental list of queries. "How did you become a Guardian?"

James' expression turns distant. "Garrett. Garrett gave me the choice."

"Garrett, your Guardian?" I ask.

He nods.

"What were your choices?" I ask softly.

"To become a Guardian or continue on to Heaven."

My eyes light up at the thought. "Heaven exists?"

James nods.

"Why didn't you choose Heaven? Why get a choice at all?"

James pauses, thinking, as his thumb traces a cold circle on my knee. "I was given a choice because I was a Ward with a life well-lived ... a Ward who died before he was supposed to. Garrett told me I could choose to become a Guardian, live in the Intermediate, and watch over my loved ones ... watch over you. So, I bound myself to the choice, despite the consequences."

I blink. "What consequences? What's a Ward?"

He smiles. "All humans are Wards. You are a Ward."

"Are you my Guardian?"

"No, but you have one."

"Does everyone have one?"

"Yes."

"Have you met mine?"

James looks amused. "Yes."

This is intriguing. "Who is it? Is it someone I know?"

"I'm not allowed to share that information. But it's someone you've never met."

He removes his hand from my knee and drapes his arm around my shoulders. The chill that glides down my spine feels like an icy stream of water, and it distracts me. I pause to think. James waits patiently, brushing his fingers back and forth over my skin.

"Can you tell me who your Ward is?" I finally ask.

He shakes his head. "I don't have one."

"Why not?"

"I haven't completed my training."

Jake bumps my foot, and I bend over to unwind his leash. "So, what is it that you do for us Wards?" I ask as I work at unwinding Jake.

"We guide and protect you."

"Like Guardian Angels?"

"Similar. Minus the wings."

When Jake is successfully unwound, I sit back up. "Do other people see and hear Guardians?"

"It's up to a Guardian how they want to reveal themselves, if at all," he explains. "I reveal myself only to you, but once I'm trained I can appear to others if necessary. You've heard of people called mediums, right? People who interact with the dead?"

I nod.

James smiles. "They're interacting with Guardians."

My mouth falls open. "Really?"

He nods. "Most Guardians work invisibly, though. You know the feeling you sometimes get when you know something is wrong or off? Like your conscience tells you 'this might be dangerous?'"

"Guardian?" I guess.

"Right," James says.

"Your intuition is really your Guardian?"

"Yes."

I think I'm catching on to this and start guessing. "Déjà vu?"

"Guardian."

"Pre-cognition?"

"Guardian."

"Creepy feeling that you saw something move out of the corner of your eye and nothing's there?"

"Guardian." James grins. "Pretty cool, huh?"

I nod, and Jake bumps my foot again. "Geez, Jake, could you stay in one spot?" I start to unwind him.

"He needs to walk. Let's keep going," James says and stands.

With Jake freed, we continue around the nature trail, following the freshly mowed curve. James walks by my side with his arm around my waist. I know it's not the most ideal situation, but I could really get used to this. We walk in silence, enjoying each other's company, until another question pops into my mind.

"What determines how long you can visit me?"

"Not what, who. Garrett calls me back when I have to go."

"What do you have to leave me for?"

"I'm in training, remember?"

"Oh yeah, the consequences."

James stops walking. I take a few steps and turn around. "What is it?"

His expression turns serious, and his blue eyes darken. He takes two strides toward me, so we're standing nearly nose to nose. He gazes at me intently. "I chose to be a Guardian, so I could stay near you," he says quietly.

"Thank you," I whisper.

"When I'm assigned a Ward, I won't be able to spend as much time with you," he admits.

"When will that be?"

"I don't know."

"Well, we'll make the most of our time while we have it." I reach up to place my hand against the side of his face. "It's too bad you can't be my Guardian. We could spend every day together."

James shakes his head no. "There are rules."

"Rules?"

His hand slides under my chin, and instinctively, I lean forward. He places a gentle kiss on my lips. "Guardians cannot be romantically involved with their Wards. If I were your Guardian, I could no longer love you, and you could not release me from my Guardianship when you die. Do you know how excruciating it would be for me to guide and protect you without being allowed to love you?"

Tears unexpectedly spring to my eyes. "Why is it so bad to love your Ward?"

"Guardians care for their Wards like a brother loves a sister. Anything stronger would cloud a Guardians judgment. A Ward must lead a life well-lived by making decisions on their own; I would be too tempted to intervene. Wards require guidance, not intervention."

I search his face. "Are there any other rules I should know about?"

"I'm bound to be a Guardian for eternity. There will be no Heaven for me."

"Until I release you," I remind him. "I'm your true love, remember?"

"*If* you release me," he says softly, his eyes giving away his worry.

"Hey, I thought we already discussed this," I gently chastise him. "I will choose you."

James gives me a sad smile. "We'll see."

A young couple rounds the corner of the trail walking hand in hand. I turn abruptly to adjust my stance and pull Jake's leash to get his attention. I steal a glance at James, and we start to walk up the trail again.

"Have you gone to see your parents?" I whisper once the people have passed us.

He wraps his cool arm around my waist. "I've checked in on them."

"How are they?"

James doesn't immediately respond. I look up to find his face impassive, his jaw tense. "They are in denial," he says flatly.

"Denial?"

His eyes lock on mine. "There is no excuse for what they said to your parents," he says sharply. "No excuse for their insensitive comments or their assumptions."

My chest constricts with sadness and guilt. Of course he would know about their visit. He shouldn't be angry with them. I did freak out at his funeral; I do blame myself for his accident. I look down and concentrate on Jake. "They are right, you know."

"Right about what?"

I glance up at him, afraid to admit what I know is true. My chest tightens further, and my lungs feel like they might burst. "I think they blame me for your accident just like I blame myself," I whisper. The tears I was able to hold back earlier start to roll down my face.

"What? Emma that's insane!" James sputters.

I close my eyes to avoid his twisted expression. I hastily wipe away the tears in case someone else passes us on the trail. "Well, it's true."

"It is not! How could you even think that?" His voice sounds panicked, and I feel him grab my arms. "Emma. Look at me."

I make myself look up. Pain is written across his face, and he tries to wipe away my tears but can't. He groans in frustration. "The accident was my fault and my fault alone."

"You wouldn't have fallen asleep if I'd gone with you." My voice breaks. "You asked me to go with you."

He wraps his arms around me. "You can't think that. I won't let you."

I don't know how long we stand together, his arms wrapped around me while tears pour down my face. Jake wraps his leash around my feet while I imitate stone. Everything I've felt over the last month overwhelms me. The sadness of losing James, the immense blame I've placed on myself, dealing with Shel and work, and the joy of his return. Figuring out where we go from here. It's a long list of conflicting emotions. "I'm sorry," I apologize through my tears.

"Do not be sorry," James says. "I won't allow it. If anyone is sorry, it's me." He releases my body to look into my eyes. "It's me."

I wipe my face and try to compose myself. I take a shaky breath and untangle my feet from Jake's leash. "We should keep going. Mike and Kate are going to think I abducted Jake."

James gives me a heartbreaking look. "Please don't blame yourself anymore," he pleads.

I inhale another shaky breath and nod. I'm not making any promises.

James grasps my hand as we walk along the trail in silence. We circle the park and finish the trail, ending where I began. I feel the coolness around my hand intensify; he's squeezing my fingers. I look up at him, and he gives me a small smile. "Do you want me to stay?"

I try to squeeze his hand back and end up digging my nails into my palm. "Without question."

Jake trots happily ahead of us as we cross the street and head up my driveway. I catch a glimpse of Shel's car and see her talking with my family. As we get closer, I notice she has something in her hands and the trunk is open. I catch their attention and Shel turns toward me. She's holding her suitcase, and she looks upset.

She's leaving.

CHAPTER 17

I pick up the pace. "What's going on?" I call out to her.

Shel sets her suitcase down and bends over to pet Jake, who makes it to her before I do. "Hi, Jakey," she says as she gives him a good scratch behind his ears. She looks up at me and sighs. "It's my uncle."

"Your uncle?"

"My mom's oldest brother," she says as she stands up. "He lives in Arizona; we got the call at the picnic. He's sick and not doing well at all."

"Oh no."

"Yeah, like they are calling in Hospice not-doing-well," she says with a frown. "My mom needs to head to Scottsdale to take care of some things, and she doesn't want to go alone. Guess who was nominated to go with her?"

"Shel to the rescue again, huh?"

"Bingo."

"Aw, I'm so sorry," I tell her.

"I'm sorry I have to leave. Trust me, I'd much rather stay here."

"Your mom needs you," my mother says, concerned. She takes Jake's leash from me and then turns to give Shel a hug. "Thank you for staying with us," she says sincerely. "You let your mother know if she needs anything to give us a call."

"I will." Shel smiles at my mom.

"Take care Shel," my dad says warmly and pats her shoulder. "Safe travels." He walks with my mom over to Mike and Kate with Jake. Jake's excited to see his parents.

I steal a glance at James, who is still standing by my side. He gives me a small encouraging smile as Shel picks up her suitcase and tosses it in the trunk.

"When are you leaving?" I ask her.

"Tomorrow. My mom is looking at flights now," she sighs. "I mean it, Em, I hate leaving you like this. I've only been here two weeks."

"It's okay," I reassure her. "I'll be fine." *Because James is here,* my mind says. "You worked your 'whip-Em-back-into-shape' magic pretty quickly," I tease. "How long do you think you'll be gone?"

"Hard to say." She shrugs and closes the trunk. "I guess you never know with these things. I'll keep in touch though, keep you updated."

"Sounds good. Are you sure you got everything?"

"Pretty sure." She gives me a weak smile. "I left a message for Kris at the course. When you see her will you tell her I'm sorry for quitting?"

"No problem. It's not going to be the same without you." I give her a hug, and she hugs me back tightly.

When we part, she holds me at arm's length and looks me in the eye. "Are you sure you're going to be okay?"

"I'm positive. You can call me every day if you want to."

"Don't put it past me," she threatens.

I follow her as she walks to the car door and opens it. "Have a safe trip. Call me when you get there."

Shel climbs into the car. "Will do." She smiles up at me.

As I close her door, she waves. I take a step back as she starts the engine and wave slowly in return as I watch her head down the driveway, turn left, and then disappear.

~

Shel arrived safely in Arizona the following evening. She immediately called to let me know how hot it was, how awkward it was, and how bored she would be. I reassured her she could call me at any time to relieve her boredom or to vent her frustration. Shel and her mother have never been what you would call close, and she was never particularly close to her ailing uncle, either. That she was put in this situation at all was odd at best.

"Hang in there. This is your go-to-Heaven deed," I encouraged her, smiling as James ran his cool fingers up and down my arm as I spoke into the phone. I wish I could tell her Heaven was indeed real – and my piece of it was sitting right here next to me.

I filled my days with work and James. Kris wasn't too impressed about Shel's abrupt departure from Bay Woods, especially since business was picking up with the string of nice weather we were having. Katie and I started to pick up some additional hours, which meant overtime for me, until Kris could hire someone new. I didn't mind; the time passed quickly and busy days meant I would see James that much sooner each night.

It was easier for James to visit me at night, easier for me to be able to talk with him without my parents hearing and becoming suspicious. We developed a routine. I'd race home from work, James would appear in my room, and I'd instantly fold myself into him. We'd spend the night talking for hours. Before I knew it, a week had passed since Shel left. I'd only spoken to her once, apart from the short text here and there; I was so wrapped up in James and in work.

Shel's irritation with me was apparent when I checked my voice mail this afternoon.

"Hey Emma, it's me. I'm at the hospital waiting for mom to finish up with Uncle Tom's appointment. Call me."

"Me again. I'm still waiting; it's been a half hour. Call me; I'm bored."

"Ooookay, we're back at the house now. Call me. Bye."

"Emma? Where are you? You could have at least texted me by now. Is something wrong? Call me as soon as you get this. I mean it!"

"Seriously?!"

"EMMA LYNN DONOHUE. Don't make me call your mother!"

That last message was left around 3:30. It's after five. I quickly dial Shel. *Pick up, pick up, pick up,* I silently chant. Unfortunately, I get her voice mail.

"Hi Shel, it's me! I'm sorry; I didn't hear my phone. I've been at work, really busy. Call me when you can. I'll have my phone glued to my hip, I promise. Hope the hospital wasn't too bad. How's your uncle doing? Call me soon. 'Kay, 'Bye."

My message comes out in a rush, and I hang up. I pray she didn't call my house, although I know my mother should have nothing negative to say. My parents appear happy that I'm happy. They haven't questioned my erratic schedule or evenings in seclusion ... yet.

I sigh and switch my phone to vibrate, shoving it into my pants pocket. There's no way I'm missing her return call.

I look up to see Kris and, to my surprise, Dane standing in front of me at the concession counter. I haven't run into him in over a week, since the pond incident. I smile at them. "Hey, guys."

"We have a temporary solution to our staffing problem," Kris says, obviously relieved. She places her hand on Dane's shoulder. "Dane here has agreed to fill in until I can find a suitable applicant."

Dane grins at me as he leans casually against the counter. I force my smile to remain in place. Dane working here? James is going to freak.

"That's great," I say slowly through my forced expression. I glance at Dane, and he looks amused by my hesitation.

"Good. I'm going to have you start training him tomorrow morning," Kris says, producing a clipboard and jotting some notes.

Me? "Oh, ah, he needs training?"

Kris nods. "I figure you two already know each other, and you've been here the longest of my new hires," she explains. She finishes writing, looks up, and smiles. "See you two tomorrow morning around nine," she says and walks away.

I stare after her stupidly. How can I get out of this? Excuse me, Kris? This isn't going to work. Not that I have a problem with Dane per se, but, um, my dead boyfriend does.

"So," Dane smiles from across the counter, "tomorrow at nine then?"

I rearrange my face to look less apprehensive. "I guess so. If you don't mind my asking, why would you need training? Your dad owns the course, right?"

He shrugs. "I've never worked here, though."

"Why not?"

"It never interested me before."

Dane flashes his cocky grin, and I try to keep the shocked expression off my face. There's no doubt in my mind he uses that perfect smile as a weapon, and I refuse to be flustered. "Oh, well, that explains it." I start to busy myself by needlessly checking the condiments. I know they're full; I just filled them less than ten minutes ago.

Dane glances at the time. "Gotta go," he says, backing away. "See you in the morning." He waves good-naturedly as he leaves.

I give him a small nod. When he's gone I let out a sigh of defeat. "I'm sorry," I whisper to the air, to James, in case he's listening.

"It's not your fault," I hear him in my ear.

I smile in relief.

"But that doesn't mean I'm happy about it."

I shoot an irritated look to no one.

At the end of my shift, I make quick work of my close-out, happy to be on my way home to James. When I get to my car, I notice something is off but can't place it right away. Confused, I walk around the vehicle. My mood instantly bottoms out when I realize I have a flat tire.

"That's just great," I exclaim and kick the rubber. I reach into my pocket to call home to ask if my dad can come help me. I have no idea how to change a tire.

"Something the matter?"

I look up to see Matt walking from the direction of the club house. What is this? Reunion day?

"My tire is flat," I complain. "I'm calling home to see if my dad can come help."

"No worries," Matt says, approaching me. "I can change it for you."

"Really?"

Matt nods and smiles. "Really. It's one of those things they teach you in Man School."

I laugh and raise my eyebrows. "Man School?"

"Open the trunk," he instructs me.

Matt makes quick work of finding and releasing my spare. He locates the lug wrench and jack and goes to work on removing my flat.

"Wow," I watch him, impressed. "Even if I did know how to do this, I don't think I could. I don't have the strength."

He remains fixated on his task. "Oh, I don't know." He places the spare tire on the car and starts to tighten the first lug nut. "You seem pretty strong to me."

Huh?

He tightens up the three remaining nuts and wipes his forehead with his arm. "That should hold you until you get home," he says as he turns to stand. "You should probably take it slow, though. Nothing over thirty," he advises.

"Got it."

Matt bends down, grabs my flat tire, and steps around the bumper to lift it into the trunk. "Oh, here's your problem," he says.

I peer around him. "What?"

"Your tire is split here." He points to a horizontal slice in the wall of the tire about an inch and a half long. "That's weird. I wonder how that happened. Brush up against any curbs or anything?"

"No, not that I'm aware of. Why?"

Matt shrugs. "It's just an odd place for a leak. Usually it's a leaky valve or a nail in the tread."

I can't help but tease him. "Listen to you, Mechanic Matt. And I thought you just filled in at the veterinary clinic."

He gives me a sarcastic look. "You know, I can put the flat tire back on the car, too."

"No, no," I protest. "I like the spare."

"That's what I thought." He smirks and places the tire in my trunk. "At the risk of sounding too mechanic-y," he turns to me, "your leak can't be patched. You'll have to buy a new tire." He slams the trunk closed.

"Figures." I frown. "Oh well, I'm working for a reason, right?"

"Guess so." He smiles as he wipes his hands on his khakis. His hand leaves a big grease smear by the pocket.

"Awww, crap."

"What?"

"Now you've ruined your pants because of me." I step forward to point out the stain.

Matt looks down at the grease, then back at me. "That does it. Now you owe me pants," he says with mock disdain.

"I'm really sorry."

"Here." He undoes the button on his shorts and then goes for the zipper. "The least you can do is wash them for me."

"Oh good God, what are you doing?" I blurt out and cover my face, dropping my car keys in the process.

Matt bursts out laughing. After a moment I hear the clink of metal as he picks up my keys. "You can uncover your face now," he chuckles.

I peer between my fingers. He's standing in front of me, holding out my keys. I drop my hands and grab them quickly. "That wasn't funny," I tell him. I try not to smile, but I fail. It was funny. It reminds me of something James would do.

"Well, now that I've thoroughly embarrassed you," Matt smiles, "I guess I'll see you around."

"'Bye," I say and head to my car door. I stop, realizing something, and turn back around. "Matt?"

"Yeah?" He's about ten steps away from me.

"Seriously, thank you. This is the second time you've saved me."

He looks down for a moment and puts his hands on his hips, then raises his head. "Anything for James' girl."

My heart melts at his response. He gives me a small smile before turning to head back to where he came from.

CHAPTER 18

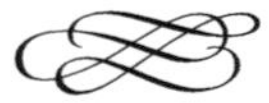

"I had to take crap from Shel, and now you're on my case too?"

James is lying on my bed following my every move as I walk around my room collecting my dirty clothes into a pile.

"I'm just saying. Listen, why do you think Matt magically showed up in the parking lot at work tonight? Did you even think to ask him what he was doing there?"

I roll my eyes. "No. I didn't subject him to Twenty Questions. He volunteered to help me and I accepted." I pause. *"I'm sorry,"* I say dramatically.

"Well," James flops on to his back, "I would bet money he was looking for you."

"Why would he be looking for me?" I throw my clothes into the basket by the door. "That makes no sense. He was probably there with Dane and stumbled upon me."

"Oh yeah, your other boyfriend," he grumbles.

"All right! That's enough." I walk over to stand in front of him and throw my hands up in the air. "What do you want me to do? Quit?"

James looks at me. "Would you?"

I sigh loudly and flop down on the bed beside him. "Yeah, that would be perfect. What would my parents think? Without Shel here they would think I'm falling back into a depression." I turn my head to look at him. "Out of the question."

He props himself up on his elbow, so he's looking down at me. "I thought you'd say something like that."

"Why can't you see they're not interested in me?" I ask, frustrated. James frowns and leans over so his face hovers above mine. I lift my head to kiss him softly. "Why can't you trust me?"

"I do trust you," he says.

"Well then, why don't you spy on Matt and Dane to see what's up? Put your mind at ease."

James smirks. "I wish I could; however, I do have other things to do with my time."

"You know," I say gently, "I am going to have people who come in and out of my life, people who are friends. When did you get so hot headed? I don't remember you ever being so jealous."

James' face twists in pain, and I immediately regret what I've said. "I have no control now," he says quietly. "Before I could just step in, like I did with Patrick."

I shudder at the memory of my psycho lab partner.

"It's like I'm out of the picture and all these men descend."

I snort. "'All these men descend?'" I quote him. "Please!" I take his face in my hands and stare into his eyes. "I love only you. For now, for forever."

He leans in to kiss me, but I stop him by pointing a finger. "Promise me we won't have this conversation again."

He shakes his head. "I can't."

"Why?" I roll my eyes.

"Because I'll never get enough of hearing you say how much you love me."

"Is that what this is about?" I make a face. "Since when did you become so greedy?"

He abruptly moves forward, passing through my pointing finger, through my hand, and kisses me. This kiss feels different, stronger. His lips feel degrees colder, and the cool air moves faster. When he stops I feel breathless.

"You don't know how badly I wish I could touch you right now," he says roughly.

His eyes follow his fingers as he traces my face from my temple to my cheek to my chin. His touch continues down my neck, brushes across my collarbone, glides to my shoulder, and then travels along my side to my waist to rest at my hip. When he looks back at me, his eyes burn.

I wish for that too, just as much. But I hold my tongue; I don't want to make him feel any worse. Instead, I reach for his hand at my hip and wrap my fingers around his. "I love you," I reassure him. I don't want to discuss jealousy or limitations anymore. James watches me as I sit up and slide to the head of my bed. I reach for him and he folds himself around me. I drift off into a fitful sleep as my mind decides to make up for one thing we can no longer have. It plays another memory.

"Hold on a sec," James whispers into my ear before he pushes himself off me. He quickly springs to the door and locks it.

"What?" I laugh. "You don't want Chad to walk in on us?" Chad is James' roommate.

"Hell no." He grins, returning to me. He puts his hands on either side of my shoulders and leans in close. "I don't get enough time alone with you," he says before kissing me deeply.

"He has a key," I remind him as his mouth leaves mine. I prop myself up so he has an easier time removing my shirt.

He pulls it off over my head. "No, he doesn't." His eyes light up, and he glances at the desk that separates their beds.

Turning my head, I see Chad's student ID connected to a Ferris lanyard along with a few keys. I turn back to James. "Well, then." I smile as I wrap my arms around his neck to pull him closer. He kisses me again, pressing me against the bed, as I run my hands along his sides and then reach around to trail them down his bare back. His lips leave mine only to reappear at the base of my throat, heading south. I close my eyes and my pulse races as he leaves a trail of kisses down the center of my body, traveling to my waist, and then burning a path to my hip. They leave my skin for mere seconds before they are on my mouth again. I grab his shoulders as he lowers his body to mine and wraps his arms beneath me. Shifting his weight, he falls to the side, pulling me with him. His back hits the wall beside the bed.

"Ow," he says against my lips.

I giggle. "Are you all right?"

He pauses to smile and then buries his mouth under my ear. He moves and traps it with his teeth sending a chill down to my toes.

"I take it that's a yes," I whisper.

He shifts forward so we're not propped against the wall anymore, and I drape my leg over his hip. As I pull myself closer his free hand roams over my naked back and then trails along my side. My mouth is on his again. I feel his hand hesitate at my hip and then reach around my waist. He grabs my side, tickling me.

"Ahhh!" I jump and push against his chest. "Stop! No tickling!"

James laughs as I try to wiggle out of his hold. He grabs my wrist with his free hand, and pins it against the bed. My leg is still looped around his. "I like to hear you laugh." He grins.

With a smirk, I wrench my hand out of his and go for his side. He rolls and I follow him, sprawling across his chest to get to my target. Laughing, he reaches up and grasps my chin, forcing me to look at him. I give up on the tickling as he takes my mouth so thoroughly my head spins. I feel his fingers leave my face and trace lightly down my back, reaching the waistline of my jeans. He works his way just inside, and the combination of his kiss and his touch winds me. I need to catch my breath. I smile and open my eyes to look into his – and see Dane's face staring back at me.

My body jolts and I snap awake, my heart pounding. I turn and reach for James, realizing the cool feeling of his body is no longer there. He has left me for the night. I roll over on my side, curl my knees to my chest, and wait for my heartbeat to slow. I try to erase the image of Dane mixed with James by clenching my eyes shut.

Holy hell. What was *that*?

~

I DUMP the unwanted milk from my cereal bowl into the sink and yawn as it flows down the drain. I'm exhausted. For the first time since James has come back to me, I did not sleep well. Our conversation and my insane dream kept resurfacing in my mind, making me feel more and more miserable. The jealousy James feels has obviously planted itself in my subconscious. I wish he didn't feel so limited. I wish he could read my mind and know, without a doubt, how much he means to me. How much he is and always will be enough for me. How can I make him see that? Will I ever be able to?

I think about James the entire drive to work. When I pull into the golf course, I have to force myself to think about maneuvering my dad's truck into a parking space. It's a Silverado, and the thing is huge. I don't like driving it, but it was my only option if I wanted a new tire put on my car today. I sigh as I turn off the engine. My training day with Dane will be sure to set James off again tonight. I shudder as the dream I had returns to me. Seeing Dane today is the last thing I want to do. I rest my chin on the steering wheel and stare out the window as I contemplate faking an illness.

As I enter the pro shop, Kris greets me cheerfully. "Good morning, Emma. Go ahead and punch in, then I'll get you two started." She nods to Dane, who is standing next to the counter wearing the requisite Bay Woods polo and khaki cargo shorts. He flashes me his all-too-familiar-grin. It irritates me, and I say nothing.

We're assigned to one of the beverage carts. Dane follows me as I head out of the pro shop to where the carts are parked. I open the coolers to make sure they were emptied from last night. "We'll need ice," I inform Dane. "This cart takes about four bags; the other about three, just so you know."

"Good morning to you, too," Dane says.

I sigh. "Good morning."

As we fill the cart with ice and bottles, I have to admit I need Dane's help. It seems like I'm getting more and more tired. His ability to do all the heavy lifting is appreciated. After we get the cart filled and the inventory list tallied, I slide behind the wheel to head out on to the course.

"Oh no," Dane objects and snatches the key from my hand. "I'll be driving."

"What? Why?"

"You're distracted and moody," he observes.

I give him a tired sigh. "I didn't sleep well."

He enters the cart, sliding behind the wheel and pushing me aside with his hip. "Obviously." He puts the key in the ignition. "Dreaming about me?" He raises an eyebrow.

What?! I try to keep a shocked expression off my face by looking away and muttering, "You wish."

"Oookay," he says as he puts the cart in reverse. "Humor is not acceptable on the beverage cart. Got it, boss."

We head out and I direct Dane around the entire course, pointing out the places I typically stop when it is crowded. There aren't many people golfing this early on a Wednesday morning, and we only manage to unload a bottle of water and a bottle of cranberry juice to some seniors. After our second tour around the course, I direct Dane to a shady spot where he parks the cart. Until the traffic picks up, we won't have much to do. I doodle on the inventory list as we sit in silence. Five minutes go by. Then ten.

"Okay," he says and turns to face me. "What's up?"

"What's up with what?"

"What's bothering you?"

I stare at him.

"It's me, isn't it?" he asks pointedly.

"Partly," slips out of my mouth before I can stop it. I wasn't expecting him to ask me that. I feel my face start to redden and quickly look away.

"At least you're honest," he says, somewhat surprised. "What exactly about me is bothering you?"

What can I say? It's not really you; it's my dead boyfriend's jealousy of you?

"Spit it out, Emma."

I really don't want to have this conversation. I look at him, frustrated. "What do you want me to say?"

"Tell me what's bothering you."

I shake my head no. "I barely know you," I snap.

He extends his hand to me, expecting a handshake. "I thought we did this already, but, hi, my name is Dane. Yours?"

I refuse to play along. I stare at his hand like it's infected.

He looks at me like I've hit him. His eyes harden. He drops his hand and turns away.

My chest starts to constrict. I know I'm acting rude as a defense. If James is watching, I don't want him to see me having a good time. The guilt of being here with Dane presses down on me because I know it hurts James, even though Dane has done nothing wrong. And now, on top of my miserable feelings about hurting James and dreaming about Dane, I can add my miserable feelings about being rude. How do I make things right?

Dane sits with his arms crossed, looking over the golf course. "Hey," I say quietly, embarrassed.

No response.

"Um, I'm trying to apologize."

Still nothing.

"Well, I'm sorry," I whisper.

Dane's mouth remains set, his face impassive, as if I'm not even there.

I don't know if it's the realization that I've truly pissed Dane off, my inability to assure James of my love for him, or my lack of sleep, but whatever the reason a sob rises in my chest and escapes me before I can do anything to catch it. I cover my face as tears pour down my cheeks and soak my hands.

"Emma!" Dane is immediately at my side. "Don't cry."

His plea makes me cry harder.

"I'm sorry. I'm not that mad, I promise."

It is as if a damn has broken. I can't speak; I can't open my eyes. I can't do anything but cry.

Dane grabs my wrists and gently tries to pull my hands from my face. "Emma, look at me."

My hands are frozen and locked into place. They won't budge with his gentle nudging. I am mortified by my behavior, and I have no energy to stop the tears.

"Please look at me?" he asks softly.

When I won't move, I feel his arms wrap around me. He pulls me against his chest and tucks my head under his chin. I feel him slide us back to lean against the seat of the cart. My entire body tenses, and he can feel it.

"Relax," he says against my hair. "Let it out."

I continue to cry as he holds me, but for entirely different reasons now. What if James is watching? This is not what I wanted to happen. Why is my body so frozen that I can't move to push him away? Why can't I speak?

Why do these arms feel warm and safe?

The shock of my last thought cuts my sobbing off with a choke. I sit back rigidly, the feeling returning to my fingers and hands. I quickly pull them from my face and try to turn away from him, pushing against his shoulder and chest as hard as I can. "Let me go." My voice sounds weak, garbled and stuck.

Dane's arms stay locked around me. "It's okay."

"No. No, it's not."

He releases me, and I shift as far away from him as possible. I wipe my eyes, silently praying for the tears to stop. When I think I have my emotions somewhat under control, I turn to face him. The look on his face is a mixture of concern and confusion.

"I'm … sorry," I apologize. "I don't know what happened." My voice is shaky.

"Don't worry about it. If you need a shoulder to cry on, I'm right here."

I smile feebly at him, thankful he is no longer upset with me. "Thanks, but I'll be all right."

"You're sure?"

I nod.

Minutes pass. Finally he asks me, "How long has it been?"

"Since what?"

"Since you lost him."

"Almost two months," I whisper.

"And he's all you think about?"

If he only knew. "Yes."

Dane studies me for a moment, which makes me uncomfortable. "Close your eyes."

"Why?"

"Just trust me."

I shake my head no.

"Are you scared?" he teases.

I roll my eyes. "No, of course not."

"Then do it."

"Fine," I huff and close my eyes. "Now what?"

Dane says nothing. After a moment, I feel his fingers wrap around my left hand. My eyes fly open, and I pull away.

Dane sighs heavily. "Close your eyes and give me your hand."

"What are you doing?"

"Just do it. You are beyond frustrating today," he complains. "I'm not going to touch anything but your hand. I promise."

I eye him warily. Should I do this? What if James is watching? He hasn't said anything so far. Maybe he wants to see what Dane is up to, so he can give me the 'I told you so' speech later. But what if he isn't up to anything? Then that speech could be coming from me. I close my eyes and comply with his request.

Dane grasps my hand and laces his fingers through mine. "Sit back and relax," he tells me. "Keep your eyes closed."

I slide back against the seat and try to relax, but this is kind of odd. I feel Dane lean against the seat next to me, but the only thing he touches is my hand, just like he said.

We sit in silence. As the minutes pass, he starts to absentmindedly rub his thumb across mine. As much as I don't want to admit it, it is comforting.

"Everything okay?" he asks.

I nod. "What are you doing?"

"Keep your eyes closed. Think of James. Use me."

CHAPTER 19

James is late. Very late. Anxiety starts to bubble in my chest. The confidence I was feeling in proving Dane is just a friend is beginning to wane; maybe James doesn't see it that way.

If he saw it at all.

I haven't heard from him once today, which is troubling. Usually, if he sees something he doesn't like, he lets me know. Not that I'm naïve to think holding Dane's hand wouldn't set him off, but the end result was positive. Dane's just trying to be a good friend to me.

It's after midnight, and I'm starting to get restless. What if James is truly angry? Anxiety scoots over and gives guilt a seat in my heart. When I curl up in bed, I lie in the darkness, my mind creating a web of unpleasant scenarios. The more I think about it, the harder it is for me to breathe. I drift unwillingly in and out of sleep. The scenario I fear the most keeps haunting me.

The one where James decides never to return.

~

My shivering body wakes me. I reach to pull my comforter higher around my shoulders when my hand passes through noticeably cooler air behind me. My eyes snap open.

"James?" I whisper.

"Sorry I'm late."

I quickly roll over and blindly throw my arms around his cool form.

"Um, you're hugging my throat."

"Sorry." I release him. "I was so worried you weren't coming. Hold on."

I lean over to turn on the light. I need to see him. When I lie down to look at him, my heart plummets. He looks tired, worn, and sad. He looks broken. Instantly, I curl myself against his stomach, and I feel his arms wrap around me. I'm scared to ask him what is wrong.

James' voice cracks. "I can't visit you for a while."

I close my eyes and take a deep breath. My gut tells me this is all my fault. I've brought this on myself. "What can I do to make it right?"

"Nothing," he responds flatly. "There's nothing you can do."

I stop breathing at the realization of his anger. My worst fear is coming true. My mind scrambles to find the right words to change his mind, to make him stay.

"Please let me explain …" I choke. "Today was … I shouldn't have …"

The chill intensifies under my chin, and I raise my head. I look James in the eye as he searches my face. "Go on."

I take a shaky breath. "I was trying to prove to you that Dane is only a friend, that he wants nothing more. He didn't try anything. I knew you'd be watching, so I agreed so you would see …"

James' face twists.

"He only held my hand, that was all. To be kind, to calm me after my crying fit, to let me pretend he was you … please … don't leave me over this."

His face falls. "He wants to pretend to be me?"

I realize how that must have sounded. "No, no, not like that. Just for that moment. Didn't you see? Weren't you watching?"

He closes his eyes as if he's trying to erase what I've said. "No. I wasn't watching."

"Then why are you leaving me?"

He opens his eyes and looks deeply into mine. "Garrett is angry. I've been spending too much time here with you. That's why I was late and that's why I have to stay away for a while." He pauses. "And now, after what you've told me, I need to be here," he mutters.

"No, no you don't. I mean, yes, you do. But you don't have anything to worry about," I say, trying to reassure him. "I don't want Garrett to get angrier with you; what if he decides you can't visit me ever again?"

James sighs in frustration. "I don't think he would do that."

"Can you be sure?"

He shakes his head no.

I lean forward to hold my forehead against his and whisper, "I don't want to take that risk."

After a moment, James asks me quietly, "What were you thinking today, with Dane?"

I lift my head, so I can see his face. "All I could think about was you," I tell him honestly. "I hate that you question yourself all the time. What can I do to make you realize you're enough for me? I analyzed every one of my actions today, everything I said, because I want to prove myself to you. Prove that you're wrong to feel threatened."

"Emma, you are blind. How can I not feel threatened? There is so much I can't do."

"There is so much you *can* do," I say. "More than I ever thought possible. What have I ever done to make you think I would bail on our relationship so easily?"

James sits and reaches for me. I rise up to face him, and he holds my hands in his. He stares at our laced fingers for a few moments, as if deciding something, and then looks at me intently. "I know with my entire being that, right now, you love me. I've never doubted it. What I doubt are the intentions of others and my ability to make you happy. Those are my issues to work through, not yours." He sighs. "I promise to be better. Please don't walk around on eggshells for me. The last thing I want to do is stress you out or push you away."

"You'll never be able to push me away," I say softly.

"I'm trying too hard to control things," he says. "That's why Guardians can't be in love with their Wards. Do you see how that would be a problem? This is one thing I have to work on. Guidance, not control."

"Is Garrett making you practice on me?"

"No, but he sees my behavior. Hence my, um, visit suspension."

I don't want to think about that. I frown. "How long will you be kept from me?"

"I don't know."

"Will you be able to speak to me? To watch me?"

"All my time with you is now limited. That's why I didn't see you today with ... him."

"Oh."

James moves to lie down, and I follow suit. He wraps himself around me, our arms and legs intertwined. "Don't forget about me while I'm away," he whispers in my ear.

"Never."

We lay in silence as the realization that we are going to be separated again sinks in. My heart feels like it's in a vise and starts to beat erratically. James raises his head to look at me, concerned. "Are you okay? I can hear your heart."

"No," I rasp. "I need you."

"And I you," he says sadly. "Just remember every second I'm allowed to be near you, I will be."

I nod because my voice is stuck in my throat.

"It won't be like before," James tries to comfort me. "I'm not gone for good."

I nod again, still trying not to hyperventilate. I don't know why this is hitting me so hard so suddenly. I try to concentrate on bringing my breathing under control.

James leans forward and kisses me. It distracts me from my sudden panic attack. His kiss is urgent. I know this because I can feel him move against me; his mouth is the coldest I've ever felt. I open my eyes to physically see him, and it's as if he's himself again, his whole self. My memory takes over as I remember what it was like to kiss him before his death. I hold on to that memory as I close my eyes again and it's as if nothing has changed from that time; he is whole.

My memory allows me to see him, through closed eyes, and I reach up and grab his shoulder to pull him closer to me. I feel his cold, freezing touch at my hip. It travels to my waist and around my lower back, as if he is trying to press me closer to him. I shift my body forward to comply, since he cannot physically move me. His chilled mouth leaves mine and finds my neck, spending time there. Eventually his mouth grazes my ear and then is back on mine, hungry.

Gradually I feel his touch begin to warm around me. As he grows warmer, it's almost like his body is transforming into his former self; I swear I can feel his weight on me. I gasp and open my eyes to see if what I'm feeling is real.

James stops kissing me and looks into my eyes. I'm shocked to see he is not becoming whole; he is becoming transparent and fading away.

"Don't," I beg and try to hold on to him.

James looks at me longingly as he becomes nearly invisible. "I love you," he tells me. "Don't forget."

"I won't. I can't."

He vanishes before my eyes.

I lie there for a moment, stunned at what I've just seen. I slowly wrap my arms around myself and then curl up on my side. My eyes and throat burn with trapped emotion, but no tears come. There is no release. My sorrow is trapped inside me.

INEVITABLY, morning comes. I have not changed position; I have not slept. My alarm goes off, making me aware of the time. I don't want to move; I don't want to leave my bed. Spending the day distracted and stumbling my way through work doesn't sound very enticing. I'm certain my irritability will carry over into my training with Dane again today. I don't feel up to making excuses as to why I'm being so difficult to work with. I just want to lie here and think about James.

My alarm continues to sound, irritating me further. My muscles protest as I try to sit up. I roll on to my back, stretching my arms above my head and my feet in the opposite direction. I feel a sharp pinch in the side of my neck that radiates down my shoulder and through my shoulder blade.

"Argh!" I wince and tense up, realizing I pinched a nerve. Damn it. I focus on relaxing so the pain will subside. After a few minutes the throbbing calms, but it still hurts. I manage to roll over slowly and shut off my annoying alarm. I stare at my bedroom ceiling, thinking about James in between the distracting throbs in my neck, until my bladder decides it's necessary that I get up.

In the bathroom, I run a hotter-than-normal shower in order to soothe my aching muscles and aching heart. The promise of seeing James is what has been carrying me through my days. It has put a smile back on my face. I know he is not gone forever, that this situation is beyond our control. It's the uncertainty of when he will be allowed to return that has made me so sad. I can't help shake the feeling I'm to blame for his restriction; if I didn't need him around so badly, he would have spent more time on his training than with me and be further along than he is. But that would only assign him a Ward sooner rather than later, which will restrict our time together indefinitely. I let out a heavy sigh. Around and around we go. This is what we're going to have to deal with for the rest of our lives ... er, my life. Reconciling our time together with the roles we've both chosen. He chose to be a Guardian. I choose to stand by him until I can release him. It sounds so simple except for my selfish need to have him all to myself all of the time. I'm going to have to get over that somehow.

I step into the steamy shower and stand motionless as the water beats down on my body. Thoughts of James roll around in my head. He doesn't blame me. I blame me. James loves me, and I love him. He will come back to me. I visualize my feelings of sadness and guilt being carried away by the water as it runs down the shower drain. Goodbye blame. Goodbye guilt. Goodbye sadness.

Goodbye hot water.

Yikes! The water has instantly turned freezing. I fumble to turn off the faucet. Shaking from the chill, I yank the curtain aside and reach for my towel. Could this day get any worse? I didn't even get a chance to wash my hair! I open the door and peek into the hall.

"Hello? Why is there no hot water?" I yell down the stairway.

"Let me check!" My father hollers up to me.

I wait impatiently as I hear him tromp down the basement stairs. Minutes pass and my hope of finishing my relaxing hot shower fades. Finally, I hear his heavy footsteps come back up the steps.

"Water heater pilot went out!" he yells up to me. "I re-lit it, but it's going to take about an hour to heat up the tank!"

My pinched nerve throbs and icy tendrils of water drip down my back from my wet yet unwashed hair. My body shakes convulsively.

That's it. I give up. I'm calling in sick today.

CHAPTER 20

BAM. BAM. BAM.

My reading is interrupted by loud thumps on the back door.

BAM. BAM. BAM.

I mark the spot in my book; I still haven't made it through *The Girl with the Dragon Tattoo.* I uncurl my legs and walk to the door, steadying the heat pack I have resting over my shoulder for my pinched nerve. It takes a minute for me to get out of the living room and into the kitchen.

BAM. BAM. BAM.

Holy impatient. "Just a minute!" I yell. Grasping the heat pack with one hand, I yank open the door with the other, simultaneously snapping, "Yes?" Blinking to clear my eyes, I see Matt standing on the step.

"Hey," he says slowly.

"What are you doing here?" falls out of my mouth.

"I came to make sure you were okay."

I stare at him confused. "How did you even know I was home?"

He shrugs. "Dane called me. Told me you're sick."

Is my life really that important to the two of them?

"So, what's wrong with you?" he asks.

"I pinched a nerve in my neck." I nod toward the heat pack. "It's no big deal."

"Hmm," he says.

Matt stands on the step as uncomfortable seconds pass. He looks at his feet as I wonder what his real motivation is for coming here. It's a sweet gesture to be concerned about me, but a phone call would have sufficed.

"Um, do you want to come in?" I ask, unsure of what more he could possibly want.

He perks up. "Can I?"

"Sure." I step back as I open the door wider. "Come on in."

He smiles and walks past me. Shutting the door, we head to the living room. I offer him a seat on the couch.

"Did I interrupt anything?" he asks as he sits.

I look at my book as I take a seat. "No, I was just reading."

"Ah, Stieg Larsson," he recognizes the author. "It's too bad he passed away; I really enjoyed that trilogy."

I look at him in surprise. Matt is such a big, athletic-looking guy, I never would have pegged him as a recreational reader.

"What?" he laughs. "I can read you know."

"I'm sorry." I shake my head. "Today has been a weird day."

He nods like he understands. The silence returns. We both look around the room in different directions. This is ridiculous. And strange.

"So," I pause. "You stopped by because ...?"

Matt gives me a small smile and looks embarrassed. He opens his mouth to speak, then closes it again, as if he is reconsidering his response. He looks down, and I notice his face start to flush.

Oh no. A ball of nerves starts to form and settle in my belly. What if James was right about him? I've always been a little slow when it comes to recognizing these things. *Please no. Please don't let this be what I think it is,* I silently pray.

Matt looks at me again. "This is really hard for me to say ..."

Aw, man.

"... but I need your advice. About Shel. I think I really like her."

I let out a heavy sigh and smile. I wish James were around to hear this. "Really?" I ask enthusiastically, relieved.

He slumps back on the couch and closes his eyes as if defeated. "I can't stop thinking about her."

"Really?" I ask him again.

He opens his eyes and smiles. "Is that the only thing you can say?"

I laugh. "No, I'm just surprised. I figured you two were into each other, but then Shel told me you weren't, so I didn't question it."

"What did she say?" he asks.

"She told me you two were okay with what happened at your house and chalked it up to being drunk. She said you talked about it and everything was sorted out."

Matt frowns.

"Except it's not?" I guess.

"I thought it was." He rubs his hand over his face. "I mean, we've always been friends; I didn't expect what happened at the barbeque to happen. But it did, and that was the first time I thought maybe we could have something more. But when she told me it was a mistake, I agreed because, well, I don't want to make things uncomfortable between us."

"I can understand that. But what about the second time you two talked? At the golf course?"

Matt chuckles. "I wanted to tell her I thought it was more, but she kept saying she was sorry and it was a mistake. I couldn't get a word in, really. She's pretty persistent."

"You think?" My eyes widen. "She's always had a way of getting what she wants."

Matt's smile fades a little. "Yeah, and I don't think she wants me."

I give him a sympathetic look. "I don't know. She was pretty upset by what happened and was adamant about making sure you weren't hurt. She seemed wrecked over the idea of ruining your friendship. Knowing Shel the way I do, I think she was trying to save herself the heartache of you possibly rejecting her."

"You think?"

"When's the last time you talked to her?"

"The day she left for Arizona. She called to ask me a favor."

"What favor?"

Matt looks at me uncomfortably. Whoops. Maybe that's too personal for me to know. "Sorry, you don't have to tell me."

"No, no. It's about you anyway."

My eyebrows shoot up. "What about me?"

He gives me a warning look. "Don't tell her I told you. She'll have my balls."

"And you want to date this girl why?" I ask him with a smile.

He laughs. "She called and asked me to keep an eye on you. To fill in for her, if you will."

Of course Shel didn't believe me when I told her I would be fine. "I take it you agreed?"

"Yes. Besides, my being around came in handy when you got that flat tire."

"Were you following me?" The thought kind of creeps me out.

Matt looks sheepish. "Kinda."

My voice raises a few octaves. "Have you *been* following me?"

Guilt is written all over his face.

"Don't you have anything better to do?"

"Shel was very specific in her request."

I shake my head in disbelief. "Lord, you have it bad for her. Listen, I'm fine. I hereby relieve you of your stalker duties."

He grimaces, unsure.

"Honestly, I'm good. Things are much better than they were. Plus, with Dane working at the golf course now, you can–wait." I stare at him accusingly. "Dane's working at the course because of me, isn't he?"

Matt holds his hands up in surrender. "Don't be mad. I can't follow you around 24/7, so I recruited a little help."

My mouth falls open in shock as I think about the breakdown I had in front of Dane a few days ago. I'm sure that was reported as *'Emma's not doing so well. Increasing mission priority to Defcon Five.'* "Are you freaking kidding me?"

"We just want to make sure you're all right. We care about you. I meant what I said the other day. Anything for James' girl."

I look down and close my eyes to process this information. I know they mean well; Shel's just being controlling like always, and Matt is doing her bidding because he likes her. Dane only agreed to work with me to help Matt out. But do they all see me as helpless? Lost without James by my side? Capable of nothing?

I open my eyes and look directly into Matt's. "How do you see me?"

I thought my question might throw him for a minute, but he responds immediately and just as pointed. "Strong."

I give him an exasperated look. "Then what's the point of all this? Do I miss James? Yes. Will I always miss him? Yes. Can I move on with my life? Yes!" Well, he doesn't need to know that moving on in life still involves James.

"The point," he sighs, "is that I miss James, too. Don't forget he was a friend to all of us. Well, not Dane. But you know what I mean." He pauses, looking at his hands to gather his thoughts. "I think ... I see you as strong because you were the closest to him. No one was closer or could have been closer. To see you survive his loss gives the rest of us the strength to do the same. This has been hard on us, but we realize it has been the hardest on you." He looks me in the eye. "Being around you is kinda like having a piece of James still here with us. We don't want to let that go. We know he would want you to be taken care of, so, here we are."

I don't know what to say. A realization hits me hard: I have amazing people in my life. And to know I can still interact with James and they can't makes me sad. I wish I could share some of him with them. I make up my mind immediately. If being around me makes Shel and Matt feel closer to James, if it makes them feel better, who am I to deny them that? We need each other.

Spontaneously, I wrap my arms around Matt and hug him tightly. The heat pack falls to the ground, my neck and shoulder throb as I irritate my nerve, but I don't care.

"Whoa," he responds as he hesitantly wraps his arms around me to pat my back.

"Thank you," I mumble into his shoulder. "I never thought of things that way."

"Well, it's true. At least for me it is, and I'm pretty sure Shel feels the same. You're her best friend. James took care of you which made her happy. Now, I think she feels a responsibility to fill some of that void. Don't be too hard on her. Or me."

I sit back, releasing him. "I won't," I promise. "But can I ask you one favor?"

"What's that?"

"Please stop following me around. It's creepy."

Matt laughs. "Well, now that you know what's up I won't have to be so covert."

I smile. "We should hang out more, now that I know what it means to you." And now that James will understand you're not a threat.

"Well ..." He looks down. "That was the other thing I wanted to talk to you about."

"Oh?"

"James' birthday is on Monday." He pauses to see my reaction.

Yes, I've realized this. "Go on," I encourage him.

"I was thinking I should have a small get-together at my place this weekend to honor the day. I was going to invite some buddies of ours, some of our friends from school. I would really like it if you could be there."

"That is really thoughtful of you." I had hoped to spend the night with James as usual but now that that can't happen, why not? "I'll be there."

He gives me a genuine smile. "Great."

"Now, back to you and Ms. Shel ..."

He looks embarrassed and rolls his eyes. "Yes?"

"You wanted advice," I remind him.

"Well, you are her best friend and the only person I know who's been in the same relationship for four years," he teases, but then catches himself. "Sorry."

"It's okay." *I'm still in that relationship,* my mind chimes. "I think you should call her. Sooner rather than later."

"And say what?"

"Let her know how you feel. Plant the seed. It's the only way to know if anything can happen. Shel is very direct. Give it to her straight; don't leave things open to interpretation."

"You think? What if I destroy our friendship?"

"If Shel lets this destroy your friendship, she's not worth having as a friend," I say with confidence. "Besides, she'll call me immediately after she talks with you, so I may be able to work a little magic."

Matt looks uncertain. "Okay, but this is really nerve-wracking."

I'm starting to think Shel may already have his balls. "It's better than sitting around and doing nothing, right?"

"Right," he concedes. Then, his face twists in thought. After a few moments, he turns to me. "Are you hungry?"

As a matter of fact I am. "Sure."

"Let's go get some lunch. My treat." He stands and holds out his hand to help me up. "Where to?"

We ended up at a small family-owned restaurant in town called Home Plate. We talked more about Shel and what he should say to her. Honestly, I started to feel like he should've been taking notes. I've never seen someone so nervous. But then again, what do I really know about dating? I've only dated one person in my entire life.

Speaking of which, I wish he were able to watch me today. My conversation with Matt has lifted a huge weight off of my shoulders. I can't wait to tell James that, for a fact, neither Matt nor Dane has any feelings for me. Knowing this makes me excited to go to work tomorrow, excited to interact with people without the fear of making James jealous. Hopefully, he will be able to look in on me and be able to remove some of the weight from his shoulders, too.

I crawl into bed, still with my trusty friend Heat Pack and a smile on my face.

Two minutes later, my cell rings. I pick the phone up off my nightstand. It's Shel.

"Hello?"

"You. Will. Never. Guess. Who. Just. Called. Me."

I smile brilliantly and ask innocently, "Who?"

CHAPTER 21

It's 8:00 p.m. and my nerves are shot. I know I promised Matt I would attend his party in honor of James' birthday, but walking up the sidewalk, I'm having second thoughts. There has to be at least fifteen to twenty cars lining the street outside his house. I can hear music and voices coming from the backyard; I can smell a fire burning. I detour toward Matt's front door and sit on the porch steps. What do I have to say to these people? Will they even want to talk to me? I wrap my arms around myself. It's been four days since I've seen or heard from James. I miss him beyond words. I'm hoping Garrett will allow him to visit me soon. So far, I've heard nothing. I pray I can keep my emotions in check tonight.

I close my eyes and imagine James is here. I imagine his voice. *"Suck it up, Em. Put your big girl panties on and do this for me."* I break out in a huge smile.

"Something funny?"

My eyes fly open. "Shel?"

"Surprise!" She grins and picks up the pace as she walks across the lawn from the street. "I heard there was a party."

I literally leap off the porch steps and run to meet her, throwing my arms around her shoulders. "What are you doing here?"

"I was invited," she responds and hugs me tight.

I let her go and step back. "When did you get in? How long are you staying?"

"Just now; I drove here from the airport." She loops her arm through mine and starts to walk me in the direction of the backyard. "I'm only able to stay until tomorrow night." She grimaces. "Uncle Tom literally has days left."

"Ugh. That's terrible. I'm so sorry."

She shakes her head. "We all know what's coming; it's just a matter of when."

We round the corner of the house, and I give her arm a squeeze. "I'm so glad you're here."

"I needed the break," she responds with a wary smile. "Trust me. I cannot wait to be back here for good."

I shoot her a knowing smirk and ask, "Any particular reason why?"

She actually blushes and looks away. I have *never* seen her do that.

"Hi," a shy male voice interrupts us. Matt is just steps away.

"Ah, the reason has found you," I say and give Matt a big smile. "Hey."

"Hey, Emma. Thanks for coming." He gives me half a hug since my other arm is looped through Shel's. He releases me and looks at my best friend. "You made it." He sounds relieved.

"Why wouldn't I?" Shel tries to sound sarcastic, but the effect is lost by the huge grin plastered on her face.

"I'll leave you two to get reacquainted," I laugh and step away from Shel. I look over toward the fire pit and see Dane waving from one of the benches.

"I'll come find you in a sec," Shel says to me.

I leave them and head over to the fire, glancing around as I walk. People are milling about, sitting in camping chairs, or standing by the pit with drinks in hand. I give small, vague smiles to the people who catch my eye. Internally, I frown as I realize I recognize none of them. I make it to Dane, who pats the empty spot on his bench.

"I saved you a seat." He smiles up at me.

"Thanks." I sit down and look around anxiously.

"Looking for someone?" he asks.

"No." I lean over and whisper, "I don't know anyone here."

He looks at me surprised.

"Where did Matt find these people?"

Dane shrugs. "I just showed up when he told me to be here."

"Why are you here?" I ask with curiosity, realizing he never even met James.

"Matt asked and I obliged," he responds. His face softens a little. "Besides I ..." he corrects himself, "*we* thought you might need an extra shoulder tonight. You know, just in case this was hard for you."

"Oh." I blink and then give him a tiny smile. "Thanks."

When I went back to work after my day off, I let Dane know I found out about Shel's request of Matt and Matt's request of him. I wanted him to know I understood his decision to work at Bay Woods and that he shouldn't feel obligated to continue; he barely knows me, after all. Dane insisted he wanted to keep working because he didn't want to disappoint Kris or his dad who, it turns out, was extremely thrilled his son was finally showing some interest in the family business. Things had been going really well between us now that I was able to relax around him, now that the true motivation for his working at the course had been revealed. Still, the thought of him and Matt talking about my well-being behind my back was a little unsettling. I'm an adult. I don't need handlers.

I catch Matt and Shel walking toward us hand in hand. As they approach, I stand and subtly wave them over to the side.

"Hey," I whisper to them. "How is it I don't recognize any of these people?"

Matt looks confused. "You should." He looks past me and nods to the left. "Most of that group over there is from the hockey team at Western, maybe a few from Ferris, I'm not sure." He points to the right. "Don't you remember Zach from high school? Brian? Kyle?"

I glance behind me. "Okay, yeah. I didn't see them before."

"Taylor's over there. Oh, and there's Olivia." He points again. Then he frowns. "There are a few people here I don't know, though. Maybe they came with the guys from the team?"

Shel gives Matt an elbow to the side. "This is what happens when you post a party invite on Facebook!"

Matt looks innocent. "Hey! I made it invite only."

Their bickering makes me smile. "I should have noticed the people from high school sooner," I tell him. "Thanks for pointing them out."

"Before I forget there's one thing I want to show you." He releases Shel's hand and turns me around by the shoulders to face the fire pit. "See that chair over there?"

I look across the flames and see an empty camping chair. People sit on either side of it, on the stone benches surrounding the pit. There appears to be a glass bottle of some sort in the cup holder, and a Western t-shirt is draped haphazardly across the back. "Yes, I see it."

"That chair is reserved for James," he says proudly. "Complete with an open bottle of …"

"... Oberon," I finish. Tears spring into my eyes. It's an obscure, micro-brewed beer made only in Michigan, but the only beer James would drink. I turn to face Matt and give him a warm smile despite my threatening tears. "I don't know what to say …" I blink rapidly as a drop escapes. "Thank you for remembering him."

"Don't cry." Matt looks a little scared. "This is supposed to be a birthday party."

Shel reaches out and rubs my arm as I brush the tear from my cheek. "I'll try, but I'm not making any promises."

"Well, so you know, I thought I would say a couple of words. I thought it would be an appropriate thing to do." He looks at me for reassurance. "Is that okay with you?"

"Of course. Stop worrying about me; this is your party."

"James' party," he corrects me.

"Hey, man!"

Someone gives Matt a hefty slap on the shoulder, and he turns to greet the newcomer. Shel apparently seems to know him as well, so I take this opportunity to return to the bench.

"Has your memory returned?" Dane asks, as he hands me a s'more sans chocolate.

"Some of it," I admit. "Thanks." I take the treat from his hand.

He gives me a square of chocolate. "Do you want something to drink?"

"Is there any …"

Dane produces a bottle of water. "Yep."

"How did you know I was going to say water?"

"I've only ever seen you drink water."

Huh. I guess that's true.

Someone appears in my periphery, and I turn my head to watch a girl take residence on the bench beside me. It doesn't surprise me that I don't recognize her. She's pretty and slender, with long, curly, dark brown hair that falls to her waist. Dressed in an oversized Western hoodie and shorts, she stares at the fire, holding her can of, well, I don't know, something.

Dane's cell rings, and he pulls it from his pocket. "I'll be right back," he says.

I nod and finish my s'more. With no one to talk to, I take a drink of water and stare at the fire with the girl next to me. She catches my eye.

"Hi."

I give her a small smile. "Hello."

She takes a drink and swallows. "This is a nice party."

"Yes," I agree.

"Did you know James for long?" she asks me.

Apparently she doesn't know who I am. Why would she? I have no idea who she is either. "Um, you could say that. Since elementary school."

"Wow." She looks impressed. "We had a couple of classes together at college, but we didn't really connect until …" she pauses, looking sadly at the fire, "until the night he died."

I think I stop breathing. "I'm sorry, what did you say?"

She looks at me. "Oh, we ran into each other that night at this bar by school. I was out with some friends, and he showed up with some friends who knew us. One thing led to another and before I knew it, we had spent most of the night together talking." She sighs, remembering. "I had no idea we would have so much in common."

Now I know I've stopped breathing. "I'm sorry, what did you say?"

Either she doesn't hear me or is too wrapped up in her memories of James to realize I can only utter that one sentence. She continues, "He was such a sweet guy. Cute, too." She smiles like I know what she's talking about. "I guess he'd had a fight with his girlfriend or something." She shrugs. "But he was the one giving out advice that night."

I manage a new sentence. "About what?"

She stares at her can. "You know, school stuff, classes. I was so comfortable with him that one topic led to another and I started spilling my guts about some personal stuff." She looks embarrassed. "But he didn't seem to care."

My mind reels. "You guys managed to have a heart-to-heart talk in a loud bar?"

"Oh no." She smiles. "We were in his car."

My breathing becomes erratic, and my ears feel hot. Is this really happening?

Mystery girl looks away from me. "James suggested we go to the car, so we could talk some more without having to yell. It was really nice of him to give me an outside perspective on my problems; talking them through made them seem easier to handle." She pauses, looking embarrassed again. "I kind of broke down a little bit while we were talking. He hugged me. That's when he realized I was freezing, and he gave me his hoodie to keep warm." She looks down at the Western hoodie she's wearing. "He'll never know it, but his concern for me that night really impacted my life." She looks distraught. "I wish I could tell him how much that night will always mean to me."

I have no words. I'm having a difficult time sorting out my emotions–and breathing. I don't know if I'm angry or just numb.

"What's your favorite memory of James?" she asks innocently.

I blink and stutter. "That's kind of hard ..."

She ignores me. "Out of that whole night, I think mine is when he kissed me goodbye."

My emotions immediately work themselves out. I know what I am. I. Am. Pissed. "Excuse me?" I snap.

My tone startles her. "Oh," she mumbles. "It was just a kiss on the top of my head. It was just a reassuring gesture, I'm sure. That's all."

"Um, everybody?" I hear Matt's voice carry. I rip my eyes away from Mystery Girl to see him standing in front of James' chair. People move to gather around the fire, and I turn my body away from Mystery-Girl-Boyfriend-Lover in time to notice Dane return to sit beside me. I'm vaguely aware that someone is standing behind me as well; my guess is it's Shel.

"Did I miss anything?" Dane asks.

Boy did you ever, I think as my blood boils.

"Everyone," Matt begins. "I just wanted to take a moment to remember why we are here tonight. We're here to honor the birthday of a close and dearly missed friend, our friend, James Davis."

Someone whistles while someone else calls out "Hear! Hear!" from behind me.

Matt turns to the empty chair. "I miss you man. We all do." He turns back to the group and holds out his drink as if making a toast. "To James! Happy 22nd Birthday, buddy. Wherever you may be."

The people gathered around raise their drinks, too. "To James!" most say and bump their drinks against those around them.

Dane bumps his beer can against my water bottle, which I now realize I have crushed between my hands. He looks at me confused.

Unexpectedly, Matt continues. "And to Emma," he says, zeroing in on me as he gestures with his drink the same way. "The love of James' life. Don't forget we love you, too."

My toast gets another "Hear! Hear!" from somewhere, but it sounds muffled to me. I need to get out of here; I need a few minutes alone.

I try to smile at the well-wishers around me, but I know it looks insincere. The guests bump their drinks again. Matt finishes, "That's all. Everyone can go back to enjoying themselves."

People return to their own conversations and some leave the area. I stand and Mystery Girl grabs my arm. I face her, and she looks absolutely horrified.

"I didn't know ..." she says. "I'm ... I'm so sorry."

"It's not your fault," I manage to say.

She stands up and strips off James' hoodie, revealing a tank top underneath. "Here. Take this."

"No." I shake my head. "He obviously wanted you to have it."

She looks shocked by my response.

"I can explain," a deep voice says.

James speaks directly into my ear, like he's standing over my shoulder. I tense up. He sounds somber.

"I have to go," I tell Mystery Girl. I turn to look at Dane and Shel who are suspiciously eyeing the girl and me. I repeat myself to them. "I have to go."

"Why?" asks Shel.

There is someone I have to deal with, I think to myself. *And he's lucky he's already dead.*

CHAPTER 22

"Your parents are still at the wedding," James says quietly.

I freeze in place, caught off guard by finding him in the kitchen. I expected he would be waiting in my room like usual. I wasn't prepared to run into him here; I still haven't sorted out what I want to say.

"You know," he continues, staring at the perfectly square ivory invitation on the counter, "I expected our names to be on something like this one day." He raises his head and looks directly into my eyes.

What is he trying to do? Distract me from what I've just discovered? I shake my head in disbelief and march past him into the living room, trying to buy some time to determine what I want my first sentence to be.

I walk to the fireplace and sit on the hearth. Resting my elbows on my knees, I hold my head in my hands and stare at the carpet. My mind races to select one of the million scathing thoughts that sear through my brain.

James' feet appear in my line of vision. "Tell me where to start. I'll tell you anything you want to know."

I snap. "Really?" Sitting upright, I look at him and spit out heavy words. "It's amazing how honest you've become all of a sudden."

He takes a deep breath. "Em, don't be like that."

"Don't be like what? Don't be angry? Or sad? Or feel betrayed? Which one?"

"You have every right to be mad," he says, crouching down in front of me.

"You think?" I ask him incredulously. "Were you ever going to tell me?"

"I didn't tell you because it meant nothing."

"To who? It means something to me! And it certainly meant the world to *her.*"

James sighs and closes his eyes. When he opens them he looks exhausted, defeated. "What I meant is it means nothing compared to what we're dealing with now."

I eye him suspiciously. "So, you never planned on telling me?"

He looks down and says nothing.

"I take it that's a yes,. I scowl.

His head snaps up. "What was I supposed to tell you? 'Hi, I'm back from the dead. By the way, the last night of my life, I ran into this girl I knew at a bar and ended up comforting her because she told me she'd considered suicide?' Sorry, but I thought we had more pressing things to discuss."

I cross my arms and look him in the eye. "Then I guess it's a miracle I ran into her tonight."

We sit in silence for a few moments staring at each other. It's hard to put my thoughts into words.

"Did you like her?" I finally ask, not sure I want to know the answer.

"What do you mean?"

"I mean, did you *like* her? Would you have seen her again? Did you think about cheat–?"

"Jesus, Emma, no!" James shouts, cutting off my insecure thoughts. "The thought of cheating on you never crossed my mind." He reaches out, grabs on to the top of my arms, and leans in to me. "I would never ... I have never cheated on you," he says solemnly.

I believe him. I do.

"I'm sorry," he continues. "Honestly, it was like comforting a sister. I couldn't just walk away from her, not after what she'd told me. I had to do something to help."

In my mind, I turn over what he is saying. "Did you have to kiss her?" I press. "Or give her your clothes?"

James looks pained. "No," he concedes quietly.

My mouth falls open.

"I can see how this looks to you," he says. "If the situation were reversed, I know how I would feel. All I can do is give you my word. I was only trying to help her." He pauses. "I love you with my whole being. I always have and I always will."

My stern expression falters. I don't doubt he's being sincere.

He releases my arms and stands. "Do you want me to leave?"

I sigh, resigned to the fact that I'd never want him to go regardless of his actions. I stand and reach for his hand. He places his in mine, and I pull him toward the stairs.

"I get to stay?" he asks as he follows me.

I turn and give him a condescending look. "Of course. Don't be stupid."

As we walk up the stairs, I hear my cell chime a message notification. I pull my phone out of my purse as soon as we make it to my room.

Are you okay? It's a text from Shel.

Everything is fine, I send back to her. *At home. Going to bed.*

I set my phone on my dresser and mechanically go about getting ready for bed. I notice my window is wide open and walk over to shut it. I don't remember opening it. James watches me as I work my way around the room. My phone chimes again.

Need me to come over?

No, I respond. *Stay with Matt. Have fun. Talk to you tomorrow.*

I get changed and crawl under the sheets. I lean over, turn out the light, and wait for James to join me. A few seconds pass and I don't feel him beside me. "Are you coming?" I ask into the darkness.

"Yes," I hear him say sadly from across the room.

A moment later, I feel the familiar cool air of him lying behind me, one arm draped over my side. Despite being upset with him, I have missed this so much. I scoot backward a little bit to press myself against him.

Minutes pass as neither of us says anything. I start to wonder if now he's angry with me. "What's wrong?"

"You're really mad at me," he says.

"How do you know?"

"You turned off the light."

"So?"

"Can't you bear to look at me?"

He's right. I always leave the light on when he's here. I don't know what I was thinking. I turn over and lean forward to turn the light back on. He immediately comes into focus as I lie back down. "Sorry," I apologize.

He presses his forehead to mine. "Please don't be mad at me. I'm sorry. I should have found a way to tell you."

"She's pretty," slips out of my mouth for some strange reason.

Without hesitation he says, "You're beautiful."

"I'm jealous," I admit.

"Of her? Why?"

"She got to spend the last night of your life with you. I didn't."

He raises his head to look at me. "You have me for eternity."

How can I argue with that? He stares at me intently and leans forward to kiss me. I respond eagerly; I have missed him so much.

"Will you forgive me?" he asks.

Even though I still have nagging feelings about what happened, I concede. "Already done."

His eyes widen with surprise.

"Don't think I won't bring it up again," I warn him. "I'm sure I'll have more questions about little Miss …."

"Rebecca."

Sarcastically, I arch a brow. "Oh, she has a name?"

James grimaces. "Can we not talk about her anymore?"

"For now."

I can see his arms move to pull me closer, so I shift toward him. "I've missed you."

"I missed you, too," he says as he kisses my hair.

"Are you learning a lot? Catching up?"

"It's been ... intense."

His lips brush my neck, and a chill courses through me. "Garrett's happy?"

"I think so."

He works his way along my jaw. "Is this the first time you've been back?" I breathe.

"Um-hmm," he murmurs under my ear.

"So you don't know about Matt and Shel? About Dane?"

James stops kissing me and meets my eyes, curious. "No."

I can't help my smile. This is going to be good. "Matt stopped by the other day. He is madly in love with Shel. Can you believe it?"

"Seriously?"

"He has it *bad* for her," I emphasize bad with a wiggle of my eyebrows. "Shel asked him to keep an eye on me while she's in Arizona, and he agreed. He recruited Dane to help since he can't be around me all day. Dane only agreed to work at the course to help Matt. So, you can stop being jealous now, Mr. Paranoid."

James laughs.

"What's so funny?"

"You."

"What about me?"

"Matt may like Shel, but his friend doesn't."

"So?"

"So? What's his obligation to help Matt land Shel? What does he care? The only thing he cares about is you."

I roll my eyes. "Whatever. I don't believe that. He's a good friend."

"Em, listen to me. I'm a guy. I've been friends with guys. We don't give up a whole summer to help out a buddy with a girl unless there's something in it for us."

Ugh. This is not how this conversation was supposed to go. "Can't you just be relieved and feel better about our situation?"

"Sure." He shrugs. "If that's what you want."

"That's what I want."

"Well ... then, done," he says.

I narrow my eyes at him. "Why don't I believe you?"

"You'll see. Dane can't keep this friend thing up forever. Trust me."

"So, you're going to drop it now just so you can say 'I told you so' later?"

"You're so stubborn it's worth it." He smiles.

"You suck." I pout. "I thought this would make you happy."

"I won't lie; the Matt thing does make me happy, although I don't get what he sees in Shel."

I scowl at him. "I would hope not."

James kisses my cheek. "I trust you. Stop worrying. A little jealousy is healthy in a relationship."

"Really? I don't care for the feeling myself."

"Let's make a deal." He props himself up on his elbow to look down at me. "I'll try very hard not to be jealous of Dane if you try very hard not to be jealous of Rebecca."

The idea rolls around in my head. Sounds easier said than done, but ... "I'm game."

James offers his free hand. I place mine in his, and we shake on our deal. He springs forward unexpectedly, passing through my fingers, and kissing me hard. The cool feeling of his hand wraps around the back of my neck and then splays up into my hair. He's trying to distract me, and it works. When his mouth stops moving against mine, I open my eyes to see him staring down at me.

"How long can you stay?" I ask him, breathless.

His eyes cloud over and he shrugs, unable to answer.

I glance at the time. It's 12:01. I'm reminded of what day it is. "Happy Birthday," I whisper.

"Thanks," he whispers back.

"I didn't get you a gift."

"Your forgiveness is enough for me."

Running my fingers through his hair, I say, "Make a wish."

His eyes close briefly and then he opens them again.

"What'd you wish for?" I ask.

He grins at me and his lips find mine.

CHAPTER 23

"Catch!" Dane shouts as he tosses me a tomato.

I manage to grab it out of the air. "Hey. Be careful!"

"Catch!" he yells again and tosses me another.

I catch that one too and look at him with his head stuck behind the refrigerator door. "Stop throwing things at me!" I say with a laugh.

"Catch!" It's a head of lettuce this time.

"Oh geez!" I yelp, as I try to catch it without dropping the two tomatoes. I fail. I catch the lettuce all right, but one tomato splatters against the tile floor while the other simply bounces.

"Catch!" he warns me again.

"No! Stop!" I laugh again. "I've already ruined the tomatoes."

He pokes his head around the door and looks at the floor. "Well, that's a mess," he snickers.

"No thanks to you."

I move to grab some paper towels. We're supposed to be prepping the sandwiches for a small golf outing the next day, but it's taking longer than necessary. Everyone who works at Bay Woods has already gone home, with the exception of Kris.

"Dude, we have to get this done," I complain as I bend down to wipe up the tomato slime. "I would like to go home sometime this century."

"Awww," he pretends to be offended. He kicks the refrigerator door shut because his hands are full with a large turkey breast, two more tomatoes, and a jar of mayonnaise. "You're that anxious to get away from me?"

"Not you, this place," I groan.

Over the last week, it seems like Kris has been working us extra hard by adding new responsibilities to our current ones, like this sandwich building fiasco.

Dane sets his items down and places the turkey on a huge, metal slicer. He turns it on and starts cutting away. "I'll be sure to go extra fast then, especially while using this." He nods toward the slicer. "Who needs five fingers anyway?"

"Stop it," I chastise him like a mother scolding a child, even though I know he's joking. "Be careful. I don't know that much first aid."

He winks at me.

I set to work slicing up the remaining tomatoes and the lettuce. When that's finished, I get the bread out and start assembling the sandwiches as Dane places handfuls of sliced turkey on the cutting board. We work as a two person assembly line. When the sandwiches are complete, and we're wrapping the last one, Kris appears out of nowhere.

"Hey, guys." She looks weary.

"What's up?" Dane asks.

"This outing for tomorrow is driving me crazy!" She slams her clipboard on the counter.

"What's wrong?" I ask.

"I just got off the phone with them. They keep changing things. Now they want to add some fruit to the lunches and a dessert."

"No problem," Dane says. "We were just about to start packing the boxes. Where's the fruit?"

"At the store," Kris sighs. "I didn't add any fruit to the delivery this week. And I need to come up with a cheap dessert."

"Cookies," I say. "Cookies are easy."

"Right!" Kris' face lights up like I just solved all of her troubles.

"So, what do you want us to do?" Dane asks.

"Could you go to the store for me? I still have to reconcile today's drawer." She frowns. "I'll give you some petty cash. Get two bags of apples and two bags of oranges and the cookies. Enough for two per person."

"Sure thing," Dane says.

Kris disappears to get the cash while we stack the completed sandwiches in the fridge. When she reappears, she beams at us. "Thank you so much for doing this. Here." She hands me the money. "I included an extra forty dollars. Get yourselves something to eat, on me, since it's so late."

"Thanks." I shrug. I'd rather just go home.

Dane grabs his keys. "Ready?" he asks.

"As ever," I reply, following him outside. At least I don't have to drive.

Dane leads me to a Chevy Camaro. A brand new, charcoal gray, leather interior, hot-rod Chevy Camaro. "When did you get this?" I ask in awe.

"I've had it," he responds like it's no big deal.

"Shows how much I pay attention," I murmur.

"Why?" He raises an eyebrow. "You like?"

"It's ... it's just ... better than my beat up car."

Dane flashes me a devious smile like he knows I'm lying. I am lying. This car is freaking awesome, and I don't even like cars.

When we make it to the grocery store, I grab a cart and we head to the produce section. "Why don't you go over to the cookie aisle?" I suggest. "Decide what to get. I'll grab the apples and oranges and meet you there."

Dane nods and walks off in the opposite direction.

I pick up the first two bags of each fruit I see, checking to make sure they're not moldy or gross. I wouldn't want to have to come back here tonight. Once I'm satisfied that the fruit is okay, I make my way to find Dane.

I turn down the first aisle – Baked Goods. I find lots of bread, but no desserts, and no Dane. I set my sights on the end of the aisle, intent on making this a fast trip.

"Emma?"

Hearing my name catches me off guard. I glance behind me and stop dead in my tracks. Standing there, staring at me, is Mrs. Davis.

"H–hi, Mrs. Davis," I say slowly.

"Catching up on some shopping?" she asks, tilting her head to look at my cart.

"Just picking up a few things for work," I mumble. I start to sweat. I haven't seen her since the night she and James' dad came over after the funeral. Even then, I didn't really see her; I just eavesdropped on the conversation. I have no idea what to say to her. My heart flutters nervously.

"Oh. Where are you working?" she asks.

"At Bay Woods, the golf course." As if there is another.

She takes a minute to assess me from head to toe. I feel as if I'm undergoing some sort of physical inspection. I stare at her in confusion as she scrutinizes me. She looks tired, haggard even. Her normally perfect, salon-styled, sandy blonde hair is unkempt, like she fell asleep and didn't bother to straighten her hair before she left the house. Her clothes even appear wrinkled, and I notice her nails are not manicured. Mrs. Davis always has her nails done; she's had a standing appointment for as long as I've known her.

"How–how've you been?" I timidly ask, afraid I'll be burned by my words. This is probably dangerous territory, but I don't want to add being rude to the top of my list of faults.

"Well. Thank you," she responds curtly as though she's rehearsed the line a thousand times.

Awkward silence. Should I just say goodbye and walk away? Or would now be an appropriate time to apologize for my behavior at the funeral? My heart pounds.

"It appears that you are doing well also," she says, breaking the silence. I can't help but notice the disdain in her voice.

Curious, I ask, "How so?"

Her blue eyes seem to darken to gray, and she narrows them

toward me. "I had a visit from your new boyfriend the other day."

My eyes widen in shocked surprise. "Excuse me?"

"Yes, I believe it was last Friday." Her expression sours. "A mutual friend of James and yours? He stopped by the house to give us his late condolences. He made sure to tell us all about how the two of you have been helping each other through such a tough time."

What is she talking about? That's impossible. I shake my head. "I'm sorry, but there has to be some confusion ..."

"Emma!" I hear Dane call my name from behind me. I turn to see him striding toward us. "What's taking you so long? I'm two aisles over and I need the cart ..." He stops talking as he reaches me, realizing he's interrupted a conversation. "Oh, I'm sorry." He holds a hand out to Mrs. Davis and smiles. "Dane Walker."

Mrs. Davis eyes Dane's hand with interest but doesn't take it. "Carol Davis," she responds coolly. She turns to me. "This isn't the same gentleman who came by our house the other day," she says. "Exactly how many boyfriends do you have *dear*?" She spits out the word "dear" like it's poisonous.

"Mrs. Davis, Dane's not ... I don't have–"

Dane senses the tension and cuts me off. "We work together. We're not dating."

James' mother chooses to ignore Dane's words and my weak protests. "That's what happened, isn't it?" she accuses me, her tone harsh and judgmental.

"I'm sorry." I shake my head again. "What are you talking about?"

"James found out, didn't he?" she sneers.

"Found out about what? Please Mrs. Davis; you're not making sense."

"About all of your men!" she hisses, raising her voice enough so the other shoppers in the aisle turn toward her, confused. "He found out about you. You broke his heart. I always knew you were to blame." She's shouting now. "You broke my poor son's heart, and now he's dead because of it!"

The blood drains from my face. I clutch the handle of the cart as tight as I can to prevent myself from collapsing. Dane moves to my side immediately. I can't speak to defend myself. I take a quick glance around. Of the few people in the aisle, some are staring at me with their mouths hanging open. I imagine others are pretending we don't exist.

"Go to the car Emma," Dane says in an authoritative tone. He holds his keys out to me without taking his eyes of James' mother.

I'm frozen. I can't move.

"I said go to the car," he says sternly again and looks at me when he says it.

I blink. Shaking, I reach into my pocket and hand him the money Kris gave us. He exchanges it with his keys. Forcing my legs to move my body forward, I start to head up the aisle, hoping to make it out of the store with a few shreds of dignity. I almost make it. Just as I turn the corner of the aisle, Mrs. Davis blasts me with one last sentiment.

"Whore!" she screams at my retreating figure.

I SIT in Dane's car, shaking. It's been twenty minutes, and I can't bring my body under control. Mrs. Davis' voice rings in my ears–*"Whore!"* How could she think that about me? I wonder what happened after I walked out of the store. Did she say anything else? My guess is yes. Did Dane jump to defend me, making it worse? I close my eyes to escape the nightmare that just took place. I could never conjure up anything like this, not in my wildest dreams.

I hear the sound of a cart arrive at the rear of the car. I fumble with the door handle and step out to help Dane with the bags.

"Get back in the car." His tone indicates he's not playing around.

I shake my head. "No. Let me help."

"Get back in the car," he says again, softer this time.

I hand him his keys and oblige. After a few moments, I hear the trunk slam shut. He walks around the side of the car, opens the door, and slides in. Dane stares at me for a few a seconds with sympathy, I think. I look out the window to avoid his gaze as the possibility of tears now threatens.

We ride in silence back to work. As we near the entrance to the course, Dane pulls off the road unexpectedly. He throws the car in park, and I turn and frown at him.

"You're shaking," he says and reaches for my hands. He manages to catch only one, and he presses it between both of his to stop its seizing.

"It's okay," I mutter lamely.

"It's not okay. That woman had no right to say what she said to you."

I give him a weak smile and state the obvious. "I'm not her favorite person."

"Evidently," he mutters as he rubs my hand.

"Listen, let's go back to work and get these lunches done." I try to remove my hand from his, but he holds it tightly.

Dane shakes his head. "You can't go back to work like this."

"Like what? Let's just do this already." I yank my hand harder. "It's not like it's brain surgery."

He lets go of my hand. "Your entire body is shaking."

"It'll stop."

"No," he says firmly, putting the car back in gear. "I'm taking you home."

"What? No. What about my car?"

Dane makes a U-turn. "Leave it. I'll pick you up in the morning."

"No! I can't go home without my car. My parents will worry especially if they see me like this," I protest. "I don't want to relive what happened with them. Take me back to work to give me time to settle down."

Dane appears to consider it because his eyes soften, but he keeps driving anyway.

"Where are we going? Kris will wonder where we are."

"We're supposed to be getting dinner, remember?" he reminds me. "I'm taking you to my place."

"Not necessary," I immediately respond as I will my body to stop shaking.

"I disagree," he says calmly.

"What are you? My father?"

Dane looks at me out of the corner of his eye. "Ah ... no."

I cross my arms in frustration and look out the window, weighing my options to get out of this. There aren't many. Jumping out of a moving vehicle doesn't really appeal to me.

Dane pulls up to a small complex of townhomes just outside of town. He parks and turns off the engine. "We're here," he says and immediately gets out of the car.

I remain seated with my arms crossed. Unfortunately, I'm still shaky. I was hoping to have stopped by the time we got here to plead my case for taking me back to Bay Woods.

He opens my door. "Come on."

I look away from him defiantly, and he sighs loudly. "If you don't get out, I swear to God, I'll make you."

I snap my head around to look at him. His expression is serious; he's not joking. I huff as I haul myself out of the car. "Happy?" I ask sarcastically.

"Extremely."

I follow him up the sidewalk to the unit on the end, #202. We go up a few concrete steps, and I wait on the small porch as he unlocks the door. He swings it open. "After you."

I tentatively walk inside and he follows me, flipping on a light switch by the door. A small living area is illuminated, and I can see a dining area at the end, which I assume is connected to a kitchen. In front of me, a flight of stairs extends upward to the darkened second floor.

Dane gestures toward the couch. "Make yourself comfortable. I'll be back soon."

I turn to face him. "You're leaving me here? What am I supposed to do?"

Dane looks exasperated. "Sit down. Relax. Take a nap. Watch TV. Snoop through my stuff. I don't care." He takes two steps back toward the door. "I'll go finish up. I'll be back within the hour and then we'll get your car."

And with that, he closes the door behind him.

CHAPTER 24

Awkwardly, I look around the room. There's a couch, a loveseat, and a coffee table. All black. I walk farther into the living room and gape at the huge flat screen TV. Who needs a television that big in a room this size? It sits on a modern looking stand that holds all the necessities–DVD, stereo, Playstation. I walk over to the small dining table that is surrounded by only two chairs. In the center is a small withering plant of some kind; it looks mistreated and thirsty. I don't think twice about entering the kitchen to find a glass to water the poor thing. Evidently, horticulture is not Dane's strong suit.

The kitchen is tiny, but holds many stainless steel appliances. On the counter, a few drinking glasses lay drying on a dish towel. I grab one and fill it, noting the stack of dirty dishes left in the sink. After I water the plant, I refill the glass and take a drink myself. When I raise the glass to my lips, I realize my shaking has subsided. Good.

What am I going to do here for an hour? I glance around the place again. I look at the dirty dishes, and my orderly instincts take over. I fill the sink with hot water and set to passing the time by washing them.

When that's done–it only takes me about ten minutes–I wander back into the living room and plop down on the couch. It's very comfy and soft; it feels like leather. I look around the room again and realize that, although the place is a little messy, there's a lot of expensive stuff in here. My eye falls on two framed pictures on a side table. I lean forward to get a better look. The first is a group of guys, Dane included, posing with their arms around one another while they sit on some bleachers. The second picture is of Dane with his arm draped casually around a beautiful dark-haired girl, both are smiling brilliantly at the camera. They favor each other. A sister, maybe? Dane doesn't talk much about his family. Come to think of it, neither do I. If he's not teasing me about something at work, our topics of discussion usually revolve around Matt and Shel, annoying customers, or how I'm feeling. That last topic of conversation is getting old.

I turn away from the pictures, spy a massive remote on the coffee table, and decide to watch TV. I play with it. How do I even work this? I find the power button and press it. The flat screen turns on but it's static. I locate the channel buttons and try to select a different station. Nothing happens. After about five minutes of this, I give up and turn the TV off. I sigh and put the remote back where I found it. There are a couple of magazines lying on the coffee table. I select an issue of *Rolling Stone* and scoot into the corner of the couch to pass the time by reading.

As I flip through the pages, my mind replays today's events and I shudder. Well, at least I know how James' parents really feel. Sadness clouds my thoughts. I always feared they disliked me, especially after James decided to leave Ferris. I mentioned my worry to James in the past, but he always blew off my thoughts telling me they loved me and I was part of his family. James doesn't have any siblings; I was the daughter they never had, he'd tell me. Boy, was he wrong. Or just covering for them. I'm leaning toward the latter.

I scoot down to lay my head against the arm rest of the couch and close my eyes. For once, I'm silently thankful for James' restriction. He didn't have to witness what happened today. He would be furious. My thoughts drift to Dane and his actions at the store. What would have happened if he wasn't there? How far would the situation have escalated? An image flashes behind my eyes; I am curled in a ball, rocking back and forth, sobbing on the floor in the Baked Goods aisle as James' mother stands above me pointing and screaming. Yeah, that very well could have happened. What did occur was bad, but it could have been much worse.

I turn on my side and realize I have to thank Dane when he returns. I need to apologize for being so difficult and thank him for diffusing the situation. I need to thank him for allowing me some time alone to process what happened and thank him for being an amazing friend when he has no reason in the world to be.

I HEAR MUFFLED VOICES, and my forehead pinches in a frown. Who's talking? I open my eyes to a hazy darkness. I blink to focus. I'm still at Dane's and the TV is on, casting the only light in the room. I must have fallen asleep. I stretch my legs out in order to turn over and end up kicking Dane in the side.

"Ugh," he whispers.

I pull my legs back and pick up my head. "Sorry," I croak out, my voice thick with sleep. Dane is sitting opposite me, not quite at the end of the couch. I move my legs over the side and sit upright just next to him. "What time is it?" I yawn.

"About midnight," he says.

I snap awake. "Midnight? We should go. I don't want to keep you any later."

"Take your time. I didn't want to wake you." I look at his profile in the changing light of the television. He's resting casually against the back of the couch. "Your car is outside."

I stare at him. "How?"

"You left your bag at the course. I found your keys and called Matt. He helped."

I shoot him a look. "You mean you went through my stuff to find my keys." Not that it matters. I should be grateful I can get up and leave.

I can see him grin through the light. "You did my dishes."

"And watered your poor plant." I look past him toward the table. "Are you killing it on purpose?"

He chuckles. "No." He pauses and smiles. "Find anything else interesting?"

I look at him quizzically. "I didn't snoop or anything, if that's what you're asking."

He pretends to pout.

"Are you disappointed?"

"Wellll," he draws out the 'L's, "I was hoping to come back and find you in my bed."

My mouth falls open.

"Sleeping, of course." I think he winks at me.

My mouth snaps shut. "I'll settle for the couch, thank you."

Dane laughs and leans forward to rest his elbows on his knees. "I'm just kidding."

Our eyes lock for an instant. He continues to look at me, and it makes me uncomfortable. It's definitely time to go. I break our stare and look away. "Where's my stuff?"

"By the door."

I look over and see my bag hanging from the doorknob, then turn back to him. "Thanks." I stand, and he follows to show me out.

Reaching my bag, I pull it off the handle and loop it over my head and across my shoulder. I turn around to find Dane right behind me. There's no time like the present to offer my apology and thanks for earlier.

"I'm sorry for being difficult," I say.

"You're entitled."

"No, I'm not. I want to thank you for stepping in at the store. Without you, I don't know what would have happened. I want to thank you for letting me stay here, too, for letting me calm down alone. It really helped."

Dane takes another step closer to me. "There's no way I wasn't getting you out of there, even if I had to pick you up and carry you out. I've never seen anyone attack someone like that, let alone a grown woman. She's clearly deranged."

"Really?" I let out a sarcastic snort. "How do you know?"

He frowns. "You can tell just by looking at her that she's not well."

I can't help my curiosity. "Did she … did you say anything else after I left?"

He regards me for a moment, apparently deciding if he should tell me or not. I can tell by his eyes when he determines I can handle it.

"She told me I should watch myself around you for my own safety, after what you supposedly did to her son." He eyes me cautiously. "Something about being in cahoots with the devil. Is there something you're not telling me?" he asks, trying to lighten what he's just shared.

I swallow. That woman loathes me. "What did you say?"

Dane takes another step forward and leans in, so our faces are only inches apart. His eyes lock on mine, so I will understand how serious he is when he speaks. He reaches out and places his hands on my shoulders. "I told her she was the one who needed to go to hell," he says solemnly. "That you are amazing to have held up the way you have, no thanks to people like her. That you loved James."

I look down, breaking his gaze. "Thank you," my voice wavers. "Thank you for defending me when I couldn't defend myself."

Dane's hand leaves my shoulder and appears under my chin to tilt my face up toward his. "You shouldn't be put into any situation where you to have to defend yourself. Ever."

My mind flashes to James and all the times I've had to defend myself to him. My love for him, my choosing to work at the course, my having Matt and Dane as friends, my choice to release him when I die.

Dane interrupts my thoughts by letting go of my chin and tucking a piece of my hair behind my ear. "Do you know what I mean?"

I nod because I do know what he means. All too clearly.

He searches my face. For what I don't know. His hazel eyes lock on mine again, and my heart starts to pound. His breath catches, and I know what he's resolved to do. He leans forward to kiss me. It's like it's happening in slow motion, and I'm powerless to stop it. My whole body tenses under his hands, and I close my eyes as if to block it out.

Dane can feel my body go rigid. I sense him pause for a second and then feel him kiss me tenderly against my forehead instead of my lips.

My eyes pop open. He searches my face again, still holding on to my shoulders. He looks cautious, maybe even a little nervous. I see a realization hit him and he steps back, releasing me suddenly. "I'm sorry," he apologizes. "I don't know what … that won't happen again."

I nod and give him a weak smile. "I'm not mad." It's the truth.

Dane looks unsure, like he's overstepped a huge boundary and there's no going back. I don't want him to be upset because, strangely, I'm not. Did I want him to kiss me? No. And he realized that. I step toward him, and he takes a step back.

"Are you afraid of me now?" I ask jokingly, referring to when he asked me that same thing weeks ago.

He appears to relax. "No." He smiles.

I step up to him, stand on the tips of my toes, and give him a quick, chaste kiss on his cheek. When I back down, I notice his puzzled expression. "Thank you for realizing everything I need."

He shoves his hands in his pockets. "That's what I do."

I turn to the door and pull it open.

"Have a nice night," he says to me as I step outside.

"You, too." I half-heartedly wave to him. "See you tomorrow?"

"See you tomorrow."

Walking down the steps, I spot my car immediately. When I slide into the driver's seat, I look up just in time to see Dane close his front door. I can still feel where he kissed my forehead, still feel his hands on my shoulders. I reach up to touch the hair he tucked behind my ear and feel myself melt a little.

Then I freeze as what happened comes crashing down on me. What am I thinking?

CHAPTER 25

It's been about a week since the "Incident." That's what I'm calling my run in with Mrs. Davis. Actually, that's what I'm calling that entire day, including what happened with Dane. "Incident" is a vague, sanitary term. That's why I like it. Thinking about what happened that day in any detail brings on overwhelming feelings of sadness, doubt, and guilt. Especially guilt.

I did end up telling my parents about Mrs. Davis–omitting a choice word or two–just in case they happen to run in to her somewhere as well. They were not impressed to say the least. My mother wanted to call her immediately and give her a piece of her mind. I begged her not to. Who wants to make things worse? She eventually agreed, but made no promises if she saw the woman in person.

Dane and I have only discussed the "Incident" once, the day after it happened. It was a brief conversation.

"Do you want to talk about yesterday?" he asked me.

"Not really." I continued to empty the beverage cart.

"You're okay with it then?"

"Yep. Already forgotten."

"Good. I'll fake amnesia, too."

After that, I had worried he might start acting differently around me, but my worries were unfounded. He kept up the same old Dane routine. Either he had truly pushed it out of his mind, or he was a great actor.

The only unresolved factor regarding the "Incident" was James. He hasn't been back to visit me since the morning of his birthday; which, as much as I hate to admit it, makes it easier to bury what happened in my subconscious. But I still wrestle with whether or not to tell him when I do see him. On one hand, I want to vent my frustrations regarding his parents and find out how long he's been lying to me about their acceptance of me in his life. But on the other hand, I don't want to cause trouble. What does it matter if his family hates me now? Would I like to vindicate myself? Sure. Will it solve anything? No.

And then there's the matter of telling him what happened at Dane's …

I sigh as the thoughts that have plagued me for the last week swirl around and around in my head. I'm not looking forward to it, but I'm going to have to tell James everything. I don't want to pull a Rebecca scenario.

My cell vibrates in my pocket, interrupting my thoughts. It's Shel.

"Hey."

"Uncle Tom died this morning." Her voice is monotone and void of any real feeling.

"Oh, Shel, I'm sorry."

"Well, the good thing is it's over and he's out of pain," she sighs.

"How's your mom?"

"She's doing well enough. She's on auto pilot right now."

"How long will it take to make arrangements? When is the funeral?"

"He didn't want a funeral or a memorial, so that part is easy," she tells me. "We do need to finish going through his things. We'd already started last week when he was moved to the hospital."

"Ugh."

She suddenly perks up. "But the good news is I'm coming home next week regardless!"

"Sweet. How'd you talk your mom into that?"

"It's getting expensive with the both of us staying out here and most of the paperwork stuff is taken care of," she says. "Plus, we've already got a renter ready for Uncle Tom's place."

I hear someone ask her a question in the background. Shel responds to them, "No, not now. Hold on." She returns to me. "Listen, I have to go. But my flight is already booked, and I'll be home for the Fourth of July. Ask for it off now; I want all of us to get together. It'll be fun." She sounds excited.

"'Kay. Just let me know."

"I will." I hear the person in the background again. "Gotta go. Can't wait to see you!"

"Me, too. Talk to you soon." I smile as I hang up. I've really missed having her around.

"Why are you grinning like that?" Dane asks when he returns to the counter.

"Shel's coming home next week for good."

"Oh, thank God," he exclaims. "I can't take anymore of Matt's whining."

I laugh. "He's that bad?"

Dane rolls his eyes and exaggerates his nod.

"When did he turn into such a girl?"

He laughs. "Memorial Day weekend."

"Shel wants us all to get together for the Fourth," I say. "I told her to let me know the plans."

"Right," Dane says, then hesitates. "Maybe it should just be the two of them? I'm not down for watching the Matt-Shel love fest." He grimaces.

I make a face, too. "Yeah, ick." I pause to think. "I doubt I'll be able to get out of it though; I haven't seen her since the birthday party."

"Hey, that reminds me. I've been meaning to ask you about that."

"About what?"

"What the heck went down between you and that girl? She looked terrified of you before you left."

Oh, that. I haven't told anyone about that. When Shel had asked, I managed to distract her with questions about her and Matt's night together. I weigh my options–keep it locked up tight or discuss it with Dane? It would be nice to get an impartial opinion on the matter.

"If I tell you, will you promise me you won't say anything to Matt or Shel? I don't feel like fending off a ton of questions."

Dane leans against the counter and raises his hand. "Scout's honor."

I take a deep breath. "The girl knew James but didn't know who I was. I didn't know her, either," I share with him. "She told me she and James really connected on the last night he was alive, that they'd met up at a bar."

Dane wasn't expecting this, and his eyes grow wide. He frowns but says nothing. I imagine his opinion of James heading south.

"James and I … we'd had a fight that night," I confess, as to defend James' reason to go out without me. "Anyway, he went out with some guys, and she was at this bar. She had a couple of classes with him, and they started talking. Turns out they talked most of the night. She started to spill some personal information and got upset." Suddenly, I feel like I'm trashing James' reputation. I tame down the story. "James consoled her and it …" I pause. "It really meant a lot to her. When she found out who I was, she felt bad for telling me, that's all."

Dane is still frowning. "And?"

"And what?"

"There's more to this story," he guesses. "Go back and fill in the parts you left out."

How does he know? I recall James' voice–*"You've never been a very good liar."*

"His words really helped her." I shrug and try to play it off. "She was grateful." Extremely grateful. I can't help myself as I grimace.

Dane looks as if he's trying to figure me out. He regards me for a moment, then asks, "That's all?"

"That's all," I say and try to end the conversation by looking around for something to do. I grab a rag and decide to wipe down the counter. For whatever reason, I don't want Dane to think less of James. Telling him was a bad idea.

"Hmm. With the way she was looking at you, I expected a juicier story."

"Sorry to disappoint you." I concentrate on wiping the clean counter, avoiding eye contact.

Dane opens the register drawer and starts to break open some rolled coins. "That's too bad," he says casually. "I was hoping you'd give me a reason to dislike her. She was cute. I got her number."

I stop wiping. I clench the rag in my fist and slowly turn to look at him. "You did not." I'm not amused and it shows. He knows he struck a nerve.

"Oh, so you don't like her?"

"I never said I did."

His eyes light up. "What's your problem with her exactly?"

I know what he's up to. He's baiting me. "I don't have a problem with her," I say through clenched teeth and go back to cleaning invisible dirt.

"Oh, okay. Good. Maybe I'll invite her to the Fourth of July thing," he eggs me on.

"You do that," I say sarcastically. I'm not falling for this.

He shuts the register drawer. "I wonder if she still needs consoling," he pretends to ponder.

"Humph," I grunt. "Go ahead. Knock yourself out."

"Not that I'd be able to do it as well as James did," he concedes. "It sounds like I could learn a thing or two from that man."

I stop wiping and glare at him. "Stop it."

"Stop what?" he asks innocently. "I'm just thinking out loud."

"Well, shut up," I snap.

"Whoa. Touchy." He pauses for a moment. "Is it that time of the month?"

Seriously? He did not go there. "Fine. You win. I don't like her. Satisfied?"

"Maybe. Tell me why."

"Why what?" I throw the rag against the counter in frustration. "Why don't I like her? Do I have to have one reason?"

He raises an eyebrow. "Ah, so there's more than one reason?"

So help me …

I take a few steps forward so I'm inches from him. If I could punch him with any effect, I would. "Stop pushing me," I hiss at him and I mean it.

"Why won't you tell me?" He cocks his head to the side. There is no way he's afraid of me.

"Because." I look around. There are only two golfers in the main area, and they're watching TV. "I'm done discussing this."

Dane looks around, too. "I don't think they're paying us much attention." He smirks. "Lame excuse. Keep talking."

"Why is this so important to you?"

"It wasn't important until you made it important. I can tell when you're lying, and I don't like being lied to."

I clench my fists and stare him straight in the eye. "He kissed her, okay? He took her out to his car, he hugged her, he kissed her, and he gave her the shirt off his back. Happy?" I can feel my chest rise and fall under my labored breathing.

Dane's face falls. "No," he says quietly.

I shake my head in frustration and walk away from him. I snatch the rag off the counter and walk over to the sink to wash it.

"Emma …"

"What?" I snap.

He walks up behind me. "I didn't get her number."

I already figured that. "That makes me feel so much better," I say sarcastically while I wring the rag to death under the faucet.

"What James did was lousy."

"You think?" I turn the faucet off. Giving the rag one last good twist, I turn to face him.

"No, I know," Dane says. "It sucks."

"You got that right." I scowl and walk around him to start wiping the other end of the counter.

"Would you stop doing that?" He follows me.

I scrub the clean counter with the same force I would use to scrub a dirty dish.

"You're going to take the finish off the laminate," he says and reaches out, grabbing my wrist, stilling my hand. I look up at him annoyed.

"Don't hold him up to be a martyr just because he's gone."

I stare at him.

"You can be mad at someone and still love them."

Don't I know it.

Dane releases my wrist. "I'm sorry I pushed you. It's getting harder for me to stop myself when it comes to you."

I'm surprised by his admission, and I don't know what to say.

Dane backs away from me. "For what it's worth, I don't like her either. And she's not that cute. In fact, she's hideous. Frankenstein-esque."

I can't help it and a snort escapes. "Don't be mean," I admonish him. Then I laugh. "Frankenstein-esque? That's the best you can do?"

He smiles and shrugs. "It's the first thing I could think of."

I relax. "Sorry for being difficult."

"What's new? You're always difficult. You've been difficult since the day I met you."

I pretend to be offended. "My apologies."

A golfer approaches the counter, momentarily distracting us. "Don't apologize," he says as he steps backward toward the register. "I enjoy a challenge."

A challenge? "What does that mean?" I ask.

Dane is interrupted by the customer, and I never get an answer.

CHAPTER 26

Shel decides she wants a pool party on the day of her homecoming. Although it's a typical American thing to do for the Fourth of July, I wish she had chosen dinner or a movie or anything else that doesn't involve me wearing a swimsuit. I search through my drawer and pull out the two suits I own and sigh. I can't remember the last time I wore one of these. I hold in my hands a bright green bikini and a sky blue one-piece with a white swirl design. Maybe I can get by with an old pair of shorts and a t-shirt.

"I'd choose the green one."

I whirl around to see James standing on the opposite side of my bed with his arms crossed.

"But that's just my opinion." He smiles and winks at me.

My heart nearly bursts. A huge grin breaks out on my face, and I drop the suits. I run around the bed to him.

He wraps his arms around me. "Hi," he says softly.

I hug him and place my head against his chest, sighing contentedly. The cool feeling of his body radiates through me.

"Happy to see me?" he murmurs.

"Yes. Very."

"I'm sorry it's been so long."

I raise my head and smile up at him. "You're here now."

"I am." He smiles and leans down to kiss me. When we part, he rests his forehead against mine. "I snuck away," he confesses.

I look up at him and frown. "You did what?"

"I had to see you."

Worry creases my brow. "What if Garrett finds out?"

He shrugs. "This," he kisses me again, "is worth it."

I'm still concerned. "What if you get caught and he decides to keep you away longer?"

James shakes his head. "He can't keep me away forever."

Raising my hand, I trace the outline of his jaw with my finger. "I don't want to chance another punishment or whatever our separation is."

He gives me a crooked smile.

"Do I amuse you?"

"I'm just happy you still want me around."

"Of course I still want you around," I say sincerely. "I want you around me always. That's why I don't think you should test your teacher."

James' smile fades slightly. "I needed to see you. I won't stay too long. Will that make you happy?"

"No. I want you to stay. But I don't want you in any trouble, either."

James releases me, running his fingers down my arms. "Have I missed anything exciting since I've been gone? Fill me in."

I study our hands, so I know where to place mine in his without passing through his form. I don't want to have the 'Your-Mother-Thinks-I'm-A-Whore' conversation right now, especially since our time is limited. I'm so happy to see him; I don't want to ruin it with crazy talk. I opt to discuss something else.

"Shel is home from Arizona. She wants to have a pool party to celebrate." I squish up my nose, making a face.

"I take it you'd rather not." He grins. Then his smile fades. "Let me guess who else will be at this party."

Shoot. How do I diffuse this?

Honesty. That's how.

I look him in the eye. "If you're referring to Dane, yes, he will be there, but late. He has to work. And you know Matt and Shel are all over each other." I make the squish-nose face again.

James gives me half a smile. "Still?"

I relax a little bit. "Still. She just got back. I'll be the third wheel," I complain.

"Then don't go," James says, like I should have thought of that sooner.

I give him a look that tells him that's not an option. "It's Shel. I have to go. Plus, I haven't seen her in a really long time. I've missed her."

James moves to raise my hands and I lift them, since he can't do it for me. He kisses my knuckles. "You'll have fun," he says. "Although it would be easier for me if you two would just have a girls' night out or something."

"Because it's all about you," I tease.

He gives me a huge smile. "Damn right."

"Come here," I laugh and move my hand through his to wrap it around his neck. He knows what I want, and he leans forward to kiss me again. His other hand leaves mine, and I feel it wrap around my waist. I move closer to him, enjoying this time we have together.

James lips leave mine, and he plants another kiss on my forehead. "Can you blame me for sneaking out?" he whispers.

I shake my head no. "Can't you bribe Garrett with something to make him release you from house arrest?" I ask as he runs his fingers up and down my back, tracing my spine. I shiver, but not because I'm cold.

James laughs. He knows the effect he has on me. "I wish."

"When do you think you'll be able to come back and stay for a while?"

"Garrett recognizes my hard work and commitment. I'll have a talk with him soon."

"Like today?" I grin at him.

"Impatient are we?" He raises an eyebrow, but I can tell my question makes him happy. Then his expression changes. "For you, anything," he says seriously. "I'll go talk to him."

"Really?" I ask, surprised.

He nods and kisses me quickly before releasing me. "I'll let you know how it goes."

"You're leaving?" I pout.

"Do you want me to talk to him about us or not?"

"Yes," I respond without hesitation.

James smiles. "I love you."

"I love you, too."

I stare at him as he fades away. It makes me feel hollow. I wrap my arms around myself and pray his conversation with Garrett goes well.

Walking back over to where I dropped my swimsuits, I hold one in each hand, deciding which one to wear, then give up and toss them on the bed.

"Oh, hey, Emma?"

James' voice is behind me. I turn around but cannot see him. I look into the room and ask, "Yes?"

"I changed my mind. I like the blue one better."

I roll my eyes sarcastically. "That's only because you know where I'm going."

He chuckles.

I lean over and pluck the blue suit off the bed. "Then blue it is."

TURNS OUT, blue it isn't. When I was putting the suit on, I heard a loud rip as I pulled the left strap over my shoulder. It's just my luck that the seam would split and leave a huge gaping hole that exposed most of my side. I had no choice but to put on the bikini. There was no comment from James; hopefully, he was in a deep, convincing conversation with Garrett.

I now sit on Matt's pool deck, still dressed in my shorts and t-shirt, brooding about wearing the green suit underneath. Not necessarily because James would disapprove, but because I'm incredibly self-conscious. I am excited to be here with Shel, though. I think I've missed her more than I realized.

"You can't get a decent tan that way you know." Shel's lying on a lounge chair beside me on her stomach, her pink bikini straps undone to prevent tan lines.

"I'm self-conscious, okay?" I defend myself. "A good tan is not that important to me anyway."

Shel squints at me because she's facing the sun. "Just take off your damn clothes," she chastises. "Be a girl with me."

I give her a look.

"There's no one here but me and Matt." She grins. "And he's taken."

I roll my eyes and sigh. "Fine," I huff as I stand and pull my shirt over my head. I drop it on the pool deck and drop my shorts on top of it. I plop back down in my lounge chair. I stretch out and lean back, closing my eyes to the blazing sun.

"*Thank you*," she says dramatically.

I open one eye and stick my tongue out at her.

"Where are Matt's parents?" I ask.

"At a veterinary conference in Chicago. They'll be gone till Saturday." She gives me a sneaky smile.

"Ew," is all I can say.

"Ladies," I hear Matt approach. I turn to look in his direction as he walks up the deck steps with two drinks, one in each hand. He steps up to us. "For you." He hands me something frozen with a straw.

"What's this?"

"Daiquiri." He smiles as he holds one out to Shel.

"Awww, you remembered," Shel says in a mushy tone. She reaches behind her back and starts to tie her straps so she can sit up.

"I got it." Matt hands me Shel's drink so he can help tie up her suit. He's all thumbs with the small strings, but he manages to get them secured.

I watch in amusement as I take a sip of my drink. Yum. Strawberry.

"Thanks, babe," Shel says as she sits up. Matt's still leaning over her, and she kisses him. What I thought would be a quick kiss turns into something deeper.

I choke on my drink.

They both turn to look at me. "Are you all right?" Shel asks.

I try to clear my throat and nod at the same time. "You two ... it's going to take ..." I cough into my arm, "a minute to get used to ..." Cough, cough. "Seeing you together," I manage to finish. Cough.

"Wrong tube?" Matt smiles as he takes Shel's drink from me and hands it to her.

I hit my chest with my fist and clear my throat again. "Yeah."

Matt checks his watch. "I'm going to go throw the chicken on the grill." He nods toward the patio. "It's going on five; Dane should be off work any minute. That way we can eat when he gets here."

Shel nods as she adjusts the back of her chair to stay upright. "Whatever you say." She beams up at him.

Matt rubs her knee as he stands and heads off the deck. "Don't think I'm not throwing you in later," he teases Shel over his shoulder.

She says nothing, and I look at her. She's absentmindedly sipping her drink. "What, no snide comment?" I ask.

"I meant you Emma," Matt laughs as he glances at me before descending the stairs.

"Ha ha. Very funny," I say sarcastically. Cough.

"So, how'd you get today off so easy?" Shel asks me.

I shrug. "I asked and I received. Why?"

She looks at me like there's something she knows but I don't. She sips her drink. "No reason."

I pin her with my eyes. "What?"

"Nothing," she protests.

"Tell me."

"I just think it's funny that the golf course owner's son is stuck working on a holiday and you're not, that's all." She takes another drink.

I frown. "Are you telling me Dane is working today because of me?"

She shrugs nonchalantly.

"You do know. Tell me."

She sighs sheepishly. "Matt might have mentioned something about Dane volunteering to work today, so you wouldn't have to. Don't tell them I said anything."

"You're the one who brought it up!" I scowl. Why did he do that? Now I'm going to owe him. One more thing to add to the list of nice things he's done for me. I take a long sip of my daiquiri. I may need more than one of these.

We sit in silence for a few minutes, sipping our cocktails. Water laps at the side of the pool, and Katy Perry sings about being in love with an alien on the radio.

"So," Shel looks at me, her face serious, "what is going on between you two?"

I stop mid-sip. "Us two who?"

"Emma!" she groans and swings her legs off the lounge, so her whole body is facing me. "You know. You and Dane."

"Nothing!" I respond without hesitation.

She eyes me suspiciously. "I think I believe you," she murmurs. "I told Matt if anything were going on you would tell me. And you haven't. Yet."

I stare at her. "There is no 'yet.' There won't be a 'yet.'"

She sips her drink again. "You two have been spending a lot of time together."

"Yeah, at *work*," I emphasize. "And we all know the reason he works there, don't we?"

Shel's eyes get wide. "I don't know what you're talking about." She tries to look innocent and turns around to put her feet back up on the lounge.

I remember my promise to Matt, the one where I wouldn't tell Shel I knew about the favor she had asked of him thus resulting in Dane's Bay Woods employment. I've already said too much. I decide to let the topic die. I take another long pull on my drink. Something bothers me.

"Do you really think I would jump into a relationship so soon after

James?" I ask her. Unbidden, Mrs. Davis' voice pops into my head. *"Whore!"*

Shel looks at me with sympathy in her eyes. "I don't. But I could see Dane making you feel better. I wouldn't think less of you if you had a connection with him."

"We're friends," I concede.

"That's good. And if it ever develops into something more, hey, you could do a lot worse." She gives me a look.

"What do you mean by that?" I shake my drink to dislodge the frozen pieces. It's almost gone.

She looks at me like I'm stupid. "Oh, so you haven't noticed he's gorgeous? And loaded on top of being a nice guy?"

"Loaded?"

"The boy's got money, Em. You didn't know?"

"I knew he had a nice car ..." I frown. If Dane is well-off, then why is he working at the course? Oh yeah. Me.

"Matt said the company Dane had an internship with his last year of college kept him on. I guess he's this amazing artist."

"He's an artist?" I ask, completely baffled.

Shel laughs. "Maybe you two should get to know each other better off the course. You can start today."

I tip my glass up to swallow the last of my drink. Yep, I know I'm going to need another one of these. I glance around the pool deck. "Where's your cabana boy?"

CHAPTER 27

About four daiquiris and three hours later, I pull myself out of the pool after being pulled in–again–by Matt and Dane. For some reason they find forcing me into the water extremely hilarious. To be fair, I did laugh really hard when Shel went in first; Matt had snuck up on her and pushed her in by surprise. When she surfaced looking like Cousin It, and heard my hysterics, she decided it was my turn to go in. From there it just turned into a vicious game of who-can-we-throw-into-the-pool-next.

I haul my dripping self to my chair to enjoy the last of the day's sunshine. Dane walks over to me and shakes his hair over my stomach.

"Hey!" I protest.

"You're already wet," he says and sits down in the lounge Shel previously occupied. He stretches out on the chair with a groan. "I'm beat."

"Hard day at work dear?" I ask and giggle. Four daiquiris may be too much for me. Wait. Make that five if you count the first one.

Dane grins. "Why yes, honey, thanks for asking." He's had a few too many as well.

He closes his eyes and places his hands behind his head, lifting his chin toward the sun. My eyes travel the length of his body of their own accord, I swear. Everything about Dane is well-defined and hard to ignore. His arms, his chest, his abs, the way his black swim shorts hang off his hips…

Bad Emma! I need to redirect my thoughts.

"So, why'd you do it?" I ask to clear my mind.

He opens his eyes and asks, "To what are you referring, Smoochie Poo?" while trying to keep a straight face.

I crack up. When my laughter subsides, I clarify. "Volunteer to work for me."

"Who told you that?" he asks. I catch his eyes dart to Matt and then back to me again.

"You've got to stop doing stuff for me," I protest and try to look serious. "I already owe you enough as it is."

Dane looks at me like he's dealing with a child. "Please," he says sarcastically. Something catches his eye and he turns to the pool. I follow his gaze to find Matt and Shel making out in the water.

"C'mon!" he yells at them and picks up a pool noodle that's laying by his chair. He tries to throw it at them, but it's too light and doesn't even make it half the distance. "Nobody wants to see that."

"Then close your eyes," is Matt's smart response. "Whose house is this anyway?"

Dane turns to me. "He's got a point," he says and makes a face.

I raise my hand to the side of my face like a blinder. "This blocks it out." I smile.

He follows my lead. Now we're turned toward each other with our hands blocking the sides of our faces. "We look stupid," he says with a laugh.

I can't help it. "You always look stupid," I say, suppressing another giggle.

"That's it!" he says and lunges forward. He grabs my arm as I try to fend him off.

"No!" I squeal as I kick.

Dane leans his shoulder toward my stomach, pulls my arm

forward and easily picks me up off the lounge chair, tossing me over his shoulder.

Yep, I'm in the pool again.

I resurface, sputtering. "Thanks a lot!" I swim over to the side where Dane is laughing. He offers his hand to pull me up.

Inspiration hits. I pretend to reach for his hand as I grab the side of the pool. Instead of taking it, though, I push myself out of the water to wrap both my arms around his leg and then let my body weight pull me back down.

"What the–"

He's caught off balance from leaning forward to help me, and he goes into the pool over my head like I'd planned. I get taken under a little, too, and when I wipe the water from my eyes, I try to contain my laughter. I know I'll be in trouble when he pops back up.

I manage to pull myself out of the water just as Dane's hand grazes my heel. I squeak and jump when I feel his touch. I don't want him to catch me. I run past the lounge chairs and right off the side of the deck. I don't know where I'm headed, but I don't want to be caught.

Rounding the side of the pool, I crouch down by the far corner. It's above-ground, so it sits slightly higher than my head. Matt and Shel are laughing, and I hear Dane's feet as he runs off the deck to find me.

"You can't out-run me!" he yells.

I don't know which way he's going to come around the pool, so I keep turning my head from side to side. When he appears at the corner directly in front of me, I let out an "Oh shit!" and take off toward the back of the house, rounding the side and heading to the front. I turn the corner and press myself against the siding. I need to catch my breath. I expect him to come right after me, so I peek around the corner of the house. I don't see him. I take some more time to breathe. The thought crosses my mind that I'm really out of shape. Or just buzzed.

I decide to slowly make my way across the front of the house, to the next corner. It never occurred to me he would backtrack and creep around that way to lie in wait. When I turn and see him casually leaning against the side of the house, I jump and let out a loud scream. I start laughing and back away with my arms out in front me.

"I'm sorry!" I laugh. "Don't throw me in again."

Dane smiles at me mockingly. "Now why would I do that?"

I keep backing up. I look around the front yard. "Leave me alone. The neighbors can see us."

He keeps advancing.

I'm not paying attention and the back of my foot hits the rubber edging on Mrs. Randall's flower bed. I stumble and the next thing I know I'm falling backward into a bunch of daylilies and mulch. I turn to try and catch myself. "Ahhhh!" I land on my side with a thud.

Dane is hysterical with laughter. Literally holding his sides. I start to crack up along with him.

"That," he walks up to me, "is better than anything I would have done to you." He offers me his hand. "Are you all right?"

I nod and wipe some tears from eyes. I grab his hand, and he pulls me to stand. Globs of mulch are stuck to my skin on my side, my stomach, my shoulder, down my leg; there's even some in my hair. I start to brush myself off. Dane helps a little.

"Are we even?" I ask, still laugh-crying.

"I think so. That. Was. Great."

"Well, my middle name is Grace," I tease.

He pauses for a minute. "Really?"

"No!" I shake my head smiling.

Dane bends down and picks up a yellow daylily I broke off a plant. He tsk-tsks like I'm going to be in trouble, then gently tucks it behind my ear.

I reach up and adjust it so it won't fall. "Can we go back and lay in the sun now?"

He nods, still laughing, and we head to the pool.

As dusk falls, Matt moves Shel, Dane, and I farther out into the yard for fireworks. We arrange our yard chairs in a line, like we're at a theater. Shel throws herself into the chair next to me after hanging our swimsuits up to dry. She has a bottle of water in her hand.

"Daiquired out?" I ask, nodding toward her water bottle.

"For now." She smiles. "This will hopefully prevent a horrid hangover in the morning." She takes a swig. "You should probably have some, too," she suggests. "I don't think I've ever seen you drink so much."

I laugh, agreeing with her. "Five drinks was probably a very bad idea," I say knowingly, although I still feel okay right now.

"Hey, Grace?" Dane asks me from the end of our theater seating. "Can you pass me a Coke please?"

Ever since my flower bed fall he's been referring to me as Grace. "Yep." The cooler is by me, so I reach in to grab a can. I pass it to Shel who passes it to Dane.

"Thanks, Grace," he snickers at me.

I roll my eyes.

"Okay!" Matt calls out from in front of us. "These fireworks are going to be fabulous. I got them at Wal-Mart."

We all laugh. Matt lights the first one and skips a few feet away from it. It's a roman candle fountain that shoots multi-color sparks into the sky. It's kind of small and lame.

"Ooooo," we all say with a laugh. "Pretty."

"It's not *that* bad," Matt says, defending his show.

Matt proceeds to light roughly seven more fireworks, and they're all the same thing.

"Jesus!" Shel yells from the chairs. "Didn't you read the box when you bought these? Are they all the same?" she complains.

"Hush woman!" Matt yells back to her. "It's the best I could do on short notice."

Matt lights two more and then tells us, "This is the last one. The Grand Finale."

"Thank God," Shel whispers to me.

Matt lights the last firework, and it's more of the same. Maybe a little larger than the others and it has some sort of noise element that every so often shrieks into the sky. When it burns out, Shel and I clap wildly for the end of the show. Dane whistles.

Matt walks up to us. "That was awesome," he says sarcastically, then changes his tone, rubbing his belly. "I'm hungry. You guys want anything?"

"I could use some food," Dane says, and I nod in agreement.

Shel stands up out of her chair. "Me, too." She looks at Matt. "I'll help you." She reaches for his hand as they walk away from us and back into the house.

Dane and I are left in our chairs, surrounded by the tiki torches we lit earlier to fend off mosquitoes. He looks over at me. "Feeling all right after your fall, Grace?"

"Yes, I'm fine." I smile and start to laugh thinking about how ridiculous I must have looked.

He laughs with me. "That was classic."

When our laughter subsides, we sit in silence staring into the yard. Suddenly, he stands and takes two steps toward me. "Walk with me?" he asks.

I give him a puzzled look. "Okay."

He takes off toward the back yard, where Matt had been just a few seconds ago. It takes me several steps to catch up with him. I walk beside him for a few feet, until we're completely out of the tiki torches light. He's uncharacteristically silent. I continue to walk beside him, deciding he'll talk when he's ready.

"Watch your step," he says and reaches out to grab my hand as he helps me over some railroad ties laying in the yard.

"What are those doing there?" I ask as I climb over them.

"I think they're left from Dr. Randall's failed attempt at a garden."

"How long have you known Matt's family?"

"A long time," he shares. "Since I was five."

Dane continues to walk farther into the backyard. How far does it go? I can barely see in the darkness, but he apparently knows where he's headed. Finally we reach our destination at the tree line, which I assume marks the edge of the Randall's property. He looks up, and I follow suit. Up in one of the larger trees I can make out the outline of a tree house.

"Matt's?" I presume.

He nods. "His and mine. We had another small one over there." He points and searches the trees for it. When he does, my arm moves, and I realize he's still holding my hand. I pull it away, and he gives me a curious look. "I guess it's gone."

Eyeing the tree house cautiously, I ask, "Are we going up in this one?"

"Oh no." Dane shakes his head, smiling. "We'd probably fall to our deaths. I just wanted to see if they were still back here."

I walk over to the tree and touch one of the boards nailed to the trunk. I look up and see several more leading up to the house. Dane remains silent. Reminiscing about his youth? I turn and open my mouth to ask him what we're doing out here, but when I look at him, he's staring at me in that way that makes me anxious.

I step away from the tree. "Well, this one's still here. Let's go back before we're eaten alive by bugs."

"Emma, I have to talk to you."

My stomach instantly knots. This sounds serious. Either that, or I'm still buzzed from my reckless drinking. Maybe I'm not processing things right. I try to lighten the mood. "I thought my name was Grace?" I tease.

He gives me a small smile and moves toward me. I retreat and bump up against the tree, feeling one of the boards at my lower back.

He steps up to me. Our bodies are nearly touching. "I don't know exactly how to say this, so I'm just going to say it."

"What?" I whisper, because I'm pretty scared I know what's coming and it won't be good.

He reaches out to touch the daylily that's still tucked behind my ear. "I know I promised you I wouldn't do this ..."

My heart starts to race and blood begins to pound behind my ears. *No, no, no, no, no!*

In one swift movement his mouth is on mine. I try to lean back and push him away, but I have nowhere to go with the tree behind me.

His hands have moved to my arms, and he holds me there as his mouth moves softly against mine. I feel like I'm falling, like my whole body has gone numb, like my limbs are jelly. Unwelcome warmth starts to spread through me. I try to resist it. I attempt to turn my head away, but Dane releases my arm and wraps his hand around the back of my neck, burning my skin where he touches me. His other arm wraps around my waist, pulling me away from the tree.

Now that I think I have some leverage, I push against his chest again, to squirm out of his grasp. He feels what I'm trying to do and his mouth leaves mine. "Please don't," he whispers.

I don't know if it's his plea or the look in his eyes; maybe it's the alcohol still left in my system. Whatever it is, in that moment, all my resolve leaves me. When his mouth crushes mine again, I want it there. The warmth I was suppressing in my chest moves outward through my body, and I wrap my arms around his neck, pulling him to me. A small part of my brain screams *"What are you doing?"* but it's a small part, and it is easily ignored. His mouth leaves mine and makes its way to my ear; his teeth graze my earlobe before I feel his lips on my neck. I'm lost in a haze. I know it's wrong, but I can't find one fiber in my being that wants to stop this.

Suddenly a sad, broken, hollow voice cracks over my shoulder. It shatters my world into a million pieces.

"Now can I say I told you so?"

CHAPTER 28

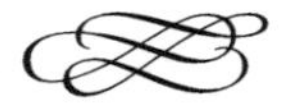

Sobriety hits me like a Mack truck. With strength I didn't know I had, I push hard against Dane's shoulders. He releases me, and I stumble backward a few steps. He reaches out to catch my fall, but I violently push his hand away.

"Don't touch me!" I snarl at him.

He looks at me bewildered. My eyes start to fill with angry tears, and I step to the side to move around him. I have to get out of here. I have to find James.

Dane backs up a few steps and attempts to stop me from leaving. He reaches out and tries to block my path with his arm, tries to grab my waist. I jerk my body out of his reach and start to walk quickly back the way we came. Dane manages to grab my forearm, and I'm forced to turn and look at him.

"Emma, wait!"

I stare at him as tears course down my face. I clench my jaw and forcefully try to pull my arm free. I see his face register my reaction and pain colors his hazel eyes. He releases my arm.

"Don't you *ever* touch me again," I growl.

I take two steps backward and then turn, picking up speed as I head back to the house. I leave Dane standing in the backyard alone. I run away from him. I run to find James.

WHEN I MAKE it home I burst through the door, leaving it open as I enter, panicked. "James!" I call out. I look around frantically, wiping the tears from my face. He's not here.

I run into the living room. "James!" I yell again, searching. I feel a sob building in my chest. I head for the stairs and take them two at a time.

I make it to my bedroom only to find it empty. "James!" I call out again. Silence. I search my room frantically for any sign he might be here. "James, please," I beg into nothingness. I have to see him. I have to beg for his forgiveness.

I wrap my arms around myself and end up sliding to the floor next to my bed. The sob in my chest continues to grow, threatening to rip through my heart and deflate my lungs. How could this happen? How could I allow this to happen? Mrs. Davis reappears in my head like the Wicked Witch of the West, staring at me disapprovingly. Everything James has done to be with me I've singlehandedly ruined. How can he forgive this? He can't. I know he can't. The sob escapes, and I hide my face in my hands. My heart breaks at the thought that I may never see him again.

I hear the back door slam shut downstairs. I anticipate my parent's voices calling up to me to let me know they're home. I try to pull myself together, hastily wiping my face and jumping up to see how terrible I look in the mirror. My eyes are red and puffy; my face is covered with red splotches. There's no hiding this. I make a hasty decision and throw myself into bed. If they come up to check on me, I can bury my face in my pillow. That's where it will be spending the night anyway.

I lie in my bed, my heart pounding, as I wait for their arrival. But they don't come. They don't call up to me, either. I glance at the clock. It's only been a few minutes since I heard the door shut. I wait impatiently; I just want to lie to them that I'm fine and get it over with. So I can cry alone. So I can hate myself in peace.

After twenty minutes pass without a word from them, I start to worry. Then my mind takes a dark turn. What if it's not my parents? What if it's Dane? Anger starts to build in my chest. How dare he? How dare he come into my house uninvited. What is he doing down there? Making himself at home?

I throw off my blankets and march out of my room and down the stairs, ready to give him a piece of my mind. I pray James is watching.

I can't see anyone when I descend the stairs. Confused, I walk through the living room and into the kitchen, prepared to blast Dane with all I have. When I turn the corner, my eyes zero in on someone seated at the table.

Someone I never expected to see again in my lifetime.

Patrick, my ex-lab partner.

"Hello, Emma." A smug smile spreads across his face. "It's been too, too long."

A jolt of anxiety rips through my body. How is this possible?

Patrick looks at me expectantly. When I don't say anything, he stands, splaying his fingers and resting the tips in front of him on the table. "Aren't you going to say hello?"

I continue to stare at him in shock, taking in his stocky build, cropped blonde hair, brown eyes, and thin-framed glasses. His overall appearance looks slightly different, but maybe my memory is hazy. He's wearing a Budweiser t-shirt and denim shorts. He starts to come around the table toward me.

"You know it's not polite to stare," he says. His mouth still wears the smile, but his eyes harden at my lack of response.

I force myself to speak. "Hello, Patrick," my voice wavers.

He continues to advance toward me. "Ah, you remember me. That's good." He nods approvingly.

My voice is nervous, rough. "What are you doing here?"

He reaches me and looks me over from head to toe. The way his gaze slides over my body makes my skin crawl. "Now that would be giving away too much too soon, don't you think?"

I take a step back. The sense that I am in danger rings loud and clear. I silently tell my Guardian I get the message. My eyes dart to the door and back to him. Is it possible for me to get away? To make a run for it?

Patrick notices my glance and clicks his tongue. "I wouldn't do that if I were you."

Oh, God. I swallow nervously.

His brown eyes turn dark as the smug smile returns. "The look on your face is priceless," he says. "Even better than I imagined."

I narrow my eyes suspiciously even though my heart threatens to hammer through my chest. "What do … what do you want?"

"Oh, I've already taken a few things," he responds, wearing a superior look. "The lock on your bedroom window is broken," he says, giving me a sly smile. He reaches into his pocket and produces a pair of my underwear.

I nearly gag at the sight. He's been in my room? How many times? Were my parents ever in danger? Anger slightly edges out my fear. It simmers, giving me a small boost of confidence. "I don't know what you think you're doing, but you are not welcome in this house. Leave. Now."

Patrick lets out a snort of laughter. "Who's going to make me? You?"

All I can do is glare at him.

He crumples my underwear in his hand and tosses them aside. "Where's your James when you need him now? Oh, that's right. He's *dead*." He twists the word dead in his mouth.

"You don't scare me." I'm lying. I'm scared as hell, but I do my best to sound convincing.

"Let's see what we can do to change that, shall we?"

He approaches me quickly and holds his face inches from mine. He's too close for my comfort, and I lean away automatically, turning my head.

"Look at me!" he shouts and grabs my arm.

Flinching, I do my best to face him. He grips my arm tightly.

"What do you see?" he demands through clenched teeth.

I don't want to make eye contact. I struggle against his grip and try to back away. He grabs my other arm to keep me in place.

"Tell me what you see!" he yells.

I try to focus on his face. I can make out two somewhat jagged, dark pink lines that cut across his left cheekbone, near his eye. Now that I'm looking at him closely, I can see the left side of his face is slightly distorted, almost swollen, even though the scars look as if they healed long ago. Is this what he wants me to see? "Your face!" I rasp. "I see your face."

"Remember that night? The night you asked your beloved James to hurt me?" he growls.

"I never asked him to do that!"

"Your boyfriend broke my cheekbone, shattered my eye socket!" He releases my arms with a twist, pushing me away. "That bastard left me partially blind."

"I'm sorry that happened to you," I choke out. "I didn't know."

"Why would you?" he sneers. "I wouldn't want to inconvenience your perfect life." He pauses and then laughs maniacally. "But that all came crashing down, didn't it?"

I say nothing; I am mute.

Patrick shakes his head, his laugh lingering. He crosses his arms. "First, James dies. I admit I was shocked to hear the news. My condolences." He leans toward me and gives me a look that mocks sympathy. "I figured you'd be pretty wrecked but that performance at the funeral," he lets out a low whistle then looks me in the eye, "that was something." He smiles knowingly.

I take a step to the side. He mirrors my move.

"After that, I thought about things, because, you know, I'm reminded *daily*." He points to his marred cheek. "And I thought, why stop there? Let's have some fun."

His twisted expression terrifies me. I start to back away from him again. "Patrick …"

"Slashing your tire was a rookie move," he admits. "It brought me no satisfaction. Breaking into your house was almost too easy," he pauses. "So I decided to pay a visit to the Davis'. *Completely* trashed your reputation there," he snickers. "Now that–that was fun."

Mrs. Davis' voice returns to me–*"I had a visit from your new boyfriend the other day."* I shudder. I don't know what to say. All I know is that I have to get away, away from here, away from him. I don't know what he's capable of. I make a split second decision. I bolt toward the back door.

"STOP!" he bellows. He runs around the kitchen island opposite me and cuts me off, blocking my way to the door.

I pant as he continues to walk toward me, pushing me back to where I came from. "You will *not* try that again," he snaps at me.

"Patrick," I plead with him. "I can't change the past. My life is broken. What more do you want?"

He tilts his head and smiles maliciously as he continues to press me backward. Before I can react, the heel of my foot collides with the dining room wall. I have nowhere to go. Patrick advances toward me and reaches out on either side of my head, pressing his hands against the wall, blocking my exit to my right and to my left. I cringe as he leans in close. I can feel his hot breath on my skin, below my ear.

"Oh, I can think of one more way to ruin you," he whispers and licks my neck.

CHAPTER 29

Time stands still. My mind fumbles to wrap around this reality, tries to comprehend the insanity. How did this day spiral so wildly out of my control? I feel my face grow hot as my heart starts to sputter spastically in my chest. My vision blurs, making the room turn fuzzy on the edges. With just that one act, I already feel violated.

Patrick moves to look me in the eye. His face twists into a lurid smile at the horror on my face. "I see you understand what I have in mind," he says and quickly grabs hold of my chin, clutching it painfully. "You. Will. Not. Move. Understand?"

I nod meekly. I understand all too well. What he doesn't know is that I'm not going down without a fight.

"Good girl," he approves. He roughly releases my chin and brings his hand down hard on my shoulder, pushing me against the wall. He takes a step closer and stares down at me as his free hand finds the bottom of my shirt and starts to make its way underneath.

It's now or never.

I slap him as hard as I can across his face. My skin hitting his sounds like a whip; my palm stings at the contact.

"Arrgh!" he growls and leans back.

I immediately spring to my right and try to take off, intent on making it to the back door. I only make it a few steps. He catches me from behind, wraps his arms around mine, and pins them to my sides at my elbows. I struggle and twist my body against his. "NO!" I scream.

Patrick turns us and starts to tow me backward against my will, pulling me toward the doorway into the living room. I'm sure he wants me as far away from an exit as possible. I plant my bare feet against the wood floor of the kitchen to try and hold on to something, anything that will provide resistance against his pull.

He realizes what I'm trying to do with my feet and lifts me off the ground slightly. He continues to walk backward, holding me up, as I struggle against him with my upper body. I can hear him huff with his efforts; he's getting winded. "Stop fighting me!" he shouts.

I start to wildly kick my legs. One of my feet ends up winding around his ankle, and I kick it out from under him. He loses his balance and stumbles. He falls backward onto the floor, taking me with him. I land hard on my back and tailbone, partially across his body. His arms release me, and I roll off him, scrambling to my hands and knees. I try to stand, but my legs are wobbly.

"DAMN IT!" I hear him yell from behind me.

Adrenaline pumps through my veins. So much so that I can barely control my movements. My mind is screaming for my limbs to cooperate, but my arms and legs are all over the place. I try to focus on coordinating my body to crawl, but it feels like I'm crawling in place, putting no distance between me and my attacker.

I manage to get a few feet away when his hand finds my ankle. My ribs and my chin smash against the floor as he yanks me backward, knocking my hands out from underneath me. Pain seers through my jaw, and I scream.

I feel myself sliding across the floor. Patrick releases my ankle and quickly crawls up my body to grab a handful of my hair. He hovers over me, straddling me on his knees, and pulls my hair painfully to lift my head up. "I said don't move," he snarls in my ear.

He releases my head violently, pushing me, and my forehead

cracks against the wood floor. Oh my God. The pain is indescribable. I can't bring myself to scream, only whimper.

Patrick rolls my body underneath him so I'm lying on my back. He remains over me, kneeling. My world swirls; I can see his face, I can see the top of the doorframe above us. I feel him move my arms to my sides and pin them against my body with his knees. I try to move them, but my head is throbbing and black spots dance across my eyes.

He leans over me, his face looming above mine. My mind registers that his glasses sit on his face askew. I feel his hands at my waist, pulling at my shorts, unfastening them. I try to move my legs to kick, but it's as if I'm paralyzed. I close my eyes to brace for what's about to happen, willing my body to recover and cooperate. I open my eyes to see if the dark spots are gone.

And see James.

He stands over us, a look of pure horror on his face. "James!" I choke out, my voice barely audible and raspy.

Patrick hears me and smiles wickedly. "James can't save you, sweetheart."

I focus on James. His face reflects everything I'm feeling–hatred, revulsion, disgust, and fear. He lunges at Patrick, wrapping his arms around his chest to pull him off of me.

It has no effect on him.

But it does on me.

The dark spots disappear and even though my head throbs with excruciating pain, I start to writhe and twist beneath Patrick. He squeezes my body tighter between his knees to stop me. When that's not enough, he removes his hands from my body and pins my shoulders to the floor. "Don't make me hurt you anymore than I already planned!"

I see James wrap his hands around Patrick's neck and squeeze. Patrick doesn't budge. James steps back and kicks Patrick repeatedly on his back, in his side. He takes another step back and side swipes Patrick's head with his foot. Still nothing. James looks at me terrified and helpless.

I return his tortured gaze. How long can I fend Patrick off? How badly is he willing to hurt me? I know the obvious, but how far will he go to incapacitate me? My only option is to keep fighting. James gives me the strength. I spit in Patrick's face.

"You bitch!" he snaps and reflexively backhands me.

All I can see are stars.

Three loud knocks at the back door make both Patrick and I jump. BAM! BAM! BAM!

Patrick looks down at me and covers my mouth with his hand. "You say nothing," he warns me.

"Emma!"

It's Dane.

"Emma! It's me!" he shouts. "We need to talk!" He pounds on the door again.

My eyes flash to James. "Scream, Emma!" he yells at me panicked. "Scream!"

I nod under Patrick's grip and bite down hard on the flesh of his palm. He snatches his hand away and lets out a loud hiss.

And I scream. I scream louder than I ever thought I was physically able.

"EMMA!" I hear Dane yell my name as Patrick slams his hand down on my mouth again. I start to twist and kick again underneath him. I hear the door handle rattle and turn, but it doesn't open. Patrick must have locked it.

"EMMA!" I hear loud thumps against the door, the sounds of Dane trying to kick it in.

Patrick looks around the room frantically weighing his options. I can see James still trying, still kicking and hitting Patrick to get him to release me.

The door gives way with a loud crack. Dane runs inside, and I make eye contact with him immediately. I'm lying in between the kitchen and the living room held down by Patrick. His eyes turn wild with fury as he registers the scene. He races toward us and dives at Patrick, knocking him off my body as they tumble to the floor.

I scramble backward as James rushes to my side. "Emma!" he yells as he reaches me. He grabs my face in his hands, and I look up to oblige him. "You have to run! You have to run now!"

I turn and look at the back door as it hangs open. I hear a loud crash, and my attention is drawn to the living room. Dane and Patrick are a tangle of arms and legs. They've hit the coffee table and shattered a crystal vase my mother had placed there. I sit transfixed for a moment as I watch Dane punch Patrick in the side repeatedly, under his ribs, as they wrestle on the floor.

"Emma!" James shifts my focus.

I look at him and nod, then stumble to my feet. My head throbs relentlessly. I take two steps toward the door and stop. I look back at Dane and Patrick. The fight has shifted; both assailants are now standing and circling each other. Patrick favors his side, and Dane's nose bleeds. I can't leave Dane. I have to help him.

James sees my decision in my eyes. "No!" he hollers at me. "Get out of here! He can handle this!"

I want to run away, but my conscience tells me no. Or my Guardian tells me no. I'm still fuzzy on how that works. "I can't just abandon him!"

"The hell you can't!" James fires at me. "You're hurt!"

"Someone's ... my Guardian is telling me to stay!"

James curses under his breath.

Dane and Patrick are too focused on each other to pay attention to my one-sided conversation. Dane swings at Patrick and misses; Patrick takes a step and turns his back toward me. I look around hurriedly to see what I can grab to hit Patrick with. My eyes fall on a heavy bronze candle base on the side table. I race forward and grab it, knocking the candle off the top. I cross the short distance to Patrick and pray I have enough strength to do some damage as I raise the base over my head. My action distracts Dane, and he catches my eye.

Alerted to my presence behind him, Patrick swings suddenly and catches me square in the chest with his forearm. It's enough to knock the wind out of me and send me flying. I trip and fall, landing on my side, my weapon knocked from my hands.

Someone lets out a guttural growl. I don't know if it's James, Dane, or Patrick. I do know that my lungs gasp for air, my head throbs mercilessly, and I'm having a hard time deciding on my next move. Blackness starts to creep into my line of vision again. I fight it. I cannot pass out.

Dane charges into Patrick, knocking him back and against the floor in front of me with a loud thud. They roll and Patrick tries holding Dane down. Dane pushes him off easily and backs up to stand. I see Patrick search the floor, smile, and reach out to grab something. He stands again and starts to advance.

"What are you going to do with that?" Dane taunts Patrick even though his breathing is labored and blood runs down his chin from his nose.

Patrick glares at Dane, sidesteps, and tries to work him into the corner. I've managed to get to my knees, but I'm having a hard time moving past kneeling. James is by my side. "Stay down!" he yells at me.

I look at Patrick and Dane again. Patrick holds a shard of the broken vase. He clutches it so tightly I can see blood starting to creep around his fingers. He jabs at Dane with it. He misses.

"Is that all you've got?" Dane taunts him again, running the back of his hand under his nose, smearing his blood across his forearm.

Patrick goes at him again. He misses the mark, but he's getting closer. I can't stop myself and yell, "Dane!" I'm sure it's anything but helpful.

"Get out of here!" he shouts without looking at me.

I can feel James' cool grip around my arm as he tries to help me stand, as he tries to pull me away.

The next time Patrick moves at Dane, Dane's ready. He grabs a hold of his forearm, the hand that holds the glass, and tries to twist it so he'll drop his crude weapon. Patrick breaks his hold and lunges forward again.

"Ugh!" Dane grunts and Patrick grins wickedly. I know Dane's been hit.

"No!" I scream from my knees.

Dane staggers trying to catch his breath, bent over and clutching at his side. Patrick shifts his gaze to me. "Already on your knees," he leers. "Perfect."

Will he never give up?

What he says enrages James. He leaps to his feet from my side, murder in his eyes. He barrels straight for Patrick.

And what happens next astounds me.

James hits Patrick hard, head on in the chest, ramming him with his shoulder. Patrick's eyes grow wide as his breath is knocked from him by an invisible force, as his body is literally knocked up into the air. He flies backward and lands on the brick hearth with a sickening crunch, his head hitting the glass fireplace doors.

James turns to me and blinks, shocked by what he's done. Dane pulls out the shard of glass embedded in his side and looks up, confused. He turns to me briefly before a moan escapes the wounded, drawing his attention back to Patrick. Patrick raises his body to his elbows, bends his knees, and tries to stand. Dane is in front of him in two strides. He reaches out, grabs Patrick's head between his hands, and slams it against the fireplace doors. Patrick slumps to the side, unconscious.

Dane instantly turns to me. His eyes look haunted as he looks me over. "Emma?"

It's only now that I realize I'm crying. I don't know when I started, but I feel the tears running down my face. My muscles ache and my head pounds. I start to feel dizzy, so I close my eyes.

"Emma!" Dane yells as I crumple to the floor. When he reaches me, I feel him touch my neck, looking for my pulse. He strokes my forehead, pushing my hair away from my face. "Hold on," he whispers and then disappears.

When I hear the familiar touch-tones of the phone, I know he's in the kitchen. For some reason I can hear the operator on the other end of the line loud and clear. "911. What's your emergency?"

As Dane quickly asks the operator to send help, I feel James' cool touch against my cheeks, my neck, and my arms. I feel his concentrated kiss on my lips and then again against my forehead. I feel his coldness slide under and around me somehow, and I manage to open my eyes to slits. I see his knee in my line of vision as he cradles my head against his leg.

"I love you," he says, his voice cracking, as he strokes my shoulder with one hand and my hair with the other. I close my eyes to try and block out the incessant pounding in my head, to make my mouth form words.

"I love you," I'm barely able to whisper. I'm not sure if he hears me.

CHAPTER 30

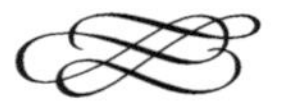

The light is too bright; it hurts my eyes. I try again, opening them slowly this time. When I see the industrial fluorescent light fixture on the ceiling, I know I'm in the hospital. My mind registers the fact that my head doesn't hurt as badly anymore; there's just a dull thrumming that matches my heartbeat. I feel tightness around my left hand and the familiar rub of a thumb against mine. I roll my head against the pillow and allow my eyes to focus on Dane, seated by my bedside, holding my hand.

"Hey, Grace." He smiles at me, relief flooding his features.

"Hey," I croak out.

"How's your head?" he asks, worried.

"It's … it doesn't hurt too bad."

He lets out a nervous laugh. "You sure know how to give a guy a heart attack, you know that?"

I smile. "I'm sorry." My eyes shift to look around the room. They catch the monitors and other medical equipment on a stand tucked against the side of the bed. None of it is attached to me. I take in the white walls, white ceiling, and the generic landscape picture on the wall. The room looks empty except for us.

"Where is everybody?" I rasp.

"Your mom and dad just left."

Images and sounds start to flood my brain. I remember heavy footsteps and unfamiliar voices asking me questions. I remember hearing my dad's frantic voice; I've never heard him so panicked in all my life. I remember lying on a stretcher, my mother's concerned face hovering above me as she walked next to me. I remember mumbling an apology, telling her I would clean the blood off the floor.

My memory flashes a picture of Dane walking toward me, holding his side and bleeding. I look at him alarmed. "Are you okay? Are you hurt?"

He gives me a reassuring smile and continues to rub my hand. "Please. I'm fine."

"No, you weren't fine," I shake my head, "I mean, aren't fine ..."

Dane lets go of my hand and pulls up the right side of his shirt, exposing a bandage. It wraps slightly around his side and extends an inch or two across his chest. "Thirteen stitches," he states matter-of-factly. He taps the dressing and then releases his shirt. "I'll live."

"Lucky thirteen, huh?" I ask and try to clear my throat. It's so dry.

Dane reaches forward and presses a button connected to the hospital bed. "I might even end up with a scar worth bragging about." He smiles, collecting my hand again. "Of course you'll be the first person I show it to." He lifts my hand and kisses my knuckles.

At first, I smile at his comment, but then my smile slowly fades. He can see me processing what he just said; he can see me remembering. I'm sure I can see my reaction to his kiss playing back in his hazel eyes. His face falls a little and he releases my hand, setting it back on the bed.

The door to my room opens and a nurse comes bustling in. "Is our patient awake?" she asks politely.

I look at her and nod. In one hand she carries a Styrofoam cup with a straw, and in the other she carries a small paper dish. "Water," she says as she hands the cup to me.

I take it from her and take a long pull from the straw. The water soothes my dry throat almost immediately. The nurse–I catch her name badge, Anne–dumps the contents of the little dish into my hand.

"Take these," she says. "They're Ibuprofen. The doctor on call will give you a script for something stronger when you're discharged."

I toss the pills in my mouth and swallow them down with a gulp of water.

"Are you hungry?" she asks.

"A little," I tell her as she places a thermometer in my mouth. "When do I get to go home?" I mumble.

"Should be this afternoon." She removes the thermometer when it beeps. She walks to my chart and scribbles something. "You were only admitted overnight for observation. Standard procedure for a mild concussion."

I nod in understanding.

"The doctor will be in shortly." She looks at Dane. "Will you be taking her home?"

"Uh, no." He shakes his head. "Her parents said they would be back in about an hour or two. I'll call them to let them know she's awake."

"Good." She smiles at us as she heads out the door. "I'll send in a snack. Feel better soon."

Dane turns to me as he stands. "I'll go, so you can rest. I'll give your parents a call; they left me the number." He starts toward the door.

He can't go. There's too much we have to talk about. "Wait."

He stops and looks at me.

I clutch my cup of water. "We have to talk."

He shakes his head and gives me half a smile. "Not now."

"Yes, now," I demand and tuck my water cup by my side. I hold my hand out to him.

He appears to think about it, then retreats a few steps and grasps my hand. He sits down next to my bed again and moves his chair closer.

"I have to thank you," I say sincerely. "Without you, who knows what–"

"Don't even think about it," he cuts me off. "I'm happy to have put that creep out of his misery."

Out of his misery? "He's not ... he's not dead, is he?"

Dane lets out a sarcastic snort. "No. But he should be."

"Where is he?"

"He's here somewhere." He frowns. "But as soon as he recovers, he'll be arrested." His face immediately shifts with concern. "Don't worry," he says, looking into my eyes. "He will *never* touch you again."

I squeeze his hand. "I held my own pretty good there for a minute."

Dane's frown deepens. "Not from what I saw. You really should have gotten out of there like I told you to."

"I'm sorry I have such creepy friends."

His eyebrows shoot up. "Are there more?"

"No, not as far as I know."

"Good," he sighs with fake relief. "I was thinking you might have to hire me as your full time bodyguard."

I laugh.

"Not that I'd mind," he adds softly.

I have to admit my heart does a little flip when he says this. But I love James. I will always love James. I've made a promise to him that I cannot break. This is going to be so hard, but things are only going to get worse if I say nothing, especially after this last incident.

Dane can sense my apprehension. "Emma, listen ..."

I take a deep breath. "I can't be anything more than your friend," I say quietly. "I wish I could be more, but ... I just can't."

Dane stares down at our hands. "I know." He meets my eyes again. "It's too soon. It was dumb of me to try what I did and for that I'm so sorry. It's just ... I needed a question answered, and I decided that was the time to ask it."

My voice is soft. "Did you get your answer?"

He nods solemnly. "Yes, unfortunately I did."

Tears jump behind my eyes. "I'm sorry about how I reacted. It's just that things are complicated ..." I can't tell him my dead boyfriend saw us kiss.

Dane rubs my hand gently. "That's not what I meant. I had a question to ask myself."

I stare at him confused.

He shakes it off. "Don't worry about it. Especially now. You need to take it easy. You need to heal. And not just your head," he gives me a crooked smile, "but your heart and mind, too. It's not going to be easy to forget what that psycho tried to do to you."

I blink to prevent any tears from appearing. "You really are too good to me."

He tilts his head to the side and smirks. "That's what I do."

"Friends?" I hopefully ask, realizing I don't think I could bear it if he says no.

He pauses for a moment, studying me. "Always." He gives me a small smile and squeezes my hand, then reaches into his pocket. He hands me his cell. "Call your parents. They'll be thrilled to hear from you."

I take the phone. "Thank you."

He shrugs.

"No, thank you for agreeing to still be friends."

"Call your parents," he says sternly, obviously done with this conversation.

I dial the number and wait for my mom to pick up. When she does, she tells me she and my dad are turning around and headed my way. As I talk to her, I can't help but catch Dane's eye. He's looking at me, but it seems as if he's looking through me. I mouth "What's wrong?" while still listening to my mother. His eyes snap to mine and he shakes his head, replacing his sad smile with a more genuine one.

I hang up and hand him his phone. "They're on their way."

"Good. I think you should rest." He stands. "I'll see you later."

"You don't have to go," I protest. "Wait with me until they get here."

He gives me a small smile. "I can't."

"Why not?"

He steps forward and leans down to me. He reaches around my neck, holding me gently, and presses a soft kiss to the top of my head. "Feel better, Grace."

He walks out the door before I can stop him.

WHEN I ARRIVE home with my parents, Mike, Kate, Matt and Shel are all waiting for me. Shel wraps me in a hug that rivals a boa constrictor.

"Jesus girl." She holds me tightly.

Matt envelops both of us in a huge bear hug. When they release me, my brother walks up awkwardly. I can tell he has a lot to say but doesn't know how to start. I make the first move and embrace him instead, followed by Kate.

"We're so glad you're all right," she says in my ear.

Mike, Kate, Shel and Matt did an amazing job of cleaning up the house after Patrick's "visit." There's almost no sign that anything happened, with the exception of the broken door and missing vase. We all end up in the living room where Shel sits protectively by my side and where the discussion, inevitably, revolves around the events of last night. Even though the room is full of familiar loving faces, I can't help but see Patrick, Dane, and James just about everywhere I look. I try to keep the details brief when I'm asked questions; I'm going to have to relive everything tomorrow morning, when the police send over an officer to collect my official statement. I spend a lot of time staring at the floor.

After about an hour or so, people start to grumble about hunger and pizza is delivered. I pick at my plate and look at the faces that surround me. My friends and family eat, smile, and laugh while the gross topic of my attack is abandoned, for now. An overwhelming feeling of love and gratitude washes over me. My heart wants to burst with the feelings I have for these people, for how much they love me, and I love them. For how much they know what I need. Then, suddenly, my heart pinches with sadness. Two very important people I love dearly are missing around my table–James and Dane.

My manager Kris calls in the middle of our impromptu dinner party to express how horrified she is by what's happened. I didn't ask, but I assume she was told by Dane. The doctor who discharged me from the hospital wrote me off of work for one week. Kris demands I take two.

"Don't worry." Shel smiles after I get off the phone. "We'll find ways to keep busy."

Our guests hang out longer than I expected, and by the time I look at the clock it's just after ten. My dad turns on the TV, and my attack makes the news. I don't know why I would expect any different, especially since we live in a relatively small town. Thankfully, the details are very generic and my name is withheld.

I decide that now is as good a time as any to call it a night. "Thanks for coming over," I tell Mike and Kate as I hug them goodbye.

"Love you, Ems." My brother squeezes me.

My mom reminds me that she'll be waking me every hour to check on me per doctor's instructions. My dad hugs me good night, as does Matt. Shel follows me to my room.

"You'd think I was leaving or something with all the hugging," I say to Shel as we step into my bedroom.

She turns to me and wraps me in another constrictor-like grasp.

"Oooookay."

She steps back. "Do you know how much you scared us?" she asks anxiously. "I mean, it wasn't your fault, but the whole idea ..." She hugs herself and shudders. "God Em, how are you handling this?"

"I don't know," I say honestly. "One minute I'm fine. Then the next my mind is replaying what happened, which creeps me out entirely. Then the next minute, I'm fine again."

Shel looks at me with sympathy. "You should have stayed with us at Matt's. Then this wouldn't have happened. Why did you leave anyway?"

I ignore her question but refute her theory. "Based on what Patrick said, he would have found another time to get to me." I look over at my bedroom window, the window that he said he came through. A chill runs down my spine. "Shel?"

"Yeah?"

"Will you stay with me tonight?"

"Of course! One sec." She leaves the room and I hear her descend the stairs, telling my parents and Matt that she'll be spending the night here.

I walk over and study myself in my bedroom mirror. The right side of my face is swollen, and there's a shadow of a bruise around my eye and a darker one across my cheek. I look like I haven't slept in weeks. I remember the feeling of Patrick's backhand and wince. Ouch.

I pull out pajamas for Shel, change into my own, and then crawl into bed, keeping an eye on the window the entire time. My dad said he repaired the lock and logic tells me Patrick's not coming back through it, but my heart still picks up its pace. I look around the room hoping to see James. I know he can't stay with Shel here, but I could really use even the briefest glimpse of his face. I expected to see him sometime today. My heart skips a beat. Is Garrett upset with him? Did his involvement in protecting me cross some sort of Guardian line? Or is he now processing the kiss with Dane?

Shel reappears in my doorway. She grabs the pj's, changes, turns out the light, and crawls in my bed to lie opposite of me.

"Thanks," I say.

"Absolutely not a problem."

We lay in silence for a few moments.

"Do you want to talk or do you want to sleep?" she asks.

"A little of both, I guess. Just ... let's not talk about Patrick."

"Done." She pauses. "Why did you leave Matt's?"

Ugh. I should have known she wouldn't leave it alone. I decide to tell her, since I've already discussed it with Dane. "Dane kissed me."

I can see the outline of her reaction in the dark. Her eyes grow wide, her mouth forms an O. "Well, then, that explains a lot."

"How do you mean?"

"When Matt and I came back with the food we found Dane sitting alone. Matt asked where you were, and he said that you had to leave. I tried to call you, but you wouldn't answer. After, like, almost an hour he just suddenly stood up, said goodbye, and left."

I make a face in the darkness. "My reaction to his kiss was ... kind of harsh."

"Emmmmma," Shel draws out my name, like she's disappointed in the way I handled things.

"You know I love James," I defend myself.

"And you know he's gone, right?" she comes back.

"Seriously? Thanks for the reminder."

She sighs. "I just want you to be happy."

"Who says I'm not happy?"

I can see her glaring at me. She makes a wise choice, though, and drops it.

"Besides, Dane and I talked this morning," I elaborate. "I told him we could only be friends."

"Hmm." Shel purses her lips. "So that's why he wasn't here tonight."

"No. We talked *this morning*. He didn't need to come by again."

Shel flops from her side to her back, making the whole bed shake. "Emma, I'm trying to remain calm."

"Please do," I say sarcastically.

She turns her head to me. "The man saves your life. Bleeds for you. Stays by your bedside for an entire night while you're under observation in a hospital. And you give him the friends line?"

"Who says he was there the entire night?"

"Um, your parents! They didn't even know who he was to begin with. He didn't even want the stitches; he just wanted to be with you."

I groan. This is worse than I thought.

"Couldn't you have at least said you could only be friends *for now?* Give the guy a little hope?"

I sigh. This is so much more involved than she knows, more involved than she can know. I look at her squarely through the darkness. "I love James. I will always love James. End of story."

She meets my stare head on and fires back. "Are you saying that to convince me ... or yourself?"

CHAPTER 31

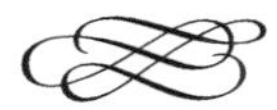

I lie on my bed and stare at the ceiling. Shel left a little while ago, and I ponder her question. I never answered it. I hate that she asked it.

"Emma."

I sit up quickly. Too quickly. My head swims a little, but I can still focus on James. My body sags with relief, Shel's question forgotten. "Hi."

He's immediately by my side, holding my face in his hands. His eyes focus on my bruises and the swelling. His face turns grim. "Are you in pain?"

Shaking my head, I smile, happy he's finally here. "I have some pretty great pills. Vicodin."

James frowns as he continues to look me over.

I place my hands on top of his. "Stop."

He stares into my eyes, and all I can see is worry and distress in his. "How badly are you hurt?"

I sigh and remove my hands from my face. He does the same. "I have a mild concussion."

James closes his eyes as if in pain himself. "I'm so sorry," he whispers.

"It's not your fault," I reassure him. "It could have been a lot worse. No one saw this coming."

"Exactly." He stands and starts to pace.

His anxiety worries me. "What's wrong?"

"Everything."

My heart plummets at his response. "Everything?" *This is it,* my mind shouts at me, *Patrick. Dane. It's all pushing him away from you.*

I stand and approach him. "Tell me what's wrong. We can make it right."

He looks at me, searching my face. "I can't protect you."

I wrap my arms around his waist. "I don't need protecting. Patrick will be arrested, and that's the end of him. And besides, you did protect me. What you did … what you're able to do … it helped save me."

He reluctantly wraps his arms around me. The cool feeling penetrates my clothes and soothes my skin. "Helped," he snorts and rests his forehead against mine. "You deserve better than that."

"I deserve you," I say adamantly. "Someone who sacrificed eternity to become a Guardian? In order to come back to me from death? I'd say that qualifies as best." James kisses my forehead, and I let out a heavy breath. "I'm the one who should be apologizing. Not you."

He steps back from me. "For kissing … him?" He can't even say Dane's name.

I look up at him, ashamed. "Yes."

James places his hands on my shoulders and gives me a concentrated stare. "I won't lie. I was angry."

I knew this, but hearing him say it feels like I've been punched in the stomach. "I … I resisted and then I don't know what happened," I sadly confess. "When I heard your voice I knew …"

"You were caught?" James finishes my sentence.

I silently pray that the floor will open up and swallow me whole. Quickly.

"I always think you're watching," I whisper. "I didn't plan for it to happen; it was never my intention …"

He wraps his arms around me, cutting me off. "It doesn't matter."

"What do you mean it doesn't matter? Of course it matters."

"You were brutally attacked in front of me. I could have lost you. If not physically then quite possibly mentally. Talk about a wakeup call," he says. "Am I upset that you kissed him? Yes." He pulls away from me. "But that doesn't make me love you any less."

I blink at him in disbelief. "Are you serious?"

He nods as his bright blue eyes cloud over. "It only makes me realize some things about myself."

I move my arms to reach around his neck. "I spoke with Dane yesterday. I told him straight out we could only be friends."

"I saw."

"You saw? Why didn't you say something?"

"You had company."

"I didn't think you came to visit me at all in the hospital. I was wondering where you were; I was worried you were in trouble again."

"No, I'm not in trouble. I was with you through the night." James pauses and shakes his head. "Me on one side of the bed and Dane on the other. It was an interesting evening." He sighs. "I can't hate the guy as much as I'd like to. Don't get me wrong; he's not my favorite person. But, he did something for you I couldn't."

"I love you. You know that, right?"

He shakes his cloudy look away and gives me a small smile. "I do." His arms encircle my waist, and he leans in to kiss me. What starts as a gentle kiss grows into something hungry. "I love you. Never forget that," he says when we part.

I don't like the sadness in his eyes. "I'll never be able to forget. You're mine for eternity, remember?"

"Emma!" my mother shouts up the stairs. "Sergeant Reynolds is here!"

"I have to give my statement to the police," I tell James. "Can you stay with me?"

"I'll stay as long as I can," he says, his eyes boring into mine.

I nod and turn to head downstairs. James follows close behind.

~

SHEL KEEPS me busy over the next week with something planned each day. If it's not lunch, it's shopping. If it's not shopping, it's a movie. If it's not a movie, it's a trip to the beach or Matt's pool. I sincerely feel like she doesn't want me left alone for any period of time. I don't know if she's worried I'll be attacked again, or if she's just trying to make the most of the time we have left this summer. Probably both. It's already mid-July. She will be returning to Ann Arbor in about two weeks; I'll be headed back to school mid-August.

I got a letter in the mail from Western approving my housing application for my senior year. While this is great news, it also brought back some bittersweet memories. I'll be residing off campus in an apartment building of sorts, an older home that has been converted into four apartments for students. This is what James and I had planned. To live together, graduate together, hurry up and start the rest of our lives together. I can't be too sad about it, though. While our relationship is anything but traditional, he is still with me. Garrett has been a little more lenient with him since the attack, and James has been able to spend almost every night of the last week in my room. He's been in a melancholy mood, however, and I can't seem to shake him out of it.

Receiving the housing letter prompts me to get in gear and get registered for the fall semester. I'm on my laptop, trying to compare the classes that are offered with the ones I need, when Shel calls.

"What are you doing?"

"Trying to register for classes."

"Oh. Well be ready at six."

"For what?"

"Dinner. I'm picking you up. You like Mario's, right?"

I roll my eyes. "Yes, I like Mario's. You know, we don't have to do something together every day. Take Matt out tonight. I'm sure he would like to spend some time with you. I can share," I laugh.

"No worries; he's coming with us."

"Oh. Well then, I really don't need to go. You two have fun."

Silence. Silence is never a good sign with Shel.

"Shel?"

"Dane will be there, too. Gotta go. See you at six," she rushes and hangs up on me.

I should have known. I shrug and end the call. It'll be nice to see the guys for a change.

Shel arrives promptly at six. It's only when she asks "You're wearing *that?*" that I realize what she's up to.

"Shelby Elizabeth Moore," I say through clenched teeth. "Please tell me you're not doing what I think you're doing."

She feigns innocence. "I'm not doing what you think I'm doing–whatever it is." She avoids my stare. "Get in the car."

I'm still suspicious. "Where are Matt and Dane?" I ask as I eye the empty vehicle.

"They're meeting us there," she says nonchalantly. "Now get in the car. We'll be late."

On our way to the restaurant, Shel receives a text from Matt. "What's up?" I ask her.

"Nothing," she says a bit too quickly. "The guys are already there."

We pull into the restaurant, park, and walk inside. I expect to see Matt and Dane waiting for us in the lobby, but they aren't there. Shel approaches the hostess and tells her we're expected. She made a reservation? My suspicion level jumps through the roof.

The hostess walks us through the restaurant to where Matt is seated. I smile and wave until I notice he's seated at a small table, a table for two. I glare at Shel as she takes the seat across from him.

"Sorry, Em," Matt says pulling my attention from Shel. "They didn't have a table available for four." He smiles like a guilty child.

I put my hands on my hips and shoot Shel a look that would probably have killed her if it could. She smiles shyly and dangles her car keys from her hand, letting me know that she drove and I'm unable leave, unless I want to walk.

"This way please," the hostess nudges me.

I begrudgingly follow her and sigh. Oh well. Shel has no idea how much this won't work. Both Dane and I know what's what.

We come upon him seated at a similar two-person table still in eyeshot of Matt and Shel.

"Hey," I say somewhat annoyed as I sink into the seat.

"Grace." He nods and looks amused.

I can't help but laugh. I haven't been called that in a while. "How did you get roped into this?"

He smiles. "Probably the same way you did."

"Well, I'm sorry," I apologize. "Shel doesn't seem to believe anything I say."

He regards me. "Friends can have dinner, right?"

"Of course." I smile and pick up the menu. "Do you know what you want?"

His eyes flash to mine and hold them for a moment before he reaches for the drink menu. "I decided what I wanted a while ago."

"My favorite is their fettuccine alfredo," I continue, ignoring his comment. My face feels hot all of a sudden.

He notices my blush. "Relax," he says. "Matt and I have been here for like fifteen minutes. I seriously know what I want."

Oh. Okay.

Our waitress appears with glasses of water and takes our order, since my favorite is the alfredo and Dane's so on top of "what he wants." He orders a Stromboli.

"How's work been?" I ask.

"Good. Boring. You know you could come up and visit."

"Sorry. Shel has me going somewhere every day. And I mean *every day*. I think she thinks I need constant supervision."

"You only have a week left off," he reminds me. "You'd better get up there to say hi sooner rather than later."

"Why the rush? You miss me that much?"

He smiles at my teasing, shaking his head. "My last day is the 20th."

Why does this news hurt my heart? My face falls before I can stop it. "You're quitting?"

He nods and takes a drink. "I have to. I thought Shel told you I have another job."

That's right. The artist thing. "Right." I shake my head to clear my thoughts. "What is your other job exactly?"

"I freelance graphic design stuff for a company called Legionnaire.

When they get an advertising contract, they call me. A big project just came through."

I'm impressed, and my face shows it. "Wow. Your dad disapproves of this job why?" I remember he told me his father was overjoyed by his late interest in Bay Woods.

"He doesn't think it's stable. The projects come when they come." He shrugs. "But it's worked out for me for three years, so I can't complain."

Huh. "Well, it won't be the same working without you." This is really bumming me out.

Dane winks at me. "You know where I live."

The waitress appears with our food, and I glance at Shel and Matt. They appear to be enjoying their dinner. Shel catches my eye and enthusiastically waves at me. I give her a small smile.

We eat in silence. For some reason, the alfredo doesn't taste as good as I remember. I swirl the noodles around my plate.

"What are you thinking about?" Dane asks me, curious.

I wasn't thinking about anything really. "Um, school," I throw out. "I got my housing acceptance. I registered today."

Dane nods, chewing. "You know, I've never been out to Western. A lot of my friends went to different schools, but not that one. Maybe I could come out and visit. When are you headed back?"

My heart beats twice, and I reprimand it. "The middle of August sometime."

"Do you need any help moving your stuff?"

No, I think. My dad and I have it covered between his truck and my car. "Sure, we could use a hand." I want to smack myself. What is wrong with me?

"Cool. Just let me know," he says conversationally.

Dane clears his plate. I have half a platter of fettuccine left. The waitress returns to ask if I want a box. I tell her yes. Maybe my dad will eat it.

"Will this be on one check or two?" she asks us.

"One."

"Two."

I look at Dane. "I can pay for my own food."

Regardless, he looks at the waitress. "One."

I shoot him an irritated look. He just smirks at me.

I turn my head to see if Shel and Matt have finished eating as well. When I look at their table, it's empty. "Are you kidding me?"

Dane laughs. "Guess I'm taking you home."

I sigh loudly and cross my arms. He pretends to pout. "You don't want me to take you home?"

"No, I'm irritated at Shel, not you."

He laughs again. "She's a crafty one. I have to give her that."

"You have no idea."

The waitress brings the bill, and I try to snatch it from his hand as he picks it up off the table. I only manage to rip the corner. Dane laughs at me. "Your injuries are making you slow."

I shoot him a look. "At least let me cover the tip."

He considers it and nods.

"How much is it?" I reach for the check.

He holds it out to show me, and I quickly grab it from his hand. "Ha!" I say victoriously and jump up from the table. I walk as quickly as I can without running to the register at the front of the restaurant. I'm pretty sure he won't chase me through a crowd.

When I make it to the counter, I pay, asking the cashier to give our waitress her portion. I feel Dane walk up behind me. I can feel his–what? Anticipation? Humor? Irritation? radiating off of him. I can't bring myself to turn around.

I walk to the front of the restaurant, and Dane reaches around me to hold the door open. I finally look at him. "After you." He smirks. It sounds more like a challenge than a pleasantry.

We walk outside and he takes the lead; I don't know where he's parked although I'd recognize his Camaro anywhere. I follow him around the back of Mario's to where he's parked in the street.

"May I open the door for you, or would you like to do that yourself as well?" he asks, amused.

I try to suppress a smile by biting my lip. "If you would be so kind. I wouldn't want to break a nail."

He opens the door in dramatic fashion, and I crawl inside the car.

The entire way to my house we don't speak, and we don't make eye contact. There's tension in the car, but it's not angry. It's more electric and fun, like who's going to break the silence first with a sarcastic comment.

When we pull into my driveway, I don't know what to say. I'm trying to think of something smart and witty, but nothing will formulate in my brain. When Dane stops the car, he surprises me by getting out and coming around to my side to open my door for me again. When he does, I step out of the car and give him a curious look.

"Your nails." He nods toward my hands. "I wouldn't want them harmed entering or exiting the vehicle."

Raising my eyebrows, I nod in agreement. "Ah. That's very thoughtful of you." I step aside, and he shuts the door.

I open my mouth to thank him for the ride and then jump as he slams both of his hands down on either side of me, against the car, boxing me in. "What …?"

He leans in close, his eyes staring directly into mine making my heart race. "You. Are. So. Difficult."

I'm speechless. All I know is my heart is flipping out, and my legs feel weak. *Stop it,* my mind screams. *Stop this!*

He pushes himself off the car and away from me. My brain is relieved he put distance between us, but my body wants him to close that distance and come back. Now.

"I have to go," I mumble and start to walk away from him. He doesn't stop me. "Thank you for falling into Shel's trap," I say as I back toward the door.

His face is dead serious. "It's not her trap I've fallen into."

Holy shit. I give him a small nervous wave, turn tail, and make a beeline for the back door.

CHAPTER 32

"Will you tell me what is bothering you already?" I ask James. This mood of his is starting to wear on me. Between his gloominess, and Shel's begging me to go visit Dane at the golf course every two minutes, I'm about ready to pull my hair out.

"It's nothing."

"That's what you always say. You've been like this for weeks. What gives?"

James simply leans forward and places a kiss on my forehead. "Don't worry about it."

I sigh in frustration. "You'd make me tell you if it were me," I complain.

James sits up and looks down at me. We've been curled up together for most of the afternoon while I read and he plays with my hair. Ever since he was able to throw Patrick he's been getting really good at physical manipulation. My hair actually moves when he touches it now. So far, it only works regularly on really light things, like hair or a piece of paper. But despite this breakthrough, something continues to bother him. He's been silent lately. When he doesn't think I'm looking he wears a far off expression, like his mind is constantly preoccupied. Whenever he catches me scrutinizing him, he quickly rearranges his face. When I ask what's wrong, he always responds with "nothing."

My cell rings again for the fiftieth time today. Okay, maybe not fiftieth, more like tenth. But it's been ten calls in the last two hours. It's Shel. Again. I let the call go to voice mail. A minute later my phone buzzes with a message.

"Maybe you should talk to her," James suggests.

"No, I know what she wants." I shrug it off. "It's not a big deal to me."

She wants me to go up to Bay Woods with her. It's Dane's last day of work. I've managed to avoid him for the last week, and I'm not going to walk into another one of her schemes again.

My phone buzzes with a text. I look at it. *Answer your phone!!*

Denied. I put the phone down.

It buzzes again. I sigh and pick it up. *Don't think I won't come get your ass!*

"Ugh!" I throw the phone down, and it bounces on the bed.

Suddenly, James jumps up. He looks wide-eyed and a little panicked.

"I didn't mean to scare you," I laugh. He doesn't look at me. "What is it?" I ask, standing, worried now.

He realizes I've asked him a question. He focuses on me and swallows. "I have to go," he whispers.

"Is it Garrett?"

"Yes. And no." He looks at me longingly. He takes my face in his hands and plants a soft, full kiss on my lips. "I'll see you later," he says as he steps back.

My mind snaps with precognition. Why don't I believe him? "Come back to me," I demand.

He nods. "I will. I promise." My phone starts to ring yet again. "Answer Shel," he says. "Do whatever it is she wants you to do. It'll pass the time until I can get back."

I eye him warily.

"I love you," he says as he fades from my vision.

"I love you, too."

~

Shel impatiently taps her fingers on the steering wheel as we sit at a stoplight. I caved in, answered her call, listened to James, and agreed to visit Bay Woods. Plus, I need to check the schedule since I start back on Monday. As we sit at the light, I try to think of all the possible scenarios she may be concocting to get me alone with Dane again. I think I should be safe, but you never know. Besides, if she does decide to leave me, this time I'll just drive a golf cart home.

"Come on!" Shel groans at the light.

"Why are you in such a hurry?" I ask.

"It's Dane's last day."

"And?"

She gives me a sarcastic stare.

I shoot her an exasperated look to match her stare. "I told you to stop with this matchmaker crap."

"Who's playing matchmaker?" She hits the gas.

"You."

She ignores me. "He asked you to stop by and see him before his last day. You never went. That's not being a very good friend," she sniffs.

"I should never have told you that."

We make it to the course in record time thanks to Shelby Andretti. She leaps from the car and waits impatiently as I take my time getting out. When we enter the pro shop, the first person I see is Kris. She gives me an enormous smile and wraps me in a warm hug.

"I'm so glad to see you! How are you feeling? Ready to come back?"

"Completely cured and ready," I say with a small smile.

"Well, well, well." I hear Dane as he enters the pro shop behind us from the concession area. I turn to see him check his watch. "Your timing is impeccable," he notes. "I'll only be employed here for another ten minutes."

Shel shoots me a nasty look.

"I wasn't sure of this one's motives." I jerk my thumb toward Shel.

She turns and starts a conversation with Kris, so she won't have to respond to my accusation. I look at Dane and he's wearing that damn grin of his. "I need to check the schedule," I tell him.

I leave the three of them and head to the office to look up my hours. Ten to four on Monday with someone named Leslie. Sounds doable. I take a glance at the rest of the week to buy time. I'm not going to lie. Seeing Dane after a week is making my pulse race. Why does he have this effect on me all of a sudden? I worked a month with him and never had this problem! This is not okay. We have to go. What excuse can I use?

"Find everything?" Dane's voice is right behind me, and I jump about a foot into the air.

"Geez!"

"Sorry," he laughs. He walks over to put his shift paperwork on Kris's desk.

"Who's Leslie?" I ask for a lack of anything better to say.

"Oh, she's new. You'll like her. Older lady." Dane walks back around me. He grabs his time card. "Well," he pauses as he stamps it in the machine, "I guess this is the end."

"The end?"

He puts his card back and turns to me. "The end of my excuse to spend time with you."

I swallow.

"Unless you can think of another one." He smiles.

"It's …" I stutter. "It's not like you won't be coming around here."

Dane looks at me, shaking his head in disbelief. "See you around then," he says as he turns to leave.

I'm having a hard time breathing as I watch him go. All I can manage to do is give him half a wave.

He walks out of the office and out of my line of vision. I look down and let my breath out in a huff. It's not like I won't ever see him again, right? We're supposed to be friends. I shake my head to clear it of my crazy thoughts. This is ridiculous. I don't need to be around him.

I decide to hang out a few extra minutes in the office, so that I can avoid running into him again on my way out. When I estimate enough time has been wasted, I walk back to the pro shop to find a seething Shel.

"What?" I ask.

She says nothing and walks out of the shop with her arms crossed. I give Kris a wave and tell her I'll see her on Monday. I follow Shel to the car and get inside. She immediately turns on me.

"He says you're not interested."

I give her an exasperated look.

"I gave him your number."

"You did what?"

She smiles sweetly at me. "You're welcome."

~

Back at home, I try to pass the time by picking up where I left off reading. Will I ever finish this damn book? I'm having a hard time concentrating on the words. Where is James? I hope everything is all right. I silently pray this won't turn into one of his prolonged absences. That will surely drive me insane.

My phone buzzes with a text. What does Shel want now? I already fulfilled her demands for the day. I roll over and pick up my phone. The text is from a number I don't recognize and contains only one word.

Grace?

I hang my head. And so it begins. I respond *Yes?*

A minute passes. *Just making sure this is really you and not the pizza joint.*

I smile. *Really me.*

My phone goes silent. I set it down and pick up the book. I actually get a chapter in before my phones buzzes again. I look at the message.

Come over.

My mouth falls open. Come over? Is he serious? My heart involuntarily starts to beat double time. No. No, no, no, no, no.

I send back: *Sorry. Can't.,* then set the phone down.

Buzz. *Why?*

Maybe I should just turn my phone off. I hit 'Reply' and stare at the empty screen trying to find a reason. The reason I want to send is 'James.' I wonder how that would go over.

I feel the hair rise on the back of my neck, like someone is watching me. I look to my right, over my shoulder, and see James has returned.

"Hey." I toss my phone aside. I swing my legs off the bed so I sit facing him. "So, what's up? Everything okay?"

James wears a haunted expression. He looks lost and anxious.

My pulse picks up as I take in his demeanor. "What's wrong?" I ask nervously as I stand and walk toward him.

His eyes focus on me and soften a little. "I've been assigned a Ward," he says quietly.

I breathe a sigh of relief. "That's … that's sooner than we thought." I try to bring my pounding heart under control. "But this is a good thing, right? It means you've done well."

He looks at me like he wants to say more, but he can't find the words.

"This means we'll see less of each other, doesn't it?" I ask sadly, remembering our conversation from weeks ago. I wrap my arms around his waist and place my head against his chest like I always do. How will we manage to see less of each other?

James makes no move to hold me. I glance down to see he hasn't moved and then look up into his face anxiously. "Does this mean you can't touch me anymore?" I ask, panicked.

"Emma." James places his hands against my shoulders and steps out of my arms. "You are my Ward."

His statement takes a moment to register. "How … how is that possible?"

"Your Guardian has been released," he says gently.

"You said that rarely ever happens." I blink, confused. My heart begins to pound as my mind races back in time. I remember how adamant James was over the idea of being my Guardian, how it was against their rules, how he wouldn't be able to love me anymore. "What does this mean?" I whisper.

James looks down and slowly takes my hands. He stares at them while he speaks. "It means I will always be bound to you. That I will be the one to guide and protect you throughout your life."

"Until I release you?" I ask hopefully, choosing not to remember that he told me it would be impossible if he were my Guardian.

He continues to look at our hands and shakes his head no. When he looks up, his expression is full of pain. "I am no longer allowed to love you."

I feel like my breath has been knocked from my chest. "How did this happen?"

"Garrett assigned me. He felt I was ready."

"Why would he assign you to me?" I ask him, distraught. "Is this a punishment?"

James closes his eyes. "When your Guardian was released, Garrett saw it as a way to help me." He stares at me again. "Ever since you were attacked I knew I couldn't bear to lose you, whether some outside force or a new love took you from me. I couldn't shake that possibility from my mind, and I let my mood overshadow everything else. Garrett saw this, and he understood it. He explained binding you to me as my Ward will keep me in your life for as long as you live. And at least I'll have that. Because the likelihood of you choosing me in the end, the likelihood of you releasing me, is ... small."

"No," I shake my head, trying to erase what is happening. "Who is he to say what I would decide? He doesn't know how I feel!"

James looks at me defeated.

"Where's *my* choice?" I demand of him, pointing to my chest. "I don't choose this!"

"It's not up to you."

I clench my fists as my eyes fill with angry tears. The pain in my face is registered in his. "I love you. I need you in my life."

"And I will be," James tries to reassure me. "I'll still be able to see you, to talk to you."

"But you won't be allowed to love me," I say flatly.

James shakes his head as he sadly responds. "No."

Tears spill over, and I hold my head in my trembling hands. James moves to wrap his arms around me. I feel his cool touch move up and down my back, comforting me. What did he say before? That protecting and guiding me without loving me would be torture. Garrett has committed him–us–to an existence of pain.

"Please don't cry," James pleads. He sounds like he is near tears himself.

"I can't do this," I say into his chest.

He whispers into my hair, holding me tighter. "I never wanted to hurt you."

I move and wrap my arms around him. "And I never want to hurt you."

James kisses my hair and continues to stroke my back. "I don't know how I'm going to stop loving you," he confesses.

We stand motionless, holding one another as time passes. It could be minutes; it could be hours. I'm not sure. My tears eventually slow, and my throat feels thick. I think about how hard this is going to be for the both of us and realize how much harder it will be for him. There are powers at work here I can't even begin to comprehend.

"What happens now?" I ask, breaking the silence.

"I go back," he says quietly. "I'll look in on you and know when I'm needed and when I'm not. I'll be capable of spending time with you, but … that will probably make things difficult."

I know what he means. "What happens if you can't stop loving me?"

James pulls away slightly, so he can look into my eyes. "I was told I would be given some time to learn to control my feelings toward you. But if I can't, I will be forced to forget. Those who rule the Intermediate, The Allegiant, will take my memories of you. They will make me forget everything we ever had."

Tears spring back into my eyes. My memories of James are my most treasured; the thought of someone forcing them from me breaks my heart. I can tell from his expression he feels the same. I would never want that for him.

I have to push myself to speak. There's not one part of me that wants this, but I have to do it for him. "I want you to stay away from me," I say quietly. "Don't visit."

He looks at me bewildered. "How could you say that?"

"I would rather you stay away than jeopardize your memory. Take all the time you need to comply with their wishes. Do you even know what else they are capable of doing to you? No," I shake my head, "I want you safe. I would never want you to forget us."

James looks heartbroken just as I'm sure I do. "I don't know if I can do that."

"Please," I ask him, tears falling again. "Please do it for me. I would die if you couldn't remember how much I love you."

He nods slowly and then leans in to kiss me softly. "I love you more than life itself. Never forget that."

I'm just about to tell him the same when his head snaps up. I know that's his cue to leave; something, someone must be calling him. I look at him frantic. When will I see him again?

"Remember I love you," I say quickly, tears pouring down my face now.

He nods and holds me tighter, as if he can stop the pull that draws him back. He fades from my vision, still wrapped around me. I can feel him grow warmer and warmer, until he disappears completely.

I don't think I've ever felt so hollow and alone. My body can't compensate for all that it's feeling, and I stand there, numb, staring into oblivion.

James has left me.

I told him to stay away.

I love him with everything in me. And he can never love me again.

MINUTES PASS. My phone vibrates, and I pick it up mechanically. *You never answered my question. Why can't you come over?*

I blink, then reply without thinking. *My heart hurts.*

Let me help.

As time passes, the need to get out of my house is overwhelming.

The silence of my room deafens me. Everywhere I look I'm reminded of James. There is an ache in my chest from a seemingly bottomless well of tears and when I close my eyes, all I can see is his haunted last expression. I feel myself slipping back into my protective shell, the one that makes my parents and friends worry. I don't want that. James wouldn't want that. I'm in desperate need of a distraction.

I try Shel first, but if I'm going to be at all honest with myself, I know where I'm going to end up. Still, delusional as I may be, I call Shel four times. And leave four messages. Evidently, she is unavailable.

I stare at my last message from Dane and take a deep breath. I type out my reply and hit send.

Be there in 15 minutes.

CHAPTER 33

I sit outside Dane's place debating whether or not to get out of the car. What in the hell am I doing here? Now that I am no longer surrounded by physical memories of James, am I really that desperate for company? James hasn't been gone but two hours, and I end up at Dane's. I can't even fathom what that says about me.

I lean back in my seat and close my eyes. If I go inside, what would James see? He'd see a friend comforting a friend. Because that's all we are. Does Dane want more? I think so. All I'm really looking for is someone to tell me everything will be all right. Is that so terrible?

A rap on my window startles me, and my eyes fly open. Dane is standing outside my car. He opens the door and leans in. "Did you drive all the way over here to sit in the parking lot?"

I shrug, giving him a weak smile. "I thought about it."

"Well, stay put," he says and closes the door. He walks around to the other side of the car and gets in.

"Are we going somewhere?"

"Yep. I figured you wouldn't mind driving since you like to do manly things, like pick up the tab at restaurants." He smirks.

"Funny. Where are we going?"

"It's a surprise."

I cross my arms. "I'm not starting the car until you tell me where we're going."

He lifts an eyebrow at me. "Is that so?"

I nod.

"Well," he sighs. "I guess we could just stay here in the car and make out ..."

I start the engine.

Dane directs me where to go and when to turn, leading us beyond the south side of town. I haven't figured out where he's taking me until we pull off the highway and turn right. My hunch is correct when he directs me to Kirby's Adventure Land, a family fun center.

"Mini-golf?" I ask him doubtfully.

"It's been scientifically proven to heal the heart."

I roll my eyes.

"Let's go," he says excitedly and hops out of the car.

We walk into the park where he pays for both of us, cutting off my protest before it leaves my lips. Our first stop is the batting cages.

"I've never done this," I say as I hold a helmet in my hands. He gives me a bat and moves me into position over the plate. He takes the helmet from me and places it on my head. "I'm going to miss," I warn him.

"Doesn't matter. The idea is to take out your anger. Pretend whatever it is that's bothering you is coming at you in the form of a baseball–and kill it."

Okay, I think. That doesn't sound so hard. He shows me how to hold the bat and then steps out of the way. The first ball is launched at me, and I automatically jump back. Hmm. I reposition myself and anticipate the next pitch. I'm a little more ready, but I still swing and miss. I miss the next four balls.

I turn around and look at Dane. "This is stupid. I can't do this."

He smiles. "Keep going."

The next ball whizzes past me. And the next. All right, this is getting serious. I refuse to look like a fool. I reposition myself yet again and concentrate harder. I imagine Garrett's face, even though I've never seen him, as the next ball. It's launched toward me, and I actually hit it–kind of. At least I made contact. I turn around and give Dane a surprised look. He gives me a thumbs up.

The next ball is Mrs. Davis. I manage to hit her and the ball goes a little farther. The next ball is Patrick. I swing and make full contact with the ball, sending it all the way back to the pitching machine.

"Not bad," I hear from behind me.

I give myself a satisfied smile. Yeah, I'm starting to like this. Garrett is up again. *Crack!* He goes flying. Mrs. Davis. *Crack!* She heads to the left. Patrick. *Miss.* Whoops. My adrenaline picks up with each swing of the bat; stress is released every time I make contact with a ball. I alternate between Garrett, Mrs. Davis, and Patrick until my pitches are spent. I must say I'm pretty proud of my performance given I hit eleven balls out of my twenty.

Dane meets me at the cage gate. "Feel better?"

"Much." I smile at him and hand him the helmet.

He gives it to the attendant. "Go Karts next?"

We head over to the karts and stand in line. I lean against the fence and watch the other driver's race around the track. My family used to come to this place when Mike and I were kids, although our main activity was mini golf. We'd always play against each other; loser was supposed to buy the ice cream. I smile as I remember how my dad always lost.

Dane turns and challenges me. "What do you say we place a little wager on this race?"

I pretend to look suspicious but grin anyway. "What do you have in mind?"

"Loser buys drinks on the way home."

I think about it and eye the track. I must be feeling over confident from the batting cages. "Deal."

We watch the rest of the race and try to determine which karts are the fastest. Dane thinks the blue one is faster and ends up behind its wheel, while I choose yellow #4. I catch his eye from across two lanes and give him a competitive nod, flexing my hands around the steering wheel.

"Bring it!" he shouts to me.

After the attendants make sure we're secure and start our karts, the countdown begins. The light turns green, and we all peel away from the starting line. I get caught up behind a little boy and his father right off. I try to maneuver around them, but don't manage it until the second turn in the track. Dane is already way ahead of me. I gain a little ground during the second lap as I push the pedal to the floor. I'm right behind him by the third lap. As we round the final turn to start the fourth, I actually start to edge around him. But toward the middle of the lap, my kart starts to sputter and lose speed.

"Noooo!" I yell in frustration as I realize the thing is probably running out of gas. I pump the pedal to make the kart move faster, but it doesn't work. It cuts off and drifts to a stop.

The rest of the racers finish the lap and pull into the starting gate to end the race as I am stuck, stalled out toward the end of the track. I notice Dane looking around to see where I finished as he gets out of his kart. When he spots me, he starts laughing. I slouch in my seat as an attendant runs out to push me off to the side. Stupid yellow #4.

"I told you the blue one was faster," Dane teases me as I walk off the track.

"Yeah, yeah," I mutter under my breath.

He laughs. "I hope you brought money."

I make a face at him but end up smiling. It would be my luck that my kart would run out of gas.

"Are you up for golf?" I ask.

"Sure."

We get our clubs and balls and take a few practice putts. It's getting dark and the whole park is lit up like a stadium. "You sure you want to do eighteen?" I bend down to retrieve my ball. "It's getting late."

"Do you have a curfew?" he asks me.

"No." I shake my head, laughing. "Just checking." Then I have an idea. I've played this putt-putt course a million times; I can completely rock it. "So," I try to ask casually. "Care to place a wager on this particular game?"

He thinks about it and smiles. "I'll play. What were you thinking?"

"If I win, the last loss is void. It never happened."

He grins. "Okay. And if I win, you kiss me."

What? That was not where I was going with this. But … I look out over the course. I remember it well. I look at him and tilt my head confidently. "Deal."

Dane looks shocked that I've actually agreed to this. He quickly rearranges his features and gestures to the first hole. "Ladies first."

After the first nine, I'm only leading by two strokes. I screwed up on six, selecting the left instead of the right hole to shoot my ball out toward the cup. Then on the ninth green, I took a bad bounce off the brick edging, putting me one over par.

"Shoot!" I say with frustration as we start on ten. I try to compensate for the slope in the green, but my ball runs too far to the right.

Dane looks amused. "You take your mini golf pretty seriously," he notes. "Or is it our little wager that has you so determined?"

I look at him annoyed. "Both."

He laughs.

Going into eighteen, we're tied. Figures. I should have known not to trust my rusty skills. Dane takes his time setting up his ball and perusing the hole, trying to figure out the best way to attack it. I wait impatiently; I know exactly how to play this hole. He finally takes his putt … and sinks a hole in one.

Damn it.

He looks at me victoriously and walks over to take the score card from my hand. He puts an overly exaggerated "1" in the box. "Your turn," he challenges me as his eyes light up.

Okay. I can do this. I give him a solid stare and walk over to place my ball. I set my feet, readjust my grip on the putter, and line up my shot. I hit the ball.

And sink another hole in one.

"Yes!" I raise my arms in victory. I walk arrogantly over to him and take the score card, putting an even more obnoxious "1" in my column. "That," I say, "was all for you."

Dane gives me a crooked smile and shakes his head in disbelief. "Excellent putt, Miss Donohue."

I take a little bow. "Why, thank you."

We head back to the beginning of the course to turn in our putters.

"So, we tied," Dane muses.

"Seems that way."

"So, you didn't win."

"Um, no." I look at him like he's crazy.

"So, you owe me a drink."

"What?"

"I didn't lose," he points out and smiles.

I make a face and concede. "Fine. Where do you want to go?"

WE END up at a small bar down the street from Adventure Land. This is somewhere I never would have come alone. The exterior is dark and dingy with a blinking "open" sign in the window. To me the Parker Lounge screams horror movie.

"Are you sure this is where you want to go?" I ask Dane cautiously as we get out of the car. I eye the motorcycles parked in the lot.

"It's not that bad." He holds the door for me.

He's right. Kind of. The inside of the bar is homier. There's a scattering of small round tables with a red jar candle lit in the center of each one. Most of the room is filled with the requisite bar, but a colorful jukebox is set at the far end. A couple dances in the small space in front of it while Elvis croons "Can't Help Falling in Love."

We take a seat at the bar. A gruff looking bartender with a bushy gray beard and kind eyes leaves a group of men at the end and comes over. He looks at us like we must be lost. "Can I help you?"

Dane looks at me. "What'll it be?"

"You won the bet." I make myself comfortable on the stool. "Order what you want."

"You're not going to get anything?"

I consider it. "Do you have Coke?" I ask Long John Silver.

He nods.

Dane scoffs. "A Coke? Really?"

"What's wrong with that?"

Dane sighs. "We'll take a Coke and a draft." He nods toward the tap in front of him.

"I.D.?" Long John Silver asks.

Dane pulls out his wallet to show him his driver's license. Long John is appeased and sets to getting our drinks. I look around the room nervously as we wait for his return.

"Why are you so on edge?" Dane asks. "It's just a bar."

"I don't know," I answer honestly. The people look nice enough.

"Out of your element?" He smiles. "Trying something new can be hard," he says with mock sympathy.

I glare at him, but then cave in and smile. "Just drink your default beer," I say as Long John returns with our fabulous order. I glance at my Coke and there's an unexpected cherry in it. I look up and smile at Long John, and he smiles back at me.

"Default beer?"

"You totally won that race by default. I only lost due to equipment failure."

He laughs. "That could be true."

"It is true."

"I guess we'll need a rematch to test your true Go Kart skills," he teases and takes a drink. "So," he pauses, "how's your heart?"

"Hmm?" I ask as I swallow.

"Your heart. How's it feeling now?"

Honestly, I forgot all about it. But that's what I wanted, what I came to him looking for. "It's much better," I admit. "Thank you."

He nods. "Mission accomplished."

I look down and swirl my drink around with my straw.

"When do you think it might be completely healed?" Dane asks, staring at his glass.

Good question. I can't tell him James was just taken from me a second time. "Eventually," I say in a small voice. It's the best answer I can give him.

He nods again, still focused on his glass, and takes another drink. "There's no set time for grief, is there?"

I shake my head. "I wish I could explain it to you."

"Oh, I don't know," he says and gives me a slight smile. "I might understand it more than you think."

My eyebrows shoot up. This is news. "How so?"

"I lost my mom when I was fourteen."

I physically wince. "I'm so sorry."

He surprises me by smiling. "She had cancer, but she was a fighter. And so stubborn." He looks at me pointedly. "Kind of like someone else I know."

I give him a sheepish look.

"Still, she had the best attitude toward everything in life, even her disease. She always found the time to laugh. If she was upset, she didn't show it much." He looks back across the bar. "It was a long time ago, but you never completely get over something like that, you know?"

I nod with sympathy and understanding. Yeah, I know.

We sit in silence for a few minutes. Dane finally turns to me. "I didn't mean to bring down the party."

I smile. "You didn't. Thanks for sharing that with me. You didn't have to."

He holds his glass to his lips. "It just goes to show you we have more in common than you think." He takes a swig of his beer. "One of the many lessons my mom taught me is that you can't let too many things pass you by. You have to be willing to take risks. If it's a mistake, it's a mistake. Learn from it and move on."

"Sounds like she was a very wise woman."

"Well," he hesitates. "She was in most things." He winks at me.

I sense there is another story there.

Dane looks over at the dancing couple. "Care to join them?"

Yes, my mind answers, but "Um, no I don't think so," comes out of my mouth.

He nods like he knew that was coming. "Promise me one thing," he says, looking directly at me.

"What's that?"

"I get one dance with you before you leave town."

That's a weird request. My brow furrows. When will we be somewhere together to dance? Probably nowhere. But then again, I never imagined us in this particular place tonight.

He looks at me expectantly, tilting his head in anticipation of my answer.

"Okaaay," I fake annoyance. "I promise."

He seems satisfied with this. He finishes his beer and sets the glass down. "Ready to go? Or would you like your other half a Coke?" He points to my barely touched drink.

I pull the cherry out of the glass and eat it. "Nope. Ready to go." I put a twenty on the bar to cover our drinks and Long John's tip. It's probably way more than necessary, but he did dress up my lame order.

When we reach Dane's place, he asks me to pull alongside the building instead of parking. He'll get out by the door.

"Thanks for tonight," I say sincerely. "I really needed it."

He smiles. "You're very welcome." He opens the door and steps out of the car, then peeks back in. "You owe me a Go Kart rematch and one dance."

I shake my head. "I only committed to the dance."

He grins. "Just making sure you remember."

CHAPTER 34

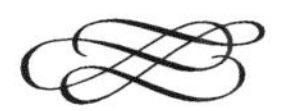

It's been four days since I started back to work. Leslie is nice and all, but it's not the same as working with Dane. I miss our bantering and sarcasm. It made the days go by faster. I decide to let him know and send him a text.

Work sucks without you.

A few minutes later he responds. *Miss you, too.*

His response makes me smile. Then I think of James and my smile vanishes. I wish I could send him a message. I picture it in my head. *Life sucks without you.*

"Emma?"

Leslie's voice brings me back to reality. "Yes?"

"Could you be a dear and hand me two waters from the cooler?"

I nod and grab what she needs. I look at the clock and sigh. Four more hours to go. I'm so bored. I decide to text Shel.

What are you doing?

She responds. *Not what, who ;)*

Gross. *TMI! Never mind.*

Something up?

No. Just bored at work.

Text Dane.

Already done.

Good girl.

I roll my eyes. Three hours and fifty-six minutes to go. I look over to see Leslie humming while she wipes the already clean slicer. Hmm. I text Dane again.

What are you doing?

Working, he responds.

Am I interrupting you?

It's a welcome interruption.

I need something to pass the time.

Something or someone?

I'm braver behind my phone. *Are you volunteering?*

Maybe. What do you have in mind?

Think, think, think. Ah ha! *Don't I owe you something?*

Yes, you do.

So?

You're killing me. Can't tonight. Busy.

My heart sinks. Bummer. I was getting brave there for a second. *Rain check?*

Absolutely.

SHEL IS LEAVING for Ann Arbor next week. I can't believe our summer together is ending. The realization that I will be completely on my own back at school in a couple of weeks is hitting me harder than I thought it would. Sure, I have a few friends on campus, but my close friends from home are the ones I will want around me. I know we can call and email, but it won't be the same. I'm already looking forward to the holiday break.

It also doesn't help that my parents are less than thrilled with my leaving and living on my own so far away after what happened with Patrick. Their anxiety feeds mine. I know Patrick is no longer a threat; he's in jail awaiting trial and has been denied bail. But I've always had James by my side. It almost feels like I'm starting college for the very first time.

Since this is our last weekend together, Shel, Matt, Dane, and I are headed out for dinner. We're supposed to meet up at Louie's Roadhouse, the scene of the infamous drunk guy fight from earlier this summer. Shel claims that night was the first time she realized she was attracted to Matt. I claim it was the drunken make-out session that pushed her over the edge. Regardless, we're headed to Louie's to celebrate. I rush to the restaurant after stopping home to change out of my work clothes into something cuter. I seriously can't wait to be done with Bay Woods. I have one more week left.

Entering the restaurant, I spot Shel waving me over. I make it to the table with a smile. "I see you managed to get a table for four this time," I say sarcastically, then change focus. "Hi, Matt."

"Hey." He smiles.

"Listen," Shel says. "If it weren't for me, you wouldn't be where you are with Dane."

"Which is where?" I ask her, making a face.

She sighs. "You know what I mean."

"Speaking of," I look around, "where is he?" I had hoped to see him tonight. We haven't been able to connect since the night at Adventure Land. We've texted each other a few times, but he's usually working or otherwise namelessly busy. Paranoia has been slowly invading my brain for days. I'm starting to think he's avoiding me.

"He should be here any minute," Matt says looking around as well.

Our waitress comes by to check on us. When she steps away, I catch sight of Dane entering the restaurant and breathe a sigh of relief.

Shel kicks me under the table.

"Ow!" I glare at her and rub my leg.

"Sorry," she says unapologetically. Then, she mouths "I saw that."

I close my eyes. Apparently, I need to be more careful.

"Sorry I'm late," Dane says as he slides into the seat next to me. He turns and smiles. "Long time, no see."

Before I can say anything, Matt distracts him with a question. "How's the project going?"

Dane looks tense. "It's turning out to be a little more challenging than I anticipated."

"I thought you liked a challenge?" I ask while I pick up a menu.

"Some more than others," he says with resignation.

Something about his tone makes me curious, and I catch his eyes darting to Matt then back to me. He leans close and looks over my shoulder at the menu. "So, what are you all having?"

When our food arrives, the conversation turns to our last time at this restaurant. Shel and Matt give a hilarious play-by-play of the fight with the drunk guy that has Dane and me rolling. Shel even reaches back into the vault to bring up the eating-strawberries-dipped-in-ketchup dare issued to her by Matt all those years ago. I haven't laughed like this is in a while. We talk about returning to school, our upcoming moves back to campus, and our wanting to be finished with it all. We tease Dane about being an old man since he finished with college two years ago. After dinner, Shel and I can't resist and order this amazing brownie covered in ice cream covered in hot fudge to share. By the time it's gone, I'm thoroughly stuffed.

"I can't move," I complain, holding my stomach.

"You have a few minutes," she says. "The DJ doesn't start playing until ten."

"We're dancing?" I ask with surprise. I guess it didn't dawn on me because there wasn't a band playing tonight. I smile. This will be fun. I haven't been dancing with Shel in years. She immediately drags me to the dance floor as soon as the DJ starts. As I pass Dane to get out of our table, he grabs my arm.

"Remember what you promised me." He cocks an eyebrow.

"I know. I haven't forgotten." My heart does a flip. I hadn't forgotten, but I'm just now putting two and two together. Man, I'm slow.

Shel and I have a blast dancing. And we don't stop. Matt and Dane watch us from the table, Shel waving to Matt every once and a while.

I yell at her over the music, "I take it he doesn't dance?"

She makes a sad face and shakes her head. "His only downfall!"

After about a half hour, when the song changes to something slow, I immediately decide it's time for a bathroom break. It's clear what I'm avoiding; I just need a minute to pull myself together. I tell Shel where I'm headed and turn. Halfway to the bathroom I'm intercepted. Someone grabs my hand from behind.

"Oh no, you don't," Dane says as I turn to face him.

"I have to pee," I tell him and try to keep a straight face.

"You're stalling," he says as he pulls me away from the restrooms and leads me back toward the dance floor.

I actually do kinda have to pee. Whatever. Let's get this over with.

He leads me into the sea of people that already occupies the floor. I look for Shel but can't find her. Dane turns and faces me, placing the hand he holds on his shoulder. He releases it and wraps his hands around my waist as I place my other hand on his other shoulder. A small space remains between us as we start to move.

"Does this make you uncomfortable?" he asks, wearing that smirk of his. The one that makes me want to hug him and slap him at the same time.

Is that his plan? To make me uncomfortable just to watch me squirm? Two can play at this game. "No," I say with confidence. I try to act indifferent as I wrap my arms higher around his neck and take a step forward pressing my body against his. He instinctively wraps his arms tightly around my waist. "Does *this* make *you* uncomfortable?" I challenge.

I actually see his breathing hitch. He rearranges his features; he knows what I'm doing. "No." He gives me a sly smile.

"Okay then." I rest my head against him, under his chin. Through his shirt, I can feel his heartbeat pick up, and it makes me smile. I may actually win this little game.

His arms loosen around me a little, and I feel his hands start to play against my lower back. My heart jumps. Dang! He probably felt that. As I try to calm my pulse, I move my fingers to his neck and start to play with the hair at his hairline. His hands stop moving against me in surprise. Ha! Another point for me.

We continue to move slowly with the music. I feel his hands start to move at my back again and then one leaves rank and starts to travel to my backside. I jerk my head up so I can look at him. He freezes. "What?"

"Don't look so innocent. I know what you're doing."

"What am I doing?" He suppresses a smile.

"You're trying to grab my ass."

He feigns confusion. "You mean like this?" He slides both his hands down and grabs two handfuls of my behind.

I jump but resist the urge to slap his hands away. He's wearing that grin of his as I try to look impassive. I calmly remove my hands from his neck and place them on his, picking them up and moving them back to my waist. I don't say anything as I wrap my arms back around him and place my head under his chin. I can feel his chest shake with laughter.

We finish the song wrapped around each other. I try not to feel comfortable in his arms, but it doesn't work. If I could've melted, I probably would have. I can lie to other people, but I can't lie to myself. I've missed this. Strong arms to hold me, arms that are real. When he steps away, I have to resist the need to hang on to him.

The music picks up again, and Shel finds me out of nowhere. Dane smiles. "Ladies," he says as he leaves my side. I give him a small smile as I watch him go.

"Really?" Shel looks at me with a sarcastic expression. "'*Nothing's going on*'," she says as she mimics my voice.

"Nothing is going on," I sigh.

"It looks mighty on from over here," she says as she starts to dance.

I try to hide my smile as I lose myself in the music, the dancing, and our laughter. I catch Dane's eye from time to time as he sits with Matt at our table. I know he's watching me, and I'm not sure if I can describe how I feel about that. But I know it's a good feeling, and I like it.

I hold out as long as I can, but eventually I need the bathroom. Shel and I head that way. As we pass our table, she stops and gives Matt a kiss. I roll my eyes at Dane. He grins as he tries to catch me around my waist, but I jump out of the way. When I look back to see if Shel is following me, I catch his expression. I think he looks hurt. What's that all about? I plan to ask him when I return, but when we get back from our break, he's gone.

"Where'd he go?" I ask Matt, confused.

Matt looks at me sympathetically, which is surprising. "He, um, had to leave."

"Why?"

Matt shrugs as Shel looks between us, confused.

What the hell? He's just going to leave without saying goodbye? Not acceptable. I reach for my phone and send him a text message.

Why did you leave???

I wait impatiently for his reply. Minutes later my phone buzzes in my hand. *I can't handle watching something I can't have.*

I frown. *Are you calling me a tease?*

If the shoe fits.

Anger wells up in my chest. That was not what I was doing! Who does he think he is? I grab my stuff.

"What did he say?" Shel asks, concerned.

"A lot," I snap.

"Well, where are you going?"

"To straighten out a certain someone." I give her a hug and then Matt. "I'll call you," I tell Shel as I head for the door.

"Be careful," she says as I leave.

"I'm not the one you need to worry about," I mutter under my breath as I step out into the night air.

I AM on a mission to give this certain person a piece of my mind. I jump out of the car and leave everything behind but myself. I won't be long. I walk up the sidewalk with my hands clenched in fists.

When I reach his door, I pound on it, then stand with my arms crossed, looking around. I notice a doorbell. I press it twice and hear it ring inside. I look around again and spot his car in the lot. He should be here.

After what seems like forever, I hear the deadbolt drop and watch the doorknob turn. Dane opens the door wide and stares at me. "Yes?" he asks. He looks pissed.

"Oh no." I shake my head and glare at him. "You don't get to be mad. I'm the one who gets to be mad! How dare you? How could you even think that? Especially after what Mrs. Davis said to me. You were there. How could you–"

In one smooth motion he cradles my head and brings his mouth down hard on mine. I lose my breath as his lips move against me, forming my mouth to his. He wraps his other arm around my waist and holds me tight. My heart pounds as my body warms; I feel myself melting beneath his touch. I search for that little part of my brain that registers logic and reason. I can't find it.

He breathes against my lips. "Do you want to come inside?"

My body has disconnected from my mind. I curl one hand around his neck and cover his mouth with mine, pressing myself against him. He takes this as a yes and moves us off the porch, over the threshold, and into his place. He shuts the door behind us, never once breaking our connection.

He leads and I follow, drawn like a magnet. We stop in the center of the room, near the couch, and his hands trace my spine. He catches my bottom lip between his teeth, and I can feel the sensation all the way to my toes. I clutch at his shoulders and run my hands over his chest to grab at the bottom of his shirt. Clenching it in my fists, I slide his shirt up only to get it caught under his arms. His mouth and his hands leave me as he steps back. He pulls his shirt over his head and tosses it aside, then returns to me, his eyes searching mine.

"Emma." My name sounds heavy and stuck in his throat. "Are you sure you want this?"

My eyes roam his toned chest until I find the small, red, inflamed line where he had his stitches. I take a step closer to him and reach out to run my finger across the mark. His breath catches in response and I whisper "Yes" almost inaudibly. I may have lost the ability to speak.

It doesn't matter because he hears me loud and clear. He hooks his fingers into my waistline, pulling me to him. He wraps his other hand behind my neck as his mouth discovers the skin there. After a moment his lips move to my ear. "Jump."

I'm confused until I feel his hands move around my back and then under me. I tighten my arms around his neck and pull myself higher, wrapping my legs around his waist. I bury my face in his neck as he carries me across the room and up the stairs. We turn, and when we reach his bed, his arms relax and I slide down his body to sit in front of him. We stare at each other intently for a moment, and I try to calm my pounding heart. Is this what I really want? My body is screaming yes, but my conscience is starting to wake up and take notice.

Dane leans over and finds my neck, trailing kisses down my throat, and silencing my inner voice. He moves against me, pressing me back, and I push myself along the mattress, toward the head of the bed. As he crawls over my body, I lose my fingers in his hair and pull his mouth to mine again. He obliges my silent request, balancing himself over me on his knees. His hands find the bottom of my shirt as he kisses me, lifting it to my shoulders, and when his mouth leaves mine I feel his lips against my chest. My eyes pop open. My conscience is screaming.

"Stop," I whisper as he moves to kiss me again. "I'm sorry. Stop."

He freezes immediately.

I push myself back and partially out from under him, pulling my shirt down over my body. I focus on his face. "I'm sorry," I say again, my voice full of remorse. "I can't."

He closes his eyes, takes a deep breath, and then opens them again. "I understand." He leans over to kiss my forehead before moving to the side to lie down on his back. He folds his hands against his stomach and turns to look at me.

I start to get up. "I should leave."

"No." He reaches across my body to pull me back into place. "Stay with me."

I give him a wary look but find myself turning toward him. He wraps his arms around me as I slide over to lie against him. "Thank you for not being angry," I murmur against his chest.

He kisses the top of my head and presses me to his side.

No other words pass between us. He holds me tight as I'm lulled to sleep by the sound of his beating heart.

CHAPTER 35

Warmth on my face awakens me. I lean into it subconsciously, moving my body toward it. I realize I feel skin beneath my cheek, and my eyes snap open. I lift my head to find myself wrapped around Dane, one leg and one arm draped across him, my head at his shoulder.

"Good morning," he says, giving me a small smile.

I squint as I look around the room. "What time is it?"

"Early." He has one arm circled around me which he moves to run his fingers lightly along my arm.

I catch the numbers of his alarm clock. 5:48. I try to sit up, and Dane tightens his arm around me to keep me in place.

"Where are you going?"

"I have to get home." I'm sure my family is freaking out that I didn't come home last night.

His eyes soften. "Stay."

I search his face and memories of last night flood my vision. My heart clenches. "I can't."

"Don't over think this," he says gently.

"I'm not." I try to sit up again and this time he lets me.

He leans up on one elbow. "You are."

I shake my head. "You forget, I have people at home who will be wondering where I am."

He gives me a defeated look, then turns to swing his legs off the side of the bed, allowing me room to slide off and stand.

"Bathroom?" I ask.

He nods toward the door and I move to open it, stepping into the small hallway at the top of the stairs. There's a room across from me that looks like an office; framed pictures hang on the wall above a computer desk. I look to my right and see another doorway. I enter the bathroom, find the light switch, and seclude myself. I catch a glimpse of my face in the mirror that stops me short. I rest my hands against the countertop and stare at my reflection. Who is this person? Do I even know her anymore?

After I finish, I find Dane leaning against the wall in the hallway. "Everything all right?"

I nod quickly. I walk past him and down the stairs as he follows me. I come across one of my sandals at the base of the stairs and bend to pick it up. I search for the other and find it a small distance away. I walk over and grab it. Holding my shoes by the straps with one hand, I make my way to leave.

"Emma," Dane says behind me.

I close my eyes and then turn toward him.

He steps forward and places his hands on my shoulders, looking me in the eye. His face is full of concern, his hazel eyes pleading. "Please don't regret what happened. Because I don't. I know it seems soon, but I think … I think I'm falling in lov …"

I press my fingers to his lips, so he will stop speaking. He can't say he loves me. Not now. Because I don't know if I can say it back. I need some space. So I can think. So I can process all of this. I step up and raise my chin to kiss him. He bends down and plants a soft kiss on my lips which starts to grow into something more. I can't let that happen. Not right now.

"I have to go."

He looks at me and then takes me into his arms. He says nothing, only kisses my hair. When he releases me, I give him a weak smile and turn toward the door. Stepping outside, I notice the sun trying to make its way above the horizon as I head down the sidewalk and to my car.

Slamming the door behind me, I look over to the passenger seat. I take my phone out of my purse. I have missed text messages. All from Shel.

Is everything okay?

Where are you?

I'm trying not to panic. I will assume you are with Dane.

CALL ME WHEN YOU GET THIS.

I sigh and put the phone down as tears cloud my vision. I start the car to make my way home. I feel like I want to crawl in a hole and die.

I STARE out over the golf course with my chin resting on the cart steering wheel. It's been three days since I've seen him. I feel like I've been in a daze ever since. When I try to sort out my feelings, my mind runs in endless circles. So, this morning, I decided to give up for now and just be a zombie. With Shel gone and between finishing up this last week of work and packing my things to move back to Western, I should be able to keep my mind off what happened.

Yeah, right.

Who am I kidding? He's all I think about.

When Shel interrogated me after that night, I did a pretty good job of convincing her all that happened was a lengthy argument and apology. I got lucky when I went home; my parents were still asleep, allowing me to sneak into my room. When I play back what happened, my feelings vacillate. I remember his hands on me, and my heart races. I remember his kiss, his smile, every kind thing he's done for me, and I have a hard time breathing. Then the guilt kicks in as James' face flashes before my eyes, twisting my heart and killing my high from the possibility of Dane loving me. I can't even bring myself to think about the likelihood that James physically saw what took place. Every time I do, tears immediately jump behind my eyes, and I feel my soul turn inside out. I still love him. But I have some very strong feelings for someone else, too.

My phone goes off, disrupting my thoughts.

Are you avoiding me? It's Dane.

Yes. *No.*

We need to talk.

I sigh. I know. *Go ahead.*

In person.

Can't. Working.

When do you get off?

6 but have plans tonight with Mike and Kate.

Tomorrow?

6 but will be packing and having dinner with parents.

Friday?

5. Still packing.

You're being impossible.

I'm not trying to be.

Saturday? Do you still want me to help you move?

I can't leave without seeing him. I don't want to leave without seeing him. *Yes.*

What time?

Whatever works for you.

He shows up at noon. I'm helping to lift a box into the bed of my dad's truck when he pulls up. My pulse instantaneously races, and I feel my ears grow hot. I focus on maintaining my composure as he gets out of the car and walks toward me.

"Dane," my dad greets him with a genuine smile. He will be forever grateful for what he did for his little girl.

"Mr. Donohue." Dane smiles at him. His smile fades slightly as he nods toward me. "Emma."

"Hey," I respond quietly.

My dad looks between us, and his expression registers that he knows something is up. "I'll go help your mother sort through those extra dishes for you," he says as he steps down from the bed of the truck. He smiles at both of us as he heads to the house.

Dane walks up to me slowly. "Where can we talk?"

I gesture for him to follow me, and we walk into the backyard. He takes my hand as we head out to my mother's flower garden where there's a small bench. I sit down and he sits beside me, our legs touching.

"I've missed you," he says sincerely.

"I've missed you, too."

His eyes search mine. "How can we make this work?"

I look down and shake my head. "I don't know."

"It's because you still have feelings for him, right?" He gently squeezes my hand. "I understand that, I do. But you can't feel bad. You've done nothing wrong."

"I know," I say quietly. "There's a huge part of me that wants this, wants you." I look up at him. "But these other feelings … the guilt. I can't escape it. It hurts."

We sit in silence, his hand holding mine. Eventually, he takes a deep breath and speaks. "I'm willing to help you through it, if you'll let me." He looks me squarely in the eyes. "The last thing I want to do is pressure you, but time is running out and there's something I need to deal with. I need you to give me an answer. Do you want me? Do you think you could ever love me? Because if the answer is yes, I'm willing to wait. However long it takes."

I want to tell him yes. So badly. But the truth is I have no idea how long it will take me to get over James, especially if it's decided that he can handle visiting me. If he even wants to visit me. Does Dane deserve that? To sit around, waiting for me to make up my mind, indefinitely? No. Not when he's already given me so much. What if I never get over James? That's not fair to him.

"I can't give you an answer right now. I'm sorry."

He clutches my hand and then lets it go. He stands to face me. "Why?" he asks. "Why is this so hard for you?"

I damn the tears that spring into my eyes. He's never been angry with me before, and I stare at him, confused.

"Yes or no Emma? It's that simple," he says, frustrated.

My voice cracks. "It's not fair to make you wait."

He crouches down before me. "But I'm willing to. Don't you see?"

No, I don't see. Why should he do that for me? If I say yes, the possibility of breaking his heart in the future is very real; the closer we grow the more painful it will be. I would never want to do that to him. No. As much as it kills me, I realize what I should have done weeks ago.

"No," I barely whisper.

"What?"

"No." I look him in the eyes as I feel tears escape mine. "My answer is no."

His face fills with disbelief and confusion. He looks so devastated I have to resist the urge to hold him. My tears start to fall faster as I come to grips with the fact that I am causing him this pain. He stands slowly, staring at me as if he doesn't know me.

"I'm so sorry," I say through my tears. "But I told you from the beginning we could only be friends ..."

His eyes flash at my last word, changing his sad expression to one of anger. "Friends? Are you kidding me?" He looks away, but then immediately turns back. He leans toward me, his eyes hard. "What happened the other night ... what was that? Last time I checked, that's not what friends do."

Ouch. I close my eyes to block out his face for a moment. When I open them, he's turned away from me with his hands on his hips. He shakes his head in disbelief and curses under his breath.

A car turns into the driveway, distracting us. We both look up to see Matt pull in and park. I hastily wipe at my face with my hands. What is he doing here?

Matt sees us and heads in our direction. When he gets close, he can tell something is wrong, and his walk slows.

"Hey, guys," he says cautiously. "I just stopped over to say goodbye before you left." He looks past Dane and at me.

My gaze falls everywhere but directly on his face. I try to force a small smile.

Dane walks up to Matt and stops. "I'm headed to the airport. Teags will be here in a few hours."

"Teags?" Matt asks, surprised.

Dane looks at me over his shoulder with a twisted expression. "Apparently I'm not needed anymore." He turns back to Matt. "I'm out."

Matt looks confused as he watches Dane leave. "Call me later, man," he says to his retreating figure and then looks at me, worried. We both watch Dane get into his car. When he backs out and turns into the street, he guns it, squealing his tires and making me jump.

Matt stares at me. "What in the hell happened?"

I try to keep it together, but a sob has been building in my chest. I hold my head in my hands as Matt tries to comfort me as best he can.

I've been in my new apartment at Western for a few days, and I'm still trying to decide where things should go. I don't have much, but I want to be as organized as possible before classes begin. Plus, I'd like to go out and get some stuff to make the place a little homier. Granted, I'm being an over achiever, but I don't have much else to do with my time.

It's very quiet around me now. I check in with my parents daily, since they are still concerned about me being so far away on my own. I keep reminding them this town is nothing new for me, just the physical location of my residence. I've met three of my four "roommates" if you will: one girl, Samantha, shares apartment one with her boyfriend Todd, and Jessica, a girl in apartment three. I haven't met the person in four yet, but Jessica tells me she thinks it's a guy. And then there's me, alone in two. Other than speaking briefly to my new housemates, the only other friend I've talked to is Shel, after I received the following text when I moved in:

WHAT DID YOU DO???

Of course she assumed I was to blame for the way things turned out with Dane, and she was right. I explained our fight to her, and she proceeded to rip me up one side and down the other. I took it like a champ because there's nothing I can do. What's done is done. He'll never forgive me. I don't forgive me. I feel absolutely wretched about everything, and I miss him more than I'd like to admit to myself. I can't wait for classes to begin, so something occupies my mind other than the memory of Dane's sad and angry face. I'm starting to think I don't deserve happiness. First James, now Dane. The image of me as the crazy cat lady James mentioned so long ago comes to mind.

My stomach rumbles, and I realize I haven't eaten anything since breakfast. It's almost four. I open the fridge to discover I have nothing appetizing to feed myself. I grab my keys and wallet and decide to walk to the small market that's close to me, about two blocks away. When I get there my hunger takes over, and I end up with two paper bags of groceries, plus some new shampoo, conditioner, and a candle I thought would look nice on my small entertainment center. You find things you wouldn't normally purchase when you have uninterrupted time to wander around a store.

I make it back to the apartments carrying both bags without incident. It's when I'm trying to unlock the door that I have a problem. I look around on the ground for a dry spot to set one of my bags; it rained this afternoon and everything is still wet.

"Need a hand?"

I turn around to see a guy approaching the door. He has brown hair that curls a little, and his skin has an olive tone. As he gets closer I notice his eyes. They're a strange mix of blue and green, almost turquoise. I've never seen anything like them. *Contacts,* I immediately think. He smiles at me in a friendly way.

"Thanks," I say gratefully and offer him one of the bags. He takes it as I dig out my key. "Do you live here?" I ask as I open the door.

"Yep, just moved in."

"I did, too. You must be apartment four." I turn and smile at him, then step inside and hold the door open. He follows me. "I'm number two."

"Hello, number two," he says and laughs a little.

We walk down the short hallway to my place, and I unlock the door. I hurry inside to set down my bag while he waits in the hallway. I return to take the other bag from him. "Sorry," I apologize.

"It's not a problem," he says. "So, number two, do you have a name?"

I shift my purchases in my arms and extend my hand. "Yes. Emma. Emma Donohue."

He regards me for a moment, then smiles and shakes my hand. "That name sounds familiar. I feel like I've met you before."

I shake my head. "If we have met, I don't remember."

He releases my hand and takes a step back. "Well, we've met now. I guess I'll be seeing you around, number two."

I laugh. "Guess so. Thanks for your help."

He nods and starts to walk away as I begin to shut the door.

"Wait." I stick my head out into the hall.

He stops and turns. "Yes?"

"I didn't catch your name."

"Oh." He smiles. "Garrett. Garrett Abernathy."

Look for the second book in The Guardian Trilogy:
Allegiant
Available now!

BONUS CONTENT

Dear Reader,

Thank you so much for taking a chance and picking up Guardian! My hope is you've fallen in love with Emma, James, and Dane's story as much as I have.

To mark the series five-year "publiversary," here are a couple of scenes that were fun to write but didn't make the original Guardian cut. By now, you know James and Emma's relationship started in high school, although they were friends long before that. These scenes are from elementary and middle school. I hope you enjoy them!

~ Yours, Sara

JAMES, Shel, Matt, and I have been friends since the third grade. Four eight year olds who didn't have a care in the world, except for maybe lunch and recess. We were drawn together by our shared love of the swings on the playground. Only four to a set and every day we claimed all four. Shel gave the best underdogs, while Matt could jump off the swing the farthest. We would twist up the chains and spin around until we were dizzy. The recess lady would eventually tell us to knock it off; we were going to ruin the equipment. Come to think of it, I don't think she liked us much. Or maybe she just didn't want to have to clean up should we puke from all the spinning.

As a matter of fact, one day I did puke at school, but not from spinning on the swings. I had felt queasy in the morning and told my mom I was sick.

"Nonsense, Em. You don't even have a temperature," she said as she felt my forehead with her magical temperature-reading palm. "You can make it."

Bouncing to school on the bus over the pothole-filled dirt back roads is probably what did it. While hanging up my coat and backpack with all the other kids, I felt my stomach start to churn. Panicked, I clamped my hand over my mouth and tried to make it to the bathroom, but there were too many kids in my way. I lost my breakfast right there on the coat room floor, in the middle of my fifth grade class.

"EW! Emma threw up!"

"Oh man, it stinks!"

"Did it get on me? Make sure it's not on me!"

"Don't step in it!"

My classmates were backing as far away from me as possible, their noses plugged while I held my stomach and prayed not to retch again. Tears were streaming down my face because my stomach hurt so badly.

"Someone go get Mrs. Clouse!"

I decided sitting down might be a good idea. I sunk to the floor by my vomit pile and bent my knees up to rest my forehead against them. At least I could hide my face this way. Still, without seeing them, I could feel my class standing around me in a circle. I could hear whispers and giggles and the occasional, "That's so gross."

I felt someone kneel down beside me. "Are you going to be okay?" It was James.

"My stomach hurts," I tell him, my face still hidden.

"Well, here." He held out some crumpled paper towel from the sink dispenser. "You might need this."

Looking up, I took the paper towel from him and managed a small thank-you smile.

"What's going on – oh dear," I hear Mrs. Clouse say. "Everyone to your seats," she said as she moved everyone out of the coatroom. "Emma, I'm going to have the office call your mother."

After a few minutes, I stood back up, surprised to see James standing there holding my coat and backpack. "Here."

I remember thinking how odd this was. How he had stepped up to help me with the paper towel, waited with me and my vomit pile, handed me my stuff, even though I was perfectly capable of getting it myself. As if I didn't feel uncomfortable enough, now one of my best friends was acting all weird. Well, weird for an eleven-year-old boy.

"Um, thanks."

He shrugged and left the room. I stood there for a few more minutes until my mother appeared, followed by an annoyed looking janitor with a mop and bucket.

"I guess you really are sick," she said, feeling my forehead again. I nodded.

"That was nice of James to stay with you," she said.

I looked at her, confused.

"I passed him in the hall. He seems like a nice boy."

Looking back, I guess you could say the day I threw up in the fifth grade coat room was the beginning. The beginning of James and me. Over the years, our names would become synonymous. If you saw one of us, the other wasn't far behind.

"I'M STARVING."

"Me, too."

"Got any money?" James asks, staring longingly at the vending machine outside our middle school cafeteria.

"Probably not. Let me see." I start to scrounge around in my back-pack. We both forgot we had to stay after school to earn volunteer hours for the honor society. We are supposed to be coming up with catchy slogans and making signs for all of the upcoming year-end events.

James searches his jeans pockets. "I have twenty cents. What do you have?"

"Looks like maybe seventy-five."

"Hold on a sec," he says and, looking around, takes off in the direction of a group of guys standing by the office.

He smiles, returning. "I managed to bum a dollar. What's in this machine that can tide us over until five?"

We survey our selection of cheesy, chocolaty, sugary, and carb-filled snacks.

"Twizzlers?" I suggest.

"What about the Cheez-Its?" he asks.

"They don't give you very many in the bag. How about the Twix? We can split it evenly."

"Sounds good." James feeds the dollar into the machine, and it actually takes it on the first try. He presses the number for the Twix. The coil that holds the candy turns and stops, but doesn't drop it. It's stuck.

"Are you kidding me?!" he exclaims.

I laugh. "I guess we donated Kyle's dollar to the school."

"No; we're getting that Twix."

"How?"

James starts banging on the glass. Nothing happens. He bends down and tries to reach up through the vending door to knock it clear. Nothing. I try to reach through the door. Not even close. James attempts to tip the machine forward from the top; it won't budge. He tries tipping it from the side. Nada. He rests his forehead on the glass, staring at the candy. "Oh, how I want you," he sighs as I laugh.

I look around the side of the machine and inspiration hits. "Wait." Spying the power cord, I unplug it. "Let's see if it resets or something."

When I plug the cord in, the lights come on in the machine and it appears to be re-starting. Then, out of the blue, change starts falling from the coin return, like we hit the jackpot in Vegas.

"Oh my gosh!" I shout and bend down to try and catch all the flying change.

James tries to help me, cracking up. "Catch it!"

Money is flying everywhere. I'm stuffing coins in as many pockets as I can find, and James is chasing the ones that managed to hit the floor and roll away.

When the money finally stops, we have tears from laughing so hard. Sitting on the ground with my back against the machine I ask, "What are going to do with all of this?" I hold up my hand full of quarters.

"Buy us two Twix," he laughs and helps me to stand.

Addressing the machine, James says, "Now, don't hold out on us this time," and he puts in the exact change. The candy falls with no problem. "Yes!" We give each other a victory high-five.

"What's going on here?" a stern male voice says. James and I look at each other, frozen.

We slowly turn to see Mr. Varner, assistant principal, standing behind us. His arms are crossed, and he's looking down at us over the top of his glasses. "I heard an awful lot of noise from you two in my office."

I try to discreetly move my hand to my jacket pocket to hide the quarters I'm holding.

"The vending machine ate our money, sir," James explains. "We were laughing about trying to get the candy to fall."

Mr. Varner doesn't look impressed. "And the metallic clinking sounds?"

We look at each other and know we've been caught. "Apparently the machine is broken," James says.

Mr. Varner looks at us expectantly, tapping his foot. I remove my hand from my pocket and reveal the quarters. "I'll take those, Ms. Donohue."

Tentatively, I dump the money into his hand. Unfortunately, this isn't the first time I've had a run-in with Mr. Varner, thanks to Shel and the food fight she dragged me into last month.

"You two weren't planning on keeping this money, were you?" he asks us.

"No, sir." We shake our heads.

"Because that would be stealing school property."

We nod.

"All right. Get back to what you're supposed to be doing."

I pick up my backpack, and James and I turn to head back to the cafeteria, the Twix forgotten. We start to walk away, and my jacket pocket jingles.

"Excuse me, Ms. Donohue," Mr. Varner says as I cringe. "I believe I need to check your other pocket."

I return to stand in front of Mr. Varner and, as I quietly apologize, relieve my other pocket of more change. "I'm sorry. I forgot there was more in there."

"Well, young lady, it looks like you've earned yourself a detention. Follow me."

I give James a defeated look and turn to follow Mr. Varner to the office.

"Wait!" James blurts out, following us. "It's my fault. I told her to put the money in her pockets."

"How noble of you, Mr. Davis. Looks like you've volunteered yourself for detention as well."

I give James a "What in the heck are you doing?" look behind Mr. Varner's back. He just smirks and shrugs his shoulders.

When we reach his office, Mr. Varner gives us each a detention slip for the following Friday afternoon, along with guaranteeing us a phone call to our parents.

As we walk back to the cafeteria, I elbow James in the side. "You didn't have to do that. Now you're stuck after school on Friday, too."

"It wasn't fair for you to take all the blame," he says matter-of-factly. "Besides, I would do anything for you."

I stop walking in order for my brain to register his last comment, a confused expression on my face.

He turns around, so he's walking backward away from me, and flashes me the biggest smile I think I've ever seen. He ducks into the cafeteria, leaving me alone in the hallway, wondering what he meant.

ABOUT THE AUTHOR

Sara Mack is a Michigan native who grew up with her nose in books. She is a wife and a hockey mom on top of being trapped in an office forty hours a week. Her spare time is spent as a chauffeur to her children, cleaning up after her adolescent puppies and elderly cat, attempting to keep her flower garden alive, and, of course, writing. She has an unnatural affinity for dark chocolate, iced tea, and bacon.

Connect with Sara:
Sign up for her newsletter
Get SMACKed

Or connect with

Made in the USA
Columbia, SC
15 October 2018